Ovid

OVID

David Wishart

All the characters and events portrayed in this work are fictitious.

OVID

A Felony & Mayhem mystery

PRINTING HISTORY
First UK edition (Hodder & Stoughton): 1995
First paperback edition (Hodder & Stoughton/Sceptre): 1996
Felony & Mayhem edition: 2006

ISBN 1-933397-39-X

For Roy *et ceteris*

Dramatis Personae

(Purely fictional characters appear in lower case.)

Agron: A large Illyrian, now resident in Rome.

ASPRENAS, Lucius Nonius: The nephew of Varus and of his sister Quinctilia.

Bathyllus: Corvinus's head slave.

Callias: Perilla's head slave.

CORVINUS (Marcus Valerius Messalla Corvinus): A rich young nobleman approached by Perilla in connection with the return of her stepfather Ovid's ashes. He was grandson to the poet's friend and patron of the same name.

COTTA (Marcus Valerius Cotta Maximus Corvinus): Corvinus's uncle.

Crispus, Caelius: An insalubrious dealer in gossip.

Daphnis: A slave in Scylax's gymnasium.

Davus: An ex-slave, first of Aemilius Paullus then of Fabius Maximus.

FABIUS MAXIMUS, Paullus: One of Augustus's closest friends and advisers, and Perilla's uncle.

Harpale: An old slave in the household of Marcia, Perilla's aunt.

Lentulus, Cornelius: A disreputable but influential old senator.

MARCIA: Widow of Augustus's friend and confidant, Fabius Maximus.

MESSALINUS (Marcus Valerius Messalla Messalinus): Corvinus's father; a politician and lawyer notable for his syco-phantic support of Tiberius.

OVID (Publius Ovidius Naso): One of Rome's greatest ever poets, and Perilla's stepfather. Exiled to Tomi by Augustus in AD 8. Despite almost constant pleas for pardon, he died there in AD 17.

PAULLUS, Lucius Aemilius: The husband of Augustus's granddaughter Julia. He was executed for treason in AD 8.

PERILLA, Rufia: Ovid's stepdaughter (her mother, Fabia Camilla, was Ovid's third wife). She was married to Publius Suillius Rufus. Her family-name (Rufia) is my own attribution.

Pertinax, Gaius Attius: An old friend and colleague of Corvinus's grandfather, now in retirement south of Rome.

Pomponius, Sextus: A decurion who once served under Corvinus's father.

QUINCTILIA: The sister of Quinctilius Varus.

RUFUS, Publius Suillius: Perilla's husband, currently serving abroad with Germanicus.

Scylax: An ex-trainer of gladiators set up by Corvinus in his own gymnasium near the Circus.

SILANUS, Decimus Junius: A Roman noble accused of adultery with Augustus's granddaughter Julia.

GERMANY

ARMINIUS: The principal German rebel leader, responsible for the Varian Massacre.

CEIONIUS, Marcus: One of Varus's staff, and also his accomplice in treason.

EGGIUS, Lucius: With Ceionius, Varus's Camp Commander and a member of his advisory staff.

VARUS, Publius Quinctilius: Augustus's military viceroy in Germany. Massacred along with the three legions he commanded in the Teutoburg Forest.

VELA, Numonius: Varus's second, and commander of the cavalry on the final march.

The icon above says you're holding a copy of a book in the Felony & Mayhem "Historical" category, which ranges from the ancient world up through the 1940s. If you enjoy this book, you may well like other "Historical" titles from Felony & Mayhem Press, including:

Man's Illegal Life, by Keith Heller
City of the Horizon, by Anton Gill
City of Dreams, by Anton Gill
The Smoke, by Tony Broadbent
The Blackheath Poisonings, by Julian Symons
Bertie and the Seven Bodies, by Peter Lovesey

For more about these books, and other Felony & Mayhem titles, or to place an order, please visit our website at:

www.FelonyAndMayhem.com

or contact us at:

Felony and Mayhem Press
156 Waverly Place
New York, NY 10014

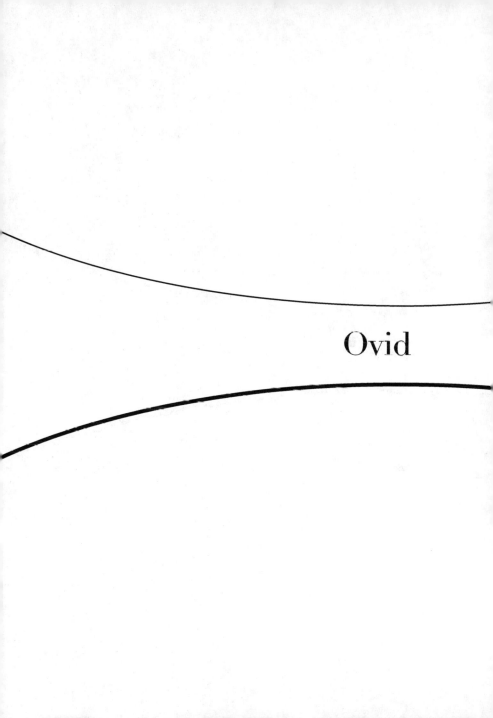

Ovid

THE IMPERIAL FAMILY

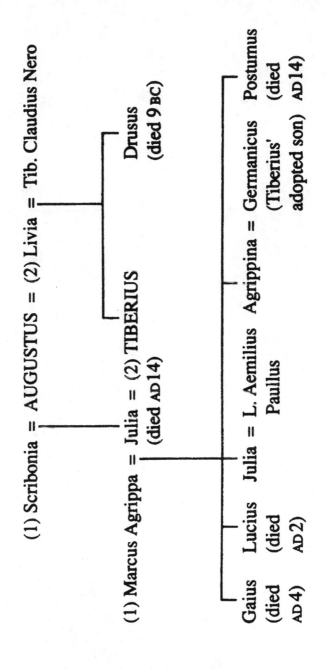

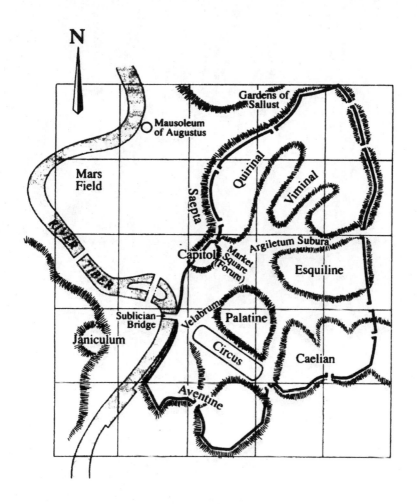

Corvinus's Rome

CHAPTER 1

I'd been at a party on the Caelian the night before. My tongue tasted like a gladiator's jockstrap, my head was pounding like Vulcan's smithy, and if you'd held up a hand and asked me how many fingers you'd got I'd've been hard put to give a definite answer without using an abacus. My usual morning condition, in other words, and hardly the best state for a first meeting with a tough cookie like the Lady Rufia Perilla.

You know the type: six feet tall, four across the shoulders, hair like wire and biceps like rocks. A cross between Penthesilea the Amazon Queen and Medusa the Gorgon before Perseus shortened her by a head, with a look and a voice that can wither a man's balls at thirty yards.

Only the woman striding towards me across the marble hall floor trailing my slave Bathyllus behind her like an arena cat's leavings wasn't like that at all. Far from it. This particular tough cookie was a stunner.

I did a quick appraisal. Early twenties (a year or so older than me), spear-straight and slim, clear-skinned, tall and tawny, with hair so bright that it hurt. On the debit side, eyes that would've nailed a basilisk and a no-nonsense perfume (I could smell it already) that reminded me unpleasantly of cold plunges, clean living and healthy exercise. Debit item three...

Item three was Bathyllus. The little guy looked chewed, and no one fazes Bathyllus. He stares down pukkah senators and deglazes dowagers, he can reduce legionary commanders to jelly, and I'd back him against anything human and maybe a step or two either side. So if this lady had taken Bathyllus apart already then she scared the shit out of me.

I tried to stand and then thought better of it. The floor wasn't too steady that morning.

'You're Marcus Valerius Messalla Corvinus.' Rufia Perilla obviously didn't believe in wasting time, or in asking questions.

'Uh... yeah.' It was less of a confirmation than a nervous twitch. I'd've said the same if she'd called me Tiberius Julius Caesar.

'Your grandfather'—she fixed me with a glare that had me checking whether I'd remembered to put a tunic on—'was my stepfather's foremost patron.'

'No kidding. Your stepfather?'

'The poet.'

'The poet?' Shit. My mind wasn't up to snappy intellectual banter this time of the morning. The only poet I could think of offhand was Homer, and I was fairly sure even in my present condition that he wasn't the guy she meant.

'The poet Ovid.'

'Oh, *that* poet!' A bell in my head was ringing faintly. Or maybe it was just my hangover. 'Yeah. Great. So you're... what's-his-name's stepdaughter? Well well well well well!'

I knew the slip was a bad one when I saw her mouth harden into a line you could've used to cut marble. Under normal circumstances, or at least when I was completely sober, which isn't quite the same thing, I'd never have made a mistake like that. I may have no interest in literature but I'm no hicko. Maybe Ovid had been rotting away in exile for ten years, but he was still the best poet we'd had since Horace hung his clogs up.

The words were out and there was no calling them back. Things went very quiet, the temperature dropped to its midwinter level, and I swear I saw ice form in the ornamental pool. Bathyllus had been watching our little exchange like Cassandra waiting for Agamemnon to speak his last line and head for the tub. Now he winced and looked away. Bathyllus never could stand the sight of blood.

The beautiful arched eyebrows came down like a chopper.

'I realise this is hard for you to follow in your present condition, Valerius Corvinus,' she said in a voice that was pure Egyptian natron, 'but do try please because it's important. My stepfather was Publius Ovidius Naso. He wrote poetry and he was exiled to Tomi on the Black Sea. You understand the word "poetry" or should I explain?'

'Uh...yeah. I mean no.' Jupiter! I wasn't up to this. Not this morning. Probably not ever. 'Look, I'm sorry. Sit down, er...'

'Perilla. Rufia Perilla. What on?'

'Hmm? Oh, yeah. Bathyllus?'

But Bathyllus was already carrying one of my best chairs through from the study. I hadn't seen the little bastard move that fast in years. Not since his hernia.

She sat, and I tried, desperately, to put my head back together again.

'You said "wrote", Lady Rufia.'

'I beg your pardon?'

'"Wrote". Past tense. He's, like, dead then. Ovid. Your stepfather.'

Yeah, I know. As a conversational gambit it stank. But you must remember I was having a hard time stopping my brain from oozing out my ears. Delicacy was the least of my problems.

She nodded and lowered her eyes. For a moment I saw the ice melt and the woman show through.

'The news came two days ago,' she said. 'He died last winter just after the sea lanes closed. The message came by the first ship.'

'Uh, I'm sorry.'

'Don't be.' The ice was back. 'He was glad to go. He hated Tomi, and that...' her teeth closed on the word. 'The emperor would never have let him come home.'

True enough, I thought. Tiberius hadn't actually been the one to exile the guy, but he'd confirmed Augustus's sentence after the old emperor fell off his perch. Became a god. Whatever. I didn't know what the reason had been for packing Ovid off to Tomi originally, nor, to my knowledge, did anyone else; but I could make an educated guess. Perilla's stepfather had had the morals and self-restraint of a priapic rabbit. One day the poor bastard had found himself hauled into Augustus's private study. There the emperor had chewed off his balls and stuffed a one-way ticket to the Black Sea up his rectum. Exit Rome's greatest living poet, with no formal charge and no trial. When Augustus died (or was promoted if you prefer) Ovid's friends had put in to the new emperor for a pardon. The Wart had refused. Now, it seemed, the guy had moved on to the Complete Works category and a pardon was academic.

Bathyllus soft-shoed across the marble floor, showing the

whites of his eyes. He set a small table beside Perilla with a bowl of fruit and some nuts on it, bowed, and sidled out again quickly. Maybe it was some weird Greek ceremony of propitiation: Bathyllus can be a superstitious sod at times. In any event it was wasted. Perilla ignored both the table and him, confining herself to straightening her exquisitely draped mantle. I gathered the shreds of my dignity together, tried to ignore whoever was sawing off the top of my skull, and got to the point.

'So how can I help?'

'I should have thought that was obvious.'

The hell with dignity. 'Look, lady, I don't read minds, right? Just give it to me straight.'

Yeah. Not exactly formal Ciceronian prose but I was getting just a little tetchy myself. Strangely, Perilla didn't seem to mind. For a moment her eyes rested on me; coolly, appraisingly.

'I'm sorry, Valerius Corvinus,' she said. 'You're perfectly correct, and I apologise. As I said, my stepfather has just died. We—my mother and I—would like his ashes to be returned to Rome for burial. As his patron it is of course your duty to put our request to the emperor.'

Yeah. Her exact words, I swear to you. I gaped. If he wants you to do something your ordinary client will spend a day or so telling you what a great guy you are, sending you the odd sturgeon, maybe a box or two of stuffed Alexandrian figs. Then when he's softened you up enough he might get round to broaching the subject in the most roundabout way he can think of. Rufia Perilla had just committed a social gaffe equivalent to asking Tiberius what he put on his boils. More, she'd done it without turning a strand of her exquisitely coiffured hair.

'I realise that you are not precisely the correct member of your family to approach,' she went on. 'Your uncle Marcus

Valerius Cotta Maximus Messalinus' (Jupiter! Did Uncle Cotta have all these names?) 'would as one of my stepfather's closest friends have been a more natural choice. Your father, too, would have been more...' She hesitated. I could see her taking in my unshaven jowls, the bags under my eyes, my slouch. 'More suitable.'

Jupiter's balls! 'Now look, lady...' I said. As a protest it was feeble, and she ignored it.

'However, I have here a letter which I think will explain everything.'

She reached under her mantle, giving me a brief glimpse of red undertunic, brought out a small scroll of paper and handed it over. I was still in shock. Without even checking that the thing was addressed to me I broke the seal and waited until the writing had stopped dancing around on the page. The letter was from my Uncle Cotta, and in his usual mind-numbing, rambling style.

> Marcus Valerius Cotta Maximus Messalinus to his nephew Marcus, Greetings.
>
> This is to introduce Rufia Perilla, the stepdaughter of my old friend Publius Ovidius Naso lately dead at Tomi. She'll scare the hell out of you, Marcus, but her heart's in the right place as well as everything else so help her as best you can, eh, boy? I've suggested you rather than your father because that pompous arselicker wouldn't be seen dead helping anyone unless he got something out of it for himself. Besides, poor Publius never could stand him and it was mutual, so his stepdaughter wouldn't get much change out of the old hypocrite either. And as you may or may

not know I'm out too, being off to Athens shortly for a few months of well-earned carnality, so you're hereby elected. Don't let the family down, eh, boy?

Farewell.

There was a PS:

She's married to an unpleasant bugger called Suillius Rufus. He's out east at present and from all accounts they can't stand each other. A nod's as good as a wink, eh? Cotta.

I raised my eyes from the letter to find that hers were fixed on me. Perhaps I'd caught her at an unguarded moment, perhaps the look was intentional. I don't know. But for the first time she looked vulnerable. Desperate and vulnerable. Now, I may be a self-indulgent overbred slob, but at least I'm a kind-hearted self-indulgent overbred slob, and that look showed me two things. First that whatever front she put on it had cost Rufia Perilla a lot to ask for help, mine or whoever's. And second (call me a sucker if you like) I knew I'd do almost anything to see her smile.

Maybe Uncle Cotta's postscript was relevant too.

'Okay,' I said. 'Consider it done.'

Which, in retrospect, was a pretty stupid thing to say. If any nasty-minded gods were listening I was just asking for the clouting of the century. Which was more or less what I was in for. Not that I'd've taken the words back even if I'd known, because as I spoke them for another precious instant the ice melted and the other Perilla showed through.

That paid for everything.

CHAPTER 2

'Consider it done.' Yeah, well, I found out how stupid that particular promise was next day.

The palace is something else, bureaucracy run mad. For a start it's huge. You can get lost, physically lost, if you're not careful. They find skeletons in there regularly, and guys who've waddled in fat as butter stagger out days later blinking like owls and thin as hay rakes. The place is full of clerks who spend most of their working day bouncing the punters between them like they were playing handball; and the worst of it is you don't realise you're getting nowhere until it's going-home time and the bastards drop you.

A typical bureaucracy, in other words.

Sure, I'm exaggerating, but not by much. And don't imagine just because I've got four names that getting something done is any easier. Especially something involving the emperor. The Wart's got better things to do (don't ask what) than sit at a desk all day scratching his boils and waiting for Rome's brightest and best to bring him their troubles. We purple-stripers have to stand in line like everyone else.

Oh, sure, if I'd been my Uncle Cotta or my father things would've been easy. Guys like that have got clout; and clout, at the palace, is everything. My father was an ex-consul and former provincial governor, which tells you something about the half-arsed way we choose our magistrates. Although Uncle Cotta hadn't made it that high yet, he was on the ladder; but with not so much as an assistant-deputy-clerkship under my belt I'd as much weight of my own to swing as the slave who mucked out the privies.

By rights my best course of action would've been to make big eyes at one of my father's friends, look helpless, and be ever so terribly grateful when the guy condescended to take me under his privileged wing. That, of course, was out, even if I could've stomached it. I hadn't seen my father for months and I wouldn't've touched most of his pals with a six-foot pole. Not that they'd've fallen over themselves to help if I had asked. My father and I weren't exactly estranged (only the marriage tie is so simply severed in pukkah families like ours), but that didn't mean to say our lives had to cross. And the last thing I wanted was to owe the bastard any favours.

So there I was, three hours down the line and making progress you couldn't've measured by the scruple. My feet hurt, my back hurt, and I'd have committed any crime short of sodomy for a cup of neat Setinian. The Sixth Assistant Secretary to the Sixth Undersecretary's Assistant had just promised me that he'd see what he could do if I would kindly wait a few months when Cornelius Lentulus hove into view.

Yeah, *hove*. 'Hove' is a good word to use of Lentulus. He had the build of a merchant ship: big, round-bellied, and inclined to wallow in anything but a flat calm. You could describe him as a friend of my father's, I suppose, but he was as far from that sharp-eyed crew as it's possible to get and stay in sight. In other words, he was human, or close enough to it to make no difference. And the old guy had clout by the barrow-load.

'Hey, young fellah-me-lad!' he shouted when he saw me (Yeah again. I never said Lentulus didn't have his faults. In my view Augustus didn't go far enough when he purged the Senate). 'Not often we see you slumming it, eh?'

I explained, and Lentulus nearly popped his clogs right there in the corridor.

'By the gods, I'll nail the bastards' foreskins to their rectums!' Oh, whoopee. Sterling stuff. 'A grandson of my old friend Messalla Corvinus left to kick his heels in the waiting-room like a commoner? Don't you worry, boy, I'll fix things for you. You just leave it to me!'

So of course I did. Willingly, and with suitable awe. Within ten minutes we'd reached the Holy of Holies itself, the imperial anteroom, where even the flies are vetted. At which point, having introduced me to one of the secretaries as something only slightly less sacred than the Palatine Shield of Mars, Lentulus buggered off.

'You must excuse me, young fellah,' he grunted, patting my arm. 'You'll be all right now, Callicrates here'll look after you. Good lad, Callicrates. I've got an early dinner engagement. Nubian girls and tame pythons. Old Gaius Sempronius always does you proud if you've got the stamina. Eh, boy? Eh?'

And, with a final elbow in the ribs, he was gone before I could thank him. A pity. I'd've liked to ask about the Nubians and the pythons. Good tasteful after-dinner entertainment's hard to come by, even in Rome.

The imperial secretary was all teeth and hair-oil.

'And now, sir,' he said. 'How may I help you?'

'A client's father has just died abroad.' I leaned against the desk, giving the guy the full benefit of my patrician nostrils. 'He was exiled under the Divine Augustus, and the client and her mother need imperial permission for his ashes to be brought back to Rome.'

The secretary smiled and reached for his pen and wax tablet. 'No problem there, sir. Not if the gentleman in question is dead. I don't think we need even bother the emperor.'

'Hey, that's great!' I said, and I meant it. Perilla would be grateful the thing had been settled so quickly; and a grateful Perilla, given Uncle Cotta's PS, might be interesting.

'Now if I may just have a few details?' The secretary held his pen poised. 'Your client's name?'

'Rufia Perilla.'

The tip of the pen moved over the wax. 'And the deceased is presumably one Rufius?'

'Actually, no. He was the lady's stepfather. His name was Naso. Publius Ovidius Naso.'

The guy stopped writing like he'd been stung.

'Ovid the poet?' he said sharply. 'The...gentleman who was exiled to Tomi?' The smarmy look was gone like it'd been wiped off his face with a sponge. I felt the first little prickle of unease.

'Yeah. That's right. He died last winter.'

The secretary laid the tablet down carefully. 'Excuse me a moment, sir.'

'Sure.' I was speaking to his back. He'd already disappeared through the curtained archway behind the desk.

I turned round and tried to look more at ease than I felt. The room wasn't exactly full but there were several people waiting behind me: two or three antediluvian senators and a clutch of fat businessmen sitting on the benches or chatting in groups.

Or rather they had been chatting. Not any longer. It was so quiet now you could've heard a mouse fart, and the way no one was looking in my direction was positively miraculous. The prickle of unease became a full-blown itch. I leaned backwards against the secretary's desk and began to whistle through my teeth. One of the senators (he must've been eighty, at least, with the physique of a rat-chewed Egyptian mummy) suddenly swallowed his spittle the wrong way and choked. I watched with interest as his friends (mummies all and only slightly less decrepit) pounded him senseless. I was laying private bets with myself which bit of him would fall off first when someone else coughed behind me, and the secretary was back.

'I'm sorry, sir, but it is felt that your client's request cannot be at present acceded to,' he said.

'You mean you won't do it?'

'Precisely, sir.'

There was something not right here. The guy was sweating. And imperial secretaries never sweat.

'Hey, what is this? You said there'd be no problem.' When in doubt go for the jugular.

Not a muscle of his face moved. 'I was mistaken, sir. I'm sorry but it simply isn't possible.'

'Look.' I was beginning to get annoyed. 'The guy's dead and buried. All I want are his ashes.'

'I know that, sir, but my instructions are—'

'Screw your instructions. I demand to see the emperor.'

I expected that to produce a result, if anything did. I had the right to a personal interview, of course. Tiberius might be a morose antisocial bugger, but he knew the power of the aristocracy. You don't mess with the cream unless you're really anxious for trouble. You can find yourself standing alone in a corner at parties, for starters.

'I don't think an interview with the First Citizen would be very productive, sir,' the secretary said smoothly. 'I assure you that—'

'Listen, sunshine.' I'd had enough of this. I wound my fingers into the neck of the man's tunic and pulled him gently towards me. 'I'm not asking your advice or your opinion. I'm telling you. My name's Marcus Valerius Messalla Corvinus, I'm a full-blown twenty-one-carat noble with a pedigree four times the length of your dick, and if you don't make the appointment forthwith I'll lop your balls off and watch you juggle them.'

He went very pale and his eyes made frantic signalling motions over my shoulder. I turned round. The two Praetorians on the door were up and running towards us as slow as they could make it without being too obvious. Shit. I let the guy go, and his sandals went thunk on the marble floor behind the desk.

He was sweating like a pig now and the small muscle at the side of his mouth had gone into spasm. 'Believe me, sir, I really don't think that an interview would be either possible or advisable. Your request has already, regrettably, been turned down at the highest possible level. Please regard this decision as final.' Taking a deep breath, he brushed at the nap of his tunic where my fingers had crushed it. 'Now, unless you agree to leave quietly...'

The rest was left hanging, but what my old grammar teacher would've called the minatory apodosis was pretty obvious. I glanced over my shoulder to confirm it. Sure enough, the guards were hovering just within lunging distance, two six-foot three-hundred-pound musclebound gorillas in gleaming armour trying their hardest to blend in with the furniture. Sure, they probably wouldn't've dared to throw me out physically, but you don't mess with these guys.

'Okay.' I held my hands up, palm out. I don't think I'd ever been so angry, or so calm. 'Okay. I'm going, sunshine. But don't think you've heard the last of this.'

I turned and walked between the two frozen-faced guards. Beyond them the senators and businessmen formed an embarrassed, grisly tableau, like a Greek chorus waiting for their cue. Even the coughing senator had shut up. He looked dead to me, but then he always had.

A thought struck me. I stopped and turned back.

'What did he do anyway?'

'I beg your pardon, sir?' The secretary looked blank.

'Ovid. What did he do to deserve exile in the first place?'

The guy's face did a good impression of cement setting. 'I really couldn't say, sir.'

'Whatever it was it must've been something pretty big, right? When they won't even allow the bastard home in a box.'

The concrete lips never stirred. The concrete eyes remained unfocused.

I wasn't taking crap like that. Not from anybody.

'Don't you worry, sunshine,' I said. 'I'll get him. I'll bring him back, one way or another. You tell your bosses that from me.'

And so saying I left, with my patrician nose held high. The family (well, some of them, anyway) would've been proud of me. It's times like this that good breeding tells.

It took me an hour to find the exit.

CHAPTER

3

Later that afternoon, I was having a pre-going-out-to-dinner nap in my study when Bathyllus put his head round the door. If ever human face showed terror, Bathyllus's did.

'I'm sorry to disturb you, sir,' he said, 'but the Lady Rufia Perilla is here.'

The effect that woman had on him was frightening. I reckoned if we could bottle it and feed it to the troops we could add Britain to the empire inside a month. Maybe Parthia as well.

'Shit!' I rolled off the couch, knocking over the statuette of Venus braiding her hair which stood on the side table. Bathyllus, tactful as ever, said nothing as he tidied up my rumpled tunic while I stood and scowled. Sure, if I'd been given official permission for the ashes to be returned I'd've been delighted to see the lady back so soon. As it was she was as welcome as a dose of fleas, and I didn't fancy having to explain what'd happened under the scalpel-like gaze of those beautiful golden eyes of hers. Not that I'd failed permanently, of course not. Perish the thought. The Valerii Messallae don't give in that easy. However, I wasn't looking forward to the next step, which was pulling a few strings in the old boy network. That meant trading favour for favour, naturally, and some of the things you get asked to do would turn your hair grey.

At least this time I was meeting her sober. Or fairly sober. Well, not exactly drunk. Well…

I stepped into the atrium like it was the arena and I was top of the menu. Rufia Perilla was standing in the open sitting area admiring the fresco I'd had done recently of Orpheus and the Maenads, and the early evening sun glinting through the portico from the garden beyond kissed her hair with red gold. She must've heard me coming because she turned round and— unbelievably—smiled. My heart gave a lurch. Or maybe it was indigestion.

'You've been to the palace,' she said.

'Yeah.' I lay down on the master couch. Bathyllus was already bringing a chair, and Perilla actually smiled at him as he set it down. He looked lost for an instant. Then he beamed. I could almost see the little bastard's hair curl.

Bathyllus is bald.

'Some wine, sir?' he murmured. Shit. The perfect butler. You could've scooped the smarm off him with a spoon.

'Yeah. Honey wine for the lady, Bathyllus. Setinian for me. The special.' It was the strongest we had, and I was going to need something pretty strong if I wanted to live through the next half-hour with my balls still attached. 'And go easy with the water, okay?'

'So we can arrange for my stepfather's remains to be brought back,' Perilla said when he had gone. 'Corvinus, that's wonderful!'

Normally her use of my last name without the addition of the more formal family one would've set me quivering. Not to mention the smile that went with it. As it was I felt sick as a dog.

'Actually, Lady Rufia...' When you're at a disadvantage, crawl.

'Oh, call me Perilla, please. Mother will be delighted. As to the funeral arrangements, we still keep up the old villa on the hillside above the Claudian-Flaminian junction. We'll bury my stepfather there, in the orchard. He'd've liked that.'

'Perilla...' Jupiter! It was like trying to dam a river with your bare hands.

'You're invited to the ceremony, of course.'

'Perilla, listen to me. I'm sorry, but...'

She waved me down. 'How long do you think it would take for a ship to go to the Black Sea and back? There must be something from Corinth, surely. Ten days? A month? We'd best say two to be on the safe side. Which means we can arrange the funeral for—'

'Wine, madam?' Bathyllus, reappearing with his tray of wine-cups, succeeded in doing what I'd been trying to do, and interrupted her.

Perilla frowned. 'I don't, normally. But perhaps just a little of the Setinian. To celebrate.'

It was now or never. I jumped in with both feet. 'Perilla, listen to me. The funeral's off. No ashes. You understand?' Her mouth opened, but I pressed on. 'They turned us down.'

There was a terrible silence, like just before Vesuvius erupts and even the birds stop singing. For one crazy moment I considered sending Bathyllus to check that my will was safe in the desk.

'I beg your pardon?'

'You can't bring your stepfather back from Tomi after all. At least, not yet. Permission's been refused.'

She was staring at me as if I'd suddenly grown two heads. 'What do you mean, permission's been refused?'

I took the flagon from Bathyllus's tray, poured myself a whopper, and drank it down. Maybe it'd be better if I tried this drunk after all. 'I saw one of the imperial secretaries. He was very apologetic, but there was nothing he could do.'

Perilla drew herself up to her full seated height. I could almost hear the ice crackling.

'Do you mean to tell me, Valerius Corvinus,' she said, and her voice was straight off a glacier, 'that you allowed a civil servant to dictate to you, a patrician from one of the oldest families in Rome?'

I temporised. 'Yeah, well, not really. He was only passing on the decision, so you—'

'And who made the decision? The emperor himself?'

'The guy didn't actually say so, not as such, not in as many words, but that was the implication, yeah.' I was beginning to sweat.

'Valerius Corvinus.' Perilla's voice was terrible. 'Did Tiberius himself refuse to grant the request or did he not?'

I poured another cup of wine and drank it off. The stuff was beginning to work. Maybe another one would do it. 'How the hell should I know?' I said.

That was a mistake. Perilla shot to her feet like a rocketing pheasant. She was stiff with anger.

'You,' she said, 'are a disgrace to your name and the memory of your grandfather. *He* would never have given up like that. Not to mention the first member of your family.'

I poured again. 'That bastard only had a Gallic champion to fight,' I muttered. 'Not a bloody harpy.'

'I beg your pardon?'

'Nothing.' Shit. I took a large swallow. 'Anyway, who says I've uppen gived?' I noticed that Bathyllus hadn't moved. He stood there with the wine things, stiff as a novelty standing-waiter bronze. 'Given up. 'Course I haven't. We'll just have to try another approach, is all.'

'Corvinus,' she said coldly, 'I think I'll go now, if you don't mind. Before you get even more beastly drunk than you are at present.'

It's good stuff, the special. I actually had the nerve to raise my wine-cup to her. She glared at me and turned to leave. As she stormed out the sunshine caught her hair again in a net of molten gold. Ah, well. You win some, you lose some.

I was just congratulating myself on getting rid of Perilla when Bathyllus told me I had another visitor. One even less welcome.

My father.

Like I said, we didn't get on and I hadn't seen him for months, barring the occasional brush in the streets when we exchanged dignified and meaningless salutes. Not, in fact, since the divorce. I was upstairs when Bathyllus announced him, getting ready for that evening's party. I changed back into my lounging tunic and went downstairs, the bile sharp in my throat. Bathyllus had left the study door open and I could see Dad's tall thin figure inside. He was standing by my desk examining the title label of a Greek novel I'd been skimming through, his lantern jaw clenched in disapproval.

'Hi, Dad. How's it going?' I said. He turned, as angry as I'd hoped he would be. My father is so uptight about the social niceties that when they burn him they'll find a poker up his rectum inscribed 'Property of the Senate and People of Rome'. 'Interested in my dirty book collection?'

He put the novel down slowly. Actually, it was pretty well written, and not dirty at all, but I wasn't going to tell him that. It would've spoiled the bastard's evening.

'How are you, Marcus?'

'Okay.' I motioned him to the study's only couch and sat myself in the desk chair. Bathyllus put his nose round the door and I sent him for the wine.

We stared at each other in silence.

'I saw your mother today,' he said finally.

'Nice of you.'

He held up a placating hand. 'She's happy enough.'

'Oh, whoopee.'

My father's mouth turned down. 'The marriage wasn't working, son. Ending it was good for both of us. You know that.'

'For you, maybe,' I said. 'Not for me. And Mother tried her best. She'd never have divorced you. If she had done it'd've been for a reason, not just because it suited her at the time. Not because a new wife would be politically convenient.'

His sallow face flushed with anger. 'It wasn't like that at all, Marcus! And I won't have you judging me!'

'Thank the gods you don't!' I shot back. He turned away.

There was a polite cough outside the door and Bathyllus reappeared. We sat in stony silence, glaring at each other while Bathyllus poured. When he'd gone, I handed my father a wine-cup.

'So what do you want?' I said. 'To what do I owe the inestimable pleasure of your fucking presence, Dad? Tell me and then get out.'

He set the cup down untasted. His hands were shaking; but then mine were, too.

'I'm here on official business, Marcus. You caused a bit of trouble at the palace this morning.'

I took a long swallow. 'You've been misinformed. I didn't cause any trouble. I made a perfectly reasonable request and when it was turned down in what I considered to be an unsatisfactory way I asked for an interview with the emperor.'

'That wasn't what I heard. I was told you got quite abusive.'

'No more abusive than the situation merited.'

'And that you assaulted an imperial secretary.'

'Come off it, Dad!' I set the wine-cup down hard on the desk, and the wine leaped up over the rim. 'What do you expect? The bastard told me he wouldn't let me see Tiberius. *He* wouldn't let me! Who the hell is a government clerk to tell a patrician noble that he can't see the emperor?'

'What he told you, and quite correctly, was that your request had already been turned down at the highest level.'

'Meaning by the emperor himself.'

'Meaning presumably just that.'

'Without doing me the courtesy of talking to me first? Without the grace at least to explain his reasons?'

'The emperor doesn't have to give a reason, Marcus. If he says a request is refused, then it's refused, and there's an end of it.'

'Oh, yeah! Sure!' I stood up and turned my back on my father. If I hadn't I think I would've hit him. 'That's your credo, isn't it? The emperor's always right, long live the emperor. If Tiberius passed a decree praising dog turds you'd have half a dozen of them in aspic on your dinner table the next day.'

'That's not fair, son.' My father's voice was calm. 'Tiberius is the First Citizen, the head of state. When he makes an executive decision...'

I turned round. 'Look, let's get this clear, right? I'm not complaining about the decision. I'm not a child. I can take no for an answer. What sticks in my throat is how the Wart's judgment—if it was his judgment—was delivered, and that I was barred from exercising my right…' I stopped, then repeated the words slowly: 'My right, Father, to a personal interview. And if you think I'm going to let the matter rest there then you can go and screw yourself.'

'Oh, yes, you will, Marcus, unless you're a complete fool!' my father snapped. 'That's why I'm here. That's what I've come to tell you, and you'd better listen or you're in real trouble. Leave it alone. You've asked and you've had your answer. Now tell that Rufia Perilla woman there's nothing you can do, and forget about her.'

I walked back over to the desk, picked up my wine-cup and emptied it at a gulp. 'How did you know about Perilla, Dad?"

'I told you. This is official.'

'Okay,' I said, turning the cup slowly in my hands. 'So just tell me one thing. What did he do? What did Ovid do, to make the Wart hate him so much?'

Now the next bit is interesting. I was looking squarely at my father when I spoke, so I saw exactly what happened to his face. It was like a door slamming shut. One moment his expression was as open as my father's ever can be, the next his eyes were blank as marble. That was interesting enough; but as I said I was looking directly at him and saw something more. It was no more than a flash, like the glimpse of lamplight behind a closing door, but there was no mistaking it. None.

What I saw was fear.

Varus to Himself

I am mad to write this. A traitor's first and cardinal rule is to commit nothing to writing, and thus far I have obeyed it scrupulously. To produce written evidence of one's treason is to raise up a witness against oneself who will shout louder than a hundred calumnies. And that is the last thing I wish to do.

So why write at all, you ask me (I ask myself?). Certainly not for the edification of posterity. Posterity can go and hang itself: my eyes will be the only ones to read this, and I will burn it as soon as it is complete. Nor is it in any way a confession, the private mortification of a spirit tortured by guilt. To hell with that. If I ever had a conscience I lost it long before puberty, and besides, in common with most traitors, I am, if not exactly proud of my treason, at least content in its company. So not that either.

Perhaps it would be best to call what I am about a justification; an appeal for understanding, by myself to myself. Oh dear, oh dear! That sounds terribly precious, but I am very much afraid that it is the truth. In extenuation, I suspect that I am not alone among traitors in wishing to justify my treason. The disease is endemic to us. Paullus was the exception, fortunately for me and for others: he died silent. Although in fairness, of course, Paullus was not a true traitor.

So call this a justification, then, of treason undertaken for the best of motives. Or wait, that is unfair and untrue. I would not have you think me a filthy altruist. No, what I am doing is, frankly, profitable and will provide materially for what I hope will be a long, comfortable and very self-indulgent retirement. The fact that it will benefit Rome is to me, alas, a comparatively minor issue, although satisfying to contemplate. Had Arminius appealed to my gentlemanly instincts (assuming, for the sake of argument, that I had any), or had he been niggardly with his rewards, I doubt very much whether venal old Varus would have cooperated. Ah me. Sad, is it not? Sad but true.

You see? I am being completely honest. But then by their own lights most traitors are.

So, then. We are agreed in calling this a justification. Now let me set the scene for you. Who are we, and where?

We are three legions. Fifteen thousand men, plus cavalry, auxiliary troops, baggage carts and mules. The pride and power of Rome and of her First Citizen, Augustus, with its impedimenta, returning south for the winter to the not-quite-province of Germany, of which I am the emperor's governor and viceroy. The campaigning season being successfully completed, we are en route from our summer camp on the Weser to Vetera on the Rhine, where (the gods help us!) my headquarters are located: a distance, as the crow flies, of some hundred and fifty miles, although as the Roman marches it is further and, alas, entails considerably greater effort.

So much is public knowledge. What follows is for your eyes only. Soon, perhaps somewhere between the Ems and the Lippe, news will reach us of trouble to the east among the large and warlike Cheruscan tribe.

And then?

And then, my gentle and imaginary confidant, the final act of my treason will begin.

CHAPTER

4

I was down to the Market Square next morning as early as my hangover would let me with a mental list of promising contacts. The list was pretty short. Like I say, I didn't use the old boy network much, and just the thought of being indebted to any of my father's cronies made me sick to my stomach. Nevertheless, there were a few strings I could tug, several favours I could call in, and if the worst came to the worst even one or two arms I could twist with a little judicious blackmail. It shouldn't be too difficult. After all, what's a handful of ashes and burned bone between friends?

Market Square was crawling like an ants' nest, and as it always does in the mornings when most of the business is done, it smelled of shaving talc and raw power. Before I'd pushed my way ten yards through the crowd I'd overheard two under-the-counter trading scams discussed, one fat senator putting the bite on another for some fancy political footwork, and a mid-ranking civil servant being bribed over a government marble tender.

Not that your average plain-mantled punter would've noticed anything, of course. These deals aren't made in straightforward Latin. To understand what's going on you have to know the special language. We patricians speak it fluently from birth, which is why so many of us are still alive even after bastards like Caesar and Augustus were through with us.

I struck lucky straight off. I'd just drawn level with the Temple of Castor when I spotted Caelius Crispus ooze down the steps of the Julian Basilica and come through the crowd towards me. I swear I could smell the guy's scent even at that distance—violets, mostly, with overtones of musk. His boyfriend at the palace must've bought him a gallon of the stuff. For my purposes, Crispus was perfect. His grandfather had been a pork butcher, he'd never held any public office, and he wasn't likely to even in these democratic, degenerate days; all of which meant that my father wouldn't've touched him with his third-best gloves on. Even so, for reasons it was best not to go into too deeply, he was one of the most influential men in Rome. Better still, he owed me one, and a pretty big one at that. I won't go into details. Suffice it to say that it involved a very young boy, a very strait-laced Gallic daddy just in from the sticks, and a very sharp dagger; and that it'd been Crispus's sheer good luck that I happened to be passing in a covered litter at the time.

'Hey, Crispus!' I shouted.

He saw me. Sure he saw me. His eyes widened and then with a piece of ham acting that wouldn't've deceived a five-year-old he looked away, waved to a non-existent friend on the steps of the Temple of Saturn and took off like a rabbit in the direction of Spain. Now that I wasn't having. No one—but no one—cuts a Valerius Messalla with impunity, not when he's calling in a favour. I piled in after the guy, stamping on a few august senatorial corns and outraging a dignity or two in the process, and ran him down with a hand on his shoulder just short of the Speakers' Platform.

'Corvinus.' He batted his eyelashes at me as if I'd sprung from nowhere. 'What a pleasant surprise.'

'Yeah, sure.' I wiped my hand on my tunic. 'Where's the fire, Crispus?'

His eyes shifted. 'What fire?'

'You were running, you bastard. So why don't you want to talk to me?'

'I was in a hurry. Am in a hurry. Someone at the Treasury. I have to talk to him urgently.'

He was frightened. I could smell his fear even above the scent, and the muscles at the sides of his mouth were twitching.

'He can wait, Crispus.' I tucked his arm firmly under mine and tried not to breathe too deeply as I led him back towards Augustus Arch. 'He can wait because I'm going to buy you a drink at Gorgo's, right? And then I'll tell you what you can do for me in exchange.'

By the time I'd got Crispus to the wineshop off the Sacred Way the guy had all the vitality and colour of two-day-old lettuce. This, mark you, before I'd so much as nibbled at him, let alone put the bite on properly. That could mean only one thing. He knew what I was after already. And that, given the bastard's reaction, was interesting.

Crispus was a trader, specialising in dirty gossip, the murkier the better. Political secrets, social scandals. Who was screwing who, or preferably what, and how and why they were doing it. He'd no scruples, no conscience, and (which was the point) no nerves. What Crispus knew may have kept him eating and surely kept him safe—because Crispus knew a hell of a lot of things about a hell of a lot of people—but it wasn't the kind of life that was good for the digestion; like walking a tightrope with your second-worst enemy throwing rocks at you and your first busy with a hacksaw. So if Crispus was scared of giving me the information I wanted (which he obviously was) then I'd give a lot to know why.

It was a cold day, but I needed privacy, so we sat down at an outside table. I ordered up a flask of Alban and a plate of cheese and dried figs, and as soon as the waiter left I got straight down to business.

'You're still attached to the imperial branch of the civil service, right?'

He nodded warily. We both knew what that 'attached' stood for.

'Good.' I took a cautious sip of my wine and swallowed carefully. Gorgo's best was still liable to go down like a handful of gravel. 'I've been having some trouble with them lately. Maybe you've heard?'

Crispus said nothing. I'd seen more expression on the face of a boiled sturgeon.

'Okay.' I played it straight-faced. 'So maybe you haven't. I want to bring the poet Ovid's ashes back to Rome and I need help to do it. You've just drawn the lucky number.'

The bastard was shaking so hard the table was moving, but I pretended not to notice.

'I'd like to, Corvinus,' he said. 'Believe me. But—'

I cut him short. 'Crispus, the poor sod's dead, okay? It's not like I was asking for an imperial pardon. I just want his ashes in a plain clay urn. Now come on, be a pal. Have a discreet word in someone's ear or whatever you diplomatic bastards do and save us all a load of trouble.'

'It's not the sort of thing my…department handles. And I'd hate to tread on anyone's toes.'

'Look, don't give me that, right?' I pushed the plate of

cheese and figs across the table towards him. He shook his head. He hadn't touched his wine, either, but maybe that was just good taste. 'It's garbage and you know it. If your friend doesn't deal with that sort of thing himself then you know someone else who does, and you're probably good enough mates to share a scraper in the baths.'

He gave me a sharp look, and I knew I'd unwittingly touched a nerve. However, the complications of Crispus's private life were no concern of mine.

'I'm not saying I wouldn't know who to talk to,' he said. 'Of course I would. But it wouldn't do any good.'

'Why not?'

His forehead was beginning to shine with sweat. He wiped it with the back of his hand. 'Look, don't push me, Corvinus. Okay? It just wouldn't. Believe me.'

'I don't. Persuade me some more.' I popped a fig into my mouth, chewed and swallowed. 'Look, Crispus. You owe me a favour. If it hadn't been for me you'd be singing soprano in the civil service glee club. I'm not asking for much and I won't take no for an answer. So fix it for me, okay?'

'You don't understand.' His face was grey now, and the twitch at the corner of his mouth was getting worse. 'The decision's already been made, and it's final.'

I lost my temper. 'Then have it unmade! Crispus, I've had about enough of this! Since when has the imperial displeasure extended to an urnful of fucking bones? That's all Ovid is now, whatever he did ten years ago. And speaking of which, if you can't help me get him back then at least you can tell me what that was.'

As I said the words I saw the fear leap into his eyes just before the shutters slammed down. This was getting monotonous. First the secretary, then my father. Now Crispus.

Seemingly everybody I talked to knew what Ovid's crime had been. It looked as if I was the only guy in Rome who didn't.

There was no point in shouting. I backed off a little; sat back, emptied my wine-cup and poured a second. Smiled, or tried to.

'Come on,' I said. 'You can tell me that, eh, Crispus? A mine of information like you? Just what crime did Ovid commit? Why's the Wart so against having the poor bastard's ashes buried in Roman soil? Just tell me that, and if the reason's a good one I swear I'll give up and go home. Debt cancelled. Okay?' He was watching me with the horrified, fascinated gaze of a rabbit watching a stoat. 'Come on, now. What did Ovid do that was so terrible?'

Crispus glanced quickly to either side of us like he expected the emperor himself to spring up from under one of the neighbouring tables and slap a treason writ on him.

'Leave it alone, Corvinus,' he muttered. 'Don't dig, don't ask questions, don't do anything. Just give this thing up right now before you live to regret it.'

And before I could stop him he was up and running: slipping from behind the table and out of the courtyard into the street fast as an Olympic sprinter. I flung a few coins in the direction of the waiter and tried to follow. But he must've wanted to get away very badly indeed, because when I looked for him he was already gone.

Round two to the bureaucrats, I thought sourly as I went back to finish the wine. If they expected me to give up that easily then they were whistling through their collective rectums.

So where were we? I knew two things so far. First of all, whatever Ovid had been guilty of was common knowledge, at least among the top brass and their 'attachments'. Secondly, it was so bad, or so politically sensitive, that even after ten years everyone was still shit-scared to talk about it. And that was interesting.

So how could I find out?

The answer was so ludicrously obvious that when I thought of it I could've kicked myself all the way back to the Palatine.

Perilla was Ovid's stepdaughter. She'd know what he'd done. Or her mother would. All I had to do was ask.

Easy, right?

Suillius Rufus's place was on the slopes of the Esquiline not far from the Maecenas Gardens. It was good sound sycophant's property—flashy enough to impress but not sufficiently grand to attract dangerous envy in these luxury-sensitive times. The slave who opened the door for me wore red. Given the look of the place, that could've only been for one of two reasons: first, the chichi visual pun on Rufus's name; second, because the Red team at the racecourse was Tiberius's favourite. Or at least everybody thought it was Tiberius's favourite. Personally I had my doubts. The Wart was quite capable of spreading a rumour like that just for the fun of watching guys like Rufus fall over themselves trying to lick his arse.

The wall mosaic in the lobby was politically correct too. Forget your bourgeois 'Beware of the Dog' tat, this was art: a more than life-size Divine Augustus, golden rays of glory streaming from his noble brow, seated on a pink cloud between the goddesses of piety and liberality, shedding his gracious lustre on the tiny city of Rome below. All beautifully and tastefully done in stones the size of my little fingernail. You could even make out the goddesses' nipples.

The thing must've cost an arm and a leg. I nearly threw up all over it.

I gave my name to the slave and he led me through the marble-pillared atrium into the garden (the pool, I noticed in passing, had a Venus and Cupids bathing in it. Another compliment to Augustus's adoptive Julian ancestors, perhaps. Or maybe Rufus was just a randy bugger). The day had brightened but it was still cold. Perilla, sitting in a chair under the shelter of an arbutus and dressed in a fetching little yellow number that looked more for show than warmth, didn't seem concerned. Scattered around her feet were half the contents of the Pollio Library; which was more or less what I'd been expecting. Since her last visit I'd done a bit of homework on sweet little Rufia Perilla. She was a pretty smart lady, not just a poet's stepdaughter but a poet herself, and a mean mind where the literary heavies were concerned. As a peace offering to one of my usual bubbleheads I'd've brought perfume or maybe a little trinket from Argyrion's in the Saepta. For Perilla I'd chosen a book: a very rare copy of some Alexandrian pansy who wrote about shepherd-boys (no, I don't know which one. He was expensive, that's all I know).

Why I should be apologising to her when she'd been the one to call me names I've no idea. But that's the way things work. Understand that and you understand women.

'Corvinus!' She looked up smiling from the scroll she was reading. 'Lovely to see you!' Good news. It seemed like I was forgiven after all, even without the book. I handed it over anyway. She looked at the title label and purred with the sort of pleasure I keep for baked sturgeon with a quince sauce. 'Oh, how absolutely marvellous! Thank you!' She turned to the slave. 'Callias, bring Valerius Corvinus a chair and some wine.'

Obviously a lady of some sensitivity. Maybe I'd misjudged her.

The slave shot off and was back in record time. He had a harried, chewed look about him that I recognised, and I felt for the poor bastard. Being a slave in Perilla's household must've been as wearing on the nerves as being chief manicurist to Cleopatra's leopards.

I sat down and sipped at the wine. It was Falernian and so ought to've been good, but it was third-rate stuff. Whatever the absent Rufus's qualities were (and he must've had some besides an ability to use his tongue to good advantage), they obviously didn't extend to a discriminating palate. Or maybe it was the fault of his cellarman. If so the guy should be crucified with a flask of the stuff up his rectum. I set the cup aside as unobtrusively as I could.

'Now.' Perilla laid the book aside and settled back, giving me the kind of smile that would have any Greek sculptor worth his salt reaching for his sketchbook. 'Don't tell me. You've seen the emperor and he's agreed.'

'Uh...actually no, Perilla. That's not why I've come.' The smile faded from her face but at least she didn't freeze up on me.

'But you're making progress.'

'I'm trying. There's just nothing doing that's all.'

"Why not?'

I shrugged. 'Your guess is as good as mine. All I get are solid refusals right down the line. I think it might have something to do with your stepfather's crime.' She didn't say anything, so I lightened it up a bit. 'What did the old guy do, Perilla? Personally promise to hand Armenia over to the

Parthians? Rape Livia? Rape Augustus? Burst one of the Wart's boils?' Silence. 'Oh, come on, lady! I'm your patron, remember?'

'I don't know,' she said at last. 'My stepfather never told us.'

Jupiter! 'What do you mean, he never told you? The guy had been punished already. The secret was out.'

She shook her head. Today the golden hair was tied up in a tight braid, simpler than was fashionable but suiting her perfectly. A single curl lay tantalisingly against each temple. I could smell roses.

'We asked him,' she said. 'At least my mother did, I was too young. But he wouldn't even tell her. He said it was too dangerous.'

My scalp tingled. 'Dangerous? Dangerous to who?'

'Himself, I suppose. Or maybe to my mother and me. Anyway, he wouldn't say.'

I couldn't believe this.

'Come on, Perilla! Sure, I know nothing was made public, but your mother must've known what he did, or be able to guess at least. They were very close, weren't they?'

'Yes. Very,' she said softly.

'And you're telling me he clammed up on her? Totally?'

'Maybe she does know.' Perilla had lowered her eyes and her voice was barely a whisper. I waited for more, but it didn't come. There was something I didn't understand here.

'Then why don't you ask her outright?'

'Because it wouldn't do any good.'

Again that phrase. I'd heard it from the secretary, and from Crispus. It sounded strange coming from Perilla. 'Didn't Ovid say anything before he left? Or give any clues in his letters? He did send letters, didn't he?'

'Oh, yes.' Perilla plucked a sprig of leaves from the bush beside her and turned it absently between her fingers. 'He talked about…whatever he'd done quite often, in fact. Not just in his letters. In his poems as well.'

Now we were getting somewhere! 'Okay. So tell me.'

'He says he made a mistake. He saw something he shouldn't have seen, and he didn't report it.'

'And?'

'That's all.'

I leaned back. Shit. The more I got into this thing, the more tantalising it became, and the more it slipped away from me. Hints and rumours. Like mist or water through the fingers.

'What do you mean that's all?'

'Just what I say. Oh, there's more, lots more, but that's the gist of it. That and what he didn't do.'

'Didn't do?' I was beginning to sound like a third-rate tragedian's chorus.

'He says he didn't profit personally from whatever it was. And he hadn't killed anyone, or committed forgery or fraud or treason.'

'That doesn't leave very much.'

'No, it doesn't.'

'So what you're saying,' I spelled it out, 'is that Ovid did nothing whatsoever? That Augustus sent him to Tomi just for seeing something he shouldn't have seen?'

'And for not reporting it. Yes, that's right.'

'But it's crazy! It makes no sense at all! Jupiter's holy prick, we're talking about exile here!'

'Nevertheless, Corvinus, that's all there is. And please don't swear. I don't like it.'

'But what could he have seen that deserved that sort of treatment? To be packed off to the Black Sea for the rest of his days, without a trial, with no reprieve. Not even to be allowed back for burial.'

'I don't know.'

'Come off it, lady! You're his f… You're his stepdaughter!'

Her lips set in a firm line, and she looked away.

'I've told you that's all there is,' she said, 'and I would be grateful if we could drop the subject.'

Now I may not know my Bion from my Moschus, but I know damn well when a woman isn't telling me the truth. And if ever a beautiful woman lied through her teeth that woman was Rufia Perilla. You expect obstructions from nit-picking bureaucrats and timeservers like my father and Crispus. You don't expect them from the client you're trying to help.

I got up. 'Okay, don't tell me. I'll find out for myself. Anyway, I've got to be going now. I've a long night of debauchery ahead of me and I need to get tanked up first. Thank you for your hospitality, Lady Rufia.'

She turned back to face me, and she had the grace to look guilty; but that was all.

'Thank you for the book,' she said. 'It was kind of you to think of it.'

"My pleasure.' I was almost as angry as I had been in the secretary's office. 'I'll see you around, okay?'

As I walked past her she laid a hand on my arm. 'I really don't know why my stepfather was exiled, Corvinus. I'm not hiding anything from you. Honestly.'

'Sure,' I said; but I'd stopped. I could no more've carried on walking back to the house with those fingers burning into my skin than thrown a party for my father and that new wife of his.

She lowered her eyes, but not before I'd seen the glint of tears. 'I may have thoughts of my own on the subject but they're just that. Thoughts of my own.'

'Care to share them?'

She shook her head. 'No, they're probably wrong anyway. Certainly they don't make much sense.'

There was a lump in my throat the size of an egg. I told you I was a kind-hearted sucker. However, I had my pride as well. Valerii Messallae don't melt easily.

'Suit yourself,' I said. I had my arm back now. There was nothing else to keep me.

'You'll still keep on trying? To get the permission, I mean?'

'Of course,' I said stiffly. 'You had my promise.'

She got up and before I knew what was happening she'd kissed me lightly on the cheek. It was the sort of bird's peck you'd expect from your kid sister, but from the effect it had on me you'd've thought she'd given me a complete no-holds-barred Corinthian tongue job. I muttered something suitably noble and patronlike about doing my best and escaped as quickly as I could.

I'd given Perilla my word that she'd have her stepfather's ashes back, and I intended to keep it, whatever the cost. But as of this afternoon I'd as much idea of how to go about it as an oyster's got of woodcarving.

Varus to Himself

Vela has just come in for the sentries' watchword. I gave him *Inflexible Vigilance*, a joke which, of course, he did not recognise as such. Numonius Vela is my second-in-command, with special responsibility for the cavalry. That, too, is a joke.

I have always viewed horses as stupid creatures. They have as much sense (and no more) as will prevent them throwing their riders in battle and ensure that they go cheerfully to possible disembowelment. In other words, they are blessed with the perfect military virtues. Horses and Vela have much in common. He is a turnip-head incapable of following a reasoned argument beyond its first most obvious premise; a nonentity of staggering blandness. Solid is the word that springs to mind— or perhaps stolid, for Vela has no stiffness, no backbone. He is thick and starchy as overcooked porridge. You could reach out your hand and knead him, body and soul. This is not to say he is a moral man. If Vela is incorruptible (and he is; oh, he most certainly is!) his virtue is a product not of choice but of mental and spiritual sloth.

In short, dear confidant, Numonius Vela is a bore of the first order. I view it as not the least of my trials that I am compelled to march through Germany in his company.

Perhaps I should give you other names, and the faces to fit them. I will not weary you with a long list—we are few, we band of brothers, despite the thousands of breathing souls who surround us. Three—not counting Vela—will be sufficient.

Egregious Eggius first, and least. My camp commander, or one of them. One of the old breed, a Roman par excellence, who might have stood with Horatius on the bridge but would have drawn the line at anything so cowardly as chopping it down. Where Vela is a cold-porridge soldier, Eggius is all pepper and fiery spices, a damn-your-eyes man destined for glory or the grave; the latter being his more likely destination, and good riddance to him so long as he does not drag the rest of us in as well. I cannot bring myself to like Eggius, but he has his uses, largely because of his natural antipathy for Vela. Which is, I may say, reciprocated and affords me much quiet amusement.

Next, Marcus Ceionius, my other camp commander and, of necessity, ally. Venal, greedy (although as you know I speak as should not), cowardly and rotten as a ten-day-old fig, which facially he unfortunately resembles. He, too, may win through to glory, but it will be glory undeserved and achieved by guile rather than merit. If, as is more likely, the grave claims him before his time, it will be with a common soldier's javelin in his back. The men hate him, and with good reason. It is rare to meet someone with no redeeming qualities. Ceionius comes as close as is humanly possible.

Third and last, your humble servant: Publius Quinctilius Varus. Ex-consul, ex-this, ex-that (I shall never, after all, see sixty again). Augustus's viceroy and general of this glorious army. Bon viveur, lover of coined gold, and (not least, this!) traitor against the state. That, I think, will do for the present. After all, I do not wish to alienate your sympathies completely.

You will notice of course that I have not described Arminius, who is the most relevant character of all. Patience. I must, like every good general, keep something in reserve. You will meet Arminius in his place, and I promise you that you will have your fill of him.

Heigh ho. Off we go.

CHAPTER

6

I didn't go straight home when I left Perilla's. I'd left a signet ring in for repair at Cadmus's in Fox Street off the Saepta, which meant another trip up town. Not that I minded. I liked walking around the city, even in weather like this. Besides, it was an excuse for a stroll through the Subura.

Yeah. I know. That's the sort of remark eager young heirs to the family fortune hope to hear their rich daddies making. It means that the old guys' lids have shaken loose and it's time to call in the lawyers and slap on a certificate of gross mental instability. No one in their right mind walks in Rome if they can avoid it. The crowds are thicker than fleas in a fourth-rate whore's mattress, the climate's boiling in summer and freezing in winter, and the streets stink all the year round of effluent, rotten vegetables and everything from cheap incense to dead dogs and month-old fish. And that's just for starters. Step off the main thoroughfares in the poorer districts and you'll find that the more enterprising locals do a line in throat-slitting, mugging, and purse-snatching that has anywhere else in the empire beaten hollow. Keep to the main drag and you've got a better-than-average chance of being hit by something thrown from a tenement. Or, if your luck's really out, hit by the tenement itself. Don't laugh. I've seen it happen.

So I like Rome. Sure, it may be a dump outside the bits that old Augustus found brick and left marble, it may stink worse than a wineshop privy in midsummer, but it's got character. Where else could you buy a pitch-black performing midget, have your fortune told by a cheiromantic goat, and catch a dose of clap from a female sword-swallower, all within twenty yards?

Like I say, Rome's strong meat. It may hurt you, it may even kill you, but it'll never bore you.

The sky was beginning to cloud over in earnest as I left the slope of the Esquiline and cut down into the Subura. This was pretty bad news. Most people who have business in that part of town can't afford raincoats let alone litters, and the chances of finding a litter-team for hire between Pullian Street and the Argiletum is about as likely as seeing the Wart do a clog-dance for coppers on the Speakers' Platform. I wrapped my cloak tighter round me, pulled up the hood to keep the wind out of my eyes, and tried to think about something other than the soaking I was going to get between here and the Saepta.

Like what I'd got on Ovid so far.

Point one. The reason for his exile was no secret among what I'd call the arselickers: people like my father and Crispus, who were on the inside of government and knew where all the dirty linen hung. If they were terrified to open their prim little mouths in case someone slapped them shut, then, whatever the secret was, ancient history or not, it was pretty sensitive.

Point two. Ovid hadn't done any of the things that usually

get you exile. Or at least claimed he hadn't. Not treason, not murder, forgery or fraud. And that, like I'd said to Perilla, didn't leave much. Sure, he could've been lying but I didn't think so. After all, why take the trouble to deny what no one was accusing him of unless he'd got a genuine axe to grind? Also Perilla had said that she and her mother still kept up the villa to the north of Rome, which meant that the emperor hadn't confiscated Ovid's property. If the crime was really serious, then that didn't make sense either.

Which brought me to the last point. Not only had Ovid not been charged with any of the crimes he'd listed, he hadn't been charged at all. No charge, no trial, no nothing, just a summons to a private interview with the emperor and a one-way ticket by imperial decree. That sort of thing just didn't happen with a run-of-the-mill crime. More, Augustus had made it clear that whatever the guy had done to put his imperial nose out of joint, the subject was closed. No questions answered, no explanations given. Stranger still, when the Wart came to power and some of the biggest men in Rome begged him to cancel the edict or at least move the poor bastard to somewhere the locals didn't trail their knuckles while they walked, Tiberius had refused. No pardon, no explanation, just that straight, bald refusal. And now the guy was dead the emperor wouldn't even make space in Italy for his bones.

Big-league stuff. And weird by any standards.

I crossed over at the junction of Pullian with Orbian and took in a family of street musicians. They were good—grampa on finger cymbals, dad on hand drum, and mum on the double flute, with a kid in a dirty brown tunic standing behind them picking his nose for light relief. The daughter—no kid by any standards—was collecting coppers. She wore a short girdle with bells, a leather bra, and an expression of total headbanging boredom. In that weather she must've been freezing. When she came round to me I slipped a silver piece under each bra cup, patted her rump and left quickly before Pa caught on to why she was grinning. Spread a little sunshine, that's my motto. Besides, she had marvellous tits. Then I cut down the first of the little alleyways that would take me through the heart of the district and, eventually, to Suburan Street itself.

So what had Ovid done? All I had to go on was his own weird, coy statement that he'd seen something he shouldn't have and hadn't told anyone about it. Not exactly earthshaking stuff, and not the sort of thing to get you permanent exile in a godforsaken hole like Tomi. Let alone stop your kin from bringing back your ashes, which was something completely off the wall. Sure, the state might take a chunk or two out of the guy's kin if his crime had been bad enough, but that was a different thing to stopping them from burying his bones when he finally died. Whatever Ovid had been guilty of, this sustained knee-jerk reaction was unique, totally savage and just plain inexplicable.

Okay, so where did that leave us? With some sort of scandal, obviously, that Augustus wanted buried deep and fast and permanent. A scandal was the only thing that would explain the secrecy and the lack of formal charges, and it could be private or political or both. My money was on the private. Ovid was no politician and like I said he'd had the moral reputation of an alley-cat. Also once he'd packed him off to Tomi, Augustus had pulled his poems off the shelves of the city's public libraries. I knew that from personal experience. I remember a few years later as a spotty kid trying to get my lecherous hands on his *Art of Love*—a step-by-step guide to seduction— and being sent off with a flea in my ear and a moth-eaten copy of Cato's *Farming Is Fun*. So. A social scandal involving sex, close enough to home for Augustus to take it as a personal insult, serious enough to get the guy exile and a strict warning to keep his mouth shut even where his wife and daughter were concerned. And it must've happened about ten years ago, about the time when...

When...

Jupiter! I stopped so suddenly that the stout woman a step or two behind me piled into my back. The pole she was carrying with two chickens dangling upside down from it caught me a stinger on the side of the head.

'You want to watch where you're going, sonny,' she said; or words to that effect. The Subura's no place to pick up refined diction.

'Yeah. Yeah. I'm sorry.' I was still dazed; and not because of the pole. The old girl gave me a funny look and moved off. The chickens didn't look too happy either.

Julia! The Julia scandal!

I couldn't remember all the details—I'd only been a kid at the time, hardly into double figures—but I knew the gist. It'd happened that same year, I was sure of that. Augustus's granddaughter Julia had been convicted of adultery and exiled to some flyspeck of an island out in the sticks. And Julia, when she hadn't been humping half of Rome, had been one of Ovid's literary patrons...

I carried on walking, my head still buzzing like a beehive. I had to be right. It couldn't be a coincidence, not the two exiles coming so close together. If Ovid had been screwing Julia and the emperor had found out, then Augustus had good reason to blow his toupé. The only problem was that I was sure some other guy had been named as having his hand down the lady's pants. Named and charged, publicly. And if Julia had been two-timing him with Ovid, then why not say so? Why not charge

Ovid as well and forget all this cloak-and-dagger crap? And if there was no cover-up involved, and Ovid simply knew Julia was on the job and didn't tell, then why not charge him publicly with that and be done with it?

Sure, I know. None of this made enough sense to fry an anchovy in. But at least it was a start; whatever Ovid's crime was, it had to be connected with the Julia affair. Had to be! It was only a question of fitting things together. More information would help, sure. The name of the adulterer for a start and what had happened to him. If I could just find someone who knew the facts and was willing to tell me, then maybe I could take it from there. The first part was easy. The second...

Yeah. The second part was the killer. The way people had been avoiding me recently had me sniffing down my tunic for body odour. If I was right about the Julia connection and started asking questions that involved embarrassing answers, then things could get worse.

I felt the first drops of rain as I reached Suburan Street. The Saepta was still a long way off, I was beginning to regret my detour, and the clouds were heaping up like a herd of elephants mating. Maybe, I thought, it might be a good idea to make a dash for Augustus Square. There were always plenty of litters touting for business there, but if the rain came on in earnest they'd all be snapped up. The streets around the square itself were always packed, and I wasn't the only pedestrian without a hat or a raincoat with money in my purse. There was just a chance, though, that I might catch a litter-team before that. Suburan Street's a main thoroughfare, and although it's still far from being a high-class area you sometimes strike lucky. I turned round and looked behind me to check for anything heading in my direction.

Fifty yards back a man was crossing over to my side of the

road. He was the sort of guy you can't help but notice, half the size of Augustus's mausoleum and twice as ugly, but without the gorilla-like shamble some really big men have. A professional sword-fighter, maybe. Or an ex-soldier. Someone, anyway, who knew his size was the other guy's problem. I saw what was going to happen before it did—in that part of town you can't make any sudden changes of direction if you want to stay popular, and even crossing the street takes time. The big guy went slap into an oil-seller, knocking him flying and drenching half a dozen peaceful citizens with lamp oil. If I'd had time I would've stuck around to broaden my vocabulary, but the rain was getting heavier and the sky directly above me was as black as a Nubian's backside.

I'd got about three more yards when the storm broke; and as storms go it was a beaut. Rain lancing down out of the black sky hissed and bounced on the pavement like hail and swarmed into the gutters. Suddenly the street was a muddy brown river full of cabbage leaves, drowned insects, and mule droppings. Everyone ran for cover, me included; only there was nowhere to run. My cloak was soaked through in seconds. My ears were full and my eyes were full, and it was sheer luck that I spotted the open doorway to a potter's shop. I shot inside like a rabbit going to ground.

The shop was dim and quiet after the chaos outside. I stood for a moment cursing and trying to wipe the rainwater out of my eyes with my already sodden cloak.

Then I turned round.

The big guy who had flattened the oil-seller was standing between me and the doorway; right between me and the doorway. And that, in the Subura, meant trouble.

I looked round. The shop was empty. Great. All the potters' shops in Rome to choose from and I had to pick the lemon.

'Your name Valerius Corvinus?' You could've taken the guy's accent and hung your boots on it. A foreigner. German, maybe.

'What's that to you?' Trying not to make it too obvious, I got my hand round the hilt of the little insurance policy I keep strapped to the underside of my left forearm.

He stepped forward without answering. Like I say, he was no beauty. Now that my eyes were used to the darkness I could see the deep, well-healed scar down the left side of his face. Part of his left ear was missing, too. I'd been right. Sword-fighter or soldier, he'd been in scraps before.

'Hey, you know what you remind me of, pal?' The dagger was free now but I didn't show it. I needed all the edge I could get. 'The gorilla they keep in Maecenas Gardens. Only he's better looking.'

Subtle as a brick, sure; intentionally so. But if I thought I could goad him into doing something he'd come to regret I was mistaken. He only grinned at me, revealing teeth like the broken tombstones on the Appian Way.

'You're Corvinus all right,' he said. 'I've been told to have a word with you, friend.'

I drew the dagger out all the way but he didn't move or even blink. That worried me like hell. I didn't expect the guy to run screaming out of the shop but a certain shift towards caution on his part would've helped my ego. As it was he still had the edge. I took a sharp look behind me and to either side to check the ground I had to work with. Could be better, could be worse. On the plus side the place was a poky little hole with cooking pots stacked up on shelves around the walls. No space to manoeuvre, so he'd have to come at me from the front. On the other hand it was one of these closed-off streetside rooms either side of the main entrance you get in most city houses, that the houseowners rent out to small retailers. So no back door, right? If I wanted to walk out of this it'd have to be over Big Fritz's dead body. Which was, as they say, a real bummer.

I held the knife out in front of me flat like I'd been taught, the point waving from side to side across the width of his belly, balanced myself on the balls of both feet, and waited for him to come at me. That would show him he was messing with a professional. He gave me a look like I was something with six legs he'd just found in his salad, turned his head aside and spat.

'Put the knife away, Corvinus,' he said. 'You won't need it. This is just a warning.'

'Yeah? Who from?' I lowered the dagger but didn't sheathe it. I wasn't that crazy. I'd already checked out his hands. They were both in view and they were empty; but then again they were the size of shovel blades and whatever this guy did for a living it wasn't play the harp. A clout with one of these would send you straight through the other end of next year's Winter Festival.

'None of your business.' He was still completely relaxed. It takes one of two qualities to look that cool when you're unarmed and facing a cornered man with a knife: either total headbanging stupidity or absolute confidence that you can take the bastard without breaking sweat. And Big Fritz for all his beer-and-barley-bread accent was no headbanger. 'You're being warned to stop asking questions, Corvinus. Do what you're told or you'll get hurt.'

'So what's Tiberius got against a dead poet, then? Or is the boil on his backside just playing him up too much?' Yeah. Cocky as hell. I should've known better.

'I told you, friend,' he said. 'You ask too many questions. Leave well alone. And just to make sure you get the point...'

I'd been watching his eyes and I swear he didn't signal the

move. One minute he was standing facing me, the next instant he was a forward-leaping blur. My hand with the knife came up years too late. His fingers closed around my wrist, pulling down and twisting outwards. The dagger rang on the stone floor and what felt like half the Capitoline Hill collided with my ribs as his shoulder thudded into my chest. Then I was flying backwards against a wall that broke and gave and showered me with a tumbling hail of earthenware.

By the time I'd picked myself up, battered and bruised but with nothing broken but my pride, Big Fritz had left.

So we were playing for real now. I was tempted to give it up then and there. Sure I was. For about fifteen seconds, while I shook the remains of half a dinner service out of my ears. Then the old Messalla blood began to stir, the legacy of twenty generations of arrogant, straight-nosed patrician bastards who'd get up from their deathbeds just to spit in an enemy's eye, and I knew that I couldn't do it. I had to see it through if it killed me.

If it killed me. Yeah, and it well might, if today was any sample. I knew that. But next time I'd be better prepared.

CHAPTER

7

I called round at Perilla's next morning. I must've looked even worse than I felt, which is saying a lot, because when she saw me her jaw dropped like she'd been sandbagged.

'Corvinus! What on earth happened?'

I eased myself into the chair her slave Callias brought. Chairs hadn't been too high on my list of favourite furniture since yesterday's little incident. Twenty pounds of shattered Best Local Domestic make a lousy cushion.

'Nothing much,' I said. 'A meeting with the security arm of the imperial civil service. They'd like us to withdraw our application.'

Perilla didn't get it at first. Then when the penny dropped she didn't believe it. 'You mean Tiberius had you beaten up?'

'Just leaned on, lady. Beaten up comes a grade higher.'

'But this is dreadful!' She got up from her chair, walked

over to the half-curtained-off sitting area, and stood looking out through it into the garden beyond. When she finally turned round her eyes were bright and her mouth set in a firm line. 'Corvinus, getting my stepfather's ashes back isn't worth this. Forget I asked you. Please.'

'And miss out on all the fun?' I tried to grin, but my mouth wasn't working too well because at some stage in yesterday's proceedings I'd tried to swallow a casserole.

She sat down facing me. I noticed that despite the usual cool calm and collected exterior her hands were clenched together. 'So what happened? Exactly?'

I told her the gory details. Maybe I embellished a little as far as numbers went, to save face. I wasn't too proud of myself.

'But what's worrying me most,' I finished, 'is whether with this fat lip I'll be able to play the double flute.'

She was instantly concerned. 'But I never knew! Is that so terribly important to you, Corvinus?'

Jupiter! A lovely girl, Perilla, read her Aristotle with the best of them no doubt, but she'd as much sense of humour as a tunny-fish. I was still explaining the joke when Callias came back in with a brimming goblet of wine. He set it on the table beside me, bowed and left. I drank as easily as my cut lip would let me.

No, it wasn't the rotgut stuff I'd had last time. I knew it wouldn't be before I let a drop of it past my bruised lips. The first thing I'd done that morning before calling on Perilla was to send Bathyllus round with a jar of my own Falernian—good stuff from the family's own vineyards six miles from Sinuessa, Faustian no less, and five years older than I was. I'd warned Bathyllus to tell Callias from me that if he served me anything else or let on to Perilla that he'd done a swap I'd personally see to it that he found himself floating down the Tiber with his prick tied in a clove hitch. I didn't mind getting leaned on for Perilla's sake but I drew the line at drinking Hubby Rufus's apology for horsepiss.

'So how well did your stepfather know Julia, then?' I said when the Falernian had begun its magic journey southwards.

'What?' Perilla's head came up like she'd sat on a wasp.

'You heard me. Julia. The old emperor's granddaughter. The one who was sent to Trimerus for adultery.'

'So you've made that connection.'

I didn't quite know what to make of her tone. She wasn't exactly angry. Maybe 'bitter' came nearest. As if somehow I'd disappointed her but she'd been expecting it.

'Oh, come on, Perilla! You must've thought about it yourself. The Julia thing's so obvious even I got it without busting a blood vessel.' She said nothing so I pressed my advantage. Or what I thought was an advantage. 'If Ovid was having an affair with Julia then her grandfather would have a right to boot him up the backside, wouldn't he? Especially since the lady was married at the time. And it'd be a private family matter, too, so it wouldn't be any concern of the state. All that worries me is why—'

'Corvinus.' You could've used Perilla's voice to make chilled grape sorbet in midsummer. 'Let us get one thing clear. There was no affair with Julia. My stepfather was a dozen years older than she was, he loved my mother, and furthermore he was the most moral man in Rome.'

I didn't laugh. It was a close-run thing, and in my present weakened state I nearly ruptured myself, but I didn't laugh.

'Oh, yeah. Sure,' I said. 'That's why Augustus banned his poetry for giving impressionable young gentlemen and ladies an itch in their drawers.'

'You're confusing the poetry with the poet!'

'Maybe. But Ovid's poetry seemed pretty autobiographical to me. From what I've read of it the guy must've gone round in a permanent crouch. Not that I'm being critical, you understand.'

'It seemed autobiographical because he was a great poet!'

'Look, no arguments, right? If you say—'

But she wasn't finished with me yet. Perilla was beautiful when she was angry.

'I knew him, Corvinus, and you didn't. He was the gentlest, faithfulest, most moderate...'

I held up my hand. 'Yeah, okay. Okay! Fair enough, I'm sorry. Birds fed out of his lily-white hand and he blushed to his socks if a girl so much as tickled his inclinations. Sure. I'll take your word for it. But come on, Perilla! There has to be a connection with Julia. Both of them exiled in the same year's too pat.'

'Stranger things have happened.'

'Don't bet on it.' I took another swig of wine. Beautiful. 'Okay, so let's take it another way. Your stepfather said he was exiled for something he saw and didn't report, right?'

She nodded briefly. Her mouth still looked like someone had cemented it up from the inside.

'So if he wasn't directly involved with Julia, what's wrong with the theory that he knew she was being humped and didn't pass the information on to Augustus?'

'Nothing, except that there would be no sense in hushing up the charge. After all, if Augustus was willing to let the crime itself become public, why should he worry about whatever Ovid saw? And why should he punish him so harshly?'

'Yeah, sure. I thought of that. But maybe what Ovid saw had other implications. Connected with the adultery but not part of it.'

'How do you mean?'

'I'm not sure myself. Maybe nothing. It's just an idea, but if there was something else then it might've made all the difference. Anyway we need more information, and that won't be easy to come by. In fact I'd bet you a basket of lampreys to a pitted olive that we'll find people's mouths sewn up tighter than a gnat's arsehole.'

Perilla was frowning—at the crudity, I thought (the phrase had slipped out), but I was wrong. 'Corvinus, is all this necessary?'

'All what?'

'This...digging into the past. Sifting through old bones. All my mother and I want is to get my stepfather's ashes back. We couldn't care less what he did.'

I sat back and stared at her in amazement. The lady was serious. She was actually serious! She honestly, genuinely, couldn't care less about trivial things like reasons. To me, now, getting the ashes was incidental; or rather it was only part of the game. I couldn't give up, whether Perilla wanted me to or not. I was hooked, I had to know what Ovid had done, for my own satisfaction if nothing else. And I knew, somehow, that the two things went together, that we'd never get imperial permission for the return of Ovid's body unless we solved the mystery of his exile.

'Yeah, it's necessary,' I said simply. 'Believe me.'

'All right.' The directness of her reply both surprised me and gave me a warm feeling inside. 'So if we do want information, then who do we ask?'

I noticed the 'we'. It seemed we were on the same side again. The warm feeling increased.

'Smack in the bull's-eye,' I said. 'That's the problem, lady.'

'And the answer?'

That's what I liked about Perilla. If there was a problem then there must be an answer. Simple. QED. Only in this case it wasn't.

'Hold on a minute,' I said. 'Let me think.'

I took a swallow of wine. This one was a real bummer. It was no use approaching any of my own age-group. Although they'd be the most amenable, like me they'd only have been kids ten years back when Julia was exiled, so none of them would be able to tell me much more than I already knew. Even if they weren't sycophantic sods like Caelius Crispus. On the other hand, the older people, the thirty-plusses who'd have the information from personal experience, were mostly my father's cronies, and I knew all I'd get from them was a blank stare and a raspberry. I couldn't risk going to a total stranger or one of my father's political enemies either, because I'd need to be sure that whoever I asked would keep his mouth shut, whether he told me anything or not. If it got around that young Corvinus was poking about for skeletons in the imperial cupboard it could net me more than just a few cuts and bruises. Tiberius was no tyrant, but that didn't mean he'd put up with some smartass bastard shoving his nose into the family secrets. That sort of thing was a short-cut to a fly-speck island of my own, or worse. So what did that leave me with? Sod all, so far as I could see.

Unless…

I suddenly remembered the fat senator who'd helped me out at the palace.

'Lentulus.'

'Who?'

'Cornelius Lentulus. You don't know Cornelius Lentulus? Down the Market Square they call him the Great White Elephant. And not just because of his size either.'

'Corvinus, I really don't know what you're talking about.'

'Lentulus knows everything. And he never forgets.' I took a long pull at the Falernian and let it trickle gently past my tonsils. 'What's more, he doesn't give a toss for anyone's opinion but his own. Lentulus is perfect. We talk to Lentulus.'

'You're sure?'

'Sure I'm sure.' I finished the wine and stood up. 'In fact I'm so sure that I'll go round to the Caelian now and catch him before he starts getting ready for his dinner party.'

'What dinner party?'

'For Lentulus there's always a dinner party. With any luck the old bugger will be half pissed already.'

'You're going straight away?' I thought I could detect disappointment in Perilla's voice, but maybe it was just wishful thinking. 'Now?'

'Yeah. Like I say, this is the best time to catch him.' Then I had another idea, completely selfish and totally unconnected with Ovid. 'Look, uh, if he does give me some information can I come back here afterwards? Maybe early this evening?'

'Of course.' Was she redder than usual or was it my imagination? 'Come for dinner. I haven't any guests tonight. Or any night for that matter.'

Perilla never ceased to surprise me. As I left I wondered which of us had made the running. I'd thought it was me, but thinking it over I wasn't so sure. And that was interesting.

I saw my mother's litter on the way—I'd forgotten that she and her new husband lived on the Caelian too. The curtains were open so I waved, but I don't think she saw me. I thought about going over and saying hello properly—I hadn't spoken to her for two months, at least—but in the end I decided against it. After my run-in with Big Fritz I wasn't exactly personable. She'd only have asked awkward questions, and worried.

Varus to Himself

I wrote last about who we are, here in the wilds of Germany. I find I have been too sparing in describing Ceionius's role. I called him, without qualification, my ally. Perhaps I should say a little more.

I do not like Ceionius. You may have guessed. As I said, he is venal, cowardly, and a thoroughly unpleasant character. However, we must all use the tools which come to hand, and that to one side the man is perfectly serviceable. He may be a louse, but he is an efficient louse, which is all I require. Ceionius has a nose for intrigue, and a talent for it, which is unique in my (extensive) experience. Generals are public men, especially when in the midst of their armies. Like it or not, when they engage in treason they must have faceless (but not faithless!) allies who can come and go on their dark business and arouse no suspicion in the breasts of the godly. Such is Ceionius, par excellence.

His faithfulness, I may say, is beyond question. I have ensured that it should be. The man has certain propensities which, were they to become known at Rome, would in the current moral climate prove the end of him militarily, politically and socially. Perhaps even physically. He is, naturally, aware that my silence on the subject is conditional on his continued co-operation.

Not that blackmail is my only hold over him. I am too old a hand to trust to that completely, and I know full well that not only are worms apt to turn but they invariably choose the most embarrassing moment to do so. Ceionius is well paid for the assistance he renders. Very well paid. Arminius is generous, and so I can afford to be generous in my turn. Between the carrot and the stick, I contrive to keep my ally moving.

So much for Ceionius. Consider yourselves properly introduced.

CHAPTER 8

Lentulus's house was the exact opposite of Rufus's. It was big, old, sprawling, and reeked of self-indulgence. There was no mosaic of Augustus in the lobby, and the slaves wore green.

There ain't no money like old money. I felt at home straight away.

I'd been right about the dinner party. The old guy was sitting on a chair in the atrium being shaved and titillated. I watched from the doorway while the barber trimmed what little thatch still covered his bald scalp, patted him with scented talc, and removed the unsightly hairs from his nostrils with tweezers. When a pause came in the disgusting proceedings I coughed.

Lentulus looked round.

'Hey, boy!' he greeted me. 'Some husband been wiping his boots on your face?'

'Yeah. Something like that.' I came forward and sat carefully on the marble rim that surrounded the ornamental pool. Lentulus would've enjoyed the real story, I knew, but I didn't want to risk scaring him off. 'So what is it tonight? More pythons?'

'Egyptian pygmy contortionists. They do it to music.' Jupiter! 'Don't sit there unless you want piles, boy. Pull up a couch.' I lay down on the guest couch, and his slave brought wine and a bowl of fruit. 'Now, young fellah, what brings you to this neck of the woods?'

'I've come to pick your brains, sir,' I said. Clichés are catching.

Lentulus snorted, and the barber, who was reaching into his right nostril with the bronze tweezers, pulled back sharply with a grunt of annoyance. Lentulus ignored him.

'Go ahead, boy,' he said. 'Not that you'll have much luck, mind you. My old schoolteacher always used to say he was frightened to beat me too hard in case he did me permanent mental damage.'

I didn't smile. The teacher had probably been serious. 'It's about Julia.'

Again the barber whipped the tweezers away just in time as Lentulus's head came round.

'What's that? Which Julia?'

'The old emperor's granddaughter. The one who was exiled ten years back for adultery.'

Lentulus took the napkin from his chest and slowly began wiping the talc and scraped-off hairs from his face.

'Bugger off, Simon,' he said to the barber. 'You can finish me later.'

The slave glared at him, gathered up the tools of his trade and stalked out.

Lentulus grinned. 'Feisty little bastard fancies himself as

some sort of artist. Been after me ever since I bought him to try a depilatory, but I don't hold with these things. Friend of mine had one once and came out in boils. Couldn't show his face in public for a month or his arse in private for two. And just in case you're wondering I don't mean the emperor.' He raised his voice. 'Hey you!'

The slave who had brought the wine hurried over.

'Let's have some of that stuff you've got there.' He finished wiping his face, threw the napkin on to the floor, and eased his bulk on to the master couch. 'And top up Valerius Corvinus's cup while you're at it, you stingy bugger.'

The slave did so and I drank appreciatively. It was Falernian again, and every bit as good as mine if not better. Lentulus might be a reactionary two shades bluer than Cato but he knew his wine.

'Now.' He turned back to me. 'Why d'you want to know about Julia, young Corvinus? Not thinking of turning historian, are you?' The way he said it made it sound like a dirty word.

I laughed. 'No. I'm just interested.'

'The hell you are. Let's have the real reason.'

I looked at him. His piggy eyes, set in rolls of fat, were pretty sharp. Lentulus might not look much but he was smart, and I knew I'd have to watch my step. Sure, I couldn't tell him the truth, but then I'd be a fool to try an outright lie, because he'd've been on to me like a stoat on a rabbit.

'I can't tell you that, sir.' I was carefully polite. 'But it's important, or I wouldn't ask.'

'This wouldn't have something to do with a certain young lady who's the stepdaughter of a certain dead poet, would it?'

Shit. So much for the eager young ingénu approach. Well, that wasn't my bag anyway.

'Okay,' I said. 'You've got me. Now tell me to push off like everyone else.'

He grunted. The slave handed him a cup of wine and he drank it down and held the cup out to be refilled.

'If I did,' he said, 'would you stop asking questions and go back to the things you spoilt young brats are supposed to be interested in?'

'Probably not. I'd just find someone else's brains to pick.'

'That's what I thought.' He gave me a long considering look over his wine-cup. 'All right, boy. It's your funeral. So long as you realise you're none too popular at the moment in certain quarters, and you don't come crying to me when you get burned. Agreed?'

'Agreed.'

'Good lad. Just remember you said it. Not that there's much to tell. Julia turned out to be a fornicating little bitch just like her mother.' Augustus's daughter, another Julia, had been exiled the year I was born for the same crime. She'd died at Rhegium four years previously. 'It happened once too often and someone reported her to Augustus. He packed her off to Trimerus. End of story.'

I felt cheated. 'I could've told you that myself. What about the details? Like who reported her?'

'Search me, boy.' Lentulus belched and kneaded his stomach. 'Mind you, I take my hat off to the little sweetie. Anyone that good at pulling the wool over people's eyes gets my vote every time.'

'How do you mean?'

'I mean you'd've taken one look at her and said "housewife". Gossip, kids and jewellery, those were sweet Julia's limits. Except for the literary nonsense, of course, but women often get these silly ideas.' I thought of Perilla. Yeah. 'On the fat side too.

Not that that means much. When these quiet well-built ones break out there's no holding them, eh?' He snickered. 'I remember a woman from Veii, Paulina her name was, big girl, tits like a bloody heifer—'

'Who was her lover? Julia's, I mean?'

"Plural, boy, plural. She'd been laid by half of Rome.'

'Names?'

'Chap called Silanus. Decimus Junius Silanus. Good family. His cousin Marcus got the daughter after the scandal broke.'

'Which daughter?'

'Her daughter. Julia's, of course. Don't they teach you youngsters anything about society these days?'

The name Decimus Silanus didn't ring any bells, but I'd heard of cousin Marcus. Sure I had. He was a real high-flyer: current consul, a friend of my father's, and an arselicker of the first order. I hadn't realised that his wife was Julia's daughter, but it didn't surprise me. We patrician families stick together.

'Who else? Who else was involved?'

'You mean who else was screwing her? Half of Rome. I told you.'

'Like who, for example?'

Lentulus opened his mouth—and then closed it again.

'Damned if I know, actually. Oh, there were plenty of rumours, and there's no smoke without fire, as they say. But Silanus is the only name I can give you for definite.'

'So what happened to Silanus? Was he chopped or did Augustus just tell him to slit his wrists?'

The old man chuckled and gulped at his wine. 'Jupiter! Nothing like that, boy! Social ostracism, that's all Silanus got. Wasn't even formally exiled, just deprived of the emperor's friendship. Mind you, the bugger left Rome pretty sharpish all the same for healthier climes. Just been let back in fact.'

I thought I'd misheard. 'Silanus is in Rome?'

'As of a few days ago, yes.' Lentulus gestured with the wine-cup, spilling a little on the tiled floor. 'His cousin swung it with the Wart. Not that he's back in public life, of course, and probably never will be. Tiberius isn't that generous. Got a little place the other side of the river, on the Janiculum. Not that little, now I come to think. Joys of the rustic life, all that sort of thing. Still, he was luckier than the bloody husband, wasn't he?'

I swear the hairs crawled on my scalp, but I kept my voice calm.

'Whose husband?'

'Clean the wax out of your ears, boy! That's the second time! Julia's husband, of course. Aemilius bloody Paullus.' Lentulus's voice was slightly slurred. There couldn't've been much water in the wine we were drinking and he'd had two full cups of the stuff straight off on top of God knows how much more. He wasn't quite pissed as a newt but he was well on the way. 'He got chopped, didn't he? Served the bastard right.'

Everything was suddenly very still and clear. I can remember staring past Lentulus at the mural on the wall, a mythological scene of Perseus with the Gorgon's head. The slave standing next to it with the wine jug shifted and the squeak of his sandals on the marble tiles went through me like a knife.

'Paullus was executed? What for?'

And Lentulus stopped. He stopped dead. Getting up, he set the wine-cup carefully on a nearby table. Then he turned to face me.

'That was the wine talking, boy,' he said. 'Forget it, eh? I've told you enough. More than enough.'

I set my own cup down. I had to. I was so excited I might've dropped it. 'Look, you can't just leave things there, you old bastard. Come on, I'll find out eventually anyway. What was Paullus chopped for?'

Lentulus was still staring at me. He looked grey and very, very sober.

'Okay, Corvinus,' he said. 'You asked for it and it's your funeral, remember. Just after Julia was sent to Trimerus, Augustus had her husband executed for treason.' He turned away. 'Now go home and leave me in peace, boy. I don't want to see you again. Ever.'

I thought about what Lentulus had told me on the way back from the Caelian. Or rather, about what he'd said he couldn't tell me: the names of the other gents besides Silanus who'd been intimate with Julia. Coming from a gossip-monger like Lentulus the admission of total ignorance was surprising, to say the least. Sure, it was possible. Anything was possible. Maybe the guy genuinely didn't know. But there was another explanation which, if it was the right one, opened up a whole new field of interesting possibilities.

Lentulus couldn't give me any more names because there were no more names to give. Forget the 'half of Rome' crap. As far as Julia's partners went Silanus was it. Full stop, end of paragraph, close the book. And *that* could mean...

Interesting, right?

CHAPTER 9

I got back to Perilla's just on dinnertime. I'd gone home to change first (never go calling on a lady with a grubby mantle), and I'd also paid another visit to Cadmus's —not for the ring (I'd got that already) but to pick up a snazzy little pair of earrings I'd seen that I thought would look great against her hair. Alexandrian poets are okay in their place but I didn't want her to think I was some sort of culture freak. It would only lead to misunderstandings later.

She'd chosen the subfusc look: a matronly mantle, the minimum of jewellery, and a hairstyle that could've come straight off the Altar of Peace. As a statement it was predictable but disappointing. I swallowed down my lust and prepared for a staid little domestic evening.

She liked the earrings, though. Even if she didn't let me put them on her myself.

Callias served the honeyed wine (I hate that stuff but I was on my best behaviour), supervised the serving of the hors d'oeuvres, and then faded into the woodwork. I made a mental note to slip him a fat tip before I left. Tact in slaves is a thing to be encouraged, especially if you've designs on their mistress.

'Well, Corvinus,' Perilla said as we settled down to the quails' eggs and stuffed dormice. 'How did your visit go?'

I gave her the salient points, glossing over, of course, the doom-and-gloom aspects of the situation. There was no need for both of us to worry about my ending up with my throat slit. 'So we've got a couple of good leads,' I finished. 'Silanus being back in Rome's a definite plus.'

'You intend going to see him?'

'Yeah. I thought I might. It seems the logical next step.'

'Why should he tell you anything?'

'He's got no reason not to. The whole thing's over and done with. And it's too good a chance to miss. After all, why mess around with middle-men? If anyone knows what your stepfather saw, our Silanus is the lad.'

'Do you know where he lives?'

'Not exactly.' I rubbed a quail's egg between my palms to remove the shell. 'But I can find out. Lentulus said he has one of those fancy farms the other side of the Tiber. It shouldn't be too difficult to track him down. And I'm interested to find out how he managed to seduce Julia and get away with it while her husband got chopped. A trick like that might come in useful some time.'

'Paullus was executed for treason, not because he was Julia's husband.'

'You're telling me there's no connection? Come on, Perilla!'

She selected a fish pickle and honey canapé. 'If so then it's certainly not an obvious one. We're talking about different crimes. In one Paullus is the victim, in the other he's the culprit.

Now if Julia had been married to Silanus, and Paullus had been the seducer, I could see your point. That is, if you consider seduction of the emperor's grandchild per se as treasonable. Which personally I don't.'

My head was beginning to hurt. I'd missed an opening there, I was sure of it. But I'm not used to discussing abstract problems over dinner. Wheel in the pygmy contortionists and stuff the Aristotle.

'Besides'—Perilla finished the canapé and picked up a baby squid filled with sausage meat—'Silanus was punished. You said yourself he'd gone into voluntary exile. And he'll never hold public office again. Surely for a man of his standing that's punishment enough.'

I frowned. 'Okay, okay. Have it your way. Maybe I've just got an over-suspicious mind, maybe everything is above board. But it won't hurt to talk to the guy at least.'

Perilla laid the squid down and turned these lovely golden eyes of hers on me. 'You will be careful, won't you? It all sounds terribly politically sensitive. Don't go treading on any more toes. You've been beaten up once already over this. I'm sorry. Leaned on.'

'Look, Perilla, the case is dead meat. It might've been sensitive five years ago when old Augustus was emperor. But Paullus is dead and buried, Tiberius is in power, and Silanus is persona grata again. Okay?'

'What about Julia? She's still alive on Trimerus, isn't she? Or have I missed something?'

I sighed. The gods preserve me from feisty women. 'Julia's nothing to the Wart, Perilla. She isn't even a relation.'

'She used to be his stepdaughter.'

'Until he divorced her mother.' Tiberius had been married to the elder Julia, the one who'd died at Rhegium. 'And from all accounts he never could stand that particular lady. It was a marriage of convenience, and you know what they're like, don't you?'

It was just a throwaway line, I swear it, but as soon as I said the words I knew they were a mistake. A bad mistake. Like asking Oedipus's wife how her son was doing these days. Perilla lowered her eyes to her plate and her long slim fingers teased at the squid in front of her. The silence grew and kept on growing.

'Shit,' I said at last. 'Look, Perilla, I'm sorry if I...'

'No, that's all right.' Her head came up. 'You aren't married, are you, Corvinus?'

'Uh-uh. I run too fast.'

She didn't smile. 'I am. But of course you know that. I've been married for six years.'

Jupiter! How the hell did I get out of this? I tried to keep the conversation light.

'Congratulations. Any kids?'

Straight in again with both feet. Maybe it was my imagination, but I think she shuddered.

'No,' she said quietly. 'No children.'

'That's...uh...that's tough.' Desperately, I looked around for something to hang a change of subject on, but there's only so much you can say about stuffed olives and raw vegetables.

'Maybe I should explain a little about...' She hesitated. 'About my relationship with my husband.'

I didn't say anything. I'm a pretty good judge of mood, especially where women are concerned. Sure, with one of my bubbleheads I'd've been crowing long before now. When a lady starts bad-mouthing her husband under conditions like these you can usually be sure that the evening will follow a pretty predictable course. But this was no come-on. The ice was back for a start, and whatever Perilla had in mind it definitely wasn't busting a mattress strap together. She was sitting stiff in her chair—no enervating couch for this Roman matron—and staring down at her plate.

'We met just after my stepfather was exiled. I must have been twelve, maybe thirteen. Rufus had been married before and his first wife had just died when he asked my mother for my hand in marriage.'

I shifted uncomfortably on my couch. I'd've welcomed Callias back at that moment with open arms, honey wine included. Even a minor incursion by German berserkers wouldn't've come amiss. However, we were stuck with no interruptions. If there were going to be confidences then I'd just have to grit my teeth and live through them. I didn't even dare risk a polite grunt.

'It was a good match.' Perilla's eyes were still lowered. 'Rufus wasn't well off but he came from a good family. He was popular with Augustus, marked for promotion and a good political career. My mother had noble connections, not very strong ones—she's a distant cousin of Marcia, Fabius Maximus's widow—but things being as they were, we were hardly popular any more at court. All in all I suppose I was very lucky really.'

I sipped my wine. The click as I set the cup down on the table top was as loud as a door slamming but she didn't seem to notice.

'We should have begun to suspect when Rufus suggested a traditional marriage,' she said. 'You know the kind I mean, where the wife's property passes to the husband absolutely.' I nodded, although she still wasn't looking at me. Marriages like that were still common enough in pukkah-patrician families, especially the ones that supplied the priesthoods, but they'd gone out of style generally for obvious reasons. 'Should have but didn't. Luckily Uncle Fabius—he was still alive then, and the head of the family—put his foot down. Rufus, as I said, wasn't particularly rich, and he had a bad reputation where money was concerned. So we compromised. He could have me after my sixteenth birthday but not my money.'

Callias put his head round the door, presumably to ask if we'd finished with the starters. Before I had a chance to signal him the bastard had worked out what was going on and shot back out of sight fast as a greased eel. I reconsidered the tip in favour of a surreptitious knee in the groin on the way out. Perilla hadn't noticed him. Her eyes were still fixed on her plate and her fingers were systematically tearing the tiny squid in front of her into smaller and smaller pieces. There wasn't a lot left of it now.

'We'd been engaged for about a year before I realised that it was the money he was interested in. Did I tell you that Augustus had left my stepfather his property when he exiled him? Anyway, Rufus had been badgering my mother from the first to let him take care of the family finances. It got quite nasty. If it hadn't been for Uncle Fabius I think he'd've had his way in the end.'

'So why not break off the engagement?' I asked quietly. 'He'd no legal right to you or your money until the wedding. Why not just tell the guy to sod off?'

Perilla shook her head. 'You haven't met my mother, Corvinus. She wasn't ill then but she still wasn't very strong-minded. And it was her money after all, not mine. Or Uncle Fabius's. My stepfather had made her caretaker of his estate.'

'But Fabius Maximus was one of Augustus's closest friends. Surely he could've done something?'

'He did what he could. But he'd no formal legal standing, only the right to advise. And Augustus had no love for my stepfather, remember. The wedding took place on schedule as agreed.'

'So Maximus just let the shit get away with it?'

Perilla smiled and nodded slowly.

'He let,' she said carefully, 'the shit get away with it. As you so graphically put it. At least as far as the marriage was concerned. He didn't have any option there. The money, luckily, was a different matter.'

I was getting interested despite myself. 'So what happened?'

'We got married. Rufus kept on at Mother but there was nothing he could actually do, not while Uncle Fabius was alive to advise her. Mother always listened to Uncle Fabius. Besides, as you say, he was a good friend of the emperor.'

'But then Augustus died.'

'That's right. Augustus died. Closely followed by Uncle Fabius. Which was what Rufus had been waiting. for. He'd been worming his way into Tiberius's favour for some time, you see. And when Tiberius became emperor Rufus went to him and asked that my stepfather's estate be formally transferred to himself as the property of a convicted criminal. We fought the claim in the courts and we won eventually, but it was a close-run thing. Now of course the estate is safe. With my stepfather dead it's my mother's absolutely, and Rufus can't touch a penny of it.' For the first time she looked up from the fragments of squid and forcemeat that lay crumbled on the table in front of her. I'd expected tears but her cheeks were dry and her eyes were hard and cold. 'So now you know, Corvinus. Now you know how I feel about my husband. Why I hate him.'

The silence stretched out between us like a windingsheet. I don't think I'd ever been so completely lost for words. Or so embarrassed. Or so bitterly sorry for another human being. Or so helplessly angry.

It was Callias who saved the situation. Forget the knee in the balls, I was really warming to that little bugger. He came in like one of these gods the Greek playwrights dangle above the stage to sort things out when they get their pricks tied in knots over a too-complex plot. Not that he was hanging from a crane, of course, but you know what I mean.

'Shall I serve the main course now, madam?' he asked.

Jupiter! I could've kissed him, and kissing male slaves isn't my bag, especially if they're as ugly as Callias. Perilla gave herself a sort of shake.

'Corvinus, I'm terribly sorry,' she said. 'I've been boring you. You should have said.'

'Hey, no, that's okay. It was fascinating.' Oh yeah! Well done, Corvinus. Another bummer in the conversation stakes. 'I mean no, it doesn't matter. Honestly.'

Callias, bless him, didn't wait for further permission. He signalled to his minions who were waiting outside, and they oozed in, cleared away the starters—most of which were untouched—and served the dinner proper. It was good plain stuff: pork in a sauce of honey and cumin, lentils with leeks, and a sea urchin ragout that made my mouth water just to look at it. Added to which Callias hadn't forgotten my instructions about the wine. I took the first cup at a swallow and held it up for more.

Perilla sat back in her chair. 'You do the talking for a change, Corvinus. Tell me about your family.'

Some particularly evil-minded god must've been hovering round the dinner table that evening. Oh, no, I thought. No way, lady. Having just lived through one downer there was no way that I was going to be responsible for the next. At some of the more literary (or pseudo-literary) dinner parties the guests produce tiny articulated silver skeletons which they jiggle while declaiming merry odes on the subjects of fate, death and bodily corruption. As a form of entertainment that's never much grabbed me. The thought of going in for a little soul-bearing of my own re my father and our relationship (or lack of one) made my balls shrink. So instead, and apropos of nothing, I began to trot out a few items from my usual store of dinner-party winners. Suitably expurgated, naturally. Which in the event proved the best thing I could've done.

I never really thought I'd ever hear Perilla laugh, but she did, especially when I told her the one about the Vestal and the vegetable marrow. We'd both had more than a few cups of wine by then and the expurgation was wearing pretty thin; in fact she'd got to the silly stage when she'd laugh at (and agree to) anything, and I suspect that if I'd really wanted to get her into bed I could've done it without much trouble. With one of my usual bubbleheads I wouldn't've thought twice, but Perilla was different. She'd hate me for it in the morning, I knew, and I suspected that I wouldn't be too popular with myself either. So just before midnight I thanked her, said goodnight, and slipped old Callias all the cash I'd got on me. Then I whistled up the lads with the torches and went home.

I wondered on the way if I was getting soft. Or had misread her. Or misread myself. All of them were possible plus a few more. No doubt I'd be feeling pretty smug and virtuous in the morning, but at that precise moment I just felt lonely.

CHAPTER

10

Forget smug and virtuous. Next morning I was too hung over to feel anything but delicate, which was a pity because I needed to go calling on Junius Silanus. Luckily finding the 'farm' Lentulus had mentioned proved to be easy-peasy, and I didn't even have to call in any favours.

If you want to know who's who in Rome and where they hang out, just ask your head slave.

I learned pretty early in life that slaves can be pretty clued-up people, and that a brand on your arm doesn't mean to say you're necessarily a thicko. Quite the reverse. I've seen senators that set next to the guy who opens my front door wouldn't even make intellectual pygmy status. And the slave grapevine has the imperial secret service beaten hollow. Try it yourself some time. Mention in your coachman's hearing that such and such a respectable octogenarian matron is screwing a gladiator, and all over Rome next day you'll see slaves sniggering at her litter.

Silanus's address was nothing. Bathyllus could've told me where the guy bought his underwear.

Once you get beyond the working-class rabbit warrens round the bridges, the west bank of the Tiber is pretty thinly populated and definitely an up-market area, especially popular with rich guys who want to give the impression of loving the simple life. The slopes of the Janiculum are sprinkled with good old-fashioned farms, each with its good old-fashioned picture gallery, plus a few more homely features old Romulus would recognise straight off. Like five or six dining-rooms (so the light's *just right* all year round), ornamental gardens, or maybe even a private zoo. You can wake up in the morning to the crying of the peacocks and the smell of the rhinos and tell yourself there's nothing quite so invigorating as being close to your ethnic roots.

Even in this company Silanus's villa was something else. Real top-of-the-market stuff, I could see that straight off: a sprawling complex of buildings in its own grounds with a riding circuit attached so the guy didn't have to mix with the plebs while exercising his thoroughbreds and a covered litter-walk so he could take the air in comfort when it rained. Silanus might be out of favour, but he wasn't exactly down to his last copper penny, that was for sure. I only hoped Julia knew. You could just about have floated her island in the carp-pond.

I presented myself at the porter's lodge. The guy on duty was squint-eyed, smelt of dank chicken feathers, and looked big enough to beat the shit out of an arena cat.

'I'm Marcus Valerius Messalla Corvinus,' I said.

'Yeah?' The porter fixed me with his good eye while the

other checked out the weather over Ostia. 'You want a round of applause maybe?'

Jupiter! Maybe the guy had trouble extrapolating. I spelled it out for him.

'I want to speak to your master.'

'He's out.'

'Look, Horace.' I stared him right in the chest. He was wearing an amulet of some god I didn't know, with pointy teeth and a big belly. Probably the patron of wall-eyed gorillas. 'Just run along like a good freak and tell your boss he has a visitor, okay? Can you manage that or should I write it down for you?'

The guy scowled, leaned his massive shoulders against the gatepost, and folded his arms. Stalemate. Scratch the friendly approach. I fell back on the old BTB gambit. Bribe the bastard.

That, it seemed, had been what he was waiting for. He made a show of examining the silver piece I gave him like it was a mint-condition Croesus original. Then he spat on it for luck, raised his tunic, and slipped it into his breech clout. As a money box I reckoned it was the safest place going.

'Okay, friend,' he grunted. 'So what was the name again?' I told him and he nodded and disappeared inside, barring the gate behind him.

Ten minutes later he was back. The grin on his face didn't improve it much but the poor bastard couldn't help that.

'About time,' I said, preparing to barge past him through the half-open gate. 'So which way…'

He stretched out his arm. It was like walking into the limb of an oak tree. The grin widened.

'The master says fuck off,' he said, and pushed.

The gate slammed in my face. It sounded pretty permanent, and I could hear the big guy walking off ho-ho'ing into the sunset.

Great. So what was I supposed to do now? Sure, I could've made a fuss, maybe kicked at the door a little and tried out a few swear-words. That might've upset the neighbours, only there weren't any neighbours to upset. Besides, the gate was studded with more nails than a battleship. There had to be another way in.

I began the long trek round the walls, looking for a convenient spot to shin over. Zilch for most of the way. Then, when I'd just about given up, I found the perfect ladder: a beech tree with a long overhanging branch. Getting up and dropping down on the other side would be easy-peasy.

I stripped off my mantle, clambered up the trunk and along the branch, then dropped down on the villa side of the wall. There was no one in sight as I walked quickly through the rose garden, past the fish-pond and over the lawn to the main building. I'd almost reached it when a young slave came out carrying a folding table. We stared at each other. Then, still carrying the table, he turned back the way he'd come.

Shit. I had to do something fast.

'Hey, you!' I bellowed. 'Yeah, you with the hair on!' There's something to be said for a rigidly enforced class system and good old tortured patrician nasal vowels. The kid skittered to a halt and drew himself up to attention. 'Yes, sir?'

'Where's your master?'

'In the north wing solar, sir.'

'Take me there now.' And when he dithered: 'Come on, lad! I haven't got a fucking room plan! And you can leave the furniture behind. I'm not a bloody money-changer.'

He dropped the table as if it were red hot. 'Yes, sir. No, sir. I'm sorry, sir.'

'Just do it, okay?'

He swallowed. 'Yes, sir. If you'd care to follow me, please?'

It was certainly some place, and I've seen some places in my time. We walked along a Parian marble colonnade, then across a courtyard with a fountain in which two rampant satyrs were doing things with a nymph that I couldn't believe. I wondered who the artist was and whether he was still around to take commissions or if he'd been packed off somewhere for gross indecency. Finally the lad stopped outside a door and stood aside to let me pass.

'Here we are, sir,' he said. 'Just go straight in.'

Junius Silanus was feeding an African parrot chained to a perch. That is, the parrot was on the perch. Silanus was sitting in a high-backed chair beside it. He was a little rat-faced bastard well into middle age. I disliked him on sight.

The feeling was obviously mutual. The guy glared at me like I was something the parrot had deposited in his dinner.

'Who the hell let you in?'

'And I'm delighted to meet you too, sir,' I said. 'What a nice garden you have. Especially the fountain.'

Silanus turned to the youngster who had brought me and who was standing goggle-eyed in the open doorway. 'Lucius, go to the front entrance and fetch Geta. Tell him we have an intruder.'

The kid shot me a quick, scared look, bowed and left.

'Come on, Silanus!' I said. 'This isn't necessary.'

'Corvinus, isn't it?' He held up a melon seed. The parrot took it gently in its beak, turning it round and round to crack the outer shell. 'I believe you were told that I wasn't at home. Common politeness demanded that you take the hint and leave. Please do so at once before I have you forcibly ejected.'

Pompous bastard. I hadn't met Latin like that since my

teacher beat me through Cicero. 'Look, it's no big deal. I just want to ask you some questions, right?'

'Your wants are immaterial.' The parrot spat out the fragments of shell and Silanus held out another seed. 'This is my house and you are trespassing.'

'Okay.' There was a stool by the door. I sat on it. 'Just tell me about your affair with Julia and I'll go.'

Silanus stared at me open-mouthed. Then he laughed. 'Young man, I may be out of touch with high society nowadays but I doubt if it's become the norm to walk into someone's house uninvited and question them about who they've been to bed with.'

'Fair enough.' I leaned back against the wall and folded my arms. 'So let's talk about your so-called "exile" instead. Where were you? Athens? Pergamon? Alexandria, maybe?'

'All of these places. And a few others.' Silanus fed the parrot another seed. 'Not that it's any business of yours. Please close the door as you leave. My porter will show you out.'

The guy was really getting up my nose. 'Hardly the back of beyond, right? Very civilised and enjoyable. No little shit-holes like Trimerus or Tomi, and a hell of a lot better than what Paullus got.' I paused. 'And speaking of Paullus, where does he fit in? Or don't you want to talk about that either?'

I'd finally got through to him. If looks could've killed I would've been a little smoking pile of ash on his Carrara marble floor.

'You're being offensive, Corvinus,' he said slowly. 'I was never formally exiled. I could go where I liked.'

'Quite right, sunshine.' I smiled. 'Why should you be punished, after all? None of it was your fault. You weren't the guilty one, were you?' I could hear running feet somewhere in the interior of the house, coming towards us. Lucius, probably, with the man-mountain Geta in tow. I didn't have much time left and I had to make the most of it. 'In fact I think it was pretty noble under the circumstances to leave Rome at all. Not to mention giving up a promising political career.'

Silanus had heard the footsteps too. His narrowed eyes were shifting back and forward between me and the door.

'How do you mean, noble?' he said. 'I had no choice in the matter.'

They were almost here now. I could distinguish between the pitter-patter of Lucius's fairy feet and the pounding of the porter's heavy nail-studded boots along the wooden corridor outside. God knows what the cost of repairing the flooring would be. Not that Silanus gave a toss about that. So much was obvious from his expression. The guy's first priority was to get me out, and fast, which was interesting. I went for the throat and prayed that I'd guessed right.

'Maybe you didn't have a choice. Maybe you just had to do as you were told. That doesn't matter. But it was pretty noble, wasn't it, to take the rap for something you never did in the first place.'

His head came round as if I'd slapped him; and simultaneously the door burst open and I found myself grabbed by two huge hairy arms and hoisted off my feet. I didn't much care because I had what I'd come for. The unmistakable look of guilt on Silanus's face told me I'd hit the bull's-eye.

'You didn't screw Julia at all, did you, you bastard?' I shouted at him as the porter hustled me towards the door. 'Nobody did! It was a put-up job!'

Silanus had risen from his chair. He was white as a sheet, with fear or anger or both. Beside him the parrot was screaming, dangling from its perch by the chain around its legs, its clipped wings beating frantically. I thought of the old woman's chickens in the Subura.

Silanus spoke quietly; so quietly I could hardly hear him over the noise of the parrot.

'Geta! Get him out of here! That's an order!'

The porter's huge hand was pressing against my mouth and his other arm encircled my ribs in a painful bear-hug. My feet left the ground and I was suddenly being carried kicking and struggling through a chain of richly decorated rooms, past knots of gaping house slaves and across the front courtyard to the main gate.

And that, when Geta had pitched me outside on to my ear, was when things began to get too interesting for comfort.

CHAPTER

11

I was on my way back for my mantle when the bastards hit me; four of them, and not Silanus's goons either, unless he employed a private army. These guys were professional knifemen.

Running was pointless—there was nowhere to go out here in the sticks—and I knew I could yell my lungs inside out before any of Silanus's slaves came to help. I reached for the knife at my wrist. Only after the general shake-up of the last few minutes it wasn't there any more.

Shit. I wished I wasn't a betting man. You find yourself working the odds out almost without thinking, and I'd've put mine at fifty to one easy. With odds like that even if the Cumaean Sibyl herself had appeared with all nine of the Books of Prophecy under her arm and given me the thumbs-up I still wouldn't've backed myself short of a place in the first five.

'Okay, lads.' I held up my hands. 'I don't want trouble. If it's my purse you want you've got it.'

They'd fanned out across the path, and they were coming slowly towards me. The guy in the centre grinned with a mouth like the exit to the Great Drain.

'Fuck that, Corvinus,' he said. 'Money's the least of your worries where you're going.'

Uhuh. So no prizes for guessing who these beauties were working for. And this time it looked like they were aiming at a permanent solution.

'Look, whatever the Wart's paying you I'll double it.' I edged backwards and sideways. 'Treble it. Okay, quadruple it.' My spine ground against the masonry of Silanus's garden wall. 'What comes after four?'

'We'd never live to collect. You're dead meat, boy.'

My eyes were on the point of the knife weaving backwards and forwards at belly height, and my guts crawled as I imagined that foot of iron ripping into me and up towards my ribs. It was now or never. Murmuring a quick prayer to whatever god protects rich young smartasses stupid enough to go out alone without a nanny, I leaned sideways and kicked the guy hard in the balls. He grunted, dropped his knife, and folded up like yesterday's copy of the *Acts of the Senate*.

Yeah. Not exactly what they teach you in the best schools—I hoped none of my ancestors was watching—but it did the job. One down, three to go.

The others closed in on me like it was the Winter Festival and I was the slave with the nuts. I stooped, snatched up a coping tile that had fallen from the top of the wall, and smashed the first guy's teeth in. Two down. Good, but not good enough.

After that things got pretty lively. There's only so much you can do if you're one against two once the element of surprise has gone, and as it was I reckoned I was about set for the death mask and the family vaults. I'd just closed with one of the bastards when someone laid a red-hot poker against my shoulder. It was a good second before I realised it was the other guy's knife. I glanced round and saw him bring his arm back for a second try. Oh, well, I thought, what the hell. It was a good life while it lasted. I'd've liked to've had Perilla, though...

At that moment what the Greeks call the Divine interposed its hand. Literally.

The guy who'd stabbed me never had a chance. A huge hairy mitt reached out of the sky, plucked him off the ground, and mashed him against the wall like a beetle. Then a second detached me gently from the bastard I'd been hugging and held him up while a fist the size and hardness of a catapult bolt scattered his teeth over half the Janiculum.

Everything was suddenly very quiet, the way it usually is after thunderbolts. I could even hear birds singing. I propped myself up against the wall with my good arm and looked around. The two knifemen I'd seen accounted for lay on the ground looking like they'd come off second equal in a fight with a blood-crazed rhino. The ones I'd dealt with myself were nowhere. Maybe they'd been eaten.

Then I saw who I had to thank for rescuing me. I suppose I'd assumed from the guy's size that it was Silanus's Geta, though why the hell he should bother I didn't know.

It wasn't. It was Big Fritz from the potter's shop, and nothing made sense any more.

'You okay, Corvinus?' He was flicking stray teeth from between his knuckles.

'Yeah,' I said. 'Never better. Apart from this hole in the shoulder you could drive a chariot through, of course.'

He grabbed my arm, inspected the wound, then thumped me on the back. It was like being mugged by the Great

Pyramid. My shoulder didn't feel a hell of a lot better for it either.

'Just a scratch. The knife must've slid off the bone. Keep it clean and it should heal okay in a few days.'

'You're a doctor then?' I tried to sound sarcastic but he only nodded.

'When I have to be.' He took a rag out of his tunic and gave it to me. I thought it'd be filthy, but it was clean and faded with washing. 'Here. Use this.'

Then suddenly without another word he was walking away, back in the direction of the Sublician Bridge. At first I just stared. Then when it was obvious he wasn't going to stop I shouted after him: 'Hey!'

No response. The big guy just kept on walking like he hadn't heard. I limped after him and pulled at his arm.

'Hey! Where the hell do you think you're going?'

I knew as soon as I'd done it that it was a mistake, like pulling a tiger back by the tail when it doesn't want your company. He whipped round and I let go, fast. We stared at each other for two or three heartbeats while I wished I was somewhere else. Like Naples, say.

Finally he growled: 'Don't push your luck, Corvinus. Just be thankful I didn't leave you to these bastards to finish off.'

Great. 'Okay. So why didn't you?'

'Nothing personal. I don't like unequal numbers is all. Which is lucky for you because, friend, I'd rather have you dead and rotten.'

Ouch. He meant it, too.

'You mind telling me why?'

He levelled a finger. 'Listen, Corvinus! Stop fucking around, okay? You could do more harm than you know. This is your last warning. Cut the questions or the next time someone comes down on you it'll be me.' He spat neatly on to the back of one of the fallen knifemen. 'And I'll do a better job than this garbage. Get me?'

And without waiting for an answer he turned and walked off down the path.

'Who are you working for?' I shouted to his retreating back. 'Who sent you?'

He didn't even break step. I doubt if he even heard me. I hobbled round to the beech tree by the back wall to pick up my mantle. So the guys who attacked me hadn't been Big Fritz's friends after all. Or if they had been they didn't need enemies. Which meant if Big Fritz was the Wart's then they couldn't have been. And vice versa. Unless of course they were...

Shit. I couldn't think. My brain was numb, my shoulder was aching and I had a lump the size of a goose egg on the side of my head where I'd landed when Geta had thrown me out.

'You could do more harm than you know.' Yeah, well, that made sense. Furkling around in the imperial dirty linen basket wasn't likely to throw up any roses, and because I hadn't the slightest idea what I was looking for, except that Tiberius didn't want it made public, I had to be grateful for whatever I could get. All the same there'd been a personal feel to Big Fritz's words. He'd said them as if he'd meant them. As if he really cared...

I grinned and shook my aching head. Oh, yeah, sure. Big Fritz is the Wart's catamite and the old bugger's using him to put the bite on. Great idea. Dream on, Corvinus.

I found my mantle and wound it round me as best I could, which wasn't exactly how Rome's best dressed were wearing it this season. Bathyllus would have a fit when I got back, he hated it when I looked sloppy. Then I set off at a fast limp for the Sublician and home.

Varus to Himself
The Farce, first act.

Vela has just left, having reported, to my immense surprise and consternation, that the Cheruscan tribe is reputedly preparing armed rebellion. I seize, of course, on the adverb. Arminius knows how important it will be for me to guard my back, and he would not want me to appear too hasty in swallowing the bait he has dangled in front of my greedy Roman jaws.

'"Reputedly"?'

'A rumour only, sir,' Vela assures me, 'brought by natives of doubtful probity under highly suspicious circumstances.'

I try not to wince. Vela has a low opinion of Germans; which tells you more about Vela than about our barbarian brothers. Ironically in this case his suspicions are well founded: the Germans have no intentions of beginning a major war. Even my treachery has its limits.

When all this is over, Vela, as my deputy, will inevitably be asked for a deposition regarding my conduct in the affair. I am therefore suitably cautious.

'You discount the rumour, then?'

'Yes, General. I do.' Just that, no more. Again I play safe, and grunt my firm agreement.

'Indeed,' I say. 'We have the army to consider, and the season. Intervention would entail a march through difficult and dangerous country.' I stiffen my jaw and look grave. 'Before I give that particular order, Vela, I will require far better evidence than unsubstantiated rumours.'

He is already nodding unqualified approval. 'Exactly, sir. My feelings entirely.'

'However.' I let the word hang. I have flung my sop to Cerberus. Now I must of necessity slip past him. 'Should that evidence be forthcoming, then that would be another matter, would it not?' Vela says nothing, but his lips tighten. 'Or do you disagree?'

He hems and haws. Finally he falls down on the side of the fence he has chosen all along.

'Yes, sir. Even then, I would distrust the reliability of even the strongest evidence. Especially in the light of what Segestes told us before we left.'

The words chill me: it is not like Vela to be so dogmatic. Or so perceptive. Segestes is the father of Arminius's wife, Thrusnelda, and a Romanophile of frightening proportions. Worse, he knows what he is talking about. Or thinks he knows. I turn my face away from the lamp, into the shadows, and keep my voice level.

'You think it's a trick? A German stratagem to draw us from our line of march?'

'Perhaps, sir.'

His voice is noncommittal; which should reassure me but does not. Can Vela suspect? Worse, can he know? If so then I am finished. As is Arminius.

'We send scouts,' I say abruptly. 'We find out the truth and take action accordingly. You agree?' Silence. 'Vela, do you agree?'

A pause; too long a pause.

'Yes, General. I agree.' A muscle in his cheek twitches. Suspicion? Distaste? Nerves?

'Good. Make the arrangements, would you?' I look down at the papers on my desk as if they are of vital interest (they deal with a complaint from the head muleteer concerning poor-quality bridle leather). When he still does not go I look up again, impatiently. 'That is all, Vela. For the moment.'

Vela throws me his pudding-soft salute and leaves me to my deliberations, which are not pleasant ones by any means.

Does he know? Can he know? Or is there some other reason for his behaviour?

The 'proof' will be forthcoming, of course. Arminius has managed this well; but then his heart is Roman, and so he has a natural flair for organisation...

It is late. I am tired, I cannot think any more, and my old bones are cold. I shall tell my orderly to warm me up some wine and then, like a man of virtue, wrap myself up in my general's cloak for sleep.

When I finally got back home more dead than alive my father was waiting for me. It put the cap on a perfect day. Bathyllus had strict standing instructions whenever I arrived and wherever I'd come from to have a full wine jug ready and waiting for me on the table by the door. I picked this up, filled the wine-cup next to it, and emptied it at a swallow.

'So what is it now, Dad?' I said. 'You on another message from the palace? Don't tell me. The Wart needs a clean lavatory sponge.'

My father was staring at the stains on my tunic (I'd shrugged off the mantle in the lobby), the crusted blood in my hair, and especially at the bloody gash on my left shoulder.

'What happened, Marcus?' he said.

'I had a run-in with a few roughs.' I eased myself on to the master couch, filled the cup again, and set the jug down on the table beside me. 'Nothing to worry about, Dad. If you are worried.'

He turned to Bathyllus, who was hovering in the doorway.

'Send for Sarpedon,' he snapped. 'Now!' Sarpedon was one of the best doctors in Rome. He'd cost Dad a small fortune when he'd bought him five years before. 'And make sure the baths are hot.'

'Look, Dad, I'm okay, right?' I stretched out carefully and sipped my wine, more slowly this time. 'Just leave it, will you?'

'Sarpedon will be the judge of that, boy. Certainly the cut in your shoulder needs attention.'

I was too tired and too sore to argue. When Bathyllus had left my father turned back to me.

'Now, what's this all about?' he said.

I shrugged, or tried to. 'I was over the other side of the river. I got jumped. They cut me and took my purse. End of story.'

'You're lying.'

I noticed with surprise that his hands and the muscles of his face were trembling. My father isn't the emotional type. At banquets he gets mistaken for the fish course. And he doesn't use straight crude words like 'lying' either. The nearest he ever comes is something like 'I don't believe that's strictly accurate' or just 'I think you're mistaken.' The flat accusation came as such a shock that I didn't even think of denying it.

'Yeah, okay. So I'm lying. So you caught me. Now what?'

He was trembling; with anger, I assumed.

'Marcus, give it up! Believe me, you don't know how dangerous what you're doing is!'

'So tell me.' I was getting pretty angry myself now. I'd had a long hard day and I wasn't taking this crap from anyone. 'You just tell me, Dad. Tell me why the emperor hates a dead poet so much he won't allow his ashes back to Rome. Tell me why when I ask questions about a scandal so old that you can't even smell it any more everyone keeps his mouth shut closer than a Vestal's kneecaps. Tell me why I nearly end up in the Tiber with my throat cut just because I go to see someone who Augustus didn't exile for not screwing his granddaughter. And if you can work out what that last little gem means, Dad, then you can explain it to me because I haven't got a clue.'

My father's face was ashen.

'I can't do that, Marcus,' he said. 'I can't trust you enough.'

That stopped me. Not, *I don't know what you're talking about* but *I can't trust you enough*. 'What the hell does that mean?'

'What it says.'

'Trust me to do what?'

'To keep the information to yourself.'

I laughed. 'Jupiter fucking Best and Greatest! Half of Rome is in on this, Dad!'

'Don't blaspheme, son. Not quite half of Rome. Only the responsible element. And the reason they don't tell is that they know it doesn't matter.'

I couldn't believe this. 'Run that one past me again. If it doesn't matter then surely there's no reason why I shouldn't be told.'

'Listen to me, Marcus!' My father's fist suddenly thudded on to the table top. 'I'm trying to save your life here! Of course you're being stonewalled! Of course there's a secret! Of course there's a conspiracy of silence! Do you expect me to deny any of that? What I'm telling you is that there's a point to it, that if the details leaked out they would do far more harm than good. And that before they let that happen the powers that be would see you or me or any other individual, no matter how well-born or powerful, go to the wall. Not because the information is important to the survival of the state but because it isn't. Now have I made myself clear?'

We stared at each other in silence. Finally, my father sat back. He was still shaking, and a droplet of sweat gleamed on his forehead. In spite of myself I was impressed: the guy really meant it. Or sounded like he did.

'Okay, Dad,' I said. 'Trust me. I swear I won't tell another living soul. Not even Perilla. And if it's as innocent as you say it is...'

My father closed his eyes and pressed his palms to them as if forcing the eyeballs back into their sockets.

'You still haven't understood, have you, son?' he said. 'There're no ifs or buts. It isn't a question of personal judgment, either yours or mine. And I never said the secret was innocent. I said it didn't matter.'

'I don't give a toss if it's innocent or not. I have to know. One way or the other, for my own satisfaction. You may as well tell me and save us both a lot of grief. I'll swear that it won't go any further, if that's what you want.'

'And that you won't use it as the basis for action? That if I tell you you'll drop this whole stupid Ovid business right now?'

I was silent. My father nodded. 'You see, Marcus? We're both trapped by our principles. I can't tell you what you want to know unless you promise not to use it; you can't make that promise until you know what the secret is. And I can't be responsible for telling you unless you do promise. That would only get both of us killed. And much though I love you, son, in spite of everything, I'm not prepared to take that risk.'

'Risk?'

'Certainty, then. It would be a certainty, Marcus. Give it up. Please! The knowledge isn't important, not now especially, I promise you that. And if you persist you won't live long enough to regret it.'

The emotional appeal impressed me. I hadn't thought my

father was capable of making one. If it was genuine, of course, and not some rhetorical trick. As an experienced orator Dad was perfectly capable of counterfeiting any emotion he pleased. Even granted that the emotion was real, however, if he had his beliefs he must allow me mine.

'I'm sorry, Dad,' I said. 'I told you. I've got to know. And if you won't tell me I'll just have to find out for myself.'

He looked at me for a long time, rather sadly I thought, but with a touch of something that could possibly have been pride. 'You're like your Uncle Cotta, son. You know that? You both think with your heart, not with your head. Other people grow out of it. He never did, and you won't either.'

'Is that so bad?'

His tone of voice didn't change. He wasn't arguing, he was just…talking.

'Of course it's bad. This is the modern world, Marcus, and it belongs to the grey bureaucrats. If you'd been born five centuries ago you'd be in the schoolbooks along with Horatius and Scaevola and all the other heroes. You're the kind that stands alone on bridges facing impossible odds or holding your hand in the fire until it withers just to prove a point. Then you'd've been called a hero. Nothing would've been too good for you. Now you're only an embarrassment.'

I said nothing. I'd never heard my father talk before. Not like this.

'Have you ever thought why Cotta's never made the consulship? Never even held one of the senior magistracies? He's from a good family. He's clever, popular, politically aware, a good speaker. A better man in every way than I am. Yet I had my consul's chair before I was thirty-five, while at forty-one he's never made it past junior finance officer. Why do you think that is?'

'Because he isn't an arselicker.' I was intentionally brutal.

My father didn't even blink.

'Just because someone is for established government,' he said quietly, 'doesn't mean to say he need automatically be labelled a sycophant. Tiberius isn't perfect, the imperial system isn't perfect, but it could be worse. Might be yet for all I know. Tiberius may not be charismatic, but he's steady, and that's what we need in an emperor. Steadiness, not heroics. Flashy isn't always best, Marcus, there's too much at stake. Look at Germanicus's histrionics in Germany. What good did they do except lose us men and reputation?'

I had to agree. Tiberius's adopted son's campaign—which Germanicus himself had trumpeted as a glorious revenge for the Varian massacre—had bombed pretty spectacularly.

'You know the story of the two bulls?' my father said suddenly.

Startled, I shook my head.

'Well, then.' He smiled: a curious, enigmatic smile I'd never seen before. 'There were two bulls, an old one and a young one, looking down into a valley at a herd of cows. The young bull says to the old one, "Look at all those cows down there, Dad! Let's run down and cover a couple." And the old bull turns to him and says, "No, son. Let's walk down and cover them all."'

It took me a moment to realise that my father had made a joke; and then another moment (because he didn't smile) to realise that it wasn't a joke at all.

'I can't help what I am, Dad,' I said. 'No more than you can. We're different people and we don't mix.'

He nodded, sadly. 'Yes, son, I know. We're different people. That is the pity of it.'

And then Sarpedon arrived with his salves and bandages, and there was no more time for talking.

CHAPTER

13

Next day before I went round to Perilla's to report developments, I dropped by the gymnasium I own near the racetrack for a word with one of my clients, an ex-trainer of gladiators called Scylax. The name (it's a nickname meaning Puppy-Dog in Greek) fits the guy perfectly. He's got the build, the facial features, and the temperament of one of those muscle-hard unkillable little brutes you see in country bullrings taking on something two or three hundred times their size and winning. That's Scylax. Once he gets his teeth into someone he won't let go, and when that happens the bastard's dead meat.

We'd met three years before at Aquilo's gym, where I went regularly to train. My usual sparring partner had broken his wrist and old Aquilo led this guy out. He may've looked like something you'd drag off with a hook at the end of the Games but Aquilo introduced him like he was less than one step down from Jupiter himself. I should've taken note of that. I didn't. Mistake number one.

We sized each other up. The top of the little runt's bald head was just about level with my chin. Shit, I remember thinking, am I supposed to fight this thing or feed it nuts?

'You ready?' I said.

He didn't answer, so I assumed he was. I feinted to the left, then brought the tip of the wooden sword round hard across the top of his belly in the sweetest little sideways slash you've ever seen: a stroke that if we'd been doing this for real should've left him staring at his own tripes. Even with a practice foil it would've hurt like hell; but then (mistake number two) I wanted to show off.

The sword never connected. Instead it was suddenly out of my hand and the little guy was lunging straight at my eyes. I jumped backwards with a scream like a fifty-year-old virgin threatened with gang rape.

Scylax lowered his sword and scowled down at me as I lay in the sand at his feet.

'Yeah, that's you upper-class bumboys all over,' he growled. 'Shit-scared your mascara gets smudged.'

I was furious. I scrambled to my feet and gave him the works.

'What the hell do you mean by going for my eyes? You could've blinded me, you little fucker!'

'Listen, boy.' His voice was barely a whisper, but I shut up as if my tongue had been nailed to the top of my mouth. 'Sword-fighting's not a game, understand? You're out to kill someone, just like he's out to kill you. There're no rules beyond that. Okay?'

'Yeah, sure, but...'

'No buts. Remember how Caesar won Thapsus, or Munda, or whatever else sodding battle it was? He told his men to cut at the enemy's faces. The patrician bumboys on the other side didn't mind dying but they couldn't stomach the thought of losing their pretty looks, so they ran. End of battle, end of story. Point taken?'

Jupiter! 'Point taken.'

'Another thing.' Without warning, he aimed a vicious kick at my groin. Instinctively my hands came down to cover my balls and I moved backwards. The kick never happened. Instead the guy's sword swung up to touch my chest. 'You can use a man's worst fear as a feint. And it may not be a feint at all. Right?'

'Right.' By this time I was staring at him like Plato must've stared at Socrates the first time they met. If there'd been any incense around I'd've had it lit and smoking.

'Okay.' He stepped back. 'Now let's start again. And pay attention this time.'

I did; and I'd been paying attention ever since.

Yeah. Scylax was worth his weight in gold; which was only slightly less than I'd paid to set him up in his own training gym behind the racetrack. I didn't regret it. He was the prime reason why I was still walking around that morning with my throat in one piece and nothing worse than a cut shoulder to beef about.

I found him working out a bald old senator with enough lard under his tunic to keep five masseurs busy for a year. The guy was gasping for breath as if he'd just run all the way from Ostia; and by his colour I'd've judged he was no more than a hair's-breadth from hanging up his sandals for keeps.

'Hey, Scylax!' I yelled.

He looked over, then lowered his sword.

'That's enough for today, sir,' he said to the fat guy. 'We don't want to overdo it, do we?'

Yeah, Scylax can be polite enough to the right person. And

there are other ways of losing a punter than work him till he turns blue and folds up on you.

The senator was reeling like a drunken pig, but he managed to bring his sword up in the military salute soldiers give their training partners on the practice ground at the end of a bout. Not a sloppy one, either. Crisp as a dream. Suddenly I saw underneath the rolls of fat and the four chins the spry young officer he must once have been; and I wondered what sort of a figure I'd cut in another thirty years.

If I lived that long.

A slave stepped forward with a towel. The fat guy rubbed the sweat from his beefsteak-red face and neck, shook some fresh air into his tunic, and turned to me grinning like a fifteen-year-old.

'Good workout, eh, boy?' he panted. 'Gets the juices going, right?'

'Yeah,' I said. 'Yeah. Great.'

He winked, waved, and stumbled off towards the bathhouse. I hoped he'd make it, but he was breathing so hard I wouldn't have given myself better than evens.

Scylax picked up the wooden swords, tucked them under his arm and began walking towards his office in the main building.

'What the hell you doing here, Corvinus?' he said. 'This isn't your usual day. I can squeeze you in, just, but it won't be for long.'

I grinned. That was another thing I liked about the guy. He knew the respect due from client to patron.

'Hey, I own this place, remember?'

'So sell it. But I still can't give you more than half an hour.'

I shook my head and fell into step beside him. 'I'm not

fighting today, Scylax. You wouldn't even raise sweat. I got jumped yesterday and one of the bastards cut me.'

Scylax stopped dead and stared at me. 'You got cut, boy? How bad?'

'Just a sliced shoulder. Sarpedon patched it up.'

'How many were there?'

'Four.'

He gave a grunt of disgust, spat on to the sand, and carried on walking.

'Only four, and they cut you? What were they, kids, women or cripples?'

'Four against one's heavy odds, and you know it. And these guys were professionals. You nearly lost yourself a patron. Would have, if I hadn't had help. Which is what I want to talk to you about.'

He sighed.

'Okay, Corvinus. Maybe I have got time to spare after all. Step over to the bath-house and I'll give you a workout.'

Jupiter! That I didn't need!

'Hey, look,' I said. 'No massage, right? I've been beaten up enough times the last few days, thanks.'

He stopped again. His eyes raked me anxiously.

'You mean it's happened more than once? What is this?'

'I'm exaggerating. But no massage.'

'Come on, boy.' He took my arm—my good one, luckily: Scylax used his hands like a crab uses its claws—and steered me towards the bath-house. 'A good massage never hurt anyone. It'll loosen you up.'

Yeah, I bet that's what they told Prometheus before they sicced the vulture on him, I thought; but I didn't say it out loud. I didn't want to hurt the little guy's feelings.

The massage room was empty although I could hear

snatches of a jolly military romp from the cold plunge next door. Somebody called Titus had evidently got hold of somebody else's towel and wouldn't give it back. I wondered how we'd managed to put together an empire in the first place, let alone keep it.

'Okay, tell me,' Scylax said when he had me face down on one of the tables and had slapped the oil on.

I told him. How much of the details were actually intelligible through the screams I don't know, but he seemed to get the gist of it. And I'm not talking about the noise from Rome's best and brightest in the next room, either.

'Why the hell did you let them all jump you at once?' Scylax demanded.

'You think maybe I should've suggested they take turns?'

Never use sarcasm on your masseur. Scylax grabbed my neck and dug his thumbs in under my shoulder-blades while I shrieked and yammered at him to stop.

'Sorry, Corvinus. That the sore arm?' he said finally, just before I passed out. The sadistic bastard could see that it was. Sarpedon's dressing covered half the bloody shoulder. 'You should've run, boy. Spaced them out and taken them one by one.'

I tried a grin. It didn't work too well.

'Oh, sure. Pheidippides is one of my middle names. I run a marathon every morning before breakfast.'

Scylax grunted. 'You say this guy was a foreigner?'

I felt a knuckle being inserted between two plates of muscle and whimpered, knowing what was coming. It came. After he'd pulled me down off the ceiling I said: 'Yeah. From the north, probably. Could be German. Good Latin, though. And no bonehead.'

Scylax's hands moulded themselves to my ribs and pulled

the flesh downwards. Great if you're into that sort of thing. I wasn't. It felt like being skinned by an octopus.

'You say he had a sword cut on his left cheek.'

'That's what it looked like. Half his ear was missing. Come on, Scylax. I need a name, okay?'

He was quiet for a long time. I could feel him thinking as the heel of his hand ground its way inch by excruciating inch up my spine. I clenched my teeth and tried not to howl. 'He's no gladiator, I'll tell you that now. A guy that big and that good would stick out a mile in the teams.' This was final. What Scylax didn't know about the professional sword-fighting world wasn't just not worth knowing; it didn't exist. 'Could be a soldier. Ex-soldier, maybe.'

'An auxiliary? What would an auxiliary be doing in Rome?'

'Who said auxiliary? The guy sounds like a legionary. You think he was German?'

'Yeah. Or maybe a Slav.'

'Slav's possible. Tiberius roped in a lot of Illyrian hayseeds the time of the troubles.'

Yeah. That fitted. Twelve years earlier the province of Illyricum had rebelled (my father was actually provincial governor at the time) and for a while it'd looked like everything between the Julian Alps and Macedon was headed down the tube. The emergency had meant that General Tiberius had had to buzz around like a blue-arsed fly grabbing all the recruits he could to stop the rebellion spreading.

'I'll buy that,' I said. 'The guy could still have connections, in fact.'

'Connections with Tiberius?' Scylax's hands paused. 'You in some sort of trouble? Official trouble?'

Shit. It had slipped out. Scylax might be a friend but the

Ovid affair was private. I covered my tracks. 'Uh-uh. Purely personal.'

'You want to tell me about it?'

'Nothing to tell. You know as much as I do. Maybe I screwed someone's sister.'

'Uhuh.' He didn't sound convinced. The hands resumed their pummelling. It wasn't so painful now I was getting used to it. Or maybe something vital had broken and I just couldn't feel any more. 'You say you've seen this guy more than once.'

'Yeah. We'd a run-in in a shop off Suburan Street a few days back. Only then he wasn't on my side.'

Scylax clicked his tongue. 'This sounds weirder by the minute, boy.'

He didn't believe me, that was sure. Which wasn't all that surprising. But at the same time he couldn't call me a liar, because it was none of his business.

'Okay,' he said finally. 'Only you need any muscle you let me know, right? Next time you may not be so lucky.'

'Thanks,' I said; and I meant it. When it came to muscle I'd've backed Scylax against a picked squad of Praetorians any day. 'But ask around, will you? I want to know who this guy is.'

'You've got it.' He was kneading and rubbing gently with his fingertips now. I almost purred. 'If the bastard's in Rome, I'll find him. And after that if you want me to I'll take him apart.'

When I finally got to Perilla's
she was out.

'The mistress is at the Lady Marcia's, sir,' Callias told me.
'She said for you please to join her there if you called round. It's
near the Temple of Cybele.'

'Yeah, I know where the Fabius place is,' I said. 'Great.
Thanks a lot, Callias.' The Lady Marcia was Fabius Maximus's
widow and, if you remember, a relative of Perilla's mother's.
She was practically a neighbour of mine, a bit further up the
hill. I could've saved myself a journey. Perilla hadn't thought
of stopping by with a message. Oh no. I was only her patron,
wasn't I?

I whistled to my four new bodyguards kicking their heels
on the corner. They lumbered across flexing their biceps and
eyeing Callias like they were wondering how far he'd bounce.
These four were the biggest, toughest guys I owned, huge
Gauls whose idea of fun was cracking nuts between thumb

and forefinger. And I don't mean the kind that grow on trees either.

I'd had it up to here with being mugged. Next time anyone wanted to try it they'd have to get past the Sunshine Boys.

The Fabius mansion was one of the biggest and oldest in Rome, taking up the space between Romulus's hut and the house of Augustus; which as far as neighbours go is pretty impressive stuff. I had one of the Sunshine Boys knock on the door, shouted my name into the septuagenarian door slave's ear, and was ushered inside. The boys settled down with their backs against the wall to play dice; at least the three who could count up to six did. The fourth seemed happy just to leer at the passing litters.

Perilla was sitting in the garden with an elderly lady I assumed was Marcia. She was wearing my earrings, I noticed, and a sky-blue cloak that went well with the peacock that was strutting up and down beside her. She smiled as I came through the colonnade.

'Oh, hello, Corvinus. You got my message, then?'

Not a trace of guilt in her lovely voice, not a spark of conscience in her lovely eyes. What the hell. I sighed and sat down on the chair the slave had brought for me.

'It must've missed me,' I said. 'Sorry I'm so late. I had to call in on a client.' I glanced sideways at the old woman. She hadn't moved, hadn't even acknowledged my presence. Her attention was fixed on the peacock, which was getting itself hyped up for a display. I remembered my manners (yeah, I do have some) and added: 'So introduce me to your aunt.'

Perilla's mouth opened to reply; but just then the peacock spread its tail with a rustling whirr and the old woman turned towards me. I saw bright mad eyes in a doughy lifeless face made even more ghastly by make-up, and a slack mouth in constant motion that dropped spittle.

'Aunt Marcia's out at the moment, Corvinus,' Perilla said quietly. 'This is my mother.'

The peacock shivered and turned in a slow circle, its tail a mass of dead staring eyes, watching me. Watching...

I carried it off somehow, don't ask me how. Jupiter knows what I said; I can't remember a word, only that I was sweating all the time. Then a female slave came out and led the old woman inside leaving us alone. We sat in silence for a while.

'It's one of her bad days,' Perilla said at last. 'She's never rational but at least sometimes she's there, at least she acknowledges your existence and talks to you.'

'How long has she been like that?' I was still shaking. If there's one thing I can't take it's madness and madmen. I can't handle the lack of contact, of common ground. It sends me to pieces every time. I knew a guy once, an army officer who'd seen active service all over and won every decoration going, who was terrified of the touch of a feather against his skin. He couldn't go near a poulterer's shop without breaking out into a cold sweat. That's how madness gets me.

'She's got worse over the last few years,' Perilla said. 'She'd never been entirely well since my stepfather was exiled. Then the strain of working for his recall, managing his estate, plus all the trouble with Rufus...' She hesitated. 'It was just too much for her. She lives here now, as she did before she was married. Aunt Marcia's very good.'

'Can't you do something for her? I mean, there must be doctors, Greek doctors...'

'We've tried. It's no use, they can't help. In a way I'm glad. I think she's happier like this, in a world of her own.'

I shook my head but said nothing. Jupiter! How could a mumbling, drooling thing like that be happy? Me, now, I'd rather slit my wrists. Or if I was beyond that have a good friend do it for me.

'Anyway.' Perilla gathered her cloak around her and smiled a brittle smile. 'You didn't come to talk about my troubles. At least not that particular one. How are the investigations going? Did you talk to Silanus?'

'Who?' I made an effort to pull myself together. 'Oh yeah. Yeah, I talked to him. In the five minutes it took him to call his tame gorilla and have me thrown out, that is.'

'Corvinus, for heaven's sake!' Her eyes widened. 'What did you say?'

'Nothing.' I rubbed the sweat from my palms. I was beginning to feel more myself again, although a large belt of neat Falernian wouldn't've gone amiss. 'At least nothing insulting. I was my usual super-polite self. Maybe the guy just didn't like my aftershave.'

'That's nonsense. He must've had some reason to send you away.'

'Well, I don't think he was too happy when I suggested he'd been paid to take the rap.' Jupiter! That was putting it mildly! 'But that was towards the end. The hit squad was already on its way by then.' I paused. 'Perilla, could I have a drink, please? I've had a pretty hard day.'

'It isn't noon yet.'

'I know, but I'd still like a drink. Please.'

'Fruit juice?' she asked sweetly.

'Oh, come on, lady!'

'You drink too much wine,' she said; but nonetheless she signalled to a hovering slave.

'I only do it to forget.'

Her brow wrinkled. 'Forget what?'

'I don't know. I've forgotten.'

I could see her working that old chestnut out. Like I say, Perilla may've been beautiful but her sense of humour was zilch. Finally she gave it up and returned to the subject.

'What did you mean "paid to take the rap"?'

'Not to make any waves over the charge of seducing Julia.'

'But Corvinus, Silanus wasn't rewarded, he was exiled.'

'Uh-uh. You've got it wrong. There wasn't any exile. Silanus left Rome voluntarily.'

'What about the ban on holding public office?'

I shrugged. 'The guy might not be interested in politics. Just because you come from a good family doesn't mean you're wetting your pants to make consul. Look at me, for instance.'

Perilla did, and I wished I'd bitten my tongue off. Shit.

'I've been wondering about that, Corvinus,' she said coolly. 'Don't you have any political ambitions? No push? No sense of duty to your family or to the state?'

I shifted ground rapidly. Lectures in self-improvement from clients I could do without. 'Yeah, well, we'll leave that aside, okay? Just admit that it does happen sometimes. A simple soul like Silanus—or a lazy bastard, if you prefer it—'

'I don't.'

'—may have decided that he prefers money and the easy life to political glory. Besides, there was a more important reason why Augustus didn't punish him.'

'That being?'

'The guy didn't screw Julia at all. No one did. This whole adultery business never happened.'

'What?'

'Sure. The charge was a fake, and everybody involved knew it.'

Perilla was staring at me like my ears'd just turned chartreuse.

'Corvinus, have you totally lost your senses? Of course Julia committed adultery!'

'Yeah? How do you know?'

'Well...' Perilla was visibly floundering. 'Everyone knows she did.'

'Everyone knows she was charged. I've just told you. The charge was a fake.'

'But Silanus admitted to seducing her!'

'Sure he did.' I was grinning. It wasn't often I was ahead of Perilla, and I was enjoying it. 'That's what he was paid for, lady.'

'What about Augustus? He laid the charge himself. He sent her to Trimerus. Corvinus, she was his own granddaughter!'

"Look, Perilla. I never said Julia was innocent. I said she hadn't committed adultery.'

'So why was she exiled, then?'

I opened my mouth—and stopped. I felt like I'd just run into a brick wall. Yeah. Good question. I just wished I knew the answer.

'I don't know,' I admitted. 'Not yet. But I'd swear on the teats of the wolf that suckled Romulus it wasn't for sleeping around.'

Perilla was quiet for a long time. Finally she said:

'Corvinus, I'm sorry I was so dismissive.'

Hey! Apologies? 'That's big of you.'

'Perhaps you're right. Perhaps Julia didn't commit adultery after all.'

I beamed. 'Yeah, well, I can be really persuasive when I get going.'

'No, that's not it. It wasn't anything you said.'

Jupiter! So much for smugness. Straight in the kisser,

without so much as the bat of an eyelid. The girl had as much tact as a sledgehammer. 'Only you're the second person to defend Julia that I've talked to today. I'd put it down to an old woman's partisanship but now I'm not so sure.'

One of us wasn't making sense any longer and I was pretty sure it wasn't me.

'Perilla,' I said, 'why don't you run that one past me again? Maybe I missed something somewhere.'

Just then the slave with the wine tray arrived. Instead of answering Perilla fixed him with her eye.

'Glaucus,' she said, 'ask Harpale to come out, would you?'

'Yes, madam.' The guy poured for both of us and left. I took a careless swallow; then as the wine hit my palate and burst into song I changed my mind rapidly and sipped. This was no swigging stuff. It was real Caecuban, pure nectar from the area around Fundi, and rare as a twenty-year-old virgin in a cathouse. Old Fabius must've laid it down about the time of Actium. Anyone who treated it with less than absolute respect deserved to be boiled in vinegar and rendered for pigswill.

'Corvinus?'

'Hmm?'

Are you all right?'

'Yeah. Uh...who's Harpale?'

'My only contribution to the investigation so far. You'll see when she arrives.'

I didn't have to wait long; not that I minded with a flask of fifty-year-old Caecuban at my elbow and Perilla to look at. Out of the house came an elderly female slave. She moved slowly and I noticed that her right foot was twisted inwards.

'You wanted me, madam?' she said.

'Yes, Harpale.' Perilla indicated a stone bench against the wall next to her. 'Have a seat, please.'

The old woman sat down and placed one hand over the other like a demure kid at her first adult party.

'This is Valerius Corvinus, the gentleman I mentioned.' The slave bobbed her head in my direction. 'Corvinus, this is Harpale. Until my Aunt Marcia acquired her she was the Lady Julia's personal maid.'

Jupiter!

CHAPTER 15

'She's beautiful.' I must've been staring at the old girl with a pretty feral grin on my face because she suddenly squirmed on the seat and looked nervous as hell. 'Absolutely beautiful. Where did you find her?'

Perilla frowned.

'I've just told you, Corvinus. My Aunt Marcia bought her when Julia was exiled. The estate was broken up and her property sold. Now please behave yourself and stop frightening the poor thing.' She turned to the slave. 'Don't worry, Harpale. He won't do you any harm. That's his natural expression.'

'Cut it out, lady.' I tried to look benign, but the old slave was watching me like a rabbit watches a snake. Her eyes were a pale washed-out blue: candid and slightly stupid. 'I only want you to answer a few questions, Harpale. Okay?'

'Yes, sir.' The woman's voice was light as a dry leaf.

'Fine. We'll start, then. You were the Lady Julia's maid. Was she a good mistress?'

The old woman's smile was surprisingly sweet and innocent.

'Oh, yes, sir,' she said. 'She was really kind. A lovely mistress the Lady Julia was.'

'Did she have many men friends?'

Harpale lowered her eyes. She might not be too smart, but
she knew what I was asking, and she stayed quiet so long that I
thought I could guess the answer.

'Some, sir. Lit'rary men like the Lady Perilla's stepfather.'

'What about Silanus?'

The thin lips pursed.

'You asked me about the Lady Julia's friends.'

'So?'

'Silanus was round at the house often enough, sir. But not
when the mistress was on her own. Only when the master was
there. They was very friendly, sir, him and Master Paullus. Not
that he came to dinner much. Not that kind of friendly. He'd
drop by at odd hours. The middle of the afternoon usually. Or
late in the evening. The mistress might be in the sitting-room as
well, she often was, but it was the master he really wanted. You
could see that, sir. Anyone with ha' an eye could see that.'

Uhuh. I glanced at Perilla.

'Tell him about the man with the ring,' she said.

Harpale turned to her. 'Oh, no, madam. He didn't have no
ring. That was the point.' The pale eyes shifted back to me. 'He
came at odd hours too, sir. Sometimes with Silanus, sometimes
on his own.'

I could feel the hairs at the back of my neck crawl.

'Did this guy have a name, Harpale?'

'Not that I knew, sir. I only saw him the once, and'—her
hand sketched a hood or a mantle-fold—'his head was covered.'

'What's this about a ring?'

'He wasn't wearing one, sir. At least'—she held out her skinny right hand and indicated the last finger—'he had the mark, see, but the ring was missing.'

'It could've been in for repair.'

'Oh, no. He never did have no ring, so Davus said.'

'Davus?'

'The door slave, sir. He used to let the gentleman in, of course. Not that he knew who he was either, even though he did see him once.'

Jupiter! 'You mean he saw him? Saw the guy's face?'

'Yes, sir. Just that one time, at the end, when the gentleman's hood slipped.'

'But he didn't recognise him?'

'Not that he'd admit to, sir. But Davus was like that, he wouldn't've told anyone, even one of us other slaves. Not if the mistress ordered him not to.'

I saw something I shouldn't've seen and didn't report it.

Like a guy who kept his face covered and visited the traitor Paullus at odd hours? Shit! The hairs on the back of my neck were crawling like I had fleas.

'Could the Lady Perilla's stepfather have seen this man too at any time, Harpale? Seen him and recognised him?'

Out of the corner of my eye, I saw Perilla shoot me a sharp look. One up for the boys. She obviously hadn't thought of that angle.

'Perhaps, sir. Davus might know that, too.'

'You mean Davus is still alive?' Beside me I heard Perilla gasp: score two. Celestial bells rang. Jupiter, I thought, if you give me this one thing...

'Oh, yes, sir. Davus is alive. Of course he is.'

I sat back in my chair. I could've grabbed the old girl and kissed her, but that would really have sent Perilla up the wall.

'So where is he now? Can we talk to him?'

The candid eyes were suddenly not candid any longer; and they were firmly fixed in the old woman's lap.

'He ran away, sir,' she said. 'Just after my mistress was arrested.'

'Where did he go?' Perilla broke in. Then, when the old woman didn't answer: 'Harpale, please tell us! This is important. You know, don't you?'

'Yes. I know.' The old woman's voice was barely audible, and I could make a good guess why. A recaptured slave gets pretty short shrift: he's branded across the face with a red-hot iron and sent to the mines, or to one of the agricultural gangs. Either way he doesn't live long, if he's lucky. 'I can't tell you where Davus is, madam. That's not my secret. But if you only want to talk to him I'll arrange it.'

I hadn't realised that I'd been holding my breath. Now I let it out.

'Yeah,' I said. 'Yeah. Okay. Any time, any place he chooses. He won't get into any trouble through me, I promise you. In fact I may be able to do the guy a favour or two.'

She was shaking her head.

'No, sir. Thank you but no,' she said firmly. 'Davus is all right, sir. He doesn't need nothing, not now. He'd like to see the mistress cleared same as I would, and if this'll help then he'll talk to you with pleasure. The Lady Julia was innocent, sir. I told them that, even when they broke my leg to get me to say different.' I glanced down at her lame foot. Yeah. That made sense. A slave's evidence against his owner is only valid under torture. 'The mistress was no whore, sir. No more than her lady mother was.'

Everything went very quiet; so quiet I could hear the sound of the fountain in the ornamental pool inside the house.

Julia's mother, the other Julia, Augustus's daughter, had been exiled too. Also for adultery...

'Uh...You mind running over that again, Harpale?' I tried to keep my voice calm. 'Just for the record?'

Harpale was quite composed. She could've been stating the most obvious fact in the world. Perhaps, to her mind, she was.

'Oh, yes, sir,' she said brightly. 'I was a present to the young Lady Julia on her marriage, but before that I was her mother's maid. That Lady Julia was innocent, too.'

CHAPTER 16

We watched Harpale limp back towards the house.

'Perilla, what the fuck is going on?'

'You're supposed to be the expert. You tell me.' She sounded a bit jaundiced, but I noticed she hadn't mentioned the language. Maybe it was my bad influence.

'Oh. Yeah. Sure.' My wine-cup was looking empty so I topped it up. 'Okay, so what do we know? First of all, Silanus never touched Julia. The whole adultery story was a lie from start to finish, a cover-up by Augustus for something else. Okay?'

'Go on.'

'But to make it plausible someone had to take the rap, and Silanus was the lucky winner—either because he volunteered at a price or because someone twisted his little arm halfway up his back. Right?'

'Yes, Corvinus. Or so it would seem.'

I may not be an intellectual giant but I know when some-one's taking the piss; and that last remark was straight out of the blunt half of a Socratic dialogue. I looked at Perilla suspiciously. Not the trace of a smile. Maybe the lady had a sense of humour after all.

'Yeah. Right. Anyway,' I went on, 'whatever reward was offered or pressure applied, the guy was promised that he'd get off lightly, and he did. He wasn't formally exiled, but all the same Augustus encouraged him to take an extended trip abroad. And just for the show of things he banned him from any future political career. That might sound pretty dire for a political whizz-kid but Lover Boy Silanus hadn't any real inter-est in politics so he wasn't unduly concerned.'

'It also meant that he wouldn't be in Rome to face embar-rassing questions.'

'Right. On the plus side, to compensate for this his cousin, who *is* a political whizz-kid, gets Julia's daughter, a marriage tie with the ruling family, and all the extra political clout that goes with it.'

'Even though Julia herself was disgraced?'

'Even then. Augustus wasn't vindictive. None of the fam-ily was penalised when their mother was exiled. Quite the reverse.'

'But if as Harpale said the elder Julia was innocent too…'

'Yeah, okay.' I frowned. 'If Harpale's right that opens up a whole new can of worms, but we'll need more than a slave's word for it. We'll need some hard evidence.'

'If it exists.'

'Don't worry. I'll dig. There's a guy I can ask about that, a friend of my grandfather's. He's retired now, lives outside the city off the Appian Way. Leave it for the moment. We've got enough headaches to be going on with.' I poured some more wine and sipped it. 'So. If there was no adultery then why was our sweet little Julia exiled? From what Harpale tells us Silanus seems to've been involved more with Paullus. And Paullus was chopped for treason, so it's reasonable to assume the other two—Julia and Silanus—were in on the same scam.'

'What was Paullus's crime exactly? Do you know?'

'Search me. A plot against Augustus, obviously. That's something else we have to find out.'

'And you think Julia was involved?'

'Yeah, why not? She was guilty of something, certainly. If the adultery charge was only a cover, then treason's as good a crime as any. Let's say she and Paullus were working as a husband-and-wife team and they got caught. Paullus was chopped but Julia, as Augustus's grandchild, was let off with exile.'

'So why weren't they both charged with treason? Why bother with adultery at all?'

'Perilla, I'm telling you. Julia was the emperor's granddaughter. You think Augustus would be willing to admit there was treason in the family?'

She nodded. 'Fair enough. You're probably right, Corvinus.'

'Sure I'm right.'

'Don't get smug. What about Silanus? You haven't mentioned him. Where does he fit in?'

'He was involved in the conspiracy too, like I said. That was obvious from what Harpale told us. If I'm right it was Silanus who blew the whole thing to Augustus. Maybe he got cold feet, maybe he just decided the game was up and he'd better save his own neck by turning informer. Either would explain why he got off so lightly, why he was so ready to admit to the fake adultery charge, and why he was given that under-the-counter reward of his.'

'And the man with the ring?'

'Ah, now.' I raised my wine-cup. Jupiter, this stuff was good! My brain was purring away like one of those fancy machines the Greeks come up with now and again for telling the time or counting votes. 'Our fourth conspirator. He gets the starring role. Why should anyone take their ring off when they go visiting?'

'Because it was distinctive?'

'Give me more, lady.'

'A gold ring would show that the man was a noble.'

True enough. Only nobles had the right to wear gold rings. That was one of these stupid rules my father could've been responsible for.

'Yeah, but anyone on calling terms with Paullus wouldn't be the type to lug fishboxes in the market, would he? Still, nobles are ten a penny. It has to be more than just any gold ring.' I held out my own right hand. 'Notice anything?'

Like all narrow- and broad-stripers I was wearing a heavy seal-ring for documents. Perilla sat back.

'Corvinus, that's brilliant! The ring would have his crest on. And if he was well known, or from a very prominent family...'

'The crest would give his name away even if his face was covered. Right.' I sipped my wine. 'Ten gets you twenty our fourth conspirator was a pretty important guy.'

'He could have changed rings, surely. Left his own at home and worn a different one.'

'Sure he could have. But he didn't. Why go to these lengths? And who worries what a slave sees? Or rather doesn't see?'

'You think that's why my stepfather was exiled? Because he saw the man and recognised him?'

'It's possible. And if he knew there was some funny business going on and didn't report it...'

I stopped. Perilla was frowning.

'No,' she said. 'No, I'm sorry, but that doesn't make sense. I'll allow you the rest, but not my stepfather's exile. Augustus had no need to be unduly harsh. After all, the plot had already failed. Paullus was executed, Julia was exiled, Silanus went abroad.' She waved her hand. 'End of story.'

I set the wine-cup down. 'Yeah. End of story. So what happened to the guy with the ring? Our fourth conspirator? Why wasn't he arrested with the others?'

Perilla opened her mouth and shut it. I'd never seen her at a loss for words. It was quite something, and I owed it all to the Caecuban. Maybe I could get old Marcia to let me have a flask of the stuff.

'I'll tell you what happened to him.' I was enjoying this. 'Nothing. Zero. Zilch. He disappears out of the picture. No execution, no exile, no nothing. Not so much as a footnote.'

'Perhaps they just never caught him.'

'Perhaps they didn't want to catch him.'

Perilla stared. 'Why shouldn't they want to catch him?'

Clever women can be incredibly thick sometimes. But then, Perilla hadn't grown up like I had in the murky world of power politics. I explained.

'Look. Silanus was the group stool-pigeon, right? He peached to Augustus. Now if Silanus knew who our fourth man was—which he must have done—the guy didn't have a hope in hell of avoiding prosecution. So if he wasn't prosecuted—which he wasn't—it means that the authorities knew who he was already.'

'But if they knew who he was, then...'

I laid it on the line.

'Sure they knew. Because our fourth man was involved in the conspiracy with their unofficial blessing.'

'You mean he was the emperor's agent?'

'Right. It was Augustus's classic ploy. Don't wait for a conspiracy to come to a head, destroy it from the inside before it gets going. Our fourth conspirator could've been Augustus's man from the start.'

'Then he can't've been the reason for my stepfather's exile.'

That stopped me.

'Yeah? Why the hell not?'

This time it was Perilla's turn to be patient. 'Because my stepfather said he'd seen something and failed to report it. If he only meant that he knew who your fourth conspirator was, and Augustus knew the man's name already, then surely it wouldn't matter very much?'

'Unless the fact that Ovid hadn't told him rubbed Augustus up the wrong way.'

'But you said Augustus wasn't vindictive. Punishing my stepfather with exile for something that happened by accident and hardly mattered in the end…well, I'd say that showed a fair degree of vindictiveness, wouldn't you?'

'Don't forget Ovid wasn't family like his daughter Julia's kids. And Augustus hated the poor guy's guts.'

'It's still completely out of proportion.'

'Yeah.' I swallowed the last of my wine and emptied the flagon into the cup. 'Okay. Maybe we're still missing something.'

'Of course there is another possibility,' Perilla said.

'Yeah?' I frowned. The wine was finally getting to me. 'What's that?'

'That the fourth man was someone really important. Too important to risk charging.'

I laughed. 'You got anyone in mind, lady? The guy would have to be pretty big to rank above the emperor's granddaughter.'

'How about Tiberius?' Perilla said quietly. 'Would he qualify?'

I stared at her in numb shock. 'Oh, no. Not the emperor, Perilla. It couldn't be the emperor.'

'Why not?'

Why not? How the hell could she be so calm about an idea like that?

'Because...' I began; and that was as far as I got.

Shit. Why not? I tried frantically to think of reasons. None of them worked. What was worse, everything that had happened in the last few days made perfect sense. If the Wart had been our fourth conspirator in the days when he'd been a not-so-humble commoner, and he knew I was busy ferreting around in that particular closet, then you could count my chances of seeing another birthday on the fingers of one foot.

'Oh, hell!' I whispered. 'Oh, hell and damnation!'

'It would make sense, wouldn't it?' Perilla said cheerfully.

I didn't answer. I couldn't. But she was right, dead right. Of course it would make sense. Ten years before the Wart had been the empire's foremost general. He had powers second only to Augustus's own, and although the old man hadn't actually named him as such, he was the only realistic candidate for the succession. Paullus and Julia would've welcomed him into their cosy little conspiracy with open arms. It would've meant giving him the purple, sure, but the chance would've been too good to miss. Paullus would've had his work cut out getting the support he'd need for the top job anyway. As an imperial candidate he wouldn't be all that convincing; but as the man responsible for the new emperor's elevation he'd have his feet firmly on the bottom step of the throne. New bosses are very grateful people...

'Corvinus? I asked you a question. Don't you think it would make sense?'

'Hmm?' Absently I swallowed the wine in my cup and reached for the jug. It was empty. Well, maybe she was right. Maybe I did drink too much. 'Yeah, it'd make sense. But would it be worth Tiberius's while? After all, the emperor was into his seventies. And the Wart was set to succeed anyway.'

'Only so long as Augustus had no alternative.'

Right again. Tiberius was never exactly the blue-eyed boy with Augustus. He'd spent years being shifted around from the wings to centre stage and back, from star billing to supporting role. The only reason he'd got to be emperor at all was that there was no one else around at the time to do the job. Maybe he'd just got tired of being the permanent second choice. Maybe he just decided he couldn't wait any longer...

'Or maybe he was playing it both ends against the middle.' I didn't realise I'd spoken the words aloud until I noticed Perilla was staring at me.

'What was that?'

The Caecuban was working again. 'Maybe the Wart wanted to have it both ways. When Paullus propositions him he lies on his back and opens his legs. Then he runs and tells Augustus he's been raped. He can't lose, right? If the conspiracy comes off, then Augustus is dead meat and he's the new emperor. If not and things aren't going too well, then he can go back to the emperor and say, "Look, I've broken up your latest gang of troublemakers for you. See how loyal I am? I could've been emperor myself but I put your interests and Rome's first. Now how about a bigger share of the action?" In the event that's what happened. Maybe he didn't feel it was worth the risk, especially with Silanus doing his political tapdance on the sidelines. So he pulled the plug on the conspiracy and bowed out gracefully.'

'And my stepfather?'

'Like I said, Ovid found out that Tiberius was involved. If he'd reported it to Augustus he would've simply been told that everything was under control and warned to keep his mouth shut. But he didn't. He didn't tell anyone. And where would that leave him with the emperor?'

Perilla leaned her chin on her hand.

'Augustus wouldn't be sure whose side Ovid was on,' she said. 'In effect my stepfather was giving his tacit support to the conspirators.'

'Right. Also, once everything was over and Tiberius had slid out from under, Ovid would be an embarrassment. Or a potential embarrassment. Augustus had to make sure he wouldn't open his mouth too far, even by accident. It wouldn't do the emperor's street cred much good if the news got out that the second man in Rome had tried to knock him off the wall, would it? Ovid had to be disappeared, fast. The Black Sea was as good a place as any, short of slitting his throat. And maybe even Augustus had a conscience.'

'It would explain something else too.'

'What's that?'

'Why Tiberius didn't allow him back when Augustus was dead.'

I nodded. 'Yeah. That's right. He could still open his mouth. And Tiberius was never a poetry lover. He's a soldier first and foremost. In fact—'

I stopped. Stopped dead.

'What's wrong?'

'Shit.'

'Corvinus! Will you tell me what's wrong? Please.'

I didn't know whether to break down and sob with relief or howl with disappointment.

'Our fourth conspirator. Whoever he is, he isn't Tiberius.'

'What? Corvinus, what are you talking about? We've just spent ten minutes working out how...'

'I don't care. The fourth man can't've been the Wart. He was out of Rome at the time, on campaign in Illyricum.'

Silence.

'Are you sure?'

'Sure I'm sure.' I put my head in my hands. 'My father was the governor.'

'Ah.' Perilla was quiet for a long time. Then she said: 'In that case your comment was quite justified.'

I looked up at her. 'What comment was that?'

'Shit.'

A surprising girl, Perilla.

CHAPTER 17

My father was waiting for me in the atrium when I came down the next morning. This was crazy. We hadn't spoken in months and now I couldn't get rid of him. He was like one of these winter colds that you just can't shake. I thought about asking him whether while he'd been governor in Illyricum Tiberius had gone back to Rome at any time, but I decided against it. He'd've seen through the question straight away and refused to answer, or just lied. Besides, just the thought of having something that big on the Wart, with the Wart knowing about it, brought me out in a cold sweat.

'Hi, Dad,' I said. 'What brings you back this time? Your pile cream run out?'

I thought that might make him lose his temper but it didn't. He'd obviously decided to play it cool as far as I was concerned.

'I was talking to Cornelius Dolabella yesterday, Marcus,' he said.

'Yeah?' I was instantly on my guard. Dolabella was a relative of Lentulus, and Lentulus, if you remember, was the guy who'd told me about Julia. I wouldn't've thought the old devil would've blabbed but evidently he had—and to the most unlikely person I could imagine. Dolabella was one of my father's most bosom cronies. I'd met him once or twice socially, although once would've been more than enough. You've seen the pigeons at Castor's Temple strutting around pecking for crumbs and shitting on the Wart's nice new marble steps? Yeah. Add a mantle and a squint and that's Dolabella.

'He had some news that may interest you,' my father was saying. 'His brother Decimus needs a replacement finance officer for Cyprus.'

So Lentulus hadn't given me away after all. I breathed again. 'Oh, whoopee, Dad. And him not halfway through the year yet. Lost the one he'd been given, did he? That was clumsy.'

My father didn't smile. Not that I'd expected him to.

'It wasn't Decimus's fault, Marcus,' he said. 'Young Rufinus was drowned in a boating accident off Paphos.'

'Oh. Oh, shit. I'm sorry.' I'd known Rufinus quite well. He wasn't exactly a friend, but he'd had more going for him than some of the other characters who inhabited Dad's world. 'I really am.'

'So is Decimus.' I can never tell whether my father is being sarcastic, drily humorous, or just plain cold-blooded. 'The point is that your name was mentioned as a replacement.'

I stared at him. 'You're not serious?'

He sat down and drew the folds of his mantle around him as if he were expecting a tame artist to wheel in a bust-sized block of marble on a trolley.

'Why not, son?' he said. 'It's about time you took an active interest in your future.'

Maybe it was telepathy. I wished I hadn't mentioned the subject when I was talking with Perilla. Now it looked as if everyone in Rome was rooting for Corvinus to make good. The sooner we knocked this on the head the better.

'I haven't done my time with a legion yet, Dad.' Young men of good family usually spent a year in the army as junior staff officers. So far I'd managed to avoid it. The thought of being cooped up somewhere out in the sticks for twelve months with a band of jolly mates whose idea of fun was a morning's pig-sticking didn't exactly thrill me to bits. A month or so of that and I'd probably get myself massacred by the locals just out of boredom.

'I dare say an exception could be made,' my father said. 'You could postpone your military service for a year. There've been plenty of precedents.'

This was serious. I sat down. 'You say my name was mentioned. Who by?'

His face took on a carefully bland expression. 'You know the system, Marcus. These decisions are taken by committees rather than by individuals.'

'Come off it!' Now the shock was over I was beginning to think of the implications, and they stank like a barrel of month-old oysters. 'Yeah, I know the system. Sure I do. You set this up, didn't you? You and your mate Dolabella.'

'Of course we didn't!'

The denial came out pat. Too pat.

'Okay. So tell me who did.'

My father's mouth shut like a trap. I didn't know which was worse: that he was lying or that he was telling the truth.

I got up and walked towards the garden colonnade. I was trying hard not to lose my temper. After all, if my father had arranged the posting then he'd done it out of what he'd see as kindness, and probably used up a valuable favour in the process. And if he hadn't there was just the chance he'd still let slip who had. And that was a name I wanted to know.

'A junior finance post in Cyprus would keep me safely out of circulation for the next couple of years, wouldn't it, Dad?' I said quietly.

'I don't know about safely, Marcus, but two years represents a normal tour of duty, yes.'

'And it couldn't come at a more convenient time, either.' My back was to him. 'After all, if someone is so bad mannered as to go around asking awkward questions…'

'Oh, for heaven's sake!' The irritation in his voice sounded unmistakably genuine. 'That nonsense has nothing to do with anything. You're being offered the most splendid start to a political career any young man could ask for and all you can think of is—'

'That's right!' I turned round. 'All I can think of is that I'm being packed off somewhere I can't do any harm in the hopes that the "nonsense," as you call it, will die a natural death. Or maybe even I will, like that poor bastard Rufinus.'

'Marcus, don't be melodramatic.'

But I wasn't going to be stopped as easily as that.

'Look, it won't work, Dad,' I said. 'Is that clear? No way! I'm staying in Rome and that's all there is to it.'

'Then you're a fool.' That came out flat as a slap. My father stood up and draped the folds of his senatorial mantle correctly over his left arm as if he were walking into court. I should've seen the speech coming. I'd had similar ones all my life. 'I won't ask you to decide straight away, Marcus. That wouldn't be fair since I've sprung it on you so suddenly. But I want you to think this over very carefully. It has nothing to do with this other stupidity of yours—you know my views on that and I won't repeat them, but it is a stupidity, nothing more and nothing less. The fact is that you're being offered a post that any other young man of your age would give his eye-teeth for. If you turn it down for no good reason then people won't forget. And when you do deign to take your responsibilities seriously you'll find they just aren't willing to trouble themselves over you.' He brushed a hair from the mantle's broad purple edging-stripe. 'I'll be seeing Dolabella later this morning and I'll tell him I haven't had a chance to speak to you yet. Tomorrow's the start of the Spring Festival, so everything will be closed down for several days. That should give even you time to give the offer more than a fleeting thought. Perhaps you'll have the courtesy to inform me of your final decision when the holidays are over.'

I knew from the tightness of the muscles around his mouth and the clipped way he delivered the final sentences that he was angry. Genuinely angry. My father was a politician's politician, and if there was one thing he could neither understand nor forgive it was for someone to refuse political advancement.

'Look, Dad,' I said as I followed him to the door, 'I'm sorry. I know you mean well. I know you've probably bust a gut trying to keep me in with the authorities.' This, I was sure, was true. He'd be concerned for the family name if nothing else. 'But I don't like being manipulated, and I don't like...'

He stopped and turned to face me. If he'd been angry before, now he was furious.

'You don't like!' he snapped. 'That's all I ever get from you, isn't it, Marcus? Perhaps if you stopped thinking of yourself for a change, of being so damned fastidious over what you will and won't allow, you'd be a better and pleasanter person and a more useful member of society. Now I have work to do, and I've spent more time on you this morning than your egotism merits. Let me know what you decide about Cyprus by the end of the festival. If you can spare a few moments of your valuable time to reach so minor a decision, naturally.'

And before I could reply he had stormed out, pulling the front door out of the door slave's hands and slamming it behind him.

After he'd gone I did a great deal of serious thinking. Dad was right about Cyprus, of course—he always was, when it came to practical politics. If I turned this job down there'd be a black mark against my name which would take a long, long time to sponge out. Cyprus-and-Crete wasn't one of the most prestigious senatorial provinces going, let alone one with the social clout of an imperial giant like Egypt; but nonetheless, to be offered the post of finance officer there was way beyond what I could reasonably expect at my age, and to spurn the offer would be to kick the Senate's teeth down its communal throat. You just didn't do that and expect to live afterwards, politically speaking. If I had any hopes of a future career in politics (and what other career was there for someone like me?), I'd have to accept. At least if it was a bribe, as it had to be, I couldn't complain that I was being undervalued.

Then there was what my father had said about me. About my egotism. That was true, too. I was honest enough with myself to admit it. And it had hurt, much more than I'd thought any comment of my father's would. Not that I could do much to change myself. We're all selfish egotistical bastards at heart, we upper-class Roman gentlemen. We always have been and we always will be. It's our weakness and our strength, it's what made Rome great and made her dirty. Even when we play the democrat it's only a questionable means to a selfish end. Selfishness is bred into us from infancy: the need to have the world as we want, to mould it to our requirements.

The trouble is the world has changed and we've had to

change with it, whether we like it or not. A hundred years ago there was no problem. We were the state, and so serving the state came naturally because we were serving ourselves. Now the state, or at least what matters of it, has been taken from us. We're like thoroughbred horses forced to work a corn mill, trudging round and round in the same never-ending circle. Yeah, sure. Sure, I know. What good's a thoroughbred except to race against other thoroughbreds and impress the yokels? Corn's a necessity, and it doesn't grind itself. So the modern state puts us to useful work. Only it expects us to behave like mules or plough-oxen, and not chafe at the traces. That's what sticks in my throat.

Sure, I was an egotist. I was selfish. I was self-opinionated. I was everything else my father thought I was. But these qualities were bred into my bones and they had their good sides as well. Determination, for a start. I'd never not seen something through in my life, and I didn't mean to begin now. Whether it hurt me or not.

That was the problem. This time it wasn't just me. Perilla was involved too. If I turned down the Cyprus posting it'd be tantamount to a declaration of war. Total commitment. And knowing what I was up against, did I have the right to put Perilla at risk as well?

That was something I had to think about.

And I was still thinking, with very little result, when Bathyllus brought me a message from Perilla. It was in two parts, the first asking me if I was free for dinner the following evening (was I! I'd've cancelled a dice lesson from Hermes himself for that!), the second to say that Harpale had arranged a meeting with Davus, Julia's ex-door slave. He'd be waiting for me at Paquius's warehouse in the Velabrum at noon on the last day of the festival.

I'd read the message and was about to dismiss Bathyllus when I remembered something.

'Bathyllus, you were with my father in Illyricum, weren't you?'

'Yes, sir. I was the general's body servant, sir.' Bathyllus was proud of what he calls his military experience. 'Myself and Nicanor, who is still with him.'

'Do you remember if Tiberius went back to Rome at all at any stage?'

He didn't even stop to think; which with Bathyllus puts any pronouncement he makes into the Delphic Oracle league.

'No, sir. Not until the winter before the last campaign, when he left Aemilius Lepidus in charge.'

That would be when Ovid had already left for Tomi, or even after he'd got there. Far too late, in any event.

'You're sure? Absolutely one-hundred-percent cast-iron swear-on-your-grandmother's-grave certain?' Best not to leave any room for doubts.

'Yes, sir.'

'Fuck.'

'Quite, sir.' Bathyllus's expression didn't change. 'Will that be all, sir?'

Ah well. As I said, I wasn't too unhappy to see it go. But the theory had been a peach while it lasted.

'Yeah. No—bring me a jug of Setinian. A large one, the best we've got. I may as well go down happy. And after that I want you to take a message round to my father's.'

I'd decided. Ovid was my problem, and I couldn't just walk away from him. Perilla would understand: she was thoroughgoing upper-class bastard too, in her own sweet way. And I knew that if I'd chosen Cyprus I'd never have had the guts to see her again.

When Bathyllus brought the wine I poured out the first cup to the war goddess Bellona. I have a soft spot for the blood-thirsty old bitch. She's Roman through and through, she's an outsider with no priest and no festival of her own, and there's no better god to call on when you're declaring a war to the knife.

I might be a selfish egotistical bastard but I'm a determined one. I don't give up. And I don't desert my friends.

Varus to Himself

The scouts I had Vela send to reconnoitre returned this morning, together with a captured Cheruscan dissident able and eager to furnish us with 'proof' of Arminius's intentions. The staff meeting which followed their return, however, was far from straightforward. Although since our interview I had antic-ipated—feared—resistance from Vela, his opposition verged upon outright mutiny; a fact which must give me pause.

There were four of us round the table: myself, Vela, Eggius and Ceionius; two of whom, of course—myself and Ceionius, if you have forgotten—knew the truth of the matter.

I hoped and prayed that the number had not risen to three.

'Well, gentlemen,' I began. 'We have our confirmation. The Cherusci are arming. What is our response?'

'Hardly confirmation, General,' Vela murmured. 'The word of a single deserter is not confirmation.'

'It's enough for me,' Ceionius growled.

'And me.' That, on cue, from the fiery Eggius.

'What would you have me do, Vela?' I spread my hands in a gesture of helpless reasonableness. 'Ignore Arminius? March past with eyes averted like a shy virgin and leave him a whole winter to gather strength?'

'Foolishness.' Ceionius nodded. So did Eggius, who was thinking already, no doubt, of the feats of valour he would perform.

'Smash him, General,' he said, so far as the clenching of his manly jaw would allow him. 'Smash him now, and when you've smashed him then smash him again. That's all barbarians understand.'

Vela was looking from one to the other. His porridge face was stubborn.

'With respect, sir,' he said to me (but there was no respect in his voice), 'we were warned that this might happen before we left the Weser. Segestes—'

'Segestes be damned.' That was Ceionius. 'Anything that two-faced German bastard chooses to tell us isn't worth a wet fart.'

Oho! The crudity was quite deliberate: Ceionius is clever and knows how to steer an argument on to safer ground. Vela, who for a professional soldier is prudish beyond belief, coloured up immediately.

'Segestes,' he stuttered, 'is a friend to Rome. He has no time for his son-in-law's schemes. If Segestes thought it important enough to warn us that Arminius was plotting treachery then—'

'Screw Segestes.' Ceionius glanced at Eggius. 'Germans are all alike, Vela. You know that. He probably told us just so we'd follow the cowardly piss-your-pants course you seem to favour.'

The warlike Eggius rose like a fish to a mayfly.

'I agree. We've a force five times anything Arminius could field against us and a hundred times better trained and disciplined. Ignore this, General, and we'll be the laughing-stock of the army from here to the eastern frontier. And quite rightly so.'

'Nevertheless,' I said, my eye upon Vela, 'it would mean a march through unfamiliar territory. And the campaigning season is almost over.'

'Are we children, to be afraid of the dark and wet?' Eggius the orator loves a fine phrase. 'Would Drusus Caesar have hesitated? Would General Tiberius?'

'Tiberius would certainly hesitate.' Vela was still punching. 'Tiberius is a soldier. And you do not have to be a child to be afraid of the Teutoburg, especially in winter.'

I temporised, again with Rome in mind. I must assume that Vela knows nothing, and continue constructing my future defence in the hope that my credibility is not already destroyed.

'Vela has a point, gentlemen,' I said. 'We must weigh our responsibilities carefully. Think. The campaigning season is over. We are leading our men back into winter quarters. If we are to investigate this matter it will mean a gruelling march late in the season through difficult and potentially hostile territory. The question is, is such a drastic and dangerous course of action justifiable?'

'Yes!' from Eggius. 'No!' from Vela; both responses immediate and decisively delivered. I turned to Ceionius, my eyebrows raised; which was the signal my louse and I had agreed on for his set speech.

'What would be the emperor's word, sir,' he said slowly, 'what would be Rome's word, for a general who put the comfort of himself and his men before the safety and integrity of the empire's borders?'

I nodded, as did Eggius. 'A fair summing-up,' I said gravely. 'Gentlemen, we have no choice. The threat is there, and, despite the undoubted danger, as loyal soldiers of Rome it is our duty'—I stressed the word—'not to ignore it.'

As a piece of ham acting in the good old austere Roman

manner I flatter myself that it was perfect. Eggius's lips were set firm, and I swear I saw a manly tear glisten in the young warrior's eye.

'However.' I paused until I was sure I had their full attention, especially Vela's. This was going to be important. 'I do not intend, gentlemen, to indulge in any death-or-glory heroics.' I let my eyes rest for a moment on Eggius. 'An investigation is one thing, prudence is another. I am quite aware of the difficulties, and of the dangers. We will take the matter as it comes and make our decisions accordingly.'

'Yet we turn east?' That, of course, from Eggius.

I was magisterial. 'We turn east.'

Vela stared at me, his hands clenching and unclenching spasmodically. Then he turned and, without a word, swept out of the tent.

CHAPTER

18

I've got a lot of time for the Floralia. For six days the whole dingy city breaks out into colour like an old oak tree bursting into spring leaf. There're flowers and garlands everywhere, even on the Speakers' Platform in the Market Square and in the dead empty eye sockets of the city tenements. Girls, too—Jupiter knows where they come from, but for some reason there're more around, and better lookers, at the Spring Festival than at any other time. And I don't mean whores either, although you'll see plenty of them about. People are friendlier. They actually smile at you, genuinely smile, and it's not uncommon to meet someone in the middle of the day who's drunker than you are. Happy drunk, I mean, not looking for a fight; Flora's a civilised goddess, the kind you wouldn't mind being parked next to at a drinking party. Even some of my father's cronies take the pokers out of their arses and unbend at the Floralia. Some of them. And not all the way. Flora may be a goddess, but even she has her limits.

I went round to Perilla's early, bright-eyed, bushy tailed, and (more to the point) clean-shaven, wearing my best mantle and carrying my party slippers. Callias led me through to the sitting-room.

By the look of her Perilla was just up. Beautiful as usual but crotchety as hell.

'Happy Floralia.' I gave her the bunch of flowers I'd had Bathyllus out gathering earlier. Added to all his other accomplishments the little guy weaves a mean garland. She wasn't as impressed as I'd hoped she'd be.

'I thought I said dinner, Corvinus.'

'Yeah, well, maybe I'm a bit early but all the same...'

'Look, I've got several very pressing things to do before I even think in terms of breakfast. Like waking up, for example. So if you'll excuse me...'

'Oh, come on, Perilla!' I wasn't giving up that easy. 'It's the Floralia! Let's go out somewhere.'

She looked at me as if I'd suggested a bump-and-grind up the steps of the Capitol.

'Corvinus,' she said slowly. 'I am married. Nominally so, I grant you, but married nonetheless. Respectable matrons don't go gadding about with young bachelors.'

'It's a beautiful day outside.'

'The weather is immaterial.'

'Separate litters.'

'Where to? Corvinus, if you were thinking of a mime...'

'No mime,' I said hastily. Mimes are traditional to the Floralia. Only to the Floralia, and understandably so. What other patron but Flora would allow actors to appear with their faces bare? And not only actors, but actresses? And not only their faces...'No mime, Perilla. I give you my solemn oath.'

I was serious. I'd more sense than to take Perilla to a mime.

She was fully capable of standing up at the first blue joke and demanding a public apology from the producer. Getting it, too.

'So what did you have in mind?' she said after a pause.

'Just a walk. I thought maybe the Sallust Gardens would be nice.' The Sallust Gardens are to the north, beyond the old Servian wall, and they make up one of the most beautiful public parks in Rome. 'Come on, Perilla! Just this once.'

'Separate litters?' I could see she was weakening.

'Yeah. Borne by octogenarian eunuchs fitted with blinkers. You have my word.'

'Just a walk in the Sallust Gardens? You're sure?'

'I saw the Chief Vestal there the other day. She goes regularly, just for the moral uplift.'

Perilla was smiling now. Genuinely smiling. I knew I'd won and was trying very hard not to crow about it.

'All right, Corvinus,' she said. 'Give me a while to do my hair.' There wasn't a thing wrong with it, but I wasn't going to argue. 'Have a seat and I'll tell Callias to bring you some wine. It's not too early for you, I take it?'

'Just this once,' I said, 'I'll make an exception.' I'd been kidding about the octogenarian eunuchs but Perilla didn't seem to mind so long as the other proprieties were observed. The four Sunshine Boys tagged along as well. I drew the line at being beaten up on holiday, and with Perilla in tow I was taking no chances. They shambled along beside the litters, two on each side, flashing their pectorals and mouthing Gallic obscenities at any passer-by who paid us the slightest bit of notice. Most people gave us a wide berth. I didn't blame them.

We got caught up with the crowds going to watch the goddess's official procession. I should've thought of that— Flora's temple is just inside the Quirinal Gate—but it was too late to do anything about it. At least with the combined muscle of the litter-bearers and my four Gauls we managed to keep the litters side by side so we could talk while the punters broke and flowed round us.

The crowds fascinated Perilla; but then the poor girl obviously didn't go out much.

'Why are there so many women, Corvinus?' she asked at one point. 'And so unusually dressed?'

She was talking about the prostitutes, of course. You get a lot of them gathering in the streets near the temple, and we seemed to be wading through a knot of about fifty, which was too close to one of my favourite fantasies for comfort. Lovely girls some of them too. If Perilla hadn't been there I'd've stopped the litter and taken a couple on board. As it was I was on my best behaviour.

I told her. She was shocked. 'What, all of them? They're all prostitutes?'

'Yeah. Well, all the women in men's mantles and make-up, anyway.' I was glad I couldn't see any guys in women's dresses in the crowd because I didn't fancy explaining them to Perilla at all.

'But there can't be work for all these girls, surely? How do they make ends meet?'

I bit my tongue. Jupiter, I thought, stand by me now in the hour of my adversity. 'They, uh, they're not all city girls, Perilla. Flora's the prostitutes' patron. They come to Rome from all over at the Spring Festival.'

'They must be very religious.' Perilla watched solemnly while I tried not to laugh. One of the best-lookers (to my horror I recognised her) slipped through the Gallic lines, planted a smacker just above my left cheekbone and stuck a flower behind my ear.

'Oh how nice!' Perilla smiled at her. Luckily she hadn't

seen what the girl's left hand was up to. 'What a lovely gesture! Corvinus, you're blushing!'

I managed to toss the girl a silver piece while Perilla wasn't looking. She caught it neatly, blew me another kiss and disappeared back into the crowd.

Good behaviour's one thing, but I had my reputation to consider.

We got to the Sallust Gardens without further mishap. I left the litters at the gate and told the Sunshine Boys to follow on discreetly and be ready if I needed them ('You understand "discreetly", boys?' 'Yeah, boss. Soft-soft. No-o-o problem.'). Mind you, that was difficult enough. Half of Rome seemed to have had the same idea as I had and the gardens were packed. We walked sedately between the lines of plane trees in the direction of the statue of Faunus.

The place smelled of spring and dry-roasted melon seeds from the hawkers' carts.

'Would you believe I've never been here before?' Perilla was looking round us with interest. 'The other parks, but not this one. I remember my stepfather taking us to the Pincian once when I was twelve. That must've been at the Floralia too. The year he was sent away.'

The last thing I wanted to talk about today was Ovid. This was a holiday, after all. I changed the subject.

'He was a hypocritical sod, old Sallust. My grandfather knew him. He spent a fortune on this place when he owned it and then had the nerve to sit out here and write about how degenerate we modern Romans are.'

'You must admit it's beautiful, though.' Perilla smiled. 'Surely it was worth the expense?'

'Tell that to the provincials that the old guy plundered to get the cash.'

Perilla glanced sideways at me. 'Corvinus, I can't make you out at all sometimes. You come from one of the best families in Rome, but you don't act like an aristocrat. Not any of the ones I know anyway. Whose side are you on?'

'I'm not on anyone's side.' I pulled a long bit of grass from the edge of the path and chewed on it. 'Because no one's really on my side. You get me?'

'No, I don't.'

'It doesn't matter. Look, let's just drop the subject, Perilla. The Spring Festival's not the time to be serious.'

'No, please. I'm interested.'

I threw the grass stem away. 'Okay. It's your decision. Take my father, then. Good public speaker. Consul at thirty-three. Successful general, well, pretty successful although he was no ball of fire. One of the committee to look after the Books of Prophecy. Bosom buddies with the emperor. And one of the biggest crawlers you're ever likely to meet outside of Aristotle's *Natural History*.'

'So?'

I stopped and looked at her in amazement. 'You don't see anything wrong in that?'

'I think you're being a little hard on him. He seems to have done remarkably well.'

'He's done remarkably well by saying the right things to the right people.'

'Would you rather he said the wrong things to the wrong people?'

'Come on, lady! That's not what I mean and you know it.'

'Or possibly the right things to the wrong people? Or the wrong things to the right people? Or…'

I grinned despite myself and carried on walking. 'Yeah, okay. Point taken. Maybe I should've put it different.'

'You don't think he might actually believe that they *are* the right things and the right people?'

She was definitely beginning to bug me, and I didn't want to quarrel. Not today of all days. 'Look, can we drop this? Please? It's the Floralia, it's too nice a day to discuss my father, and I shouldn't have mentioned the bastard in the first place. Okay?'

'Very well.' We walked on in silence and turned the corner of the box hedge. 'Corvinus, look at the narcissi! Aren't they beautiful?'

Ahead of us the grass was a mass of white and yellow. It was, I had to admit, pretty impressive, although the flowers were way past their best.

'You were right. It was a good idea to come.' Perilla had left the path and was walking over the grass away from me towards the blanket of petals. For an instant the vivid green of the grass, the yellow and white flowers, and the sky-blue of her cloak combined in a single picture which could have come straight from a mural painter's sample book: Flora, golden-haired goddess of spring and blossom, walking in the meadows of the clean, fresh-minted world, her head half turned over her shoulder to look behind her, one hand holding a flower to her cheek, the other reaching behind for whoever was following...

'Come on, Corvinus!'

The picture dissolved. I don't get these poetic fancies often, but then maybe I'm missing something. I caught her up and took the outstretched hand.

How it happened, neither of us knew. Maybe Flora had something to do with it. Certainly she would've approved. We'd lost the Gauls, or they'd lost us, either through tact or monumental stupidity (No prizes for guessing which. These guys couldn't've mustered an ounce of tact among them if they'd sweated over it for a month). We'd left the path, of course, and plunged into what a certain breed of poets would call a sylvan grot, which has always sounded pretty disgusting to me. You know the sort of thing. Carefully manicured wilderness, purling stream overhung with ferns, rude statue (politely rude) of the Rustic Pan. Nooks and crannies...

I especially remember the nooks and crannies, or one of them at least. Whether it was a nook or a cranny, the real miracle was that it was empty. What I don't remember is if I kissed her first or she kissed me. In any case the question soon became academic. Whoever started it, kissing Perilla was like being hit on the head with a triumphal arch, then smothered in rose petals. After about a century or two I came up for air. The conversation thereafter was about one per cent monosyllabic and ninety-nine per cent tactile.

'Corvinus, I really don't think we should be...'

'Let me just...'

'There's a tree root in my back. Do you think you could...?'

'That better?'

'Mmmm.' (Long pause.) 'Mmmm!' (Longer, more energetic pause on both sides.) 'Mmmmm!'

We were just getting into the swing of things when she sat up.

'This is not,' she said, 'a good idea.'

I pushed her down again.

She sat up. 'I don't mind so much being seduced, Corvinus, but I'm certainly not going to ruin a perfectly good cloak in the process. Now stop it this minute.'

Easier said than done. Some things you just can't stop. You have to let them run their course...

She socked me in the jaw. With her fist. Hard.

When the Sallust Gardens had reassembled themselves from the shower of scintillating flashes they'd suddenly become, I looked up and saw Perilla bending over me. She was, unbelievably, crying.

'I'm sorry, Marcus,' she said. 'Are you all right?'

A silly question, under the circumstances. Instead of answering I tried moving my lower jaw around. She hadn't broken it, luckily, and I couldn't see any teeth lying around. Mind you, my eyes still weren't functioning too well and I could've missed one or two.

Perilla kissed me; a gentle, brushing kiss, her eyelashes wet against my face. Then she stood up.

'We'd best get back.'

'Separate litters?'

She smiled, lowered her eyes and shook her head.

CHAPTER

19

We didn't have dinner. We made love instead. She cried out when I entered her, and I was so surprised that I drew back; but she pulled me closer and we finished it. It was only afterwards, when our hearts slowed and we talked before the next time, that I realised that it had been a cry of pain and that Perilla had been a virgin.

'I wouldn't let him touch me,' she whispered, and her eyes were wet against the hollow of my shoulder. 'Not even on the first night. Not knowing what I knew, why he wanted me.' I kissed the tears, saying nothing, and my lips tasted salt. 'So you see, Marcus, in the end he got nothing at all, apart from hatred.'

'Why didn't he divorce you?'

'Pride, maybe. Maybe hope. Greed certainly. With Mother dead or declared insane the estate would come to me, and he was my husband. He had certain rights.'

Something tickled at the back of my mind. I reached for it but it was gone.

'Can't you divorce him?'

'I might. Now.' I felt her smile against my skin, her lips pluck against me. 'Do you want me to?'

I swallowed. 'Yes.'

'All right. Then I will. There was no reason before, and he's a friend of the emperor.'

'Not of the emperor. He's Germanicus's friend, not Tiberius's.'

'Germanicus is the emperor's son.'

'Adopted, not natural. There's a difference.' The mental itch was back. There was something…I was close, so close! As if I were looking down at a ruined section of mosaic flooring and held all the missing pieces in my hands. It was only a matter of where each piece fitted…

'Marcus?'

'Hmmm?'

'What are you thinking about?'

'Nothing. Nothing important.'

She moved under me. We were still locked together. I felt myself stiffen as she guided me back into the wet warmth between her thighs. We took it more slowly the second time around, as if each of us were already matching our rhythms to suit the other person. Her sharp little teeth nipped my shoulder once, and then her head was moving from side to side and she was making faint mewing noises like a blind kitten. This time she came first, in a sudden, shuddering spasm, straightening her whole upper body, gripping me hard with her arms twined round my back and the inside of her thighs clenched about my hips.

We lay quiet when I'd finished. Then I rolled to one side and lifted her head into the hollow of my shoulder. Her hair had the scent of wildflower honey as I buried my face in it.

'You learn pretty quickly for a beginner,' I said.

'I'll improve with practice.'

I kissed her. 'Good.'

She smiled and snuggled closer. I lay still for a long time, staring at the inlaid panelling above the bed.

'Will you do something for me, Marcus?' she said at last.

'Yes.'

'No ifs or buts?'

'No ifs or buts. Only if you want a repeat performance you'll have to wait.'

This time she didn't smile.

'Okay. So what is it? A first edition of Homer? Cleopatra's best necklace? One of the Wart's boils set in rock crystal? Just ask me and you've got it.'

'Make your peace with your father.'

Whatever I'd been expecting, it wasn't that. I raised myself on one elbow and stared down at her. She was looking at me very seriously.

'I don't mean like him,' she said. 'Let alone be like him. You couldn't do that even if you wanted to. But admit he's a person too, with as much right to his opinions as you have. You're different people but that doesn't mean you have to be enemies.'

I remembered the conversation I'd had with my father a few days before. *Different people...*

'It isn't as easy as that, Perilla.'

'Why not? What's so very difficult?'

'It's...what he did. To my mother.'

She waited: no questions, no comments. I was having difficulty breathing. I'd never told this to anyone and the words didn't come easily.

'It happened three years ago. My mother was pregnant—

a late pregnancy. No one expected it, no one even thought the child would come to term. My parents had been talking about a separation before that, before my mother knew; but the pregnancy didn't make a blind bit of difference. Dad wanted the divorce, and he got it.'

'Why?'

'It was a political marriage, of course. Not like yours, not for money. Our kind don't marry for money, it's not considered proper.' The word felt sour on my tongue. 'Family connections now, that's different. That's respectable. My mother was fourteen at the time, and her daddy was Agrippa's nephew. Marrying her gave Father an in with the new ruling families, or so he thought, with Agrippa being Augustus's right-hand man. But then it all went wrong. A year after the wedding Agrippa died, Augustus forced Tiberius to divorce the old man's daughter, and Dad realised his own marriage was a blind alley. Then, twenty-seven years further down the line—twenty-seven years, Perilla!—when Tiberius became emperor he finally cut his losses, divorced her, and took a new wife. One more "politically relevant". End of marriage, end of story.'

By this time Perilla was sitting up. Her hair spilled across her breasts like liquid gold.

'What happened to the child?' she said.

'He was born dead a month later. The only brother I ever had. Am ever likely to have.'

'And your mother?'

'She survived, but the birth nearly killed her. She married again last year. A senator called Priscus. He's okay. His first wife died of a stroke.'

'Is she happy?'

'Yeah, I think so. I don't see her very often, but yes, I think she's happy.'

'Then it was all for the best in the end, wasn't it? Despite the mess.'

When I didn't answer she kissed me gently and laid her head on my chest.

'Is there all that much difference between your parents and us, Marcus?' she asked quietly. 'I have a husband, too, remember. We don't get on either. How can divorce be wrong for your mother yet right for me? Or do you think adultery's more "proper"?'

'You were a virgin. You don't have a husband, not really. Let alone children.'

She raised her head.

'Don't play with words, Corvinus! You know what I mean!'

'I'm not playing with words. You don't just dislike Rufus, you hate his guts and always have done. You said so yourself.'

'And does that make your role any more respectable?'

The question had come back sharp as a beesting. We were heading for our first quarrel. I knew that, but there wasn't anything I could do about it because despite my anger I could see that she was right. For a moment I was tempted to get out of bed, get dressed, and walk out of her life for ever. Only for a moment. That was something I knew I could never do, whatever she said, however angry I was. I'm not that much of an egotist, and I'm not that kind of bastard either. Besides, Perilla was part of me. I could no more walk out on her than cut my own arm off.

I took a deep breath and held it. 'I'm sorry. Yeah, okay, maybe there isn't all that much of a difference.'

'You'll try to understand your father, then? To make it up with him? Please, Marcus!'

I was silent for a long time. I thought of my father, of his pompous way of speaking, his political hypocrisy and the cold way he'd put my mother aside. Then I thought back to earlier years, when we'd been much closer. Little things. How he'd taught me to swim when I was six years old. Summer at our villa in the Alban Hills. His attempts even when we hardly spoke to each other any more to smooth out a career for me. Sure, maybe he'd done it partly for the sake of the family name, but the fact remained that he'd tried his best according to his lights. As Perilla said, if my mother was happy enough with the situation, then what did it matter? And wasn't I just as much of a hypocrite as my father? Not politically, but where Perilla was concerned?

Maybe we weren't such different people after all. Or at least in ways that were really important.

'Okay,' I said. 'Okay. I'll try. It won't be easy but I'll try.'

She kissed my cheek and snuggled down against me; and when we made love again later I felt strangely peaceful.

CHAPTER 20

I knew from the start that it was useless trying to stop Perilla from coming with me to meet Davus, but I had to do my best anyway.

'Look, do you know what the Velabrum's like?' I couldn't even sit down, I was so uptight. I paced back and forwards across the marble-floored atrium while she sat by the pool filing her nails with a slip of pumice.

'Of course, Marcus,' she said calmly. 'Not very pleasant, I do realise that, but it can't be as bad as the Subura surely.'

Jupiter! This from the woman who hadn't even been to the Gardens of bloody Sallust!

'Don't you bet on it. The Velabrum's got its moments. I wouldn't fancy a female *cat's* chances of getting in and out of there intact, let alone a hot little stunner like you.'

Yeah, sure, I was exaggerating. The Velabrum's Rome's docklands area, the centre of the wholesale trade occupying the low ground between the Palatine and the Tiber. Although it's nothing compared to the Subura, the part I'd have to go through to get where I was going was pretty rough, and you're just as likely to find a pearl in a privy as a well-born lady in that part of town. So I didn't want Perilla tagging along. I'd got enough things to worry about without playing the macho protector.

Perilla was smiling.

'I appreciate your concern, Corvinus,' she said, 'but I'm sure you can provide any security that's necessary.'

Shit! Didn't the woman ever listen? I could feel the steam leaking out of my ears. 'I'd need a bloody company of Praetorians to do that! And even then we'd have fifty per cent casualties!'

'Nonsense. You go walking in the Subura quite happily, or so you tell me. Why should a trip to the Velabrum be any more dangerous?'

I counted to ten. Then to twenty. 'You haven't listened to a word I've been saying, have you, lady? Sure I go walking in the Subura. And I can walk pretty safely anywhere I like in the Velabrum, too. But I don't happen to be built like a souped-up Praxiteles Venus with mammaries that'd knock an eighty-year-old Chief Priest's eyes out at forty yards.'

The slip of pumice didn't even pause. 'Even Chief Priests can't see through the sides of a closed litter, Corvinus. And as you are very well aware my breasts are no bigger than average. Smaller if anything.'

'Okay, strike the Venus. But you can forget the closed litter idea as well. Take one of these things through the Velabrum and you might as well carry a big sign with "Come and Get Your Rich Smartass Here" painted on the side. You'd draw every wide-boy for miles.'

She frowned.

'All right,' she said. 'No litter. But I can still go disguised.'

I stopped pacing. I didn't believe this. It was straight out of a third-rate Alexandrian bodice-ripper. 'What as, for God's sake? A Numidian all-in wrestler? A performing elephant?'

'Don't be silly. Just wearing a thick cloak and hood should be quite sufficient.'

Jupiter who guides and guards the fortunes of the Roman state, I prayed, strike me dead or give me patience!

'Look, Perilla,' I said. 'Just listen to me, okay? These guys may not be up to reading Plato in the original but they're not stupid. You go down to the river wrapped up like something out of a Greek melodrama and you won't get five yards before someone starts wondering what's beneath the wrappings. And he'll probably have a dozen pals with him to help open the parcel. You understand?'

She laid the pumice stone aside and stood up.

'Marcus, this is pointless. I'm coming with you and that's the end of it. Asking Harpale was my idea, not yours. And besides I gave her my word I'd personally see that no harm came to her friend.'

I felt the way Pyrrhus must've done when he did a head count of his troops after the Battle of Beneventum and decided if this was victory he'd be better off at home. I made one last try.

'Okay. So get her to tell Davus we've changed the venue. Make it somewhere respectable. Or get him to come here, or round to my place. It's not much further to the Palatine, after all.'

She sighed. 'Davus is a runaway slave, Marcus. He can't go anywhere near the Palatine or any other high-class district on his own. He'd stick out like a sore thumb. You know that.'

'So let me meet him by myself. I gave Harpale my word too, remember.'

'Now we're arguing in circles.' She came over and kissed

me. 'Harpale was my find, Davus is her friend, and as such he's my responsibility. Besides, you're doing this for me and I want to be involved, not sit at home like a prim little matron. So I'm coming with you and that's that. All right?'

'No one could accuse you of being a prim little matron, Perilla.'

'Don't change the subject.'

I knew when I was beaten.

'Fair enough,' I said. 'If you want to come you can, only no closed litters and no mysterious strangers, right? So how are you going to play it?'

If I'd hoped that putting the onus on her might make her change her mind I was on to a loser from the start. She had it all worked out already.

'Easy,' she said. 'I'll go dressed as a boy.'

I stared at her. 'Perilla, you're crazy!'

'Why not? I think it's a marvellous idea.'

'Have you looked at yourself recently? Since puberty, I mean?'

'I don't see why it shouldn't be possible.' She lifted up her beautiful hair. 'If I tie this in a bun and wear a cap people will never notice.'

'Come off it! You'd stick out a mile.' We were really into Alexandrian bodice-ripper territory now. 'And I mean that quite literally.'

'There are such things as bras, Corvinus. An over-tight one will be rather uncomfortable, but that won't matter for a couple of hours. And I can wear a looseish tunic and a cloak.'

'It'll never work.'

'Yes it will.'

'No it won't. If the local knife gangs weren't bad enough you'll have every pederast in the city trailing us.'

'Nonsense.'

'Believe it, lady!'

She drew herself up for what I suspected might be a major no-holds-barred frontal assault. I backed off hastily.

'Okay. Okay.' I held up my hands. 'I'll make a bargain with you. Go and get dressed up. If you pass with me you can come. If not I go on my own. Deal?'

She hesitated. Perilla, unlike me, was no gambler, but she knew when she was being called. And she didn't give her promise lightly.

'Look, Perilla,' I said. 'I'm not doing this for fun, right? I want to get in there, find Davus, and then get out again. Full stop, end of sentence, no fancy clauses. If you tag along life gets complicated. So put up or shut up, okay?'

Her mouth set in a firm line. 'All right, Corvinus,' she said slowly. 'You have a deal. I'll see what Lalage and I can fix up between us.' Lalage was her maid.

'We have to be there at noon, remember.'

'That's fine. Give me an hour.'

I didn't recognise her when she came back down. She was wearing a thick homespun cloak, heavily darned, and under it a beltless green slave's tunic that was a good two sizes too large for her. Her beautiful hair was hidden completely under a freedman's cap and her face was darkened with walnut juice.

'Well?' she said. 'How do I look?'

I stared.

'Not bad.' It was an understatement, but I wasn't going to give up that easily. 'Not bad at all. Let's see you walk.'

She walked across the room. The result was sexy as hell. I groaned.

'Jupiter, Perilla! What's that supposed to be? Get your head down. Slouch. And try not to move your hips.'

'I am trying.'

'Try harder, then. Walk through the streets like that and you'll be arrested on sight. Or propositioned. Probably both at once, knowing some of those buggers in the Watch.'

'All right. How's this?'

She tried again. It was better this time, but I knew at least a dozen guys in Rome who'd pay a fortune for an introduction. They'd be in for a disappointment later, mind, but that was neither here nor there.

'Look, watch me,' I said. I walked towards the door and back. 'Bigger steps. Loosen up a bit, and keep your eyes on the ground.'

She had hidden talents, that girl. And I don't mean the obvious ones. After four or five turns around the room I couldn't've sworn with absolute certainty that she wasn't what she pretended to be. So long as she could keep it up we were home and dry. Shit.

'Do I win the bet?' she said.

'Yeah, you win. Come over here first, though.'

She did. I kissed her. She co-operated long enough for things to reach the interesting stage before turning her face aside.

'Marcus! Stop it! You're smudging my make-up!'

Reluctantly I let her go.

When you check, you check. It was Perilla all right.

We didn't walk all the way. Perilla needed the practice, but I didn't want to be too hard on her so we used one of her litters as far as Tuscan Road. Naturally I took the four Sunshine Boys with us; I'd've liked to have taken more muscle, but it would've made us too conspicuous, and I reckoned the boys could take on anything short of a minor riot. All the same I had a quiet word with them before we left to make sure they knew where their priorities lay, and what exactly would happen if they got them wrong. I'd never actually seen a matching set of six-foot Gallic eunuchs on the market but there was a first time for everything.

I also made the situation very clear to Perilla.

'Listen,' I said. 'There're certain ground rules which are non-negotiable. Agree to them now or stay at home. Right?'

I must've looked unusually impressive because she just nodded.

'Okay. First of all, I can look after myself. If there's any trouble you run.'

'Yes, Corvinus.'

'Second. You do what you're told, exactly what you're told, straight away, with no arguments and no fancy heroics. Got it?'

'Yes, Corvinus.'

I glanced at her suspiciously.

'Perilla, are you laughing at me?'

'No, Corvinus.' Her lips twitched, but she kept her eyes modestly cast down.

'Yes you are.' This was no time for messing around. 'Look, I'm serious. There's no way I'm taking you down to the docks unless we get something clear before we start. I know what I'm doing here, you don't. You may be a very gutsy lady but if we get into trouble the high-handed patrician act isn't going to get us anywhere. This isn't a game and if you think it is you'll land both of us in deep shit. Okay?'

Silence. Finally, she nodded. 'All right. I'm sorry, Marcus. You're quite right. What else?'

'Third and last, no talking. Not when we're on foot in a built-up area, anyway. We've got enough problems with what you look like without worrying about what you sound like as well, and the less interest we draw the better. Agree to all three conditions now or you can stay at home bottling pickles.'

'I love you, Corvinus. You know that?'

There's no answer to that one. Not in words, anyway. Once she'd wiped the walnut juice off my face with the edge of her cloak we set off for our appointment with Davus.

CHAPTER

21

We left the litter at the western edge of the Palatine, crossed Tuscan Road and plunged into the maze of markets and slum property that was the eastern Velabrum. To my relief no one paid Perilla much attention—at least, no more than they paid me. The Sunshine Boys stuck close and made no attempt to fade into the woodwork, which was probably a good idea: I saw more than one suspicious-looking character zero in on my patrician tunic and veer off at the last moment before a granite shoulder mashed him to pulp against the nearest wall.

At least the boys were enjoying themselves. Maybe, I thought, I should take them walkies more often.

I didn't know the Velabrum all that well, certainly not as well as the Subura, apart from the bit around Cattlemarket Square. Like I said, it's the area where most of the wholesale trading goes on, and because it's the city's main link with Ostia most of the traffic between the Market Square and the river passes through it. Senators are barred by law from trade, so you don't see many broad-stripers down that way. Not that the ban would be all that difficult to get round. All it'd need, for example, would be to set up dummy companies through one or two of your freedmen and cream off the profits. However, for a senator to dirty his hands with trade is another of these things that's just not proper. We broad-stripers make our money respectably in other ways. Like from letting out rooms at sky-high rents in gimcrack tenements, for example. There're always plenty of punters looking for four walls and a floor to sleep on. And when the tenements collapse or burn down about their ears you can always shark up a few more and replace the dead tenants with new ones.

Property's a seller's market that never loses its edge. Why get your hands dirty when you don't have to?

Thanks to the boys we got through the built-up eastern and central sections of the Velabrum with no serious problems and moved out into the main docklands area near the river itself; streets of granaries and warehouses where the wholesalers keep the consignments of grain, olive oil, and fish sauce that come upriver on barges from Ostia. Most other days the district would've been swarming like a lump of maggoty meat, but because it was the Spring Festival everything was shut up and the streets and alleyways were deserted. They still smelled, though—a pleasant, storeroomy smell that was a mixture of wine and cheese and oil, with the faint musty overlay of drying corn.

'How much further?' Perilla asked.

'Not far now.' I'd found out where Paquius's warehouse was from Bathyllus (who else?). 'It's just downstream from the Sublician Bridge.'

'Oh, good. So long as it's *the* Sublician we're talking about, of course, and not another one I don't know about five miles upriver.'

The crabbiness was understandable, and I made the necessary allowances. We'd come a fair way that morning.

'Getting tired, eh?'

'Just a little.'

I pointed 'That's the river ahead of us.'

'I'd never have guessed, Marcus. Does it always smell of roses?'

Jupiter, she was crotchety! Still, I had to admit that the tendrils that were reaching out to us were pretty ripe. Pound for pound Tiber mud must be one of the evillest substances known to man.

'Yeah, well. Just be grateful we're still upstream from the Drain. The water's so thick there you can practically walk to the other side without a bridge. So long as you don't look down to see what you're standing in.'

She shuddered.

'Stop it, Corvinus.'

'You think I'm exaggerating?'

'I don't care. I just don't want to know, that's all.' We walked on until we reached a junction, then turned right along a street of warehouses backing on to the riverbank.

'That's it up ahead,' I said. There was no name painted that I could see, but Bathyllus had told me what to look for—a building set out slightly from the rest with a dilapidated wagon mouldering against the side wall. 'See anyone?'

'No.'

'Me neither.' The place, like its neighbours, looked deserted. 'You wait here with the boys and I'll have a look round.'

'Nonsense. We'll go in together.'

'Ground rules, remember.'

'But Corvinus…'

'Don't worry. If Davus is there I'll come back out and get you.'

'Be careful, then.'

'Yeah, sure.' I grinned.

'Marcus, I mean it!'

'I know. I'll be careful.'

I took the knife from its scabbard at my left wrist—I'd got a new one since my brush with the muggers—and walked towards the gates. My left shoulder was still stiff, but Scylax's massage had worked wonders and I reckoned I could handle myself pretty well if anything did go wrong. Not that anything would go wrong, of course.

I paused at the entrance to the warehouse. The double doors were unbarred, which was curious: like I said, everything we'd passed had been locked up tight for the holidays. But then again I didn't know why Davus had chosen this place. Maybe he worked here. Maybe he could come and go when he felt like it and had left the front door open for us. All the same I held the knife ready and went in carefully.

'Davus?' I shouted.

No answer. It was dark, of course, after the sunlight outside. I stood still and waited for my eyes to become adjusted. Then I looked around me.

Paquius was obviously in the grain trade like his neighbours. Down each long wall of the shed stood a line of corn bins. Their lids were open and I could see that most of them were full of dried grain. At the back was an industrial-size mill with bags of (I supposed) flour stacked against the wall beside it ready for distribution when the warehouse reopened the next day.

I shouted again. 'Davus!' Still no answer. Maybe he was hiding until he knew it was safe to come out. Not that there was anywhere in that place to hide. 'Hey, it's okay. I'm a friend. Valerius Corvinus. Harpale sent me.'

Something scuffled to my left and I whipped round, knife levelled; but it was only a rat. I walked up the centre of the warehouse towards the mill at the end.

The gate of the last bin had been lifted and the grain was lying in a pile on the stone floor. Resting on the side of the pile, its sole turned towards me, was a sandal. Or maybe not just a sandal. I went over for a closer look, the hairs lifting on the back of my neck because I already knew what I would find.

I was right; but I moved the grain away, just to make sure.

How he'd died was obvious enough as soon as I turned him over and saw the gaping flap below his grey-stubbled chin. His throat had been cut from ear to ear with one slash of a very sharp knife. I checked the grain beneath him. It was dry, and there was no sign of blood. While I did it his eyes stared up at me, blankly, accusingly.

So much for getting the name of our fourth conspirator. If Julia's door slave had known who the guy was he wasn't going to pass it on now. I'd come to a dead end. Literally.

'Fuck,' I whispered.

I heard footsteps behind me, and spun round. 'Corvinus, if you expect me to stand around outside while you...' Perilla began.

Then she saw what was left of Davus, and it was too late for explanations.

CHAPTER

22

The journey back was hellish, even with the boys to help. I had to half-carry Perilla most of the way to where we'd left the litter, which caused quite a stir at times. Then even when I'd got her under a familiar roof—the Fabius place had been the nearest—it took two cups of neat wine and a lot of quiet talking before she looked even half herself.

I never wanted to go through anything like that again. Ever.

The iron was back in her spine now, and she was sitting up straight in her chair and talking rationally; but her eyes were still strange and I knew it would be a long time before the lost look disappeared from them.

'Marcus, who'd want to kill Davus?' she said. 'He was only a harmless slave.'

I sipped carefully at my own wine, holding the cup with both hands so it didn't spill. Finding the old guy had shaken me too, more than I'd've liked to admit.

'Davus wasn't harmless, Perilla,' I said. 'Or at least what he knew wasn't. And he was killed as a warning to me. That's clear enough.'

'What makes you think that?'

'It wasn't done at the warehouse. There was no blood. Someone brought him there specially and left him for us to find.'

Perilla shuddered. 'Let's give this up,' she said. 'It isn't worth it.'

I shook my head. 'I can't. Especially not now. Davus may not've been a client of mine but I was responsible for him. He trusted me and I let him down. The least I can do is find his killer.'

Her eyes suddenly opened wide.

'How are we going to tell Harpale?' she whispered. 'I gave her my word nothing would happen to him.'

Yeah, I'd been wondering that too, and I wasn't looking forward to it, although the old girl probably knew already through the slave grapevine. Not the details, only that Davus was dead.

'Send for her now. Please, Marcus!'

I signalled to the wine slave, who was shifting nervously from foot to foot as close to the door as he could get. He left quickly.

'It wasn't your fault,' I said. 'If anyone was responsible I was. I knew I was being watched. It wouldn't've been difficult for whoever was tailing me to follow Harpale when she took the message.'

'Then they could've killed you as well. They could have been there waiting.'

'And had the Gauls to face? No, like I said, this was just a warning. Davus was the important one. Our only witness, and I pointed them straight at him.' Brilliant, right? I thought bitterly. Smart move, Corvinus. Score one for the home team.

The slave came back in with Harpale. She knew, that much was obvious from her eyes. Their accusing look reminded me of Davus's.

'I'm sorry, Harpale,' Perilla said.

'He was dead when we got there.' I couldn't face the old woman's eyes. I got up from where I'd been kneeling beside Perilla and crossed over to my own chair.

Harpale ignored me.

'What happened, madam?' she said quietly.

'His throat was cut. They left him for us to find.' The old woman nodded, as if she'd been expecting it. Maybe she had.

Then she turned to me.

'You promised, sir. You promised.' No accusation in her voice; she was stating a fact. 'You promised he'd be in no danger.'

Shit. 'I know I did,' I said. 'But there was nothing I could do.'

Suddenly, without warning, the old woman folded up like someone had pulled the bones out. Perilla caught her as she fell and steered her towards her own chair. We watched guiltily— neither of us touching her—until she came round.

'I'm sorry, madam,' she said. Her voice was thin as a ghost's.

'That's all right. Just…'

'You see, Davus was my brother.'

Perilla shot me a startled look. I signed to the wine slave hovering in the background. Perilla took the cup he handed her and held it to Harpale's lips. She shook her head.

'I'm all right, madam. Just give me a moment. Please.' We waited until her breathing calmed. 'He always knew they'd find him. After he ran away he got work down at the docks, where they don't ask too many questions. I was the only one who knew where he lived.' She looked straight at me. 'It was my fault, wasn't it, sir? I led them to him.'

'No,' I said. 'You were just the messenger, Harpale. Whoever's fault it was, it wasn't yours.'

But the old woman wasn't listening. She'd begun to rock back and forwards gently; the way peasant women do at a death.

'He knew he shouldn't have seen the gentleman's face,' she said. 'He told me. Told me he knew him. That was all, he wouldn't tell me the name. Then when the master was took, the selfsame day, he packed his bag and left the house. Said it was-n't safe any more. He was always clever, was my Davus. Too clever for a slave.'

'The master.' That would be Paullus. Davus had run away the day Paullus had been arrested for treason. So he'd known how important his information was. And what it could do to him. Clever for a slave right enough.

'Did they look for him?' I said. 'The emperor's men?'

She nodded. 'But he hadn't told no one he was going, sir. Not even me. I didn't know where he was till months after, when we met in the vegetable market. And he made me swear not to say nothing about him, even to the other slaves.' She start-ed to cry; not holding her hands over her face, but openly, the tears running down her cheeks like the slow sap trickling down runnels in a tree trunk. 'Then the mistress was sent away and I came to the Lady Marcia's. We didn't see each other often because he said it wasn't safe. Just now and again in the Velabrum market, or maybe at a festival when we were both free. He was working for Paquius by then, unloading grain and working the mill. I wanted to find him a better job but he wouldn't allow it. He said it might be harder work than what he was used to but at least it was safe. And then when they got the master, of course, I knew he was right.'

There was something wrong somewhere. I looked at Perilla, but her hand was stroking the old woman's hair.

'What do you mean they got the master, Harpale?' I said. 'Sure they got Paullus. You told us he was arrested the day Davus ran.'

Maybe she'd just mixed the times up, I thought. Maybe it was the slip of an overwrought old woman's memory.

Her next words pulled the ground out from under my feet.

'Oh, no, sir,' she said; and her eyes, even through the tears, were bright and guileless. 'I didn't mean Master Paullus. I meant my new master, Lady Marcia's husband. The Lord Fabius.'

Time seemed to stop. Perilla's hand lay frozen against the old woman's forehead, and she stared at me in shock. The hairs lifted at the back of my neck.

When they got the master...

Oh, shit. Not another corpse. We'd got enough and to spare without any more bodies scattered around.

'But Fabius wasn't arrested.' I tried to keep my voice calm and reasonable. 'And he wasn't accused of any crime, let alone executed. Fabius was an old man, and he died a natural death.'

Harpale's eyes went blank.

'Yes, sir,' she said. 'You're right. Of course you are. I made a mistake. I meant the Lord Paullus.'

Yeah, I thought, like hell you did. But Perilla got in first.

'Harpale.' I could hear the iron in her voice. 'How did my Uncle Fabius die? Let me have the truth, please.'

The old woman looked at her for a long time. Then, in a voice so low I could hardly make the words out, she said: 'The master killed himself, madam.'

'He did what?'

'Killed himself. Slit his wrists.'

'Why?'

'I don't know. You'll have to ask the Lady Marcia.'

'You mean my aunt knows?'

'Yes, madam. Of course she knows.'

'And she never told me?'

The old woman's lips tightened and she said nothing.

'You said "they", Harpale.' My head still hadn't stopped spinning. 'Who were they? The emperor's men?' I meant Tiberius's: Fabius had died barely a month after Augustus, just after the Wart had come to power. 'Why should the emperor want a harmless old guy like Fabius dead?'

Harmless old guy. Yeah. I thought of Davus. He'd been a harmless old guy too.

Harpale's lips were still set firm. She refused to look at me. Her eyes were on Perilla.

'I'm sorry, madam. I shouldn't've said anything. I'm only a silly slave. Don't listen to anything I say.'

'Harpale, please!' Perilla had got over her shock. Now she was kneeling beside the old woman's chair. 'You want us to find who killed your brother, don't you?'

The lips trembled.

'So this is important. We can't go any further. If my uncle's death is important in any way then we have to know. And we won't know unless you tell us about it.'

The old slave was quiet for a long time. Then she said: 'You weren't at the master's funeral, were you, madam?'

Perilla frowned. 'No, I was too young. What does that have to do with—'

'Please, madam. Let me speak, please. I was there with the mistress. The Lady Marcia. She was in a terrible state. Wouldn't eat, wouldn't sleep. Wouldn't even speak most of the time.'

'But that's quite natural, Harpale. After all, they'd been married for—'

'Please, madam!' The old woman's bird-claw fingers clutched at Perilla's arm. She was trembling. 'Listen, please! We go to the funeral, the mistress and me. When the torch is thrown on the mistress suddenly runs forwards like she's going to fling herself in after it, shouting that she's killed him. Killed your uncle.'

Shit. This didn't make sense.

'You said the guy committed suicide,' I said. 'Why the hell should Marcia think she'd killed him?'

Harpale hesitated. 'He did kill himself, sir. I'm not quite sure what the Lady Marcia meant.'

Perilla was glaring at me.

'Be quiet, Marcus,' she said. 'Please.'

'Thank you, madam.' Harpale paused. 'Anyway, half a dozen of the mourners pulled her back and I took her to the coach. She talked to me on the way home. At least, she didn't really talk. It was more of a ramble, like. As if I wasn't there. You understand, madam?'

Perilla nodded. 'Yes, Harpale. I understand. What did she say?'

'Mostly it was about a trip that the master had made with the old emperor. The Divine Augustus I should say. A trip that no one was to know about, to some island or other...'

'Trimerus?' I couldn't stop myself. My scalp prickled. The old woman frowned.

'No, not Trimerus, sir. That's where the Lady Julia is. This place was different. Plan- something.'

Oh, Jupiter! Oh, Jupiter Best and Greatest! There was only one Plan- island that I knew of. And that was where Augustus had exiled his grandson, Julia's brother, for gross immorality...

'Planasia?'

'That was it, sir. "To see the Exile," the mistress said.'

'Augustus went to see Postumus?'

'I don't know, sir. "To see the Exile on Planasia," that's all she said. And she'd given away the secret. That's what was upsetting her.'

I sat back in my chair, waiting for the world to right itself again and let me think. Postumus had been Julia's younger brother, exiled the year before Julia's own disgrace. He'd been executed—supposedly on Augustus's orders—immediately after the old emperor's death. But if Augustus had gone to see Postumus only a few months before, and secretly, then...

'Who did she tell?' I whispered. The old woman stared at me. 'For Jupiter's sake, Harpale, you must know that! Who did Marcia tell?'

The thin lips parted. Quietly, matter-of-factly, she said: 'Of course I know, sir. She told her friend the empress.'

Marcia had told Tiberius's mother!

Varus to Himself

Let me tell you now (yes! At long last!) about Arminius: dread leader of the Cheruscan tribe, flaming spearhead of German resistance, Rome's arch-enemy, and, of course, my current employer.

I first met him three years ago in Rome, at one of my nephew Lucius's dinner parties. It was an all-male, all-military affair: myself, Lucius, Marcus Vinicius, the ex-governor of Germany, Fabius Maximus. And, of course, Arminius.

I had known that Lucius had invited him, and I expected... what? A barbarian, certainly; someone with a veneer of civilisation, a performing bear in a mantle, dense of wit, halting of speech; a clod of German earth with the manners of a slave and the arrogance of a savage. I should have known better. Arminius's father had sent him to Augustus in childhood, and he had been reared as a Roman gentleman.

Lucius introduced us. The young man—he can have been no more than twenty—rose politely from his couch. He was slim, his blond hair cut short in the Roman manner, and he wore his knight's mantle with more grace than I did my own.

We shook hands, and I said in German (I was with Tiberius when he reduced the Sugambri): 'I'm delighted to meet you, Prince Hermann.'

'Your accent's better than mine, sir.' The young man smiled. His Latin was flawless. 'Perhaps we can arrange lessons?'

There was general laughter.

'Don't show off, Publius,' Fabius grunted. 'The lad's as Roman as you are. More so.'

I could believe it. If it had not been for the colour of his hair he would have passed anywhere for a young Roman nobleman.

We reclined, and slaves brought the first course. I noticed that Arminius ate sparingly, and had the wine waiter add extra water to his cup. Then someone (I think it was Lucius) brought up the subject of Illyria.

It was a natural topic at the time, especially in that company: the whole country was up in revolt, Rome's back was to the wall and the soundness of our entire frontier policy was being seriously questioned. Not to mention the soundness of the ageing emperor's judgment.

'The problem is'—Fabius fixed us with a levelled quail's egg—'it's a matter of security. Augustus can't just let Illyria drop. She's vital to the empire's safety.'

'No one's disputing that, old boy.' Vinicius, I remember, had the unpleasant nasal twang of a third-rate harpist. 'The trouble is he's gone too far and too fast. He's botched the job and now we're suffering the consequences.'

Vinicius was absolutely correct, of course. As was Fabius. We needed Illyria. We needed the land route to Macedonia and Greece and control of the eastern passes through the Alps. Without Illyria Italy was vulnerable and the empire split in half. And the initial stages of the conquest had been skimped.

Fabius shifted uncomfortably. He was the emperor's man and one of his most trusted advisers; criticism of Augustus did not sit well with him.

'You may be right,' he conceded. 'Certainly we don't have the men for an armed occupation. But we must have a secure northern border somehow. It's a question of balance, the optimal use of the forces available. The Illyrian revolt has simply shown how difficult establishing that balance is.'

'It would be easier if we pushed north to the Elbe,' Lucius said. 'That would shorten our lines of communication and give us an almost total natural frontier.'

Fabius nodded. 'Oh, I agree, absolutely. And so does Augustus. However, there's one glaringly obvious problem.'

Vinicius grinned. 'The Germans,' he said. 'These bastards—saving your presence, Arminius—would rather not be part of the Roman empire, thank you very much. And who's to blame them?'

'I, for one.' Arminius set down his cup. 'The tribes between the Rhine and the Elbe are an undisciplined rabble.'

'And long may they continue to be so.' That was Vinicius again. 'So long as they're knocking each other's heads together they leave ours alone.'

'Quite.' I reached for an olive. 'Divide and rule is the obvious policy where the German tribes are concerned.'

'I disagree.' Arminius frowned. 'What have we achieved so far? Certainly not Roman rule. A stalemate at best. Granted, unless we keep them firmly under control the Germans will always cause trouble; but, as Fabius says, we haven't the forces for an armed occupation.'

'And your solution to this paradox?' Fabius's smile was tolerant.

'Perhaps it's time to rethink our policies completely, sir. The answer may not be to fragment the tribes but to unite them.'

'You mean like Maroboduus?'

Vinicius's quiet comment brought a shout of laughter. Maroboduus was a German chieftain who, having established a power-base in Bohemia, had extended his influence over neighbouring Saxony and Silesia. The situation was still unresolved.

Arminius was waiting calmly for the laughter to die down. When it did, he said: 'Yes, in a way. I do mean like Maroboduus.'

I noticed that Fabius was looking at him keenly.

'Go on, young man,' he said.

'It's quite simple. In theory at least. At present most of the chiefs can't see past their petty local affairs. They hate Rome because they don't understand her, and they'd rather die than be part of the empire. But if they could be united under one of their own people, a single strong leader, one sympathetic to Rome, then—'

'Just a moment,' Vinicius put in. 'That's a sizeable if, old boy. I know the Germans. A Roman sympathiser—such as yourself, for example'—the words were silkily neutral—'wouldn't have a hope in hell of gathering the support he needed. And if we tried to impose him from outside he wouldn't last a month.'

Arminius turned to him.

'You're right, sir, of course,' he said. 'I did say I was speaking theoretically. But if it were somehow possible, then it would solve Rome's problems at a stroke, wouldn't it?'

'Yes, it would. If your theoretical leader could be trusted.'

The young man's eyes flashed. He half rose from the couch, and I thought that blood would be spilled, at any rate metaphorically. However at that moment the slaves came in with the main course and amity was restored.

I looked across at Fabius, who, as I say, was one of Augustus's closest advisers. He was looking unusually thoughtful, and more than once during the remainder of the evening I saw his eyes resting on the young German with what was certainly speculation. But he did not raise the subject again, at least in my hearing.

I saw Arminius often after that—mostly at Lucius's, since the lad with his passion for things military had adopted my nephew almost as a mentor. He continued to impress me. He had sense, intelligence, good breeding, and, above all, a clear devotion to Rome and Roman values. Together with his idealism, this made him, as Fabius had said, more Roman than I was, especially where the last two qualities are concerned. When he was finally sent back to his people we lost touch for almost a year; until, in fact, I was given Germany and he came to me at Vetera with other tribal representatives to pay his respects. He was wearing German dress, and his hair was long in the German manner. Although he was perfectly polite, his greeting was perfunctory, and I was, I admit, more than a little offended.

I should have known better. As I was to discover before the day was out, Arminius's patent unfriendliness had a purpose.

I was relaxing in my private quarters after bathing when a tall German strode in. He was muffled to the eyebrows in his cloak, but of course I recognised him: Arminius, without a doubt. Once he had unwrapped himself we shook hands for the second time that day; on his side, warmly.

'Varus, I'm sorry,' he said. 'My behaviour earlier was dreadful.'

'On the contrary, my boy.' I was beginning to thaw out. Despite his appearance this was the Arminius I knew. 'Your German manners were impeccable.'

He laughed and sat down on the desk stool. These might be the quarters of the governor of Germany and the commander of the armies of the Rhine, but they were spartan in the extreme, and would be until my full complement of furniture arrived from Rome.

'What do you think of the fancy dress?' he said. 'And the hairstyle?'

He was smiling; I was not.

'Strangely enough,' I said, 'they suit you.' They did. In Rome he had looked like a Roman. Here he looked more German than the Germans. 'But I wasn't aware that it was the German fashion to wrap one's head in one's cloak. Especially indoors.'

'It was necessary, sir.' He spoke gravely. 'I had rather that no one knew of this conversation. Roman or German.'

'Is it such a crime, then, for old friends to talk in private?'

'Possibly. Given the circumstances.'

I didn't like the smell of this at all. I was cautious, and turned to the tray of wine-things to cover my caution.

'Explain,' I said.

'You remember the plan I talked about, sir? When we first met?'

'Your grand design to turn Germany into a western client-kingdom? Yes, of course I do.'

'Perhaps we should talk about it again. More seriously this time.'

I am by nature a diplomat rather than a soldier. As I poured the wine and handed it to him I kept my expression neutral.

'Go on.'

Arminius took a single sip and set the cup aside. 'Very shortly, sir,' he said, 'I will break with Rome. I will begin to gather support first among the young men of my own tribe, then among other tribes. I will tell them that only by banding together can we Germans resist you Romans and live as we have always lived outside your boundaries.'

I was staring at him, too shocked even to interrupt. 'When the peacemakers shout, I will shout louder. I will keep on shouting until the hotheads believe that I am more against Rome than they are, and give me their trust and their allegiance. And you, sir, will help me.'

I got up; what I intended to do I am not sure, because at that moment I was incapable of thinking clearly at all. Call the guards, perhaps. In any case he pulled me back.

'Hear me out,' he said. 'Please.'

I sat down, as did he. When he spoke again it was in the same quiet, reasonable voice he had used to condemn himself.

'Believe me, sir. I am no traitor to Rome. The fact that I've told you this proves it. Give me a free hand between here and the Elbe and I'll unite the tribes into a federation which I control. I control!'

My brain was spinning.

'Arminius. You are telling me—me, the Roman governor—that you are planning a rebellion?' I expected him to deny it, but he said nothing. 'You're mad!'

He shook his head sharply. 'No, sir. Not mad. And rebellion is not the proper word.'

'What is, then? Treason?'

'Not that either,' he said stubbornly. 'There will be no trouble. No real trouble. I promise you that.'

I was at a loss for words. I simply stared at him.

'Think, Varus!' He bent towards me, his eyes shining. 'Rome wants Upper Germany and a secure northern border. The Germans want to be left alone to govern themselves. At the moment the objectives clash. The Germans provide a constant threat, we Romans haven't the forces to take and hold the territory we need. Stalemate. I'm offering Rome a solution. I'm offering a way out.'

'By uniting the tribes and increasing the threat?'

'No!' His hand came down so hard upon the desk top that I thought the wood had split. 'I told you! To break the stalemate in Rome's favour! In the long term Rome can only benefit.'

'And in the short term? You'd be a rebel. Any Roman who helped you would be a traitor.'

To be honest, I was quibbling for appearance's sake. He already had half of me convinced; and the other half (ah, me! I may as well admit to it now, and make of it what you will) scented gold, which is the most exciting smell on earth.

Oh dear, oh dear! What it is to be venal! Yet blessed is the man who will admit to his infirmities, and indulge them when in good conscience he can. After all, what Arminius was proposing was for the good of Rome, was it not? And who was I to balk him of his laudable ambition? Especially if in the process I could turn an honest penny for myself.

'In the short term, Varus,' Arminius said in answer to my question, 'you must simply trust me.'

I remembered Vinicius's words at the dinner party, and how the young man had reacted to them.

'So,' I said, 'it comes down to trust.'

'Yes, sir,' Arminius said carefully, his eyes on mine. 'It comes down to trust.'

I stared at him for a long time, weighing him. Not simply his words on this occasion, but what I recalled of our conversations in the past. Then I weighed his manner, his conviction, and last but not least his indefinable aura. I may be greedy, but I am not a fool; and if the rewards of treachery are high, then so are its corresponding dangers.

Finally I nodded.

'Very well, Prince Arminius,' I said. 'You have your traitor.'

Neither of us had mentioned payment, of course. That came later, when the terms of my treachery were discussed in a civilised fashion, as if they were unimportant. Which, to him at least, I am sure they were. As I said, the lad has good breeding, and in this if nothing else Arminius the German is a better Roman than I am.

CHAPTER

23

When Harpale had gone I sent the wine slave for another jug. After what she'd told us I needed it.

'You didn't know that Fabius had killed himself?' I asked Perilla. 'You never even suspected?'

'No.' She still looked grey. Shit, she'd had enough shocks that day to floor anyone with twice her guts. 'Aunt Marcia never even hinted at it. I thought that Uncle was found dead in his study, which would have been true enough I suppose. I don't think even Mother knew the death wasn't natural.'

'You think Marcia would confirm the story if you asked her straight out?'

'I doubt it. And don't ask me to try, Marcus, because I won't. It would be terribly painful for her. If she's kept the secret for so long she must have a good reason.'

'Oh, yeah,' I said. 'She's got a good reason all right. If what Harpale says is true the Wart has at least two deaths on his conscience that he wouldn't want made public. Sure, Postumus had to go. As Augustus's last male relative he'd be about as welcome politically as a flea in a barber's shop, and if he was the bastard they say he was then nobody would shed many tears. But Fabius is different. He wasn't guilty of anything. And if the news had got out that Augustus had talked to his grandson just a few months before he died, then as far as the Wart was concerned it'd be embarrassing as hell.'

'Why should it be embarrassing? After all, if Augustus gave the order himself for Postumus's death then...'

'Oh, come on, Perilla! Act your age! It would've shown that he *didn't* give the order, that killing Postumus was Tiberius's own idea. Why do you think the old guy went to Planasia anyway? Just to make faces at his grandson through the bars?'

'You tell me, Corvinus.'

'Okay. We'll take it slowly. Augustus was old and sick, yet he took the trouble to visit Postumus in person. So why should he do that?'

'Because what he had to say was too secret to trust to a messenger?'

'Right. And possibly too personal. Say the guy wanted to apologise. To admit that he'd made a mistake, a bad mistake.'

'But he'd exiled Postumus himself! Why should he change his mind?'

'I don't know, but one gets you five I'm right. He went to patch up the quarrel and give his grandson his personal assurance that he'd put things right as soon as he could.'

'You mentioned a mistake. What kind of mistake?'

'Maybe Postumus wasn't the bastard he was made out to be. Maybe Augustus found out that someone had been bad-mouthing him all along and wanted to make amends.'

Perilla looked at me, appalled. 'Tiberius?'

'Sure. It makes sense. The Wart got rid of Postumus pretty smartly as soon as he got the chance. And your Uncle Fabius had to die too because he was the only one still alive who knew the truth. The secrecy angle's pretty obvious, too. As Augustus's heir, Tiberius'd be chewing bricks if he thought Granddad intended bringing little Postumus home. It all fits. It fits perfectly. And it explains what Julia and Paullus were up to as well.'

'Julia was exiled six years before all this happened, Marcus. How could Postumus's death have had anything to do with the Paullus plot?'

'Listen. Postumus is the missing strand. With Gaius and Lucius dead he was Julia's only surviving brother and Augustus's only direct male descendant, right?'

'Yes, but I still don't see what...'

'You gave me the idea yourself, that first night we were together. You said that a husband has certain rights. Sure, Julia may've been the emperor's granddaughter but she was still a woman. She couldn't hope for any sort of power through her relationship with Augustus, not direct power, anyway. But her husband could!'

'Corvinus, we know Paullus conspired against Augustus. There's no secret about that.'

'Yeah, but what chance would he have on his own? Augustus had been the kingpin for two generations. You think Paullus only had to put himself forward with Julia beside him for the whole state to fall into his lap like a ripe plum? A political lightweight whose only claim was that he'd married the emperor's granddaughter?'

'Of course not. We talked about that before. That's why you said he needed Tiberius.'

'Right. But that was when we thought the Wart was our

fourth man. We know now he couldn't have been. What if Paullus had Augustus's only surviving male descendant on the team?'

'You're saying the man with the ring was Postumus?'

I shook my head. 'No, Postumus was already exiled. But his sister Julia was there to represent his interests.'

'But Augustus banished him in the first place. He'd only be a contender if the emperor were already dead.'

'That's right. It makes sense like before, only for Tiberius read Postumus. Paullus and Julia knock off Augustus and bring Postumus back to Rome. Then either Postumus becomes emperor with Paullus as his right-hand man or they do a deal to carve up the state between them.'

Perilla sighed. 'I'm sorry, Corvinus, but it won't work. As an argument it's got too many holes.'

'Oh, yeah?' I sat back and folded my arms. 'Name some.'

'Very well. For a start you can't have it both ways. On the one hand you're saying that Augustus decided Postumus had been slandered by Tiberius, and on the other that he had been involved in a bona fide conspiracy against Augustus. Now isn't that just a little inconsistent?'

'Not necessarily. Postumus needn't've known anything about the conspiracy himself. If it had come off he wouldn't be the first ruler to be set up as a figurehead. Once Augustus was dead…'

'Exactly. That's when the problems would start. First of all the death would have to look natural. That would be difficult enough. Second, why should Postumus be the one to take Augustus's place? He'd never held office of any kind. He'd been disinherited and exiled by Augustus himself, and Tiberius was already earmarked to succeed. The Senate would choose him over Postumus any time, unless Paullus and Julia could produce a will that was a good enough forgery to stand against the official one. Third, even if by some miracle the Senate did accept him as Augustus's heir, Paullus and Julia would still need physical force to back his claim. Where was that to come from? Or do you think Tiberius would simply stand aside and let them get away with it?'

'Uh, yeah.' Jupiter! Well, I'd asked her after all. 'Yeah, well done, Perilla. Maybe there are a few holes. Still, Paullus must've been pretty sure of his ground.'

'How do we know that?'

'He had to be, because the conspiracy happened. Paullus may not have got away with it, but he sure as hell didn't just wake up one morning and say, "What a nice day, I think I'll have a conspiracy"!'

'Now you're being flippant, Marcus.'

'No, I'm not. Something must have made the guy reasonably sure he'd have the backing he needed, political and military. Yeah, sure, I accept your arguments but there must be some way of getting round them because the Paullus plot happened. The question is, if he didn't have Postumus on the team, then who did he have?'

'Davus's stranger. The fourth conspirator.'

I nodded. 'Right. He's the key, I'm certain of it. We always come back to him.'

'So who could he have been, if not Postumus?'

'Someone pretty high up. We know that, because that was why he got in in the first place.' I frowned and drank my wine. 'Okay. How about this for a set-up? Postumus provides the figurehead, Paullus is the ringleader with Julia as his dynastic link. Silanus has the good blue-blood connections they'll need to bring the old senatorial families round when the thing comes off. And our fourth man makes it all possible. He provides the real political and military muscle that guarantees all the rest. Or at least, if his job was to bust up the plot for Augustus from the inside, he pretends to guarantee it.'

'So who was he?'

I put my head between my hands.

'Perilla, I don't know! The Wart would've been ideal. Nobody else even comes close. But even if the Wart had been in Rome at the right time he couldn't be the one we're looking for, not now we know about Postumus. Paullus and Julia wouldn't've trusted him as far as you can spit. So we're still stuck. Whoever could deliver the high-grade backing the conspiracy needed ought to stand out a mile, but he doesn't. And he doesn't because there wasn't anyone that big around.'

'Oh, come on, Corvinus,' Perilla said sharply. 'It's not that bad. At least we have the Postumus connection now. I wish I'd known before that—'

She stopped.

I sat up. 'You thought of something?'

'No. No, it's not that. Nothing directly to do with Postumus, anyway. It's just I've remembered something my stepfather wrote in one of his poems that might fit in with what Harpale told us about my uncle's death.'

'Yeah? What sort of thing?'

'I can't quote the lines offhand. I'd need the book.' She got up. 'Wait a moment. Uncle Fabius had all my stepfather's works. There'll be a copy in his study.'

While I was waiting I poured myself another cupful of wine from the new jug. I hadn't been holding out on Perilla. Apart from Tiberius there was no one who had the sort of power we were looking for—especially since, if push came to shove, Paullus and his friends would've had to take on the Wart himself. In which case they were on a hiding to nothing. And even if the fourth guy had been a double he'd still have had to put his money where his mouth was as far as the others were concerned. No, I was stymied. My only chance was that something else would turn up. Like Scylax tracing the big lunk with the sawblade accent...

'Here it is, Marcus.' Perilla was back with a partially unrolled book. She handed me it and leaned over the back of my chair as I read, her sharp little chin resting in the hollow between my neck and shoulder.

> You'd been certain, Maximus, pride of the Fabii,
> To plead for me with the God Augustus
> But died before you made your plea.
>
> I think
> Maximus
> That I caused your death
> (I, who was of so little worth).
> Now I am afraid to trust my safety to anyone.
> With your death help itself is dead.
> Augustus had begun to pardon my deceitful fault
> When he died too, leaving
> At a single stroke
> The earth, and all my hopes,
> Barren.

'It doesn't make sense, does it?' Perilla said as I laid the book down. 'How could my stepfather have thought he was responsible? He'd been shut away in Tomi for six years when Uncle Fabius died.'

I said nothing. I was thinking of Marcia. She'd taken the blame for Fabius's death too. Two people independently claiming they'd caused a death that on the surface was no one's fault:

the natural death of a tired old man. Even if Fabius had been forced into suicide they still couldn't both be right.

Unless, of course, they were.

'Marcus!' I suddenly realised that Perilla was digging me in the shoulder. 'I asked you a question!'

'Hmm?' I blinked. Maybe I'd had too much wine again. 'Oh, yeah. Sorry. Run it past me again.'

'How could my stepfather have caused Uncle Fabius's death when he was in Tomi?'

'Jupiter knows, Perilla. But it has to connect with what Marcia told Harpale. Maybe...' I stopped as the first tingle of the idea hit me.

'Maybe what?'

'Maybe Fabius wasn't killed just because he knew about Augustus's visit to Planasia. Maybe there was another reason. An extra one.'

'Corvinus, why should...?'

'No, wait. Let me work this out. Sure, Planasia would be a good enough reason for Tiberius to want to shut your uncle up permanently. But let's say Fabius had put the Wart's nose out of joint in another way. Say he'd almost caused something to happen that didn't, but could well have if Augustus hadn't died when he did.'

'Are you being intentionally obscure, or is it my fault?'

'Just look at the lines again and answer me one question. Who died first? Augustus or Fabius?'

'I can tell you that now. My uncle outlived the emperor by a month. You know that.'

'Sure. So read the poem again.' She did, and her startled eyes stared into mine. 'You see? Now tell me again.'

'But this reads as though it was Uncle Fabius!'

'Yeah, that's right. Ovid got the deaths back to front.'

'But why should he do that?'

I shrugged. 'Tomi's a long way from Rome. News travels slowly, sometimes it gets garbled. What's a month either way? There're a dozen reasons. But that's not the point.'

'So what is?'

'Your stepfather's reaction. He says Augustus was already beginning to waver but Fabius's plea-in-form for a pardon never got made, so the whole thing came to nothing. We know that that was because the emperor died first, but Ovid took it the other way round.'

'Marcus, I still don't see what you're getting at.'

'It's simple. Ovid thought your uncle had been the first to go and blamed himself for his death, right?'

'Yes, but...'

I stopped her. 'So what made him assume that Fabius's death was connected with a plea for his recall? And because he knew what his own crime was, why shouldn't he be right?'

CHAPTER
24

I found a letter waiting for me from Gaius Pertinax when I got home.

Pertinax was the guy I'd thought might know the inside story on the Julia scandal. Not Paullus's Julia. Her mother, Augustus's daughter, who'd been exiled when the City Watch had caught her putting it around one night in the Market Square while her husband Tiberius was off sulking in Rhodes. Harpale had claimed that she'd been innocent, too. What she had to do with our little mystery I wasn't sure—that particular scandal had broken ten years before Ovid went to Tomi—but it was a lead all the same. And we had less of them than a eunuch has hard-ons.

I'd known Pertinax all my life. He was an ex-subordinate of my grandfather's when the old man had been city prefect forty-odd years back, and the two had hit it off like fish sauce on broad beans. Not that Granddad had held the job for long. According to family tradition (Uncle Cotta, not my father), he'd thrown it up because it was, and I quote, 'a major pain in the arse'. Not that that was how he'd expressed it to Augustus. The official reason he gave was that it was 'undemocratic'. Which I suppose was as strong as he could make it without putting a knot in the imperial knickers.

Unlike Granddad, Pertinax had his daily bread to earn. He'd stuck with the city service and when the elder Julia had been arrested he'd had one of the top jobs with the Watch. As a regional commander no less. For Region Eight, the Market Square area...

Yeah. Pure gold, right? If Uncle Gaius couldn't tell me what had happened that night then no one could.

He was retired now, of course. Long retired, to a farm in the country about thirty miles down the Appian Way, where he grew the best pears and apples you've ever tasted. I used to go there with my grandfather at harvest time when I was a kid, and Pertinax took quite a shine to me. He still sent me a bushel or two out of his crop in the autumn, and I'd call in whenever I was down that way to see how the old guy was doing.

So when the Julia thing came up I'd sent a runner to Pertinax's place with a note asking him if I could come down and milk his brains, subject unspecified. This was the reply. It was short and snappy: Uncle Gaius could've given a Spartan lessons in prose style.

Gaius Attius Pertinax to Marcus Valerius Messalla Corvinus.
Greetings.

Come when you like. Bring fish.

I grinned as I read it. Some people's weakness is money, others power, others women. Pertinax's was fish, and he would sell his soul for a sturgeon. When he came to dinner with my grandfather (which he did on average about once a month) Old Corvinus would send Philip his cook down to scour the fish-market in the Argiletum for the widest and best selection money could buy. It cost him, too—good fish costs an arm and a leg in Rome and always has done—but then my granddad was generous to his friends. I'd never understood why Pertinax hadn't settled further south when he retired; at Naples, say, where the seafood would draw Jupiter himself down banging his dinner pail. Maybe he'd thought too much perfection was dangerous. Or maybe he just liked growing good apples better.

When I'd read the note I sent Bathyllus out for a barrel of Baian oysters and the biggest sturgeon he could lug home without giving himself another hernia, packed off a minion to tell Perilla where I was going and why, and ordered up the carriage.

The journey was uneventful. Not knowing how busy the Appian Way would be after the holiday (it wasn't, especially), I'd taken the big sleeping coach. Thirty-odd miles may not seem a lot, but I'd been caught out before on a slow road, and unless you want to risk being rolled or eaten alive by fleas at a quaint wayside inn or have acquaintances en route (I didn't unfortunately. Or not ones I'd've willingly spent an evening with, anyway) it's a sensible way to travel. Apart from the coachman and my body slave Flavus I took the four Sunshine Boys. Three of them could ride without falling off. The fourth usually landed on his head, which didn't seem to worry him much and provided harmless amusement for the rest of us. I had a private bet with myself (which I won easily) that he'd go arse over tip at least once per mile.

Pertinax was looking pretty fit for his seventy-odd years, brown as a berry and with less of a gut on him than I had.

When he saw the sturgeon his eyes lit up like a twenty-lamp candelabrum.

'Slow-steamed with coriander,' he murmured as two of his lads levered the fish out of the boot. 'Perhaps with a celery-mint sauce. What do you think, Marcus?'

'It's your fish, Uncle. Have it how you like.'

'I'm your debtor, boy. Let's see what Nestor has to say.' Nestor was his cook. 'What's in the barrel? Sea-urchins?'

'Oysters.'

'Baian oysters?'

'Would I stick you with less?'

'Jupiter! I haven't had Baian oyster stew since the Winter Festival. You're a true Roman, lad. And a gentleman, which isn't the same thing.' Pertinax was from Cremona. 'Come inside. I've a jug or two of good Rhodian that's just asking to be drunk.'

I followed him in. The place looked different from the last time I'd been there.

'You've made some changes,' I said.

'That's right, boy. I've had another solar built on, to catch the afternoon sun. We'll go in there now. Rejigged the baths at the same time, so you can wash the dust off properly before we eat.'

Maybe Pertinax's farm was a working one, but he'd never been a sour-faced Cato. And taking an interest in building had kept him going since his wife had died three years before.

'Decoration in the dining-room's new too. Chap I got in from Naples. Tell me what you think.'

'Let's have the wine first,' I said. 'I've got a throat like a short-legged camel's scrotum.'

Pertinax chuckled. 'You've your grandfather's turn of phrase, boy. And his priorities. Make yourself comfortable while

I have a word with Nestor about dinner. I'll send in the wine, don't you worry.'

I lay down on one of the couches in the solar and examined the wall paintings. Pertinax's late wife wouldn't have approved. She had gone in, I remembered, for still lifes. Grapes and hanging pheasants, those were her limits. Nymphs and satyrs were definitely out. And these nymphs and satyrs would have had her reaching for the whitewash. I wondered if Uncle Gaius was fitter even than he looked.

The wine came, with a bowl of last season's apples—wizened now, but hard and sweet inside. They brought back memories.

'Good? The wine, I mean.'

I looked up. Uncle Gaius had come in while I wasn't looking and was helping himself to a cup from the jug.

'Very good,' I said, and meant it. 'I always think Rhodian's overrated but this stuff's not. Where do you get it?'

'Another chap in Naples. The architect's cousin. Clannish lot the Greeks.'

'Did he do the mural as well? The architect?'

'That's right. Do you like it? I thought it was pretty good myself.'

'You'll have to give me his name before I go. The guy's talented.'

'Wait till you see the dining-room. That'll really knock your eyes out.' He settled down on the couch and selected an apple. 'So. The baths are heating up nicely and we've got a couple of hours to kill before dinner. Now do you really want to discuss pornographic art or would you like to tell me what this is all about?'

I sipped my wine. 'Talk to me about Julia,' I said.

'Which Julia?'

'The old emperor's daughter.'

'Ah.' He set his cup down carefully on the table beside him. 'I thought it might be something like that, young Marcus.'

Shit. We were a long way from Rome, but Uncle Gaius still had his contacts.

'What's that supposed to mean?'

'Exactly what it says.' He wasn't giving anything away, that was for sure. 'How badly do you want to know?'

'Very badly. Very badly indeed.'

Pertinax stared into his cup. 'I do hear things stuck out here, Marcus. And I may be old but I'm not a fool. What would you say if I told you that what happened to Julia isn't important now, but that you'd be better off not knowing?'

Yeah. I'd heard that one before. It looked like this was going to be a wasted journey.

'I'd say that was for me to decide, Uncle. And that I have to know for my own peace of mind if nothing else.'

His eyes came up level with mine. 'You're like your grandfather, Marcus. Very like. That could've been him talking.' He hesitated. 'There's a woman involved in this, isn't there?'

I didn't even think of lying. I owed him that, at least. 'Yeah. There's a woman. A client. Her name's Rufia Perilla. She's Ovid's stepdaughter.'

'You love her?'

My throat was dry. 'Yes.'

'Enough to sacrifice your political career?'

'Yes.'

'You're sure, Marcus? Absolutely sure?'

'Yes.'

'Because it may come to that, you know. And it may not be worth it in the end. I don't mean her. I mean what comes of just

having the information without being cleared for it. You understand?'

'Yes, I understand.'

'And you still want me to answer your question?'

'Yes.'

He sighed and turned away. 'Then you're a fool, boy. Still,
I'll give you what I can.'

I relaxed. 'Thanks, Uncle. I'm grateful. Really.'

'I don't want gratitude. Your father would kill me for this
if he knew. But then I never could stand young Messalinus and
I think your grandfather would've approved, which is far more
important. Besides, I'm too old to care. So ask away, son.'

'I think she was innocent. Julia, I mean.'

'That's not a question.'

'Was she?'

He hesitated for a long time. A very long time. 'Yes,' he
said at last. 'Julia was innocent. Of adultery, at least.'

I was tired of fencing. I just wanted hard facts. 'Just tell me
what happened that night, Uncle Gaius. Please.'

He got up and went over to where the slave had left the
wine jug. He didn't look at me as he carefully filled his cup.

'Very well, Marcus. I'll tell you what happened. Exactly
what happened. You know our company was responsible for the
Eighth Region—the Market Square area?'

'Yes. That's why I'm asking you.'

'Right. So I'd gone out with the lads. We started our patrol
at dusk, just as usual. We picked up a couple of disorderly
drunks near Marcellus's Theatre and banged their heads together. Then we walked up towards Pallacina Street. One of the lads
thought he saw someone breaking into a wineshop but it turned
out to be a cat. We came back along the north side of the Capitol,
down past the edge of the Citadel and into the Market Square.

Then we went up the Sacred Way. Young Publius Afer had a stone in his boot so we stopped while he leaned against a shop wall and got rid of it.'

Shit. What was going on here? It wasn't like Pertinax to spin a story out. He spoke like he wrote. Give the guy a nut to crack and he went straight to the middle.

'Look,' I said. 'I just want to know about Julia, right? Remember her? The hot little number being gang-banged on the Speakers' Platform?'

'And I'm telling you what happened, Marcus. Exactly. When Publius got his boot back on we went up towards the Subura. It was pretty quiet...'

By this time I'd caught on.

'You mean nothing happened? Nothing at all?'

Pertinax brought the cup back to his couch and lay down. Now his eyes were sharp as chips of marble.

'Nothing happened, boy. Not a thing. If the emperor's daughter got herself laid in the Market Square then it wasn't that night. Or whoever saw her it wasn't us.'

'But she must've been there! Everybody says...'

I stopped. Yeah, sure. Perilla had tried that argument with me when we were talking about the other Julia. It didn't cut any ice then, either.

Pertinax was nodding. 'That's right, Marcus. Circular logic. Everybody says she was there so she was there. QED.' He took a large swallow of his wine. 'Only she wasn't. The orgy story's a myth. Believe me.'

'But what about the men she was with? She was screwing some of the top guys in Rome!'

'Give me names, Marcus.'

'Uh.' I thought. 'Sulpicianus. One of the Scipios. Sempronius Gracchus. The others I can't remember, but they're on record. And Iullus, of course.' Iullus Antonius had been cited as Julia's principal lover.

'Of course,' Pertinax said drily. 'You notice anything?'

'What's to notice? Like I said, they're all big names but...'

'Not good enough, boy. Listen.' He ticked the guys off on his fingers. 'Cornelius Scipio. Grandson of the emperor's first wife, Scribonia, and so Julia's first cousin. Gracchus. A "persistent adulterer" according to the charge-sheet. Supposed to have been sleeping with Julia when she was Agrippa's wife. Helped her compose a certain letter of complaint to Augustus. Sulpicianus. Consul seven years before. Quiet man, no previous convictions except for a deep devotion to the emperor.' He paused. 'Are you getting the idea yet?'

My scalp was beginning to tingle. 'I might be. Go on.'

'I could give you a few more you haven't mentioned, but let's just settle for Iullus. Iullus Antonius, adulterer-in-chief. Mark Antony's son. Brought up by Augustus's sister Octavia like he was her own. Deeply devoted to Augustus. Married to the emperor's niece Marcella, with three children. Full political career under Augustus's personal supervision. As a child he was even included on the Altar of Peace along with the rest of the imperial family, with his hand on Julia's head. Come on, Marcus! Do you want me to spell it out for you?'

Something cold with lots of legs was running up my spine. 'They're all political. Attached to the imperial family, by blood or obligation.'

'The imperial family?'

Shit!

'Augustus, then. Augustus personally. Or his first wife.'

'Remember that, boy! Now, you say they're all attached to Augustus personally. All of them?'

'Yeah. Apart from Gracchus.'

'So what was special about Gracchus? Come on, you can do it! You can do it, boy! How did they describe him? What did I say was on the charge-sheet?'

The sweat was pouring off me in bucketfuls. 'He was a "persistent adulterer". Julia's long-standing lover.'

'That word persistent sound familiar?'

Persistent depravity. Holy shit! 'Postumus?'

'You're doing well, boy. So who's Postumus?'

'Augustus's grandson.' The Augustus connection again! Jupiter!

'And whose son?'

'Julia's. Our Julia's. The emperor's daughter.'

'That's right. So let's get back to Gracchus. Anything else? Come on, boy! What about that letter to Augustus I mentioned? The letter Gracchus helped Julia write? Who was she complaining about?'

My head was bursting. 'For God's sake! How the hell should I know?'

'All right. She was complaining about her husband, Marcus. And her husband was...?'

The answer hit me between the eyes like a butcher's hammer. 'Tiberius! Julia's husband was Tiberius!'

Pertinax leaned back with a smile of satisfaction.

'Give the man a handful of nuts,' he said.

I sat stunned. So there was a connection after all. We always came back to Tiberius, to the emperor. The elder Julia. Her daughter. Paullus. Fabius and Postumus...

Ovid?

'You mean it was Tiberius? Tiberius framed Julia? His own wife?'

The smile disappeared. I'd missed something, obviously. But I couldn't see what it was.

'Marcus,' Pertinax said carefully, 'I don't usually talk politics. I crawled out of that particular sewer years ago and I've never regretted it. But I'm going to educate you, son. You've asked for it and you're going to get it. Tiberius is only half the story, and you're going to get the whole thing. Even if it kills you. As it well might if you're not careful. Very careful indeed. Remember that.'

I said nothing. Pertinax rose from the couch, brought over the wine jug and filled first my cup and then his own. 'The only reason—the only reason, boy!—that I'm telling you this is because you remind me so much of your grandfather. I think he would've trusted you and I think he would've wanted you to know. So pin your stupid privileged Roman-patrician ears back and listen.'

Varus to Himself

We were talking of treachery.

Mine, as you have seen, is a harmless thing, and hardly worth the name; a piece of diplomacy of which I am sure the emperor will approve but of which I am loath as yet to inform him. In the long run it will turn to Rome's benefit as well as being—rather more immediately, I hope—profitable to myself: to my mind, the perfect combination. I am certainly not a traitor in the grand style, as is Livia. If the gods regard treason and murder as crimes of any weight, then Augustus' wife is damned.

I am revealing no secrets here. The facts are known to most of the inner circle, not excluding Augustus. No doubt the empress, in common with most traitors (such as myself!) would say that she has acted for the good of the state. Perhaps she could even argue her point. One can also understand a mother's preference for her own son over the offspring of her predecessor. However, for Livia to further Tiberius's interests through subterfuge and false accusations is quite another matter. To put it plainly, the empress is a treacherous, murdering bitch.

Where are they all now, the Julians? Where are they, Augustus's own family, who should have followed him in honour? Call the roll. His only child, Julia, accused of a filthy crime she never committed, rotting in exile at Rhegium. Her sons Gaius and Lucius, whom Augustus was grooming for empire, dead, poisoned by their stepmother's agents. Their younger brother Postumus, slandered, disgraced and banished to Planasia. But for young Agrippina, a clean sweep...

Bitch!

Finally, a year past, the other Julia, Augustus's grandchild. Like her mother, exiled on a trumped-up charge, her husband executed for a conspiracy that was no conspiracy at all...

Bitch!

If there is any justice then Livia will burn, and her bastard of a son with her. And if I am a traitor then I thank the gods that at least I am a clean one.

CHAPTER

25

║ left Pertinax's early the next morning, my head still buzzing. I was glad now I'd brought the big sleeping carriage because it gave me the chance to think in comfort.

Oh, sure, the old guy hadn't told me anything I didn't know already, not as far as the facts went. How they all connected up was something else: like looking at a complex piece of embroidery from the back. I'd always known that the old empress was a callous bitch, but just how callous she was, and how much of a bitch, I hadn't even begun to suspect.

Yeah. So to get her blue-eyed boy's boil-encrusted bum on the throne Livia had stalked the Julians one by one and knocked them off their perches. That was fun to know, but, as my father had tried to tell me, it just wasn't relevant any more. After all, the Wart had become emperor, everything was sweetness and light, and only a fool bucks the system. The trouble was that something *wasn't* irrelevant. It hadn't lost its smell over the years, it wasn't common knowledge, and it had something to do with the Paullus plot. If I could just work out what that thing was then we were home and dry.

I was still thinking when the coachman gave a shout and the carriage stopped. I threw open the door and looked out.

That one look was enough. We were in trouble. Real trouble. We still had half a mile to go before joining the Appian Way and the track led over boggy ground across a line of wooden piles. Fifty yards ahead of us it had been blocked with a hurdle of sharpened stakes. We'd got zero room to turn, backing off was impossible, and from the look of the ground on either side, even the Sunshine Boys' horses wouldn't've made it more than a yard or so. Behind the hurdle stood a dozen mean-looking bastards wearing leather armour and holding short swords.

I ducked back inside. At least this time I'd come prepared. There're stiff penalties for arming slaves; have been ever since Spartacus's time. If we'd been in Rome I'd never have risked it, but out here in the sticks was another matter. In the baggage compartment under the seat were six cavalry longswords, which are serious weapons in anybody's book.

'Hey, boys!' I yelled to my Gauls. 'Look what Daddy's got!'

The guys' eyes lit up like fifty-lamp candelabra and they were already champing on their moustaches and grinding their teeth before they so much as touched the things. That figured. Put a Gaul within reach of a sword and it's like you've taken the lid off Tartarus. We might still be outnumbered two to one—the coachman and my body slave hardly counted—but things were looking brighter. Or so I thought when I drew my own sword and jumped down from the carriage to grab my bit of the action.

Mistake. I knew that as soon as the first guy went for me. The vicious punching stab was straight from the army manual, and it nearly spitted me. I slammed the carriage door sideways, catching him on the left shoulder and spinning him round, then brought my own sword up and shoved it in under the armpit where his jerkin would give no protection. One down. I glanced anxiously towards the Sunshine Boys. I needn't've worried. They were happily slogging it out on foot Gallic-style: no points for finesse, several million for enthusiasm. Three more of the bastards fell apart like carved chickens before you could say Vercingetorix.

The ones who were left shifted tactics, working as a team, which again was pure army. Out of the corner of my eye I saw Flavus, my body slave, go down to a thrust that turned his throat into a bloody mash. Then two of them jumped me at once and I felt the edge of a blade slice along my ribs. No pain, not yet. Without thinking I brought the heavy pommel of my sword down hard. It connected with the guy's wrist. Bone crunched, and he screamed. Before he could recover I buried the dagger I was holding in my left hand hilt-deep in his groin.

I stepped back just as what looked like a beanpole flew past my shoulder and thudded into the woodwork of the carriage. The second guy, sword drawn back to stab, saw it too. He looked behind me, eyes wide, then turned and ran. A second javelin spitted him like a hare.

I risked a look myself.

I couldn't believe it either.

'Hey, good shot, Titus!'

'Bull's-eye!'

'Ti-tus! Ti-tus! Ti—'

'Watch me! Hey, you guys, watch me!'

They swarmed over and around the barricade like a pack of frisky wolf-cubs, squeaky clean in their nice new armour. None of them could've been more than nineteen or less than five-ten, except for the decurion bringing up the rear, who was small and grey-haired, and red as a beetroot with yelling orders no one was listening to: 'Hey, you bastards! Keep together! You there, Marcus Sedilius, get that effing point up! Quintus, not the effing edge, you little bugger! If I've told you once I've told you a thousand times…'

It wasn't the time or place for it, I knew, but I couldn't help myself. Maybe it was hysteria. I sat down with my back against one of the coach wheels and laughed until the tears came while those kids took the bastards apart. Not that it was any great deal. The few still on their feet after the javelin volley probably didn't know what day it was or which way was up, let alone what had hit them. I only saw the youngsters in trouble once when a big guy with shoulders hunched like a bear had one of them backed up against the barricade. The decurion was between the two before you could say 'knife', and he finished the bastard off with as nice a parry, feint and thrust as I'd seen outside a demonstration bout.

When it was over he wiped his sword neatly on a clump of reeds, slid it back into a well-worn scabbard and came across to me.

'You all right, sir?' he said.

'Yeah. Yeah, I think so.' I looked round to check my team. Apart from Flavus we'd all made it out the other end. One of the Gauls had a cut shoulder, another was bleeding from a head wound and a third was limping, but they were all on their feet and I couldn't see any stray bits lying about the place. Not Gallic bits, anyway. Lysias the coachman had stayed well out of it, snug in his box. I made a mental note to dock the bugger of his perquisites when we got home. 'Thanks, friend.'

The decurion spat modestly. ''S nothing, sir. Lucky the lads and me was passing.'

'Recruits, are they?'

His boot of a face split into a grin that revealed teeth like tombstones.

''S right, sir. Trained 'em myself. We're on our way to Puteoli. Young Titus there heard the ruckus from the road.'

I saw something move out of the corner of my eye and spun round with my sword raised. One of the bodies at the edge of the group was up and sprinting back down the track, his hand pressed to the side of his blood-soaked jerkin.

'Marcus!' the decurion growled.

'No! Wait!' I shouted; but I was too late. The javelin had already caught the guy in the back of the neck and pitched him forwards like a struck rabbit.

'Wheee-ooh!'

'Way to go, Marcus!'

Evidently the star pupil. The decurion hadn't moved.

''Scuse me, sir,' he said politely. Then, turning on the cheering kids: 'How many effing times do I have to tell you buggers? Before you relax check your effing bodies. Whose was he?'

'Sorry, decurion.'

'Sorry's no use, young Quintus. Sorry don't butter no beans. You're on report, lad.' He turned back to me. 'Now, sir. Care to tell me what happened?'

I shrugged. 'They jumped us. That's about all I can tell you.' I wasn't going to give much away if I could help it. Even if the guy had saved my life.

The decurion cast an expert eye over the barricade. 'Waiting for you, sir, from the looks of things. Big gang too, and well armed. 'S not often you see something like that so close to a main road. You sure they wasn't after you special?'

'Why should they be after me?'

'You'd know that better than I would, sir.' A careful

answer, carefully delivered. The guy wasn't stupid, that was for sure. Not that he'd press the issue. I'd seen from the first that he'd taken in the quality of the carriage and the broad purple stripe on my tunic. He wasn't showing any interest in the swords my lads were holding, either. Which meant he'd noticed them, too.

'No reason that I can think of, decurion.'

He rubbed his nose with a finger that looked like it had been hacked from an olive stump. He didn't believe me, that was for sure. But disbelief is one thing. Calling a senatorial a liar to his face is another.

'Then it's a mystery, sir,' he said. 'Maybe we should've taken that last sod in and kicked his balls until he talked.'

Oh, yeah, I thought. Great. So now tell me something I don't know.

'Maybe it's not too late at that.' He wheeled round. 'Hey, you bastards! Any more live ones there?'

'Just stiffs, decurion,' the kid who'd thrown the javelin called back cheerfully.

'You sure this time, young Marcus?'

'Yes, decurion.'

'Shit!' He turned back to me. 'Never mind, sir. Can't be helped. Can I have your name, please? For the report, like?'

I knew better than to lie this time. Names were too easy to check up on.

'Corvinus,' I said. 'Valerius Messalla Corvinus.'

His eyes widened. 'Any relation to the consular, sir? Valerius Messalla Messalinus?'

'Yeah. He's my father.'

The decurion's face lit up. He threw me a flawless military salute.

'Sextus Pomponius, sir. Ex-PFC, third century, Twentieth Valerians. I served under your father in Illyria.'

Oh, whoopee. Just what I needed, an old boys' reunion. Still, the guy had done me a big favour. The least I could do was give him the courtesy of some small talk. 'You were in the Rebellion?'

''S right. When we near lost the whole effing province and then some. Pardon my language, sir.'

'How was my father? As a general?' I really wanted to know. If you believed what Dad said, when he'd fought his way through the Illyrian Revolt with the Wart he was Caesar and Alexander rolled into one. I'd be interested to know what the guys at the bottom had thought of him.

Pomponius's face set like concrete.

'He was okay, sir,' he said cautiously.

'But nothing special?'

'Doesn't apply, sir. The governor wasn't a soldier. Begging your pardon. Not his fault if he was more of a bum-on-the...more of an administrator, sir.'

I grinned. Oh, beautiful! He'd got Dad to a T. 'Sure. Go ahead, Pomponius. A bum-on-the-bench type describes my father perfectly.'

I got no answering smile. The decurion gave me a look like an old-fashioned matron whose pet parrot has just told her to piss off.

'Like I said, sir. The governor was okay. For a...for an administrator, sir.'

'What about Tiberius?'

Pomponius relaxed visibly.

'Tiberius,' he said simply, 'was the best effing general I ever served under, sir. Bar none.'

High praise, coming from this little guy. Pomponius had probably cut his first tooth chewing on a helmet.

'I'd heard he wasn't too popular with the men,' I said.

'Sure, he was hard, sir. Maybe too hard. But you knew

where you were with the general. Even when we was belly-aching the years before the frontiers blew up there was never a word against Tiberius personal. Maybe he's First Citizen now, sir, but the general's got the Eagles in his blood. He's army first and last, no flash, a real professional. You can't catch fish by grabbing their tails, you've got to take things careful. Look at old Varus, he…'

'Hey, decurion! Come and see this!' It was smartass Marcus again. The javelin king. He was crouching over the guy I'd killed by the coach.

We went over. The dead man was lying face-up, his right arm thrown out sideways with the hand bent back.

'Look at his wrist.' The kid pointed. On the inside of the forearm was a blue ram.

'Fuck,' Pomponius said softly.

I'd only seen this sort of thing on Gauls before. They go in for it a lot, even in the more civilised parts. The skin's punctured with needles in the shape of a design and then dye rubbed into the wounds. It doesn't come off even with scraping. My four lads were covered in the stuff.

'Mean something to you, decurion?' I tried to keep my voice level.

'Sure. It's a legionary badge, sir. Fifth Alaudae.'

Yeah. That made sense. The Larks, being a Gallic legion, would go in for tattoos. So the guy had been army right enough.

'You know where the Fifth's based these days?'

It was like asking a baker if he'd ever heard of bread. The decurion gave me a withering look.

'Sure I know, sir. Vetera.'

Vetera. In Germany.

The guy had served with a legion on the Rhine.

I sat back on my heels and thought.

CHAPTER 26

It was late when I got back, so I had the coachman drop me off at Perilla's.

We turned in early, as soon as I'd made my report. She was worried at first about the sword-slice along my ribs, but at Pomponius's insistence I'd had the wound looked at on the way and it wasn't too bad. Certainly not bad enough to cramp my style after a two days' absence.

'It must be all that fresh air, Marcus,' she said after we'd finished. 'Either that or being ambushed agrees with you.'

'It's the oyster stew. Pertinax insisted I have three helpings.'

I could feel her laughing. 'Pig!'

'Pigs don't eat oysters.'

'Anyway, they'd've worn off by now.'

'Not Baian ones. They're the best in the world.'

Her arms tightened round me, and she kissed the side of my neck.

'I love you,' she said.

'Uhuh.'

We lay quiet for a long time.

'Perilla,' I said. 'I've had a thought.'

'Hmmm?'

'About the Paullus plot. Maybe…'

She groaned. 'Not now, Marcus! Please!'

'You don't want to hear it?'

'You haven't got a single ounce of romance in you. Did you know that?'

'I'm just exhausted. I think better when I'm exhausted.'

She smiled up at me. 'Very well. So what's this great thought of yours?'

'No. If you don't want to hear, you don't want to hear.'

'Corvinus…'

'Okay. Okay,' I said hastily. 'You're sure?'

'I'm sure.'

'Fine.' I turned over and lay on my back, hands behind my head. 'We're assuming the plot was against Augustus, right?'

'Of course. Who else could it be against?'

'The empress.'

Perilla lifted herself on her elbow and stared down at me. 'Livia?'

'Why not? If she was systematically knocking off the Julians you'd expect them to turn sooner or later. They wouldn't just lie back and take it.'

'Corvinus, that's silly!'

'No it isn't. Listen. Say the main aim was to put the skids under Livia. Gaius and Lucius are already dead, but the elder Julia and Postumus are both sitting on their islands twiddling their thumbs. So what would happen if someone sprung them and smuggled them off somewhere Livia couldn't get at them?'

Perilla sighed. 'Absolutely nothing.'

Wrong answer.

'Why the hell not?'

'Because Augustus may not have liked the idea of Tiberius as a successor, but by this time he didn't have much choice. Even if he knew that Livia was manipulating things, which I personally doubt.'

I shook my head. 'You're missing the point. Livia had got away with it so far either because she operated an under-the-counter scam or because she used Augustus to do her dirty work for her. The poor guy had no choice but to play the patsy because she'd cancelled all his other options.'

Perilla turned over on her side.

'I've changed my mind,' she said. 'Could we leave this for the morning please?'

'No, listen.' I tugged at the blanket. 'The only way the Julians could fight back was to change the rules. If they could find a sympathetic military commander on one of the frontiers and manage to get to him, then they'd be home free where Livia couldn't touch them.'

Perilla groaned. 'Corvinus, come on! You know perfectly well that the emperor controls military appointments. Commanders have to be loyal before they're chosen. Completely loyal. And even if one wasn't, he'd be cutting his own throat to take in political escapees. Now let's leave this, please. You may not need your sleep, but I do.'

She pulled the blanket over her head. I pulled it off her.

'Okay,' I said. 'But there's another angle we haven't thought of. That Augustus knew about the plot from the beginning.'

The eyes opened. Perilla sat up.

'But we know he did! Silanus was the emperor's agent!'

'From the beginning, I said. Not when it'd already been set up. Maybe even from before the beginning.'

'I'm sorry. I don't understand.'

'Look.' I pulled myself up and leaned my back against the headboard. 'We're assuming the plot was directed against Livia, right?'

'Fair enough.'

'Augustus knows she had his grandsons Gaius and Lucius murdered. He knows she fixed it so he was persuaded to exile his daughter Julia and Postumus. He knows all this, but like you said he can't do a thing about it. It's too late, he's hamstrung. Livia's won, and all he has left is the Wart.'

'But why does he go along with her? He's still the emperor.'

'Okay, so Augustus has Livia arrested. He goes to the Senate, denounces her as a murderess and traitor, reverses the sentences on Julia and Postumus, and sends the Wart off to pick his boils in Corsica. What happens then?'

She was frowning. 'He'd destroy his own credibility completely.'

'Yeah. Right. And in the end what would he be left with? Livia exiled or dead. The Wart disgraced, maybe even in armed revolt. Postumus too young for real power. Oh, sure, he'd have the satisfaction of knowing that justice had been done, but he'd've pulled up the beans with the weeds pretty thoroughly.'

'But if Augustus wanted to stop Livia he wouldn't have done it that way.'

'So how would he have done it?'

'Not openly. He would have—' Perilla stopped. Her jaw sagged and I knew the point had gone home.

'That's right. He'd've acted secretly, set up a conspiracy of his own.'

'For heaven's sake, Marcus! That's crazy!'

'No, it fits. Look. Julia and her grandfather come to an

arrangement. Augustus can't do anything directly, but he promises her and Paullus his support. He'll turn a blind eye to the Julian "conspiracy" while it's in preparation, and he'll help them in the final stages.'

'Help them how?'

'I told you. By making sure they have somewhere to go. Somewhere they'll be safe and give him room to breathe at the same time, maybe work out some way of making things up to them.' My brain was racing. 'Perilla, that explains our fourth conspirator! Remember we said whoever it was would have to be pretty powerful to give them the clout they needed for the thing to work? What if the fourth conspirator was Augustus himself?'

'Oh, for Jupiter's sake!'

'You think that's too far-fetched? Okay, so maybe our guy isn't Augustus in person. But he's someone who could stand as his accredited rep. One of the big legionary commanders, say, or the soon-to-be commanders. Even a military governor. Maybe someone like...'

I stopped.

'Someone like who?'

'Someone like Quinctilius Varus,' I said quietly.

'Marcus, I repeat. This is crazy!'

I shook my head. 'No it isn't. Varus would be perfect, and the timing's right. He's the emperor's man, he's even married to Augustus's grand-niece. With him on the team the Julians will have somewhere to go, because when Paullus springs the others Augustus will already have given Varus Germany.'

Perilla was holding her head in her hands as if it would burst.

'All right,' she said. 'So if the conspiracy had the emperor's secret support, then why did he destroy it?'

'Because he was forced to. Because he had to cut his losses and get out of the game. Because someone peached to Livia.'

'Someone? Like who?'

'Our original stool-pigeon, of course. Junius Silanus.'

'Corvinus, that's nonsense. You told me that Augustus rewarded Silanus. Would he have done that if the man had double-crossed him?'

'Sure he would. Even if it meant sacrificing Julia. He didn't have any choice. He had to cut himself off from the conspiracy completely, which meant siding with the guy who betrayed it. Maybe Silanus's silence was part of the deal.'

Perilla had turned on to her side.

'Marcus, I'm tired and this is complicated,' she said. 'Perhaps it'll all sound better in the morning.'

I ignored her. 'There's another thing. We already have a German connection. The dead guy with the tattoo on his wrist served in a German legion.'

'Tell me tomorrow,' she murmured.

'But in that case who sent him and his mates, and why? Livia? The Wart? Someone else?'

There was no answer; and when I looked Perilla was asleep.

Varus to Himself

Arminius and I have kept in touch, of course, through Ceionius's good offices. I was right to use him. The man is a natural conspirator. Our partnership has been a profitable one for all parties: for Arminius, for myself, and, potentially, for Rome. Under the guise of fulfilling my military obligations I have managed in this campaigning season to draw the teeth of his private enemies among the German chieftains; with the result that he is well on his way to the pre-eminence which is our aim.

The last stage of the plan is the most difficult of all. The first part is over. As agreed, I have allowed myself and my army to be drawn off our line of march towards the Teutoburg. On the fringes of the forest, Arminius will attack us in full force. I will order a withdrawal, and Arminius will claim to have inflicted a defeat and proved himself to his allies beyond a doubt. My army will be intact, and I will lead it back to the Rhine. The Germans will give the credit to Arminius and spill more beer at the victory feast than they did blood in the battle. Germans love a winner, and a Roman 'defeat', no matter how token, will do more to unite the tribes under Arminius's aegis than a hundred speeches.

Naturally there will be questions asked in Rome. My defence will be unanswerable: that I reassessed the situation and the risks and decided reluctantly to abandon the advance. I will be criticised, but not overly blamed. Then I will withdraw quietly from public life (my old carcass, after all, can have very few years left in it) and enjoy the rewards of a career tarnished only slightly at its close. Arminius's gold will be a great solace to me in my misfortune. I wish him well, and every success.

Tomorrow we should enter the Teutoburg proper. My scouts report no hostile forces so far, yet the 'battle' cannot be far off—half a day's march, at most. It cannot come too soon for me—the weather is worsening and these German forests are terrible places, even when one does not believe in what superstitious natives call the *Waldgespenst*. Let us hope that Arminius does not keep us waiting long.

The night is cold, and I can hear the rain battering on the roof and walls of my tent. I have told Agron to warm me some wine. Perhaps it will help me sleep.

CHAPTER 27

When I got home next morning there was a slave kicking his heels outside my front door.

'Master wants to see you,' he said.

I groaned. After last night I'd been looking forward to a quiet day loafing in the garden, followed by another few dozen Baian oysters. 'This master of yours got a name?'

'Sure. Scylax.'

I felt the first prickle of excitement. 'He say what it was about?'

'Nah.'

I recognised the guy now: the big Spaniard who kept the sand raked in Scylax's exercise yard. 'You didn't think of telling my slave Bathyllus, I suppose? He knew where I was.'

The sarcasm bounced off like dried chickpeas from a breastplate. The guy didn't even blink.

'Master said I was to see you personal,' he said. 'You weren't in, so I waited. Till you were in, like.'

This boy was wasted raking sand. I could've used him as a doorstop.

'Okay, sunshine,' I said. 'Give me a chance to fetch the lads and I'll be right with you.'

Scylax was binding a new grip on a wooden training sword when we walked in. His eyes shifted from me to my four Gauls and I saw them widen. Three of the lads looked pretty chewed, but they were happy as hell after their scrap and I hadn't had the heart to trade them in for new models.

'Daphnis found you all right, then,' he said.

'Daphnis?'

Scylax shrugged. 'Not my fault. The poor bastard had the name when I bought him.' He laid the sword aside. 'I've got the information you wanted.'

I could feel my heart speeding up. 'You've found Big Fritz?'

'Yeah. Pure fluke. His name's Agron and he's got a metalsmith's shop in the Subura.'

'Whereabouts in the Subura?'

'Let me get my boots on and I'll take you.'

I shook my head. 'Oh, no. I'm grateful, believe me, but this is my business. I'll take care of things from here on in myself.'

'No chance.' Scylax stood up. In his bare feet he was even shorter than usual. 'I've found your boy for you. Now I want a piece of the action. Or at least an explanation.'

'Look, Scylax, don't crowd me, okay? I'll tell you later. Promise.'

'Screw your later.' He stood square in front of me like a concrete block. 'Come on, Corvinus. You owe me. And whatever trouble you're in is getting worse. So now tell me I'm wrong.'

'Things're hotting up, yeah,' I said reluctantly.

'Another fight?'

'Just a titchy one.'

'Titchy one, hell.' Scylax's slabwood face split in a grin and he nodded towards the Sunshine Boys. 'It'd only take me a month to turn any one of these marblecrushers into a first-rate gladiator. That's a four-man army you've got there, boy, and it still gets dented. Who were the opposition? Praetorians?'

'Near enough.' I hesitated, wondering how little I could get away with. 'You ever heard of a gang of legionaries turning bandit?'

Scylax's jaw dropped. 'You got mugged by legionaries?'

'Only one of them qualified for sure that I know of. But the rest had regular army stamped all over them.'

'Fuck!' He spat on to the bare boards at his feet. 'How many?'

'A dozen. Maybe more. I didn't count.'

'No wonder you got creased.' He was staring at me. 'You're lucky to be alive, friend.'

'We had help. A squad of Rome's finest who happened to be passing and needed the exercise.' I told him the story. 'So what's your explanation?'

'You get them sometimes. Men who've been drummed out. Thieves. Cowards. Runners. But not that many, not in Italy, and not bunched together in dozens.' He paused. 'Not freelance, anyway.'

'That's what I thought.'

'You got someone's back up recently, boy? Someone bigger even than you are, with military connections?'

'I might've done. Look, Scylax, I'm not holding out on you but I don't want you involved.'

'Screw that.' Scylax had picked up a pair of thick hobnail soldier's boots and was putting them on. 'From what you tell me this Agron guy could be trouble, private army or not. And I'm not having my patron carried home on a board for nobody. Okay?'

'Okay.' I conceded defeat. Not that I had much option. 'Suit yourself. Only if you find in the near future that you and your balls have parted company don't say I didn't warn you.'

He grinned, and we set off for the Subura.

We were walking along Tuscan Road, the Sunshine Boys doing their battering-ram routine with the crowds so we could actually move in a straight line at a decent speed. Mind you, we'd've been okay even without the lads. No one crowds Scylax.

'You want to tell me how you tracked the guy down?' I said.

'It was a fluke.' Scylax frowned. 'Couple of days ago this friend of mine gets involved with a knifeman outside the Shrine of Libera and busts the hilt of his dagger on the guy's front teeth. He goes into the nearest metalsmith's to get it fixed and guess who's swinging the hammer?'

'Your friend didn't give himself away, I hope.'

'Nah.' Scylax spat into the roadway. 'He's subtle, old Bassus. Just got his knife fixed, paid for it and left. We won't be expected, don't you worry.'

We'd passed the spice-sellers now and were into the per-fume-makers' stretch. I stopped at one of the better-class booths and poked about a bit, but there wasn't anything Perilla would touch with a ten-foot pole. Scylax bought a tub of bright yellow cream from a guy squatting on the pavement.

'Piss-awful stuff, but it keeps off the flies when you sweat.' He passed it over. 'You want to try some?'

I took a cautious sniff and nearly threw up.

'What the hell is that?'

'Jupiter knows. Guy calls it Gorilla Juice.'

'I'll take the flies any day.' I passed the box back. 'What did you say Big Fritz's name was?'

'Agron. Bassus got that much. The guy's an Illyrian, like we thought.' Scylax stopped suddenly. 'Okay, I've done my bit, boy, and now it's your turn. Let's take some time out for explanations.'

I sighed. 'Look, I can't tell you, okay? Not yet. Later, maybe, when this thing starts to make more sense. But not now.'

Scylax shook his head and carried on walking. 'You're in trouble all right, boy,' he said. 'Right up to the eyeballs.'

We were well into the Subura by now, and I could see the Shrine of Libera up ahead, half hidden in the ramshackle chaos of the hawkers' booths and the swarming crowds of Rome's poorest citizens. No wonder Scylax hadn't been able to track the guy down. Even leaving numbers aside, the Subura's a law to itself. If you're part of it you can disappear like water into sand, and it'll lie itself blue to hide you.

'That's Metalsmiths' Row on the left,' Scylax said. 'Agron's shop should be about halfway down.'

We found it, and it was closed. Seriously closed. Heavy wooden shutters had been pulled across the entrance and fixed with a metal padlock.

'Maybe he just took the day off.' Scylax sounded guilty.

'Oh, sure! Like for his grandmother's funeral. We're just through with the Floralia, for Jupiter's sake! Who the hell takes a day off at this time of year?'

'You looking for Agron?'

I turned round. A little fat guy had come out of the cook-shop next door holding a slathery bunch of what I hoped were sausage skins.

'Yeah. Know where he is, friend?'

'Your name Corvinus?'

Shit. 'Yeah, that's me.'

The guy gave me a look like I'd just sodomised his pet cat.

'He said you might be round after your friend called to get his knife fixed.' So much for Scylax's Bassus. Sure, he was subtle all right. Subtle as a ton of concrete. 'Said to tell you he was sorry to've missed you but that he'll be in touch if your nose is still troubling you. That make sense?'

Despite myself, I laughed.

'What's funny?' Scylax demanded.

'Nothing. Private joke.' The guy might be an enemy but he had style. Style and brains. Ovid's last name was Naso, the Nose, so it was a double pun.

'You know where he went?' Scylax turned back to the sausage seller.

'Nah.' The man disappeared back into his shop. Scylax was going in after him but I pulled him back.

'Let's take this easy,' I said. 'You'll scare him off.'

'I'll feed the little fucker to his own customers. They won't know the difference.'

'Easy!' I pushed past him and went into the shop. The guy was already stuffing the skins with a disgusting mess from a cracked bowl. His shop smelt of burned grease, cheap olive oil, and long-dead meat. 'You sell them, friend, or just make them?'

The man scowled. 'Blood puddings, meatballs or Lucanian sausage?'

'Real Lucanian sausage? All the way from Luca?'

The fat fingers gave the filled tube a vicious twist. 'You on the stage or something, pal?'

'Okay. Just grill us up a couple of your best, right?' I remembered the Sunshine Boys waiting patiently outside. 'Make it a dozen.'

I took a gold piece from my pouch and threw it on the table. The shopkeeper's eyes went straight to it, but he kept his hands in the bowl.

'Sausages're two coppers each,' he said. His eyes never left the coin. He wouldn't make that much, I knew, in a month.

'So we're rich mugs,' I said. 'Now tell us about Agron. And don't forget the sausages because my lads outside get nervous when they're hungry, okay?'

'You're wasting your time.' He reached up to the hook above his head, pulled down a string of sausages, and laid them on the grease-blackened grill. 'I don't know nothing.'

'Come on, Corvinus, let me handle this.' Scylax spoke quietly. He didn't move a muscle but the fat cook showed the whites of his eyes. Scylax has that effect on people.

'Last chance, sunshine,' I said. 'Before I let my friend here ask the questions. What's your name anyway?'

'Tarquin.'

'Fuck!' Scylax muttered.

I ignored him. 'Right, Tarquin. Take it slow and easy and just tell us what you know.'

'Look, I've told you, I don't know nothing!'

'That's right. Start at the beginning, take us through the middle and stop when you come to the end. The guy's Illyrian, right?'

The fat man sighed.

'Yeah,' he said. 'Comes from Singidunum, wherever the hell that is.'

'On the Danube, west of Sirmium.'

'Yeah. Right. Whatever. If you say so. He came here first about nine, ten years back. Maybe twelve, I can't remember. Patron bought him the business and set him up nicely.'

'Who's his patron?'

'How the hell should I know? You purple-striped bastards're all the same.'

'Watch your mouth,' Scylax grunted.

'So he's an ex-slave?' I said.

Tarquin eased the tip of a spatula beneath the half-cooked
sausages and flipped them over with a deft twist of the wrist.
'Nah. Soldier. Patron used to be a military man out that way.
When he got his discharge he tagged along with the guy to
Rome.'

Jupiter Best and Greatest! 'You ever see him? The patron,
I mean?'

'Nah. What'd one of your lot be doing round here? Present
company excepted, of course.'

'Agron ever mention his name?'

'Nah. And I never asked neither.'

'He's still around?'

'The patron? Search me. Maybe he is, maybe he isn't.' He
reached into a crock and pulled out two greasy, stale-looking
loaves. 'Maybe he's pushing up the daisies someplace. How
many plates you want?'

'We'll take them with us. That's all you can tell us?'

'That's it.' He picked up the gold piece and slipped it into
the pouch round his waist. 'Enjoy your meal, gents.'

We fed the bread and sausages to the Sunshine Boys, who
wolfed them down as if they hadn't seen food for a month. I
thought they'd toss their guts up on the way home but they did-
n't. Gauls must have cast-iron stomachs. Or maybe they just like
five-day-old dog.

So Big Fritz had been a soldier. And his patron had been a
military man who'd held a command 'out that way'. Although
it was tantalising, that particular gobbet of information didn't
get me very far. 'Out that way' to a guy like Tarquin could mean

anywhere from the Rhine to Thrace. Or even at a push south to Spain or Egypt. And the 'military man' could've been anyone from Tiberius down to Pomponius the decurion. He could even be my father...

I dropped Scylax off back at the gym and went home. I didn't go round to Perilla's that evening. Bathyllus couldn't find any oysters and anyway I didn't have the energy.

Varus to Himself

We have been marching all day. The weather is worsening, the road is no more than a track. The attack should have come this morning, at the edge of the forest, but there has been nothing, there has been nothing, only minor skirmishing between my outriders and an enemy who slip back into the trees like ghosts and draw them on to their deaths...

Where is the German army? Where is Arminius? He has betrayed me. Set it down, Varus. Set it down, you fool. He has betrayed me.

Trust. Yet he is Roman. Fabius said it. Fabius said it. Arminius is more Roman than I am...

I believed in him!

Traitor. Traitor. Venal, gullible traitor!

We could go back. We could still go back. But then what of Rome? I have let him gather his army, I have helped him unite the tribes. I am responsible, no one else, and I must be the one to destroy him. If we can pass this forest we will be in his own heartland, and we are still three legions. If we only had a map. Guides...

Vela has come and gone, asking—begging—for orders. I smelled his fear, the forest-fear that he has kept bottled up throughout the march, which I mistook for knowledge of my treachery. I told him to burn the surplus baggage carts. If we are to come through this and smash Arminius then we must move quickly. We are still an army...

I am deceiving myself. We are dead. All of us.

Traitor!

CHAPTER

28

My head was so full that night that I couldn't sleep. Instead I sent Bathyllus for a flask of mulled wine and settled down in my study to think things over.

The Illyrian Rebellion had almost crippled us. Sure, we pulled through eventually—the good old Roman Eagle always does, somehow—but it had taken two years for the situation to be normalised; which means we smashed the buggers. End of story, and hooray for us.

Only it wasn't the end. A year or so later Quinctilius Varus is massacred with three full legions in the Teutoburg, the northern frontier defences are suddenly non-existent, and the Roman Eagle is up the creek without a paddle for the second time in three years.

And in between the two disasters Augustus's granddaughter gets caught with her pants down while her husband Paullus goes for broke conspiring against the emperor. Or whoever...

There had to be a link. The Paullus conspiracy had to fit in somewhere. And how it fitted in, I was sure, hinged on the identity of our fourth conspirator.

So what about Varus as a candidate? Standing in, as I'd suggested to Perilla, for Augustus himself? I sipped the mulled wine and went over in my mind what I knew about the guy. Exconsul. Governor of Africa, then military governor of Syria, where he put down the Jewish revolt. Finally appointed by Augustus to be his personal viceroy in Germany...

Of which task he made the most almighty balls-up within living memory.

I shook my head. It didn't make sense. Oh, sure, given that Augustus was playing the conspirators' game, or pretending to, Varus was the natural choice for the job. He was the emperor's man beyond question, and he had a lifetime's experience as a diplomat and a general. A good all-rounder, experienced, tried and tested over a career stretching back thirty-odd years...

So how the hell had a guy like that managed to make such an almighty cock-up? How had the man who'd put down the Jewish revolt practically single-handed let himself be outgeneralled by a pack of unshaven louts who couldn't form a tortoise to save themselves?

The usual excuse was Arminius: a clever, smooth-talking Romanised bastard who'd twisted the poor senile governor round his little finger and then stamped on his balls. But that, I felt, wouldn't wash. Varus wasn't senile, he wasn't a military tyro, and as an ex-governor of Syria he'd dealt with guys that would've run rings round Arminius without so much as working up a sweat. So there had to be another explanation, and the obvious one was good enough to be going on with.

Varus's cock-up was intentional, and something had gone wrong.

The jug was almost empty. I tipped the last of the mulled wine into my cup and considered shouting for Bathyllus to bring me some more; but it was late, I'd already sent the little guy to bed, and I suspected that another jugful would be one too much for me. I sipped at what was left, spinning it out.

Say at the start Varus had been quite genuinely Augustus's agent, his job being to guarantee the conspirators the protection of the Rhine legions. Only then Augustus tells the old guy that he's changed his mind, and that now Varus will be stringing the conspirators along. No legionary backing, no final bolthole. The whole thing's suddenly a sham. But maybe the scam's too tempting. Maybe Varus thinks that the way things are going the conspirators have a better-than-even chance of pulling it off. And even although it involves a certain amount of risk his treason's in a good cause because Augustus would secretly welcome the chance to throw the Wart out on his boil-studded arse. Also, if Postumus makes it past the starting gate then Varus is going to be very, very popular with the new regime. So Varus decides to carry on playing it for real. He sets out to screw up Germany, alienate the army, and force the emperor to do what the poor bastard really wants to do all along.

Yeah, I thought. I'd go for that as a working theory. Except that if Varus had double-crossed Augustus, then why should the emperor cover up for him instead of nailing him by his foreskin to the Senate House gates?

Shit. I swallowed the last of the mulled wine at a gulp. Varus was too good a candidate to pass up that easily. It was a shame the old bastard was dead. Maybe I could find a Babylonian necromancer and get him to call his spirit up from Tartarus or wherever. Bathyllus would know at least a dozen…

Then I remembered. I had one more valid option. Varus himself might be dead but his sister Quinctilia was still alive.

Maybe she could tell me something. I thought of waking Bathyllus and sending him round to arrange a meeting, but of course it was far too late. Anyway, I was finally getting sleepy. That last mouthful of mulled wine had been one too many. Tomorrow morning would be early enough. I settled back on the couch and closed my eyes.

I was at a dinner party. Round the central table, lit by hanging oil lamps, reclined three figures. Silanus I recognised at once. He lay on the couch to my left dressed in an expensive party mantle, his arm draped across the shoulder of a naked woman who stared up at him with dead, empty eyes. The other guy, on the host's couch, was propped up on his left elbow, his pose stiff and formal, like the figure on an old tomb. His face was covered by a wax death mask.

They were waiting, I knew, for the principal guest to arrive. The dining-room doors swung open and a fourth man came in. He moved stiffly as if his limbs were not flesh and blood but stone. Silanus rose to his feet and led the man formally to the guest couch. He reclined, and in the light of the lamps I saw his face for the first time. It was cold, chiselled marble—the face of the dead emperor who stares down with fish-white eyes from the top of his mausoleum in the Field of Mars.

Augustus.

Silanus clapped his hands, once, and went back to his place. The doors opened again and Davus came in, the wound in his throat gaping and bloodless. He carried a tray down the length of the room and set it on the table. On the tray was a pastry map of the world and a cavalry longsword. Without a word he handed the sword hilt first to Augustus.

As the marble hand took the sword the atmosphere changed. Silanus and the woman leaned across the table, their eyes fixed on the pastry map. The dead man didn't move, but his wax mask seemed to take on an air of expectancy. The Augustus-statue rose to its feet, the sword held in a two-handed grip, its point hovering above the map's centre. Everything was suddenly very still.

Then the sword swung once... twice. Blood spurted on to the map, soaking the pastry, and two heads bounced and rolled across the table, one with a woman's braids, the other still wearing its mask. Silanus hadn't moved. Now he smiled up at the Augustus figure and nodded.

The statue raised its eyes and looked straight at me. It, too, was smiling. Slowly, horribly, with the grating sound of stone on stone, the head began to turn on the marble column that was its neck. Further and further it turned, beyond what I knew was humanly possible, until the face was in complete profile and I saw that it was not one face but two...

Two faces, one looking forward, the other back, like the statues of the door god Janus.

The head continued to turn, like the upper stone of a mill. The room faded and there was only the head and the terrible grating noise. I screamed...

And woke, sweating. Grey half-light shone through my study window, bringing with it the rumble of iron cartwheels on the stone surface of the street beyond.

CHAPTER

29

I thought about the dream while Bathyllus hot-footed it round to old Quinctilia's. Most of it was pretty obvious. The naked woman was Julia, the guy with the death mask Paullus. Even Augustus was no surprise. I'd've expected the fourth man to be Varus, but after all he was only the emperor's stand-in. The only thing I didn't get was the business with the head. That was weird.

Maybe, I thought, I should see an augur.

Bathyllus came back with the news that the Lady Quinctilia would see me right away. That sounded promising. I whistled up the lads and set off for the Caelian. For once I took a litter. I was still pretty whacked after my disturbed night, and anyway I wanted to think about how I was going to play this. You don't just stroll into a Roman matron's house, accuse her dead brother of five different kinds of treason, and expect to be asked to stay to dinner.

Not that Quinctilia would have any illusions, of course.

Politicians need scapegoats, and Varus had carried the can for the whole German fiasco. Still, incompetence was one thing, outright treachery another. I'd have to be careful where I put my feet with Quinctilia.

We pulled up outside the door in great style. I rearranged my freshly laundered mantle—Quinctilia was one of the old breed and wouldn't appreciate a caller with gravy stains down his front—and signed to one of the litter-bearers to knock. I gave my name to the door slave and was ushered straight into the atrium.

The old girl had obviously decided on a formal reception. She was sitting by the ornamental pool dressed in an impeccably draped mantle and elaborate wig. Behind her a guy in late middle age stood with his hand on her shoulder. Probably her son, I thought. Certainly, given the heavy jowls which were common to both of them, a close relative. Neither was smiling, and in front of them set square on was an empty chair.

Shit. So much for the softly-softly approach. I felt suddenly like a man accused of murder walking into a courtroom where the judge is itching to try out a new kind of axe.

'Valerius Corvinus.'

No salutation. No 'Pleased to meet you'. Just the name, delivered in tones that'd freeze the arse off an Alpine chamois. I reckoned the Lady Quinctilia could give even Perilla lessons.

'That's right, Lady Quinctilia. I've come...'

'I know why you've come. Sit down. This is my nephew Lucius Asprenas.'

Fat Face nodded. You couldn't've prised his lips apart with a crowbar.

I eased myself into the chair. The old woman bent forwards to stare at me as if she were about to whisper a secret; but when she did speak it wasn't to me. And she didn't whisper either.

'You're there, Agron?'

'Yes, madam.'

'Then you had better join us as well.'

I whipped round. There was Big Fritz, large as life and twice as ugly, standing behind my chair. He must've followed me in and I hadn't heard a thing. The guy could've given a panther lessons and worn hobnail boots while he did it.

'Sit still, Corvinus,' he said. 'No one's going to hurt you if you behave yourself.'

'That's quite enough, Agron.' Quinctilia turned back to me. Her eyes were curiously pale and empty. 'Forgive him, young man. You're quite safe here, I assure you.'

Oh, yeah. Sure. Safe as a lamb chop in a wolf's den. I cursed myself for having left the Sunshine Boys outside; but there again who'd've thought I'd need them against a respectable old biddy like Quinctilia? It just showed you that you can't go by appearances.

'So I'm right,' I said. 'Varus was our fourth conspirator.'

Fat Face Asprenas shot me a look that would've curdled milk. I didn't see Agron's reaction, but from the hiss of indrawn breath you can bet he wasn't choking back a belly-laugh.

'I'm afraid I don't quite follow you,' Quinctilia said coldly. She was staring at a point about six inches past my left ear.

I sat more easily on my chair. Lounged, almost. When you have your back to the wall and there's no place else to go, look confident.

'Come on, lady,' I said. 'You know what I mean. Your brother was Augustus's agent in the Paullus plot. Only he got greedy and sold the emperor out.'

'Watch your mouth, Corvinus!' Agron whispered.

The old woman's expression was a mixture of distaste and puzzlement. 'I really must insist that you explain, young man.'

Jupiter! She'd got this respectable elderly dowager act polished to perfection!

'Okay.' I sat up straighter. 'If that's how you want to play it then fine. Augustus got your brother to offer a safe haven to the elder Julia and Postumus when they'd been sprung from exile. It was a put-up job because the emperor wanted to pull the teeth of the Julian faction. Only Varus had his own ideas. He played it for real and went over to the Opposition.' No reaction. I decided to up the aggro. 'So what did Paullus and Julia promise him, lady? For screwing up the northern frontier and putting the bite on the emperor? Money? A share of the political action? Or maybe just another lucrative governorship out east somewhere?'

Quinctilia turned to her nephew. 'Lucius? Will you answer the young man or shall I?'

Her expression hadn't changed. Fat Face, on the other hand, was staring at me as if I'd thrown up into the ornamental pool.

'Go on, Corvinus,' he said. 'Let's hear you prove it.' Something about his voice told me he didn't think I could; but both of them listened without expression or comment as I took them through the main points.

I'd expected flat denials, outrage, maybe even a veiled threat or two. What I got was silence.

Then Quinctilia stood up. Although she stooped she was taller than I'd thought, and from the set of her mouth I reckoned even in her old age she was one hell of a strong-minded lady. I began for the first time to feel less sure of myself. I'd've felt happier in a way if they'd denied everything and had the door slave pitch me out on my ear.

'Excuse us for a moment, Valerius Corvinus.' She reached out and gripped Asprenas's arm. 'My nephew and I have things to discuss. Agron, entertain our guest, please.'

I half rose to my feet, but the big Illyrian's hand pushed me back down.

'You heard the mistress,' he said. 'Just take it easy, right?'

Quinctilia, with Fat Face supporting her by the arm, disappeared into the living quarters proper at the back of the house. Agron took the chair she'd been sitting in, pulled it over until I was within reach, and sat down facing me.

'You're a real shit, you know that, Corvinus?' he said. 'I should've killed you when I had the chance. Or left you to these knifemen to finish.'

Good start. Obviously the guy had eccentric notions of entertainment.

'So why didn't you?'

'I told you that at the time. I didn't like the odds. And the mistress wouldn't've been pleased.'

'You were Varus's protégé, weren't you?' So long as we were having this cosy few minutes to ourselves I reckoned I might as well fill myself in with a bit of the background. 'Where did you meet up? Germany?'

'That's right.' He smiled without humour. 'I got into the legions by the back door when Tiberius was recruiting around Sirmium.' So Scylax had been right about that as well. I only hoped I'd live long enough to tell him. 'After the troubles were over we were sent to the Rhineland. I was the general's orderly.'

This was something I hadn't expected. 'You were on the final march?'

'Sure. Don't be so surprised. Some of us survived. Not many.'

'I thought the Germans didn't take any prisoners.'

'They didn't. Not ones that lived long anyway. I survived because I hid and then fought my way back to the Rhine. It pays sometimes to be good at killing. And I'm good, Corvinus, believe me. Very good.'

I let that last bit go. 'You mean you were a deserter.'

'No,' he said quietly. 'By the time I decided it was no use fighting any more there wasn't an army to desert from. And don't ever call me that again, friend.'

'Uh, yeah.' Jupiter! Why didn't I keep my big mouth shut? 'So you saw what happened? At the end?'

He regarded me levelly before answering; and when the answer came it was slow and considered.

'Sure, I saw. And I'll tell you something for free, Corvinus. It's important and I want you to remember it. The general may've had his faults, he may have made mistakes, but whatever they were he paid for them. He fought to the end and he died well. You understand me?'

'Yeah.' My palms were sweating. This quiet-spoken guy scared the shit out of me, and I'm not ashamed to admit it. 'Yeah, I understand. You want to tell me what happened?'

He shrugged and turned away. 'Why not? But don't expect a word against the general. Like I say, Varus has paid his dues already. Maybe it'll save the mistress some pain later. If you've got a later.'

This guy was a real bundle of fun. Trouble was, it sounded like he meant it. My throat was dry and there wasn't a cup of wine in sight.

'Okay.' Agron leaned back. 'So we're on our way back from the Weser to Vetera. The general gets reports that the Cherusci are arming. He decides to follow them up and we turn east towards the Teutoburg...'

'Just like that? Cut across dangerous country that late in the season to check out a local disturbance?'

Agron scowled. 'Look, Corvinus, I've already told you I

won't bad-mouth the general. I'm telling this because you asked and it passes the time, okay? You got any smartass comments to make, you can keep them to yourself.'

'Okay, okay!' I held up my hands. 'Forget I spoke.' Jupiter! And I'd thought Perilla was touchy!

'Then lose the commentary, boy.' I didn't answer. 'So the weather gets worse—wind, rain, you name it. Visibility's down to nothing, the road's a sea of mud with fallen trees every hundred yards. We're well into the forest before they hit us. Not a full-scale attack, we could've handled that easy. Small groups, individuals even, slingers and spear-throwers. Picking off stragglers. Thinning us out. Chase them and they melt into the forest, follow and you don't come back. The first day's bad, but we're committed. At the end of it we pitch a proper camp and the general orders some of the baggage to be burned so it won't slow us down. The next day things get worse, and we know we're not going to make it.' He paused; his eyes shifted. 'The third day's the last.'

'What happened?'

He was looking through me rather than at me, and it made the skin crawl on my spine. He didn't answer at first, and when he did it wasn't an answer at all. 'You ever been there, boy? In the German forests?'

'No.'

'There's no light, the trees shut you in. Off the path they're set so close together it's like being in a cage with a black roof. You can't breathe, there's no wind, no sound. You can't even hear your own footsteps. It's as if everything's dead, and you're dead with it.' Now his eyes held mine. 'You believe in spirits?'

I shook my head, but I had the sense not to laugh. The guy was serious. Deathly serious.

'Nor did I, once. But that place was haunted by Jupiter

knows what bitch of a demon that moved with us every step of the way. It ate our hearts out and then it killed us piece by fucking piece.'

I swallowed. His eyes were on mine, and they were hard as knives.

'So there wasn't a lot left of us by the third day. Not a proper army, for sure. We'd been split up, carved into bits no bigger than a company. Then Vela, the second-in-command, decides he'll go it alone with the cavalry, cut and run for the Rhine. He's been twitchy for days, poor bastard, and it's got worse. The forest takes some people that way. "Go ahead," says the general. "Tell them I'm sorry." Not that Vela gets very far, there's Germans everywhere by then. With the cavalry gone the rest of us don't have a hope. The Germans attack in force at last, they break our square, and the lads go down like pigs in a slaughterhouse. That's the end. That's all there is, Corvinus. Finish.'

He was shaking. The big guy was shaking, and his eyes were fixed on something I couldn't see. Shit. No wonder the poor bastard believed in demons. After listening to him I half believed in them myself.

'What happened to Varus?'

'He killed himself. Him and most of the staff officers. It was that or be taken alive. The Germans hacked the heads off and used them for footballs. Then they burned what was left. Or half burned it.'

'You saw that?'

'Yeah. Like I said, I hid. I found a hole where a tree had come down, crawled into it and pulled some brushwood on top. There was nothing else I could've done. The army was dead and the Germans were rounding up the prisoners. Nailing the poor bastards to the trees for their gods to look at.

When the screaming stopped and the Germans left I slipped off south towards the Rhine. It took me a month to get back.' He took a deep breath. 'You see now why I don't like unfair odds, Corvinus? And why I don't want spoilt young smart-asses like you stirring things up again for your own pissing pleasure?'

'But if the whole thing was Varus's fault, then…'

He reached over and gripped the neck of my tunic, his fist pushing me backwards into the chair and pressing so hard into my larynx that I couldn't breathe.

'You think that's news to me?' he said softly. 'You think it was news to Varus? Three Eagles lost, Corvinus! You know what losing an Eagle means to a general? To any soldier? Leave the general alone, boy. He paid all he had to give, and he doesn't owe any more. Least of all to bastards like you.'

'Agron!' Asprenas's voice slashed across the room. The fingers at my throat loosened without haste and I fell forwards gasping. Agron stood up and wiped his hand on his tunic. He didn't look at me.

Fat Face, with Quinctilia on his arm, looked pretty unhappy. Jupiter knew what they'd been talking about back there, but he'd clearly lost the argument and I suspect he would've been just as happy to see the big guy twist my head off. Quinctilia, on the other hand, didn't look any different. It would've taken an earthquake to throw her out of kilter. Maybe not even that.

'I'm sorry to have kept you,' she said, 'but my nephew and I had things to talk about and decisions to make. I'm happy to say we've decided to tell you the truth. The whole truth.' I wondered if that whole was for Fat Face's benefit. Certainly the guy looked as though he'd just swallowed a neat half-pint of vinegar. 'Lucius, help me to my chair please.'

She sat down slowly but with great dignity, like a queen preparing to give audience. Agron and Asprenas took up their positions on either side, like the rod-and-axe men round a magistrate.

'You are quite right, young man,' Quinctilia said. 'My brother was a traitor.'

CHAPTER 30

I stared at her; but I noticed that Agron didn't bat an eyelid, let alone Fat Face Asprenas. Obviously whatever Varus had done wasn't news as far as they were concerned.

Quinctilia was still completely relaxed. She had guts, that lady; guts and perfect poise.

'I should make it clear from the start,' she said, 'that Lucius here is against my telling you this and that I do so on my own responsibility. You are of course free to make use of the information as you like.' Agron shifted and swore under his breath, but she ignored him. 'However, I would ask you please to think carefully before taking any action that would bring further disgrace on the family.'

There was no pleading in her voice. Nothing beyond the words themselves. I nodded, and felt like five different kinds of rat.

The old lady took a firm grip of the arm of her chair. I

noticed that her fingers tightened and slackened spasmodically. Whatever the impression of calmness she wanted to convey she wasn't finding this easy. Like I said, Quinctilia had guts.

'I knew nothing of Publius's...arrangement with Aemilius Paullus,' she said. 'Let alone with the Divine Augustus. However, as you have described the situation it seems eminently probable and agrees well with what I do know. Publius was a traitor, certainly. But I had always thought his treachery arose from greed, not political ambition. It appears now that I was wrong. Or rather it appears that love of money may not have been his only motive.'

'Aunt Quinctilia, I really think you should reconsider this.' Asprenas laid a hand on her shoulder, but she shook her head.

'It's better that Valerius Corvinus knows everything,' she said. 'Bring him the letter, Lucius. Please.'

Fat Face wasn't happy. I could see that. He gave me a look like he might something very dead and very rotten that his dog had dug up, and left the room. Quinctilia turned back to me.

'My brother was always greedy, even as a child,' she said. 'He had to have the biggest slice of cake, the stickiest sweet on the plate. When he grew up it was money, of course. He should have been prosecuted after Syria, but then he was married to Augustus's grand-niece. And my late husband being the emperor's nephew...' She hesitated. 'Well, I realise these things shouldn't happen, but they do.'

'You mean the emperor intervened?'

'Not as such, no. Augustus was always careful not to play favourites, at least overtly. But the relationships were sufficiently well known to cause a certain...reluctance, shall we say, to prosecute. Besides. Publius got on extremely well with the emperor, and he was a very capable administrator.'

'Except in Germany.'

Agron growled something I didn't catch, but the old lady ignored it.

'Except, as you say, in Germany; but of course there was a reason for that, as you know.'

'He'd been bribed by Paullus to let things slide.'

'Indeed? Two reasons, then.'

I was puzzled. Something, somewhere, didn't add up. 'Lady, you've lost me. If that wasn't the reason you had in mind, then what else was there?'

'It's very simple.' The old girl's filmy eyes held mine. 'Publius may well have been involved with the Julian faction, for all I know. But as Augustus's governor in Germany he was certainly taking money from Arminius.'

I sat back. This was a twist I hadn't thought of; but given the old guy's character it made sense, a lot of sense. Having the Roman governor on the payroll would've been a real coup for the Germans, and Arminius would've been happy to pay through the nose for the privilege. Meanwhile Varus could report to the conspirators that he was fulfilling his part of the deal to destabilise Germany for Julia and Postumus. As a plan it was beautiful. Maximum returns, minimum risk. With two paying clients, neither knowing of the other's existence, a gold-mine that would set him up for life. And if things did go wrong the most he could be charged with was poor governorship.

Except that in the end things hadn't just gone wrong. The conspiracy had bombed and Arminius had cancelled out on any arrangement he'd made with a vengeance.

'You know this for a fact, Quinctilia?' I said. 'That Varus and Arminius had a deal going?'

'Of course. The proof came from Numonius Vela. He died with Publius, naturally, but before the army had left the Weser he had passed it on to me. Vela was a good friend of the family, and of my brother. I will always be grateful that he chose me as the recipient of the information rather than the emperor.'

Yeah. Sure. Vela might've died with Varus but I remembered what Agron had said about him running out on the old man when things got tough. With that kind of friend who needs enemies? I wondered if Quinctilia knew; but then she probably did. The old girl didn't miss much.

Just then Asprenas came back carrying a worn-looking message tablet. He handed it without a word to his aunt. I thought she'd open it but she didn't. Instead she passed it straight to me.

'Before you ask, young man,' she said, 'there is no possibility of forgery. The handwriting is quite certainly my brother's.'

I undid the fragile lacings and opened the tablet. The wax surfaces were in good condition although the writing was cramped: the guy had had a lot to say and not much room to say it in. Like she'd said, it was a letter, and at first glance I didn't see anything strange about it except that the usual first line giving the names of sender and addressee was missing. It was bread-and-butter admin stuff, general to staff: a list of forces and their order of march, together with details of the route to be taken, including the all-important detour...

I stopped.

Including the all-important detour!

Shit! Quinctilia had said that Vela had sent her the tablet before the army left the Weser. And at that point Varus had known nothing of any trouble to the south. Which meant...

Feverishly, I skimmed through the rest of the text. At the bottom of the second page my eyes came skidding to a halt. Even when they'd read the last sentence twice I couldn't believe what they were telling me:

> I suggest that the attack be made at this point since it will restrict the movements of my cavalry and provide me with a reasonable excuse for withdrawal.

Varus had known! He'd known all the time!

'You see the implications, of course,' Quinctilia said softly.

'Varus was in league with Arminius.' I still hadn't taken this in. 'He set the massacre up himself.'

'Correct. Vela had suspected Publius for some time. How he came by that letter I don't know. But I do know that it is genuine.'

'But this is crazy!' I held up the message tablet. 'You're telling me that Varus arranged his own death?'

'No,' Asprenas said. 'Of course not. You'll notice that my uncle mentions a withdrawal. An ambush was arranged, certainly. But not the massacre itself.'

I thought about that. Yeah, it would make sense. Especially if the guy thought he had a standing deal. 'Varus and Arminius had agreed on a military embarrassment? A limited defeat?'

'That's right.' Asprenas nodded. 'Arminius gets the kudos and my uncle provides the emperor with an excuse for a change of policy. Expansion of the empire as such beyond the Rhine is too risky to attempt. The territory is difficult to police, the natives intractable, and the forces for a long-term occupation unavailable. Under the circumstances it wouldn't be hard to persuade Augustus to rest content with what he had, especially if he knew Arminius to be a secret sympathiser.'

'You think the emperor knew, then? That Varus was acting under instructions?'

'No.' Asprenas shook his head. 'I would like to say that,

Corvinus, but no. This was a private arrangement between Arminius and my uncle. Perhaps, had he known of it, Augustus would have approved, but he did not.'

'So Varus had agreed to let Arminius grab himself a little glory? Only Arminius took the idea one step further.' Jupiter! It made sense. 'He let the arrangement stand but double-crossed Varus at the last minute. What was supposed to be a limited military action became a full-scale attack and three whole legions went down the tube.'

'Correct.'

'But the old guy must've suspected something, surely. He was taking a hell of a risk relying on Arminius to pull his punches like that, and he was no fool.'

Asprenas shrugged. 'I'm not my uncle,' he said. 'I can't say what his reasons were. He knew Arminius well. Maybe he had a blind spot for him, trusted him just that bit too much. The man was no ordinary native, remember. He was Roman-educated and Roman-trained. He would have known the right words and the right arguments to use. Most important, we don't know what my uncle was promised in return.'

'So the whole thing was a mistake,' I said. 'Varus believed he'd some sort of gentleman's agreement with Arminius while Arminius was planning all the time to make sure Rome pulled out of Germany beyond the Rhine altogether.'

'That's right.' Asprenas reached over and took the wax tablet from me. 'Which of course is virtually what happened. The loss of three legions tipped the balance. I doubt if we've the forces for a major expansion beyond the Rhine now even if we wanted to try. Maybe we never will have.' He paused. 'So you've got it all now, Corvinus. The whole dirty truth. We're in your hands. What do you intend to do with us?'

I'd been hoping no one would ask that question, because I

had no answer to give. Quinctilia, too, was watching me, as was Agron. I could see the old lady wanted desperately for me to make the certain decision but that unlike her nephew she was too proud to ask. They'd been open with me. The least I could do was be honest in return.

I gave it to them straight. 'I don't know. I honestly don't know. But, believe me, I won't use the information unless I have to.'

The tension in the room relaxed. Even Agron stopped scowling.

'That is all we can reasonably ask, young man.' Quinctilia smiled for the first time.

'There's only one thing that still puzzles me,' I said.

'And what is that?'

'It has nothing to do with what happened in Germany. At least not directly. All I'd like to know is why Augustus didn't pull your brother in with the rest of the conspirators.'

'I'm sorry. I don't follow.'

'If Varus was involved in the Paullus plot—genuinely involved—how come he got away with it? Initially he'd have Augustus's protection, of course, but that would've been withdrawn when the emperor found he'd been freelancing. So if the fourth conspirator was your brother, what was it that protected him?'

'Maybe he simply wasn't identified,' Asprenas said.

I shook my head. 'No, that won't wash. Not with Junius Silanus playing kiss and tell. And Varus's connections wouldn't've helped him this time because even Julia got exile. Unless of course he had some major hold over Silanus that kept the guy's mouth shut...'

'I'm sorry, Corvinus.' Quinctilia stood up. 'I'm afraid we can't help you any further. As I told you, we knew nothing of my brother's involvement in the Paullus plot. No doubt there is an explanation but I'm afraid you must look elsewhere for it.'

So that was it. Still, I had to be grateful for what I'd got. As I rose to my feet and prepared to murmur the polite phrases I noticed a child's wax tablet lying beside the ornamental pool. I picked it up. Scratched on to the surface was a drawing of an old man's face.

'You have grandchildren, Lady Quinctilia?'

'Great-grandchildren.' She peered at the tablet in my hand. 'That must be Hateria's. She's quite the little artist, so I'm told.'

'It's very good.' I was lying through my teeth. The thing was a travesty. There was something wrong with the lower part of the face, the eyes were too far down, and the forehead was a confused mess.

'My Greek secretary showed her the trick. It's very clever, really. Turn it round and you'll see what I mean.'

I turned the crude drawing round. The lines seemed to flow and change, one face becoming another. The smiling old man was suddenly metamorphosed into a frowning old woman. One head, two faces. I remembered the figure of Augustus in my dream, and something shifted...

The world suddenly turned itself inside out.

'It's not a man after all,' I whispered.

'I beg your pardon?'

'The drawing.' I held the tablet out towards her. 'I thought it was a man, but it isn't. It's a woman.'

'Of course it is. But only when you look at it in a certain way. That's the whole point.'

I began to laugh; and once I'd started I couldn't stop.

'Corvinus! For Jupiter's sake!' Asprenas grabbed me. 'What's got into you?'

'It wasn't Augustus at all!' I managed to get out. 'It was never Augustus! It was sodding Livia!'

Asprenas froze. 'What?'

I had a hold of myself now; only I had to sit down. I was shaking so badly that I would've fallen if the chair hadn't been there.

I understood! Finally I understood! Why hadn't I listened to Perilla when she'd suggested that I had the Paullus plot upside down, that it had been aimed at Julia all along? Or maybe I had. Maybe that's why I'd had the dream in the first place...

Quinctilia had drawn herself up to her full height, her stoop forgotten.

'Young man,' she said. 'That was the most disgraceful display of bad manners and bad language that it has ever been my misfortune to witness. You will please leave my house at once.'

'No.' I shook my head. 'No. I'm sorry, Lady Quinctilia. Deeply sorry. I apologise for my bad manners, I really do. But I can't leave yet.'

'If the mistress says you leave, Corvinus, then you leave.' Agron hadn't moved from where he'd been standing behind Quinctilia's chair. 'You want to do it feet first that's your decision.'

'No, Agron. Wait.' Quinctilia turned back to me. 'I don't understand. Why should you suddenly be so anxious to stay?'

'Because I haven't finished,' I said. 'Because I've just realised how the whole thing fits together.'

CHAPTER

31

They stared at me. All three of them. Then the questions began.

I held up my hand. 'Do you think I could have a cup of wine first? Please?'

My throat was parched. Keeping up the politenesses was one thing, but after what I'd been through I'd've killed for a drink. Besides, this was a celebration. Although the puzzle wasn't complete, at least I could see now where the missing pieces had to fit in.

'Of course.' Quinctilia was trying hard to preserve her impassive dignity. 'Of course you may. Agron, find one of the slaves and tell him to bring a flask of the guest reserve.' She turned back to me as the big guy went out. 'It is my turn to apologise, young man. My lack of hospitality was unforgivable. I told the servants to stay out of earshot until our…discussions were completed, but I should at least have offered you wine.'

'Forget the wine.' Asprenas's eyes were boring into me. 'What did you mean, Corvinus? About the empress?'

'Just that I've been looking at things the wrong way up,' I said. 'Oh, sure, it was a natural mistake to make. I'd assumed because the Paullus plot was infiltrated and Augustus was the one to take action then he must've known what was going on all along. Maybe he didn't. Maybe Livia was the one to bust it up and Augustus didn't know a thing about it until she chose to tell him.' Gods! Where was that wine?

Asprenas was still staring at me like I'd made an indecent suggestion. 'Why should the empress keep Augustus ignorant of a plot against the state, Corvinus?'

But Agron had arrived back at last with the wine slave. I grabbed the cup from the guy's hand and drained it, then refilled it from the flask. Agron jerked his head towards the door and the man scuttled out.

I turned back to Asprenas.

'But it wasn't a plot against the state,' I said. 'That's the whole point. The conspirators didn't want to organise a rebellion, they wanted to put the skids under Livia and Tiberius. It was Julians against Claudians. So who had the biggest vested interest in seeing the plot bomb? A big enough interest actually to get it off and running just so she could pull the floor out from under?'

I could see that I'd rocked Asprenas. 'You're saying that Livia *encouraged* the Paullus plot? The empress?'

'Sure. Why not? She provided the rope and watched the poor bastards hang themselves.'

'So how did it work?'

I took another swallow of wine. It was good stuff. I was beginning to glow already. 'Okay. First of all it had to have the emperor's backing, right? Paullus and Julia had to think that Augustus was secretly sympathetic.'

'That would make sense, I suppose.'

Not exactly a ball of fire, old Fat Face. 'So we have three conspirators. Paullus, Julia, and Silanus. Silanus is a double, but the others don't know that. Also there's a fourth guy who Julia and Paullus think represents the emperor.'

'This fourth conspirator, presumably, being my uncle.'

'Yeah.' I glanced at Quinctilia. She was sitting frozen-faced. 'Yeah. Anyway it's Varus's job to deliver the goods. He's their guarantee of a safe haven, their insurance policy. Clear?'

Asprenas nodded. Quinctilia was frowning. Maybe, I thought, I'd lost her already. The old girl had had a busy day.

'So now comes the twist,' I said. 'Augustus doesn't know a thing about the conspiracy. Varus isn't his man at all. Nor is Silanus, for that matter. Both of them are working for Livia. Of course—'

'I'm sorry to interrupt, young man,' Quinctilia said. 'But that is impossible.'

I stopped dead as if I'd run into a brick wall. 'Oh yeah? Now why would that be, lady?'

Not exactly politely phrased, but I hadn't expected any opposition from that quarter, and it threw me.

'Because Publius got on abominably with the empress,' she said. 'He would certainly never have involved himself with her, whatever the reasons. And equally certainly Livia would never have trusted him to act so blatantly against Augustus, even if he had made the offer. Whoever my brother was working for it was not Livia. Or conversely, if the empress was behind things then her agent would not have been Publius.'

'You're sure about that?'

'Of course I'm sure. When you said that Publius was working for the emperor and subsequently for himself I had no reason to disbelieve you. But to have him working for Livia is another matter.'

'Under no circumstances?'

'Under *no* circumstances.' The words had the finality of a door slamming.

Shit. 'So where does that leave me with my fourth conspirator?'

'Not with my brother. I'm afraid, Corvinus, that you will have to look elsewhere.'

I reached for the flask and filled my cup to cover the sudden silence. I needed to think. Sure, Quinctilia had been pretty dogmatic, but she was a pretty dogmatic person. That didn't mean she had to be right. I wasn't ready to give up on Varus yet, not by a long chalk. He fitted in too well, and anyway I had the hard truth of the letter now to back me up. I knew there were pressures that Livia could've exerted if she'd wanted the guy particularly badly. Like blackmail, perhaps. Varus seemed the kind of guy who'd be a natural for blackmail.

I realised that Fat Face was talking to me.

'So where does the massacre fit into all this, Corvinus?'

I felt almost relieved. I was on firmer ground there as far as Varus was concerned. He'd stage-managed the whole thing, even if it had gone wrong. And given the Livia connection his reasons were pretty obvious.

'Okay,' I said. 'Forget the Julians for the moment and look at it from Livia's point of view. She's been out from the start to get her baby boy into the purple. She wants him to shine, for people to notice him. The only problem is that young Tiberius isn't the shining type. He's got boils, halitosis, dandruff, all the personal problems you can think of, and to cap it all his manner would make a rhino look sociable. Also Augustus hates his guts.'

'You're talking about the emperor, Corvinus.' Fat Face

wasn't looking too happy. 'Let's have a little more respect please.'

'Oh, don't be so stuffy, Lucius!' Quinctilia said sharply. 'Corvinus is perfectly right. Tiberius may have many excellent qualities but the man's a boor and always has been. Carry on, young man.'

Jupiter! The old girl never ceased to surprise me. Asprenas stiffened as if she'd run a needle into his backside and his mouth closed so fast I could hear his teeth snap together.

'Okay,' I said. 'Now, the Wart may not look much but he's a grade-A general. The only problem is that even when he's winning victories nobody notices. And recently he hasn't been shining all that much on the military side either. In fact he's been coming in for quite a bit of stick back home over his conduct of the Illyrian campaign. You'd agree?'

Asprenas inclined his head stiffly, but I could see that I had him hooked. Agron, too.

'So the empress has a problem. Somehow she has to manoeuvre things so that her baby boy can come up smelling like roses. Only he has to do it in his own right, not as step-daddy's deputy. Diplomacy is out. The Wart hasn't got the charisma. A big military success, now, that's a different thing, and it's right up Tiberius's street. The trouble is he's had them before and they haven't got him anywhere. The only way this one is going to be any different is if it fulfils two requirements.'

'Which are?' Fat Face's lips hardly moved.

'One.' I held down a finger. 'The Wart gets full credit, not just a pat on the back as Augustus's stand-in. Two. Connected with this.' I held the second finger down. 'The campaign's necessary to clear up a mess for which Augustus was personally responsible.' I paused. You could've cut the silence with a knife.

'Germany was perfect. If Livia could arrange for a disaster and a recovery there she'd really be cooking. Frontier policy was Augustus's baby. Also Varus was the emperor's personal choice for the German command.'

'And if he were shown to be incompetent,' Quinctilia said, 'Augustus would share the blame. How very ingenious.'

'It worked, too.' Asprenas had finally got his mouth unstuck. 'The massacre nearly broke him. He thought of suicide, did you know that?' I shook my head. No, I hadn't known, but it didn't surprise me. 'It's not common knowledge, for obvious reasons, but it's fact. And then of course you're right about the outcome. When the crisis was over and Tiberius came back to Rome he got his co-regency. I apologise, Corvinus. And I agree with my aunt. Your theory is both ingenious and plausible.'

Quinctilia cleared her throat. 'There is only one flaw, young man,' she said. 'I must reiterate what I said earlier, even if my opinion is totally contradicted by the facts. Assuming he knew what he was doing, my brother would certainly not have involved himself in a scheme such as you have described.'

We stared at her; and she stared back, completely unmoved. I wondered if Perilla would look like her in another fifty years.

'What I said in regard to the Paullus conspiracy applies here also.' Her voice was firm. 'Doubly so. Publius may have been greedy, he may have betrayed his trust, but he was certainly not capable of treachery to that degree. Especially if the empress was involved.'

It was time for a bit of tact. 'Lady Quinctilia.' I laid my hand on her arm. 'I realise that you must have cared for your brother very deeply, but...'

She pulled the arm away. 'Publius was a greedy, self-indulgent pig with a grossly overdeveloped sense of his own importance. I never could stand him. Nevertheless, there were things at which even he drew the line. And treachery such as you have described would have been one of them.'

Jupiter! 'Then maybe he was pressured into it, lady. Blackmailed, even. Whatever his reasons...'

She held up her hand. I stopped.

'Valerius Corvinus,' she said. 'You are a very clever and able young man. You also, as far as I can tell, have all the facts of the matter firmly on your side. That is not in dispute. However, I knew Publius all his life and you did not. I tell you now that he could no more have consciously been involved in such a scheme as you describe than renounced his patrician's stripe and joined the mob.' She stood up. 'And now I think that you had better go.'

There was grief and pride in her voice as well as certainty. I set my wine-cup down on the table.

'I'm sorry, Lady Quinctilia,' I said, and meant it. 'I'd like to believe you. But you must see that it's impossible.'

She drew herself up a finger's-breadth straighter. She was so tall that her pale eyes were almost on a level with mine.

'And do you think, Corvinus,' she said slowly, 'that I don't know that?'

There was no more to be said. I thanked them and left.

CHAPTER 32

I'll say one thing for litters. They give you a chance to think things through in comfort, which is just what I did on the way home. Quinctilia had rattled me more than I liked to admit even to myself. Yeah, sure, the facts pointed clearly to Varus being guilty—after all, a traitor is a traitor is a traitor—but the old girl had been convincing as hell. Maybe I was wrong about Varus after all, or at least half wrong, despite the letter. Maybe he had been set up. The question was how?

Okay, I thought. Let's say he isn't our fourth man. Call the guy X. X's job is to get Varus into bed with Arminius. Obviously he has to be someone Varus trusts and will listen to. And he needs to be on the spot, because the scam's tricky and he has to keep a close personal eye on how things are going.

In other words, X is a high-up member of Varus's staff who's also a personal friend.

Okay. So X moves on to the first part of the plan. He

arranges for the two to come together. That's easy. Varus already knows Arminius from Rome, they've even met socially. Out there in the sticks with his polished Roman manners Arminius stands out like a rose in a desert. Compared to the other locals he's okay, he's civilised, he's one of the club. So when Arminius tells Varus that he's got a proposition to make, one that's in Rome's interests and incidentally will make Varus a penny or two for himself, the old guy's half won over already.

So Arminius and Varus set up a private bargain. North of the river, where Roman writ stops, Germany's a loose collection of hostile tribes, one of which is Arminius's. Up to now they've been nothing but a pain in the arse, which is why we've had to keep the Rhine garrisons up to strength. Arminius proposes, with Varus's help, to weld them into a federation with himself at the head. With Arminius in charge, that would leave us with a friendly client kingdom on the far bank, which would take the pressure off our northern frontier. Sure, he tells Varus, it'll be dangerous in the short term. I'll have to pretend that I'm acting against Rome. Only you'll know the truth. You'll know I'm on your side. So all it needs is for Varus to turn a blind eye, maybe kick in now and again by using Roman troops against tribes that wouldn't play ball. And then there would be the money; lots and lots of money, because Roman military governors don't come cheap...

Yeah. The greedy old sod would've jumped at it.

So who was X, the lad who starts the ball rolling? Like I said, he had to be someone close to Varus and one of the imperial admin team. Someone high up.

Varus's deputy? Numonius Vela?

It fitted. Vela was a family friend, Quinctilia had told me that. He was also the second most important man in the province after the governor. And when it came time to shift the blame—the time of the final march—he would've made sure he had the hard evidence to clear himself if necessary and incriminate his boss: Quinctilia's letter. Short of a signed confession witnessed by all six Vestals and half the College of Augurs, no one could ask for better. With the finger pointing at his own choice for governor Augustus himself was down the tube without a lifebelt. I'd've bet he'd oppose the detour to the Teutoburg, too, knowing that Varus would overrule him.

The last stage of the plan fitted as well. Varus would've thought the German trap was only another part of the scam: one last bit of propaganda to get things really cooking: a victory over a Roman army in the field. Only Vela knew better. He'd made his own deal with Arminius. Sure, the engagement would be limited, but not all the blood would be fake. The Germans would let Varus into the Teutoburg, but they wouldn't attack at once like he expected them to. They'd wait until he was too far in to get himself out and then they'd hit him hard and keep hitting him until he didn't know which end was up any more…

At which point they'd stop. That was the crucial difference between how X had arranged things with Arminius and how they'd actually happened. There would be no massacre. Varus would surrender, or be allowed to come out of the forest with his army in shreds. The result would be the same either way. Varus's reputation would be down the tube and Augustus's with it.

Only, of course, it didn't happen that way either. Arminius had been playing a game of his own. He'd double-crossed both Varus and Livia's agent and gone straight for the jugular. No wonder Vela was twitchy. He must've realised that he'd been had long before the last day when he'd cut his losses and tried to make it on his own back to the Rhine. Maybe he thought Arminius would let him through; or maybe he just panicked. In any case it hadn't done him any good. Exit Varus. And exit our fourth conspirator.

Leaving, of course, the prime movers behind the scam, Livia and Tiberius, in the shit up to their imperial eyeballs.

I leaned back against the litter cushions feeling pretty smug. Yeah. It worked, it hung together. I had to find out more about Vela, though. At the moment the guy was no more than a name. Maybe Perilla could help.

But when I stopped off to talk to her the door slave said she was out, visiting her mother.

Which reminded me of my own filial duties. I hadn't been round to my mother's in over two months, not even during the Floralia. Now might be as good a time as any. At least I looked sober and presentable: I'd put on my sharpest mantle for the visit to Quinctilia's and I still had my best litter out. It was hard luck on the litter-team that Mother happened to live out on the Caelian, where we'd just been, but with my eccentric preference for walking the guys could afford to lose a few pounds anyway.

After the divorce Mother had married a widower, Helvius Priscus. Apart from the wedding ceremony itself, when I'd given the bride away, I'd only seen the old guy twice, and I doubted if my mother had seen him much oftener, because his hobby took him away from home a lot. Priscus's bag was tombs and tomb inscriptions. Etruscan and early Republican tombs especially. Try to get him to talk about normal things, like how the Blues are doing these days racewise or who said what to who at last night's party and all you get is grunts. Ask him about the development of orthography from its primitive beginnings to the modern day, tied in with the epigraphic evidence for a vowel shift in the vernacular, and you can't shut the guy up. Ah, well. It takes all types.

Mother was looking well: she'd lost a lot of weight after the stillbirth and never put it back on. When I came in she was discussing floral arrangements with one of the house slaves.

'Marcus! Lovely to see you!' She came over and kissed me on the cheek, and I smelled the scent she has specially mixed for her by the best perfumer in Alexandria. 'Where have you been these last few months?'

'Only two, Mother.'

'Then it seems longer.' She stepped back. I saw her eyes go to the bruise beside my ear, where I'd landed when Silanus's porter threw me out. 'You've hurt yourself.'

'Nothing serious. I fell down some steps, that's all.'

'You drink too much, dear.'

'It had nothing to do with anything I drank.'

'Nonsense.' The smile in her eyes took the sting from her words. 'Come and sit down.'

I stretched myself out on the guest couch as she gave the house slave his final instructions. Then, sitting down herself, she turned back to me.

'So, Marcus,' she said. 'And what's been happening with you?'

'Nothing particular.' I wasn't going to tell her about the Ovid affair; and with Priscus being strictly the butt end of high society I doubted if she'd have heard from anyone else.

'Have you seen your father recently?'

'Maybe. Why?'

She lifted an elegant shoulder. 'Just curiosity. I saw him myself not too long ago. We had quite a civilised little chat.'

'You spoke to him?' I remembered Dad mentioning that he'd seen Mother, but not that they'd actually talked.

'Of course I spoke to him. Why shouldn't I? We may be divorced, but we aren't enemies.'

I didn't answer.

'He's worried about you, Marcus. He thinks you're wasting yourself.'

'Nice of him.'

'I wish you wouldn't run your father down so much, dear. It isn't fair. We don't get on, of course, but he's well-meaning enough in his own dull way. And if you must know in this at least I agree with him.'

I stared at her. I'd never heard Mother say she agreed with Dad in my life. Sure, she'd never actually said she disagreed either; she'd simply, separately and without comment, given her own opinion, which happened never to be his. That isn't the same thing at all.

'Oh, I know,' she went on. 'You're of age and can decide things for yourself. I also realise that because my father was misguided enough to leave you a large slice of his estate you're financially independent. But these things are beside the point.'

'I'm not interested in politics, Mother. Not Dad's kind, anyway, and there doesn't seem to be any alternative.'

'I said your father thinks you're wasting yourself and that I agree. I didn't say we wanted to force you into public office.'

'You may not want to, but Dad does. And anyway what else is there?'

'Marcus, I don't know! That's for you to decide. You're twenty-one now, twenty-two next month. Old enough surely to know what you want to do with your life.'

'I do know. I want to enjoy it.'

She sighed. 'Don't be melodramatic, dear. You'll be bored silly before you're thirty. Anyway, I'm not going to lecture you, it's your own business, not mine. I've told you what I think and whether or not you pay attention to it is up to you.'

We were getting on to dangerous ground. I changed the subject. 'How's Stepfather?'

'Oh, Titus is well enough. He's in Veii at the moment on a genealogical binge.' Her brow furrowed. 'At least I think it's Veii. But I'm absolutely sure the binge is genealogical.'

'You don't find the old guy dull?'

'Unlike your father, Titus has hidden depths.' She smiled in a very unmatronly way. I wondered if maybe I hadn't misjudged Helvius Priscus. 'You'd be surprised. At least not you personally, but you know what I mean. Speaking of which, why don't you tell me about this girl of yours.'

'What?'

I must've looked as shocked as I felt because she laughed.

'Oh, yes, I know all about young Rufia Perilla, Marcus. You've caused quite a little scandal between the two of you. Not that I mind personally. From all accounts the poor girl needed taking out of herself. That Suillius Rufus is a shit.'

'How did you know about Perilla, Mother? Who told you?'

'I don't think I can remember all the names, dear. But I shouldn't worry. Sympathy seems to be on your side. Is she applying for a divorce?'

'Yes.'

'I hope she gets it, then. It may be a little difficult with her husband being so close to the emperor's son, but there's nothing worse, Marcus, than being married to someone you don't like. Let alone love. Wherever the faults lie. Do you understand me, dear?'

I stared back at her, woodenly. 'Yes. I think so, Mother.'

'Good.' She settled back into her chair. 'Now tell me about Perilla.'

I did. Not the personal stuff, of course, nor what had brought us together originally: if Mother knew anything about that she had the good sense not to mention it. They'd've got on well together, I thought, although they were completely different characters. Mother was glass to Perilla's marble.

'You must bring her round for dinner some evening,' she said when I'd finished. 'I'm sure Titus would enjoy talking to her too. Rufius is such an unusual family name.' I glanced at her sharply, and sure enough there was laughter in her eyes and at the corners of her mouth. 'No, but I'm serious, Marcus. I'd love to meet her and so would Titus. Don't worry, I'll keep the old bore on a tight leash. Perhaps we should invite your father and his new wife as well.'

'Mother!'

'Just a joke, dear! If you insist we take it as such. It would make for a rather turgid evening, but I'm sure Perilla wouldn't mind.'

No, I had to admit she probably wouldn't. However, although I'd promised her I'd try to get along with my father I drew the line at dining with him. I was shocked that Mother had suggested it.

We talked for a bit longer, about this and that. I enjoy talking with my mother. She has a jay's quickness, a brightness and irreverence that is a complete contrast to my father's ponderous dignity. Then I caught the sound of footsteps behind me. A slave had entered the room carrying a tray with a wine jug and cups.

'Thank you, Glaucus. Just pour for us and go, would you?' My mother turned back to me and smiled. 'I got this in specially for you, Marcus. I couldn't resist it.'

Knowing Mother, I should've had my suspicions. However, it had been a long hard day. I could feel the nectar bathe my tonsils already. 'Really? What is it?'

The smile broadened. 'Pomegranate juice, dear,' she said. 'With a touch of cassia.'

Yeah, that was Mother. To pretend I'd missed the point (not that that fooled her) I had to drink some of the stuff. When the time came to go back home I still hadn't got the taste out of my mouth.

Perilla was out the next morning, too; and when I checked with Callias it turned out she hadn't been home at all.

'Why the hell didn't you tell me last night?' I yelled at him.

'I'm sorry, sir. I just assumed...'

'You assumed what?'

The guy was grey with worry, and I made a mental note to ease off. Shouting at the slaves wouldn't help, and it wasn't Callias's fault.

'When the mistress didn't come home I confirmed with the Lady Marcia that she had in fact left. Such being the case, sir, I assumed, erroneously, that...ah...'

He subsided into embarrassed silence.

'Callias, if you thought she was at my place, then why didn't you send someone to make sure?'

'Sir.' The old slave drew himself up with what I had to admit was great dignity. 'I am my master's property, not my mistress's, and my primary responsibility is to him. Accordingly, there are some things that I would rather not know about or if I do know about them that I would rather not acknowledge. You understand me, sir.'

'Yeah, sure. I'm sorry.' I stopped striding about the reception hall and sat down on the marble lip of the pool. I noticed with interest that my hands were shaking, and that however hard I tried I couldn't make them stop. 'So what time did she leave her aunt's house?'

'An hour before dusk, sir.'

'In a litter?'

'Yes, sir.'

'And the litter-team haven't returned either?'

'No, sir.'

'Your own litter? Or hired?'

Callias's mouth pursed.

'A house litter, sir, of course. I would never permit the mistress to go out in a hired litter.'

Despite my anxiety, I grinned. Slaves can be snobbish as hell; and I'd back a snobbish slave against a patrician dowager any day.

'Okay. You've...ah...you've checked with the Watch?' The question had to be asked.

'Yes, sir. Of course. No fatalities whatsoever in this region last night, sir.'

I breathed a sigh of relief. It wasn't likely she'd been attacked, not that early in the evening, not between the Esquiline and the Palatine. Still, it was a load off my mind to have murder ruled out as a possibility.

'Where else would she go?'

'Nowhere else, sir. Not without telling us. And the Lady Rufia Perilla doesn't... didn't go out very often. Certainly not overnight.'

So what the hell does that leave? I asked myself. It wasn't a question I cared to answer. 'Let me know immediately she comes back, okay, Callias? Immediately!'

He inclined his head. 'Yes, sir.'

It took me three nail-biting hours of fruitless waiting before I shelved my pride and went round to my father's. He was in his study, writing. When his chief slave Phaedrus showed me in he laid the pen down and simply stared at me without speaking.

I wasn't surprised. It'd been three years since I'd set foot in that house. Never since the divorce, in fact. When I'd walked out (I'd had a house of my own to go to for about a year by then) I'd sworn an oath by the family spirits not to come back. Ever.

'Welcome, Marcus.' My father rose and came towards me, his hands outstretched. I thought he was going to hug me, but he didn't. The hands dropped to his sides. 'It's good to see you here.'

'Perilla's disappeared,' I said. 'I think she's been kid-napped.'

'What?'

'Dad, if you know anything about this, anything at all, please tell me.'

He stiffened. 'Why should I know anything of the where-abouts of the Lady Rufia Perilla?'

'Look, don't play games, okay? I didn't ask you where she was, I asked you if you knew what could've happened to her.'

'Of course I don't.'

'You swear it?'

'Marcus, for heaven's sake, what's got into you?'

'Swear it!'

My father stared at me for several heartbeats. Then he sighed.

'Very well, son. If that's what you want.' He walked over to the family shrine and placed his right hand on top of it. 'I swear I had no knowledge, until you came in here just a moment ago, either of the whereabouts or of the disappearance of Rufia Perilla.'

'Or who might be responsible?'

'Marcus!'

'Swear!'

'Or of who might be responsible. I so swear.' He took his hand away. 'Now, Marcus, will you please sit down and tell me what's going on.'

'Can I have a cup of wine?'

'Of course.' He pushed past me, opened the study door and shouted: 'Phaedrus! A jug of wine, here. Now, please.'

I heard the acknowledgment, and the slave's feet padding off over the marble tiles.

'So tell me what happened.' My father closed the door behind him.

I sat down on the couch. My hands were still shaking. They hadn't stopped all day. I slipped them beneath my thighs to keep them still.

'She went out yesterday afternoon to the Fabius place to visit her mother,' I said. 'She left well before dark and she still hasn't come home. That's all I know.'

'Where do you mean by home? Your house or hers?'

'Father!'

I'm sorry, son. That was uncalled for, and it's none of my business. Could she have spent the night anywhere else?'

'Callias is sure not—he's her head house slave. He says she would've told him. She'd certainly have told me.'

'And Callias is telling the truth?'

'I assume so. Why should he lie?'

'I don't know. You haven't quarrelled, you and the Lady Rufia?'

'Of course we haven't sodding quarrelled!'

'Softly, Marcus, I'm only trying to help. She didn't mention going to visit anyone else? No one at all?'

'No. Not that I know of.'

The door opened. Phaedrus with the wine. I took the cup from his hands, drank it off, and held it out for more.

'Leave the jug on the desk and go, Phaedrus,' my father said. Then, as the door closed again: 'Marcus, why did you think I might have known about this?'

I shook my head. 'I made a mistake.'

'You did. The emperor doesn't deal in kidnapping. Whatever the provocation. And neither do I.'

'Yeah? And what about the empress?' I couldn't stop myself. 'Don't tell me Livia's above that sort of thing, Dad. It'd be about the only crime she hasn't committed, wouldn't it?'

The silence was sudden and total. I hadn't meant to say the words. They'd slipped out and it was too late now to call them back.

'Who told you?' My father's voice was no more than a whisper. 'Marcus, who told you?'

'That doesn't matter.' I was having to hold the wine-cup with both hands. 'I know, Dad. I know the whole story. About Gaius and Lucius. The two Julias. But I also know you were right. It's all water under the bridge, it's not important, it doesn't matter.' I looked at him. 'Father, why couldn't you trust me?'

He shook his head and said nothing. He looked grey.

'There's only one thing I don't know, or not for sure,' I went on. 'Who was the fourth conspirator? The guy Ovid saw at Paullus's? Was it Quinctilius Varus, or Vela, or someone else? Come on, you can tell me now, Dad.'

My father's head came up, and he stared at me. His face was blank, completely blank. He couldn't've been acting. The reaction was far too natural and unrehearsed for that.

He simply didn't know what I was talking about. 'Ovid was exiled because he found out the truth behind Julia's adultery. It had nothing to do with Paullus's conspiracy. And why should Varus be involved?'

'But Julia didn't commit adultery.' I'd been living with the problem so long that the simple statement came out as self-evident, almost naïve.

'Of course she did! Silanus seduced her on Livia's instructions. Then Livia reported her to the emperor.'

It was my turn to shake my head. 'No, Dad. That wasn't how it happened. There was no adultery. None at all. Paullus and Julia were conspiring to bring back Postumus and take him to the Rhine legions.'

'But...'

I had never seen my father look so confused, so lost; but I'd no time for sympathy, or for explanations. It wasn't important now anyway. 'Look, Dad, none of this matters. The important thing is that Perilla's missing and I think the imperials may be responsible. I'm asking you please, Father, to do your best to find her. I'll do anything they want, anything you want, I'll give up asking questions. Anything! Just get her back!'

He hesitated. 'Very well, Marcus. I'll do my best. I don't accept that the emperor is responsible, mind. Or the Empress Livia. But I can at least make enquiries through the proper channels.'

I felt my face flush. 'And how the hell long is that going to take?'

'I don't know, son.' My father's voice was gentle. 'Several days, probably, at least.'

'Several days?'

'Marcus, I can't just go to the palace, demand an audience with Tiberius and Livia, and accuse them both to their faces of kidnapping. It has to be done diplomatically.'

'Oh, sure!' I turned away. 'We wouldn't want to put anyone's nose out of joint, now, would we?'

My father sighed. 'I'll do my best, son, believe me. But I'm not going to go storming in there casting unfounded accusations around right left and centre for you or for anyone. Especially where the empress is concerned.'

I was facing him again. 'A bit too close to the bone, right?'

'If you choose to see it that way, yes. Far too close to the bone.'

I looked at his stiff expression and remembered my promise to Perilla. 'Hey, I'm sorry, Dad. Yeah, anything you can do, I'd be grateful. However you do it, however long it takes, and whether it works or not.'

His expression softened.

'We'll get her back, Marcus,' he said. 'Don't worry. If she's still...' He stopped. 'We'll get her back for you.'

I left the house in a better frame of mind than I'd entered it. All the same I couldn't help thinking of the words my father so carefully *hadn't* said at our parting; and I prayed to every god I knew, and any that I didn't who might be listening, that Perilla wasn't already dead.

I didn't sleep that night.

CHAPTER 35

My next stop was the gym, to talk to Scylax. Dad would handle the official side of things, but if the emperor was responsible, short of waving the white flag for me I knew there wasn't a lot he could do. With Scylax's help I could start from the other end. Scylax had contacts that spread throughout the city's underground as deep and as far as an oak tree's roots. If anyone could track Perilla down or put the finger on who'd taken her, then Scylax could. First, though, I had to persuade the guy I was serious. In Scylax's book women ranked somewhere between mules and chickens. Even then, on a good day the chickens had them beat three times out of four.

I found him in the tackle-room he used as an office, putting an edge on a dagger.

'What makes you so sure she's been kidnapped?' His leathery thumb worked spittle into the whetstone's surface. 'Time's nothing to these bubbleheads. Maybe she just decided to stay over with friends and forgot to mention it.'

'She didn't.'

He scowled. 'Hey, that's good, Corvinus! Nice touch in certainties! You got your own Thessalian witch tucked away somewhere? Or do you do the palm readings yourself?'

Before I knew what I was doing I'd grabbed the whetstone away from him and thrown it into a corner.

'Look, you bastard,' I shouted. 'Are you going to help me or not?'

He didn't move; just looked at me and held out his hand until I'd picked up the stone and given it back.

'Take it easy, boy,' he said quietly. 'That was a joke. Remember jokes, Corvinus?'

I swallowed; my nerves were scraped raw. 'Yeah. Okay. I'm sorry. No, I don't know that she's been kidnapped. Not for sure. But she has disappeared. And if she was visiting friends she'd've told me, or at least told her house slaves. That I am certain of.'

Scylax frowned. The dagger slid across the stone with a *swchhh! swchhh!* that set my teeth on edge.

'Okay,' he said at last. 'I'll help. Sure I will. Only if I end up looking ten kinds of fool when she comes home tomorrow trailing a new boyfriend I'll break your neck.'

'She won't. She won't, believe me.'

'You'd better be right, boy, because that's no joke. So let's have the details.'

I told him as much as I knew, which wasn't a lot.

'You've checked with the Watch?'

'Of course I've bloody—' I stopped. 'Yeah. No corpses.'

'And you haven't been contacted?'

'No. Nor have her family.'

'Early days yet. They want you to sweat.'

I stood up and moved to the door. Out on the sand, Scylax's

chief trainer was giving a dandified young narrow-striper hell for dropping his guard. I watched with dull eyes.

'So who took her, Corvinus?' Scylax spoke softly.

I spun round.

'How the hell should I know? That's what I want you to find out!'

'You know, boy. Not the names of the guys who actually grabbed her, no. That's my end. The big guy, though, the one who gives the orders, the guy you've been having all this trouble with. You know who he is, don't you?'

'Maybe.' I'd no intentions of springing the names Tiberius and Livia on him, not unless I had to.

'There's no maybe about it.' Scylax tested the edge of the dagger against his thumb and laid it aside. 'Listen, Corvinus, because I'll only say this once. I don't turn my back on a friend, and if he asks me to hold my tongue then I don't blab. But it cuts both ways. You want my help, you pay my price.'

'Which is?'

'Trust me. Tell me the whole thing from the beginning. The whole thing, boy, not the edited highlights. Then we'll see where we stand.'

'We've been through that already. I can't do it.'

He shrugged and got up.

'Okay,' he said. 'If that's the way you want it.'

'Look, you don't understand! Just knowing about this could get you killed. There're big names involved.'

'I said it was okay.' He picked up a wooden training-sword and made for the door. 'Good luck anyway, boy. I'll see you around.'

I stood in the doorway, blocking his path.

'You mean you're not going to help?' He said nothing, just kept on coming. 'Answer me, you bastard!'

His shoulder caught me in the side of the chest like the business end of a battering-ram. I fell winded, and he stepped over me. I thought he'd simply keep on going but he stopped and looked back.

'Never mind the names, Marcus,' he said. 'Just trust me. That's all I ask.'

I lay on the dirt floor gasping and kneading my ribs. They felt like they'd been crushed by a runaway Doric column.

'Okay,' I said when I could talk again. 'Okay, you've asked for it. But don't blame me if you wake up tomorrow with your throat cut.'

He grinned and pulled me to my feet. 'I'm a light sleeper, Corvinus. Besides, who wants to be old anyway?'

So I told him. The whole story from the beginning, with nothing missed out. I thought maybe he'd balk at the political stuff, but he didn't: Scylax had been around, and he wasn't stupid.

'You sure the imperials're behind this?'

'They have to be. I was stonewalled that first day at the palace, and no one else has that kind of clout. Anyway, it's in their interests.' I glanced at him. 'Worried?'

'Yeah. Shit-scared, if you want the truth. Who wouldn't be?'

'Does it make a difference?'

Scylax inspected the blade of his dagger and laid it down. 'I gave you my word, remember? I don't do that often, boy, and when I do no one questions it, not even you. You get me?'

I swallowed and said nothing.

'Okay. So Tiberius and Livia wouldn't involve themselves directly in something as dirty as this. If we want to find your girlfriend we're looking for a middle-man. I'll put the word out. Meanwhile we stake you out. Watch you, watch your house.'

'What good will that do?'

'Jupiter, Corvinus!' He spat. 'What do you use for a brain? You say these guys haven't made contact yet?'

'Not yet, no.'

'They will. And when they do we have a face we can follow.'

'Yeah, but they—the imperials, whoever—they just want the investigation killed, right? They don't have to contact me to tell me the obvious.'

'You got a better idea, boy?'

'No, but...'

'So shut up and trust me. I've done this before, and I know what I'm doing. When—not if, when—someone puts the bite on you I'll know it. Know it without him knowing I know. And then we'll find the guy and take him apart piece by fucking piece.' He grinned. 'Unless it's Tiberius himself in a big black cloak and false beard, in which case you're on your own. So sod off and let me organise things, okay?'

I checked Perilla's house before I went home, just on the off-chance; but there was still no news.

I was getting ready for bed when Bathyllus shoved his head round the door to tell me Agron was outside and wanted to talk to me privately.

Privately. Yeah. Sure. I could quote him now. We've got your girlfriend, pal. Stop screwing around or you can kiss her goodbye. It looked as if old Quinctilia had been spinning me a line after all. Shit, I'd believed in her and that fat-faced nephew of hers, and I didn't think my judgment could be that much out. Sure, Asprenas I could understand: Fat Face had struck me as the sort of guy who wouldn't balk at kidnapping if he decided it was the only way to shut me up. But not Quinctilia. I'd've thought the old girl would've had more pride.

I got my sword out and told Bathyllus to wheel the big guy in and make sure the Sunshine Boys made themselves conspicuous in the lobby. The Illyrian walked past them as if they were part of the furniture. If he'd been wearing a hat I swear he'd've used one of them to hang it on.

'Sorry to hear about your girlfriend, Corvinus,' he said.

I set the point of the sword against his chest.

'Okay. So where is she? You've got three seconds.'

Although I must've looked pretty mean Agron didn't bat an eyelid. He brushed the sword aside, drew up a chair and sat down.

'Put that pig-sticker away, boy, you look ridiculous. If you can't look after your women it's no concern of mine.'

Slowly, I sheathed the sword and sat down facing him. The guy had more guts than I had, I'll say that for him; but I wasn't going to leave things there.

'If she's come to any harm,' I said carefully, 'you're dead meat, understand? You and Chubby-chops Asprenas both. I'm telling you that now.'

He laughed. 'Think you can do any better than last time? And what's Asprenas got to do with it?'

I made a sign to the Sunshine Boys, who were hovering in the open doorway. They trooped inside grinning and nudging each other, cracking knuckles and flexing biceps. As a performance it was subtle as a Suburan mugging, but that suited me. This was one message I wanted spelled out in capitals.

Agron didn't even look round. 'Look, Corvinus. We may not particularly like each other but I don't need the hassle and I don't want to bait you, okay? I'm telling you now that I've no more idea where the girl is or who took her than you do. Nor has Asprenas and nor has the mistress. So call off your performing monkeys back there before you make yourself out to be a bigger fool than you are already.'

He could've been lying, but somehow I didn't think so. In any case, like I said, I admired his nerve.

'Okay, boys.' I held up my hand. 'Change of plan. Scram. Go play with your toys next door.'

The knuckle-cracking and biceps-flexing trailed off and the grins disappeared. I've seen kids look like that when someone stops them torturing the cat. 'And tell Bathyllus to bring us a jug of mulled wine.'

'That's better.' Agron folded his arms and watched me as the last of the Gauls trooped out again and banged the door behind him. 'Now tell me what happened.'

'Hold on. First you tell me how you knew the lady was missing.'

'Not me. The mistress. And before you go jumping to any more half-baked conclusions, most of Rome knows. You can thank Daddy for that.'

Yeah. That made sense. My father wouldn't've had any reason to keep the news quiet, quite the reverse. I'd asked for his help and the first thing any self-respecting purple-striper would do under the circumstances was put the call out on the grapevine. The old patron-client relationship might be shakier now than it had been in the past, but when it came to getting results it still left official channels nowhere. I was surprised that he'd gone to so much trouble. Grateful, too.

'Okay,' I said. 'For what it's worth, she went out visiting a couple of nights ago and didn't come home. The day we had our little chat about Varus.'

If he noticed the tone of the last sentence he didn't show it.

'Kidnapped?'

'It looks that way.'

'You had any ransom demands?'

'Not yet. But I doubt if whoever took her is interested in money.'

'What, then?'

'What do you think? They want me to stop asking questions, same as you did.'

'We didn't go beyond a pretty please, Corvinus. You think it's that important?'

'Yeah,' I said. 'I'd say it was important. Or wouldn't you agree?'

There was a knock on the door and Bathyllus came in with the tray. He gave the big guy his best disapproving stare, poured, and left.

'So what brings you here?' I sipped at the hot wine. 'Apart from curiosity.'

'Screw the curiosity. I told you, if you can't keep your women it's none of my business. The mistress sent me to ask if there's anything she can do.'

'I can manage. Thank her anyway.'

Agron frowned and set his cup down on the floor untasted 'Look, Corvinus. This isn't my idea. Quinctilia feels responsible. She wants to help, right? Asprenas, too. Sure, they tried to shut you up, but they know now it was a mistake. And don't blame the mistress for what happened that day in the Subura. That wasn't part of the orders.'

'Using your personal initiative?'

'Yeah, if you like. I was told to follow you, keep an eye on you, maybe scare you a little. But no violence. And I saved your life, remember.'

The guy had a point. And what he was saying came as close to an apology as I could see him ever making.

'Okay,' I said. 'So let's call it quits, then. For the moment.'

'You still think the general was your fourth man?' The question came straight out of the blue, without any signalling; but then that seemed to be the way Agron operated.

I hesitated. Just because the big guy had stopped threatening to belt the hell out of me didn't mean I had to confide in him. And if he was working for the Opposition it'd be a real mistake.

'Come on, Corvinus! This is important.'

Sure it was. 'Who to?'

'To me.'

I nursed my wine while he waited in patient silence. If Asprenas was mixed up in this somehow then he could've sent his tame gorilla round to sound me out, maybe drop a few hints on how he wanted me to play things. All the same it didn't feel right. Agron might be a bastard, but I was willing to bet that he was an honest bastard.

'Okay,' I said finally. 'I don't know. I honestly don't know. Sure, Varus was involved. He must've been, the letter proves that. But there's a good chance that he was set up. Or at least used.'

He relaxed. 'That's what I hoped you'd say. Who by?'

'If I knew that, friend, I'd know the whole thing. What's it to you, anyway?'

'You know what I think of the general, Corvinus. He may've been greedy, he may've been taking bribes from the Germans, but like I told you, when the time came, he paid and paid hard. That bit of it's over. If Varus is your traitor I don't want to know about it and I sure as hell won't help you prove it. You get me?'

I thought I could see what he was driving at. 'I get you. So let's have the but.'

He nodded. 'Right. If it wasn't the general, if Varus was set up somehow, then I want the man who did it. I want him just as much as you do, Corvinus, maybe more. Not just for Varus but for fifteen thousand other poor sods and three golden Eagles. So if that's the direction you're headed in then maybe— just maybe—we're on the same side after all.'

As a peace offer I'd heard better, but it had a genuine feel to it. An honest bastard, right enough.

'Everything so far points to Varus being guilty,' I said. 'You know that, don't you?'

He nodded. 'Yeah. But I'm like the mistress. I can't believe the general was that kind of traitor, and I'm gambling that I'm right.'

'And if you aren't?'

'I don't make wild bets, Corvinus. Varus was set up. I know he was.'

Maybe I was making one of the worst mistakes of my life, but my gut feeling told me the guy was on the level. I raised my wine-cup.

'Fair enough. Truce?'

Slowly he reached for his own cup. Then, his eyes on mine, he took the barest sip and put the cup back down.

'Truce.'

'Okay,' I said. 'So start helping. If Varus wasn't our man what about the other possibilities?'

'Such as?'

'Let's start with Numonius Vela.'

His brow furrowed. 'You got reasons for that, Corvinus, or are you just dropping names?'

'Reasons. If our traitor wasn't Varus he must've worked pretty closely with him and been pretty high in the hierarchy. Vela was the general's deputy, and you don't get better placed than a deputy to frame a boss.' I sipped my wine. 'So tell me about Vela. What sort of guy was he?'

'Not the conspiring type.'

That came out flat. Too flat. 'You sure?'

'Not unless he was a good actor. Vela was straight as a die but he'd no spunk and no imagination. A brainless nobody who turned out a coward into the bargain. Count him out, Corvinus. You won't see me shed any tears for Vela, but he isn't the man you want.'

'Hold on. You don't ditch the guy that easy. Vela was the one told Quinctilia her brother was a traitor. He gave her the letter that proved it. If Varus was set up I'd say that made his second a pretty strong candidate.'

Agron's brows came down. 'Sure he gave the mistress the letter. That's the point. If he'd been the one who framed the general he would've hung on to it, but he didn't. He sent it straight to Asprenas by special courier.'

Something cold touched the back of my neck.

'Run that past me again, will you? Slowly this time.'

He stared at me. 'What the hell's got into you, boy? You okay?'

'You say Vela sent the letter to Asprenas?'

'Yeah. To Mainz, where he was stationed.' Agron looked blank. 'What's this about?'

'Asprenas was in Germany?'

'Sure he was in Germany. I thought you knew that.'

'No,' I said slowly. 'I didn't know that.'

Jupiter! If Asprenas was in Germany, then...

'He had a couple of Eagles. Not ones involved in the massacre, further up the Rhine. If it hadn't been for Asprenas the whole frontier would've collapsed.'

'Yeah?' Jupiter! 'Tell me.'

He was still staring at me, which was pretty understandable. I must've looked as if I'd just seen the ghost of old Julius march in and do a slow strip on the table.

'Asprenas was one of the general's staff,' he said. 'He was upriver on garrison duty at Mainz. When he got the news of the massacre he force-marched his two Eagles back to protect the south bank of the Rhine. Like I said, if it hadn't been for him the Germans would've crossed over and chased us all the way to Gaul.' He paused, then said deliberately: 'Nonius Asprenas was the only hero we had, Corvinus. So if you've got him in mind for your traitor you can stick it.'

I sat back and tried to stay calm. I could see what the guy meant, but he'd got it wrong. Sure, if his job had been to wreck the Rhine frontier totally Asprenas would only have had to put off his march for a day or so and watch the whole thing fall apart. Safe, no risks, and completely effective. Only that wasn't the idea, not at all. Not even Livia would go that far. She'd only wanted to disgrace Augustus. If I was right, and the massacre had been a double-cross on Arminius's part, then her agent wouldn't have expected it any more than Varus had. Fat Face's prompt action was an argument for guilt just as much as for innocence.

Then I had another thought; and it wasn't a pleasant one. If Asprenas was the traitor then it explained why Perilla had been snatched so fast. I'd given him his reasons myself. I'd shown him just how close to the truth I was. And how important it was to stop me before I made the final connections...

Fool!

Agron was still staring. The big guy didn't know, I was sure of that, unless he was the best actor I'd ever come across; nor did Quinctilia. And I couldn't tell them, because I didn't know which way they'd jump if they knew. Certainly not yet, not until I had proof...

The door opened. Bathyllus came in holding a scrap of paper.

'I'm sorry to disturb you, sir,' he said, 'but I feel you should see this.'

Domestic hassles I could do without at the moment. 'Bathyllus, look, we're busy, right? Tell me tomorrow.'

Then I saw the expression on the little guy's face, and I knew it was serious.

'From the kidnappers?'

He nodded. 'One of the slaves found it in the garden, sir.'

I grabbed the paper and spread it out on the desk. I'd never actually seen Perilla's handwriting, but there wasn't any reason why this shouldn't be genuine. I felt, suddenly, very cold.

'It was wrapped round a stone,' Bathyllus was saying. 'Someone must have thrown it over the wall.'

'When?'

'I don't know. It was lying beneath one of the rose bushes.'

The message was short and to the point:

> Marcus: They say that if you haven't left Rome by
> the day after tomorrow they'll kill me.

There was no signature. Just that.

I'd seen the gardener weeding the rose garden myself, three days ago. Since then there'd been no reason for any of the slaves to have been outside, barring chance. This could've come at any time since Perilla had gone missing. And if it had been delivered before Scylax could set up his stake-out, then maybe I was too late already. Maybe Perilla was already dead...

My hand clenched, crushing the paper into a tight ball.

Fool!

CHAPTER

37

The gym wasn't open when I got there early next morning, but I hadn't been waiting long when I saw the big Spaniard who'd brought me Scylax's message a few days before coming up the street chewing on a hunk of barley bread. Seeing me standing there didn't seem to hurry him any. He ambled over, glanced at me from beneath brows that could've doubled as an outcrop of the Capitol, then produced a key from inside his greasy tunic and unbarred the gate. All this without a word or even a spark of recognition. Conversation obviously wasn't his strong point. Or maybe his vocabulary just didn't extend to good morning.

'Hey, Adonis,' I said.

'Daphnis.'

I'd been close, anyway. At least it wasn't Hyacinth.

'Whatever. Scylax due in?'

'Yeah.'

That was all I was getting, seemingly. He stood aside to let me pass, then took a rake from behind the gate and began moving sand around the training ground grain by grain. I left the guy to his executive duties and wandered over to sit down on the bench beneath the portico.

I was feeling pretty light-headed, not to mention depressed. I hadn't slept much the night before, and I'd come to a decision. Bathyllus was already busy packing. Given the choice between carrying the thing through and getting Perilla back, I had to choose Perilla, even though the very thought of doing a runner set my teeth on edge. Staying in the city was just too risky. A few months in Athens with Uncle Cotta wouldn't be so bad. If...when...Perilla got free she might join me. We might even settle there, because Jupiter knew there'd be nothing more for me in Rome. Nothing I'd have the stomach for, anyway. But first I had to tell Scylax to call off his dogs. He wouldn't like it, I knew—that was putting it mildly—but it had to be done.

This whole business had turned sour as hell. If I was right and Asprenas had set his uncle up, then unless I had hard and fast proof there wasn't a thing I could do about it. The guy was a war hero, a highly respected politician, and a personal friend of the emperor. If I were stupid enough to confront him he'd laugh in my face; and if I decided to do something really stupid like go direct to Tiberius I wouldn't have a face left to laugh in.

That was the clincher. Tiberius. With the Wart in on this I was way out of my league. Try to take the lid off this thing, accuse the emperor and Livia of multiple dynastic murder and high treason, and I'd be floating down the Tiber with a knife in my back before you could say 'liquidation'; and Perilla would be floating along beside me.

Slice it whichever way you liked, I was beaten, and I knew it. No proof, no clout, no nothing. All I could do now was wave the white flag and hope it wasn't too late.

Shit. And I'd been so close! I leaned back against the wall and closed my eyes...

I must've nodded off, because the next thing I remember was being shaken awake and Scylax's ugly mug grinning down at me.

'Hard night, Corvinus?' he said. 'She must've been good.'

I was still dopey. 'Yeah, she was. Who're we talking about?'

'Never mind. You look like you've been rolled the length of the Sacred Way and pegged out for the crows.'

I rubbed my eyes to squeeze out the sleep. 'They made contact. We have to talk.'

He was still grinning.

'I know that, Corvinus. Don't worry, we've got the bastard cold.'

The words took a moment to get through to me. When they did it was as if someone had dunked me in the public cistern.

'You've what? What did you say?'

'I said we've got the guy cold. Daphnis saw him heave a brick over your wall last night and followed him home.'

'Daphnis saw him? Daphnis?'

'Sure. I told you, you were staked. Daphnis was stretched out under a builder's cart in the alleyway behind your house, and I'd two more lads round the front.'

I was wide awake now. 'Then why the hell didn't he tell me as soon as I got here?'

'Maybe he's shy.'

'Maybe he's a sadistic sod.'

'Yeah, that too. Anyway, he saw the whole thing. Tailed the guy all the way home, like I told you.'

'You mean you know where Perilla is?'

'Could be. We won't know until we've looked. But at least we've got an address. It's a start.'

I was on my feet by this time. My depression was gone. If we'd found Perilla then I might be back in the game again. Once, that is, we got her back safely. That was the priority. The only priority.

'So what're we waiting for?'

'Hold on a minute.' Scylax's hand against my chest was like a brick wall. 'We've got to work out how to play this.'

'Screw that. It's simple. I get the Sunshine Boys, you whistle up a few sympathetic greasers, and we tear the bastard into inch-square pieces.'

Scylax was shaking his head. 'Uh-uh. Daphnis only found the messenger, remember. We don't know that he's got the girl himself.'

'Okay. So we walk on his balls until he tells us all he does know and then we tear him up.'

The hand against my chest increased its pressure. I felt myself pushed backwards and down on to the bench.

'Listen, Corvinus. I know how you feel, believe me. But if you think about it you'll realise that taking this guy out isn't going to solve anything.'

I was beginning to calm down now. Scylax was right. Of course he was. We wanted the boss, not the errand boy. Charging in with hobnail boots on would do more harm than good.

'So who is he?'

'Use your head, Corvinus! We know where he is and what he looks like, that's enough. Daphnis didn't stop to ask questions, especially at that time of night. If the guy found out we were on to him he'd be off like a scalded cat.'

I was beginning to suspect that Scylax's executive assistant wasn't the chicken-brain I'd thought he was. The guy obviously had hidden talents.

'So what part of town are we talking about? You can tell me that, anyway.'

'Sure. Launderers' Street. Third tenement along, second floor up.'

Definitely no chicken-brain. As an investigator Daphnis must be red-hot. I wouldn't have fancied my chances following anyone up the stairs of a city tenement, especially at night. There's plenty of cover in the open street, but once you're inside one of these places you'd need to be a cockroach to pass notice. A resident cockroach, at that.

'Good address.' The Subura again. And not one of its best parts, either.

'It's not the Palatine. But then our friend is no purple-striper.'

'So what's the plan?'

'Another stake-out. We watch him, follow him when he leaves, mark where he goes, check up on any visitors. I doubt if we'll see the actual boss at the tenement—any purple-striper'd stand out like a sore thumb in that district—but our friend will lead us to him. If we're lucky, that is.'

The boss could be Asprenas. I was pretty sure he was, but not sure enough to put Perilla's life on the line by going for him direct. I wanted hard proof first. 'What if we aren't lucky?'

'Then we walk on his balls and listen to him squeal. But we try this way first, right?'

'Okay.' I got to my feet. 'So let's go.'

Scylax pushed me back. 'Hold on. When I said "we" I didn't mean *we*.'

'Run that one past me again. Maybe I missed something.'

'You're not invited, Corvinus. Daphnis and I can handle this on our own.'

'The hell you can!'

'You want this to work or not?'

His hand was gripping my tunic. I shook it off. 'Scylax, this is non-negotiable. Include me in. I mean it.'

'I said any purple-striper would stand out. Have you looked at the edge of your tunic recently, boy?'

'Come on! I can borrow another tunic if that's all that's worrying you.'

'Screw the tunic. You've got patrician written all over you, friend. Or do you think you've time for a nose job?'

'Oh, let him come, boss.' I turned round. Unbelievably, it was Daphnis. Slapped all over his face was the evillest grin I'd seen in a long time. 'The guy's a born piss-merchant.'

Humour, now. Puns, even. Launderers' Street meant laundries; and city laundries send their slaves round the public privies to collect the stale urine. Not the most salubrious job in the world, but one appropriate for where we were going. Daphnis was definitely rounding out into someone I might grow to dislike. All the same I kept my mouth shut. I wasn't about to pass up an ally just for the sake of a cheap retort. And after all I owed the guy.

Scylax shrugged. 'Okay. Fair enough, Corvinus. If Daphnis says you're in then you're in. Just don't blow it, right?'

'Why should I blow it?' I hoped I sounded more confident than I felt. 'There's one more thing. I want someone else along.'

'Jupiter, boy!' Scylax growled. 'Why don't we just take a fucking army and be done with it?'

'This guy might qualify. Anyway, we can split up two and two in case we have to cover another entrance.'

'What other entrance? This is a tenement. Unless you think the guy can fly.'

'Stranger things have happened.'

'Not in my book.' It was a token protest. I was right and Scylax knew it. Two pairs were better than a group of three. One man from each to stay put, the other to cut loose if necessary.

'You won't regret it,' I said. 'Agron's good.' Scylax stared at me like I'd grown an extra head. 'We're talking about the Illyrian? The guy who beat you up?'

'That's him.'

'And you say I won't regret taking him along?'

'Yeah.'

He shook his head slowly. 'Corvinus, you've got even less between the ears than I thought you had.'

'It's my responsibility, Scylax.'

'It could also be your funeral. And your girlfriend's.'

'Let me worry about that.'

He agreed. It was touch and go, but finally he agreed. I just hoped that neither of us was making a mistake.

Launderers' Street was off the Corneta, right next to Tannery Row and not far from the knackers' yards and the meatmarket. Not a salubrious area, in other words. There was a breeze of sorts, but that was no help. Wherever it was blowing from smelled worse.

We'd split up already. Scylax and Daphnis had gone on ahead while I stopped round at the blacksmith's shop to pick up Agron. That was tactics. In Rome, apart from purple-stripers with their retinues at one end of the scale and gangs of wide-boys looking for trouble at the other, only Egyptian tourists go round in threes or more. And any tourist stupid enough to go sightseeing in the Subura is asking to come out minus his purse, if he comes out at all.

The other two were already in place when we got there, lounging in the shade of a dusty oleander opposite one of the high-rise tenements: 'slaves' killing time while their master's mantle was being cleaned in one of the shops nearby. As we passed, Scylax raised his hand as if he were brushing a fly from his face.

'So how about that jug of wine?' Agron said.

I'd worked out a compromise with Scylax; not very flattering, but I had to agree it was sensible. I could tag along and bring Agron with me, but we had to stay out of the way until we were needed. Daphnis had suggested a wineshop on the opposite side further down the street because (and I quote) 'if the bastard can't blend in there he can't blend in anyplace.'

Daphnis was really beginning to get up my nose.

The wineshop was empty. I didn't realise why until the fat Syrian who owned the place brought us our wine. It looked, smelled, and tasted like the spillage you get on the floor of a vintner's cellar, murky rotgut stuff I wouldn't've passed off on my slaves. As I sipped it I looked out and down the street towards the tenement. We'd picked a table just inside the door but set slightly back, which meant we could see out but we were under the shadow of the lintel. The street wasn't too crowded and I doubted if we'd miss much. Barring the quality of the wine, we couldn't've had a better place to watch from.

'So tell me about your life, Agron,' I said. 'You came straight to Rome right after Germany?'

He poured himself a cupful of the rat-piss from the jug. 'Yeah. I was with the Eighteenth. After the massacre what was left of it was disbanded. No Eagle, right?' A legion's Eagle is sacred. Totally and absolutely. Lose the Eagle and the legion's dead for ever. Dishonourably dead. 'Sure, I could've got a transfer, but I'd had enough of the army by then. And survivors weren't popular.'

'How do you mean?'

'You've never been a soldier. A defeat as total as that, if you live it says something about you.' His voice was bitter. 'The best die, the worst survive.'

'That's garbage.'

'Sure it's garbage, but it's what everyone believes. Not just the know-nothings in the wineshops, either. The survivors were barred from Rome. Officers, anyway. The rest of us had a pretty bad time of it too.'

Yeah. I'd heard of that. The blanket ban of exile showed how hard the disaster had hit Augustus. How personally the old man had taken it.

'Were there that many? Survivors, I mean.'

'There were a few. Some of them were runners, sure. But others like me just happened to be lucky. If you can call it luck. Anyway, I came to Rome, and the mistress got Asprenas to set me up in the blacksmith's shop.'

'Generous of him.'

Agron shrugged. 'He gets his cut, like patrons usually do. And it didn't cost him anything; he was left it by a friend who died. Anyway, I've had the business ever since. That's it. You want more, friend, you tell it yourself.'

I glanced down the street towards the small square where Scylax and Daphnis were sitting. Daphnis was facing us with his back against the tree, his eyes half closed.

'So you're Asprenas's client now?' I was pussy-footing. I still wasn't sure where the big guy's real sympathies lay; and if Asprenas was our man I'd have to find out fast.

'The general was my real patron, but yeah, I look after the family's interests. Run errands now and again.' He grinned. 'Lean on young smartasses.'

'Save their lives, too.' I'd never actually thanked the big guy for that. Maybe it was time I did.

'That had nothing to do with you, Corvinus. I told you.'

'You know who these guys were? Or who sent them?'

'No. It wasn't any of my business.' He frowned. 'You ever wonder why Tiberius should use garbage like that?'

'How do you mean?'

'Where's your brain, Corvinus? The guy's an emperor. If he wants you stopped then why aren't you coughing your guts up in the Tullianum?'

I sat back. It was a simple enough question; so simple that it rocked me. The Tullianum was the old prison off the Market Square, reserved for guests of the state waiting for the authorities to get round to shortening them by a head.

Also, of course, for any private citizen the emperor took a violent personal dislike to, although that function wasn't exactly public knowledge.

'Maybe he just didn't dare,' I said.

'Oh, yeah. Sure. Daddy's Little Boy's got clout. So forget the Tullianum. There're still a dozen other ways the Wart could've used. If it'd been me giving the orders I could've got rid of you long since. The Wart doesn't. He sends in the local knifemen and the sweepings from the legions to do his dirty work on the quiet. So the question I'm asking is why.'

'Easier. Quicker.' I was making excuses, and I knew it.

'Screw that. I told you, there're neater ways. Official channels. Why not use them?'

The guy was right. This was a top-level scam, an imperial-level scam. It had to be, for everything to fit in. Even if Asprenas was involved it could only be as a middle-man, an agent for Tiberius and Livia. There'd been a dozen ways I could've been stopped dead officially, with the minimum of risk and the minimum of fuss; but none of them had been used. And that could mean...

I had to think this through.

Maybe I was wrong. Maybe this wasn't an official cover-up at all. The Wart and his mother didn't get on too well these days. I knew that. So if Livia was acting behind the Wart's back it would explain why she hadn't been able to use official channels to shut me up...

Yeah. Only that didn't make sense either, right? Tiberius needed the cover-up just as much as Livia. Maybe even more so. After all, the guy had to know about how his mother had got him the throne. He had to know about the murders and the exiles. And of course he had to know about...

About...

I stopped.

Oh, Jupiter! Jupiter Best and Greatest!

Agron was staring at me. 'Corvinus?'

'Hold on.' If I was right, I was saved, I was home and dry! 'Hold on. Let me think! Just let me think, okay?'

What was it Pomponius had said about Tiberius?

He was the best. Maybe he's First Citizen now, but the general's army first and last. A real professional.

A real professional. A soldier. The highest compliment Pomponius could pay anyone. Jupiter, it made sense! It made all kinds of sense! The Wart was army. And yet he'd agreed— must have agreed—to a scheme that might send a whole province and the security of the Rhine frontier down the tube.

Three Eagles lost! Three sacred Eagles...

The Wart would never have done that, not to win a dozen empires. Never in a million years. And that meant...

'He doesn't know,' I whispered. 'Jupiter Best and Greatest, the emperor doesn't know!'

'Corvinus, what the hell...!' Agron was gripping my arm. 'Get a hold on yourself!'

The landlord was staring at us and absently wiping a

wine-cup with a rag. I turned away from him, towards the street. I tried to keep my voice low, but I was trembling with excitement.

'Listen! The Wart wasn't involved in the Varus scam! The rest, the murders, yeah, sure, maybe even the Paullus plot, I don't know and it doesn't matter. But he didn't know about Germany!'

'Jupiter, Corvinus, will you shut up? Everyone's—'

'No, listen!' I had to get this out or I'd burst. 'He doesn't know there even *was* a scam! The whole German idea was Livia's, only it went wrong. And now the empress is pissing acid that her son will find out, because if he ever does he'll nail the bitch's hide to the palace gates! That's who's been trying to stop me! Not Tiberius and Livia! Livia!'

And that's when it happened.

Like I said, we were sitting in the shadows just inside the wineshop door with the pavement only a step or so beyond. As I spoke the empress's name a nondescript guy who was slouching past stopped as if I'd planted a hook in his neck. His head whipped round...

For the space of two heartbeats he stared straight at us, his eyes wide, his unshaven jaw slack. Then he turned and was off like a hare up the street back the way he'd come, in the other direction from the tenement. I saw Scylax and Daphnis spring to their feet, but they were a good hundred yards away and unless they sprouted wings they didn't have a hope in hell of catching him.

'Fuck!' I was on my feet myself now. I knew we'd blown it and that it was my fault. The guy would've known what I looked like. Sure he would. Scylax had been right. I should've stayed at home. 'Agron, for...'

That was as far as I got. The big Illyrian was still sitting in his chair, his eyes wide and his face drained of colour. Then, suddenly, he was up, pushing past me and sprinting down the street after the fleeing man. There wasn't much else I could do so I went after him, although I knew I couldn't match his speed or his skill at dodging between pedestrians. I was in time to see the guy throw a frantic look over his shoulder and duck into one of the little side alleys.

Someone—a woman—screamed just as Agron half rounded the alley corner. He pulled up sharp like he'd found there was no alley there at all, just a brick wall; and everything, suddenly, went very quiet.

I saw why when I caught up, by which time Scylax and Daphnis were right behind me. When they saw they stopped too. Daphnis took one look and threw up all over the pavement.

The guy was dead. Very dead. On the corner just inside the alley's mouth was a scythe-sharpener's booth. The owner must've hefted a scythe butt down just at the wrong moment and the upturned blade had taken the running man square across the throat. I thought of Davus, although this time there was more blood. A lot more blood. A crowd had collected from nowhere, the way crowds do after an accident. Through the ringing in my ears I could hear the booth proprietor saying over and over again, like some kind of charm: 'I couldn't do nothing. I couldn't do nothing.' A young girl in her early teens sat huddled in the corner between the alley wall and the booth making little grunting noises like a pig with asthma. Her cloak was drenched with red as if someone had poured a full jug of wine over it. The ringing in my head changed to a hot buzz, and the sounds of the street suddenly faded to nothing.

I felt my arm gripped. Scylax steered me out of the alleyway.

'Come on, boy.' he said. 'We're not involved in this.'

'Yeah, but we can't just…'

'You want to explain things to the magistrates?'

That got through. I stumbled after him back up the street. The others followed. They looked pretty shaken, too. You expect decapitations in the arena, they don't shock there, but street corners are different.

'I need a drink,' Scylax said. 'Any wine left in that jug, Corvinus?'

'What jug?'

'Come on, boy! Where you are there's always a jug!'

'Oh yeah. Sure.' I still couldn't get my brain to move. 'That jug. Help yourself.'

We went back to the wineshop in a bunch. There was no point now in pretending we weren't together, not with the guy we were trailing lying in two bits down an alleyway.

The fat Syrian shot us a suspicious look when we walked in, which was understandable under the circumstances; but Suburans learn pretty young to mind their own business if they want to keep breathing, and when Scylax met his gaze he suddenly lost interest. I ordered another round of the rotgut and paid with a silver piece. The Syrian didn't offer any change but I didn't make a fuss. After what we'd just seen even rotgut at ten times the proper price was welcome.

'Some shave, eh?' Daphnis was getting some of his bounce back, and a lot of his basic nastiness.

'I noticed you lost your breakfast pretty quick, friend,' Agron said sourly. Daphnis shut up and sat scowling. The Syrian, oiling over with the wine, gave him a quick look from under his thick scented eyebrows and left us to it. That's another thing Suburans are good at. Gauging situations.

'So what happened?' Scylax set down his empty cup. I reckoned he'd sunk a good half-pint at one go.

'The guy spotted Corvinus,' Daphnis grunted. 'I was watching him. He took one look inside here and turned tail.'

Scylax turned to me. He looked dangerous. 'That right, boy?'

I had my mouth open to answer, but Agron beat me to it.

'Wrong. It wasn't Corvinus he recognised. It was me.'

'What?'

'I recognised him too, which is why he ran. He was dead before the scythe touched him. Ten years dead.'

CHAPTER 39

Whe someone says something like that the flesh crawls on your bones. Daphnis's hand came up to make the sign against bad luck and even Scylax drew in his breath.

'What the hell's that supposed to mean?' he said. Agron lifted the wine-cup to his lips and set it down empty. His eyes were staring into space.

'His name was Ceionius,' he said. 'He was one of Varus's camp commanders. And he died in the Teutoburg along with the rest of them.'

You could've heard a pin drop.

'Screw that,' Scylax said at last. 'He was no ghost. The guy was flesh and blood. Especially blood.'

Agron's face was expressionless. 'Maybe so. But I saw him captured myself. And the Germans weren't taking prisoners.'

'Where were you at the time?' Daphnis sneered. 'Hiding?'

Agron turned towards him slowly.

'That's right, friend,' he said. 'I was hiding. You want to comment, maybe?'

'Cut that out, Daphnis!' Scylax growled. 'So who was this Ceionius guy?'

'Like I told you. One of the camp commanders. A slimy little bastard who'd have sold his grandmother for a copper coin. If the Germans hadn't killed him his own men would've, eventually. I'd've done it myself.'

I'd started to pour more wine into my cup and decided against it. Treatment for shock's one thing, but I didn't want to take the lining off my palate. 'You say he was in the massacre?'

'Yeah. He was one of the officers who suggested surrender.'

'Tell me.'

Agron shrugged.

'What's to tell? A bunch of them came to the general's tent second day demanding he ask the Germans for terms. Ceionius was the spokesman.'

That fitted with the theory I'd worked out for Vela. Asprenas, of course, wasn't on the march, but he'd've needed an agent to make the right suggestions at the right times. Varus might've survived a surrender to Arminius physically. Politically it would've left him, and Augustus, dead meat. Which was the object of the exercise.

'So what happened?'

'The general told him to piss off. He tried again the next day but it was too late. Arminius had us where he wanted us and it was all over bar the shouting. He threw down his sword and surrendered when the Germans broke our line.'

'Just like that?'

'Just like that.'

'Consistent bastard, anyway,' Scylax grunted.

'If you saw him surrender,' I said, 'how come you were so convinced he was dead?'

'I told you. The Germans weren't taking prisoners. Anyone left alive had his guts wound round a tree trunk.'

'He could've escaped.'

Agron shook his head. 'Not likely. Ceionius didn't escape, not the way you mean. The Germans let him go. And there's only one reason they should do that I know of.'

'Because that was the agreement,' I said softly. 'Because he was on their side.'

Scylax's mouth twisted. 'So you finally got your fourth man, Corvinus. Congratulations.'

I wasn't ready yet to put the finger on Asprenas, not in Agron's hearing, anyway. Still, I was feeling pretty sick. I needed proof desperately and for about five minutes I'd had it. I'd had Fat Face, or whoever, cold. We could've made Ceionius talk, and instead the bastard goes and gets himself killed...

'No,' I said. 'The fourth guy wasn't Ceionius. But I'll bet you a gold piece to a used corn plaster he was working for him and being well paid into the bargain. After all, why shut yourself away in a Suburan tenement unless...' I stopped as the enormity of my stupidity hit me.

Perilla!

The place stank of cabbage water, soiled nappies, and poverty. I took the stairs two at a time. Like all tenement staircases they were filthy with urine and worse, and the walls were scarred with knife marks and savage, hopeless graffiti.

There were four doors on the second floor.

'Which one?' I yelled. Daphnis was half a flight behind me,

and blowing like a bellows. As he cleared the last step I grabbed him by the neck of his tunic. 'Daphnis! Which sodding flat?'

He knocked my hand away. Maybe he'd've landed me one, but Scylax and Agron were close behind him and he thought better of it. Instead he simply pointed.

The door was locked. I threw myself against it and almost dislocated my shoulder. Agron raised his hobnailed boot and drove hard at the crosspiece above the lower panelling where the lock was. The door burst open and we piled inside.

Nothing. The room was empty except for a cot against the wall, a rickety ironwork table, a cheap wooden stool and—incongruously—a bookcase. No tied-up prisoner. No Perilla.

No Perilla...

'Never mind, Corvinus.' Scylax was frowning. 'Maybe we can find...'

Agron had raised his hand.

'Listen!'

Something was making a regular bumping noise. Bump...bump...bump. The noise was coming from behind the bookcase. I rushed over to it, got my fingers into the crevice between bookcase and wall, and heaved.

It came back easily. A long erect bundle swathed in a sheet and with rags tied round its upper part toppled out of the cupboard which it fronted. Daphnis, who was close behind me, caught it before it could fall and damage itself.

Carefully, carefully, I unwound the rags, revealing a red, very indignant face.

'Well, you took your time, Corvinus!' Perilla snapped.

I took her home. I won't say any more about that day because it isn't relevant and concerns no one but ourselves.

I took her home.

W e were in the garden hav-
ing a late breakfast the next morning when my father came
round. I'd thought he'd be embarrassed at finding Perilla there,
but he didn't seem surprised at all.

'I heard that the Lady Rufia was back safely,' he said, 'so I
stopped by to offer my congratulations.'

Perilla gave him one of her dazzling smiles. 'That was
kind of you, Valerius Messalinus.'

I signalled Bathyllus to lay another place, but my father
stopped him. 'No, Marcus. I only called in to introduce myself.
And possibly to learn first-hand what happened.'

'You sure you want to know, Dad?' I said. Even to me the
words sounded sharper than I'd meant.

'Yes, son.' My father sat down on the chair Bathyllus had
brought. 'I would like to know. Unless the Lady Rufia doesn't
wish me to, of course.'

'Not at all.' Perilla's hand briefly touched my arm. 'Marcus is being his usual boorish self. Aren't you, Marcus?'

I flushed. She was right. After all he'd done to help the guy deserved better.

'Yeah,' I said. 'Sorry, Dad.'

'Not that there's much to tell.' Perilla scooped honey on to a piece of bread. She was looking okay this morning, a lot better, I knew, than I was. Glowing almost. Maybe she should get herself kidnapped and shut up behind a bookcase in a Suburan tenement more often. 'It was my own stupid fault. I know the way home from Aunt Marcia's perfectly well, but it still didn't occur to me that the litter-team were making a detour until it was too late.'

'They took her towards the Caelian.' I pitted an olive. 'It's more open there. Then they jumped her and tied her up.'

'You mean your own slaves did this?' I could understand the incredulity in my father's voice. If you can't trust your own slaves, then who can you trust? Besides, for a slave to turn against his master is a short-cut to the arena.

'They weren't family slaves, not really. We'd only had them for about a month. Callias bought them.'

'Who from?'

Yeah, good question. That was an angle I hadn't thought of. I shot my father an approving look.

'I don't know,' Perilla said. 'I could ask.'

'Do that.' My father was frowning. 'I'd be willing to bet the first approach came from the seller. And that the offer was a good one.'

'You think they were planted, Dad?'

'It would seem a safe assumption, yes. Although I doubt if the slaves themselves will ever be found to verify it.'

That made sense, too. The guys would either have been hustled away from Rome with fake manumission certificates and money in their pouches or, which was more likely, they were at the bottom of the river with their feet in concrete sandals. I hoped it was the latter.

'Anyway,' Perilla went on, 'they took me to the tenement and handed me over to Ceionius. Not that I knew his name then, of course.'

'Ceionius?'

'Yeah, that's right,' I said. 'Ring a bell, Dad?'

'Varus's Ceionius?'

'Bull's-eye.'

'But that's impossible! Ceionius is dead, surely. He died with Varus in the massacre.'

'The rumour was exaggerated. He's been hiding out in the Subura.'

'Why should he do that? Oh, I know Augustus wouldn't have let him back to Rome, but if his only crime was cowardice, then...'

'It wasn't,' I said bluntly. 'The guy was a traitor. He was working with the Germans.'

'What?'

'The massacre was planned, Dad. And not just by Arminius. There were Romans involved too. Bigger Romans than that bastard.'

I'd rocked him, obviously. He genuinely hadn't known anything about this, and I was glad of it.

'Marcus, you can't be serious,' he said. 'You're claiming that the Varian disaster was engineered?'

'That's right. It's pretty complicated and I don't understand it all myself yet, but basically Varus had done a deal with Arminius.'

'Varus had done a deal? I thought you said Ceionius was the traitor.'

'He was. Or one of them, anyway. But Varus was involved too, only he was set up. At least I think so. Like I said, it's complicated.'

'Where's Ceionius now?' My father was on his feet. I'd never seen him so shocked, or so angry. 'The emperor will want to know about this. Come with me and I'll...'

'Hang on, Dad. There's no point. He's dead. Really dead this time.'

'You killed him? Marcus, that was stupid. Monumentally stupid!'

I glanced at Perilla. I hadn't told her how Ceionius had died. 'We never touched the guy, Dad. He tried to escape and there was an accident.'

My father sat down again, slowly.

'Tell me about it,' he said.

I told him. The whole story, from Bathyllus's finding of the note to the shambles in the alleyway. By the time I'd finished his lips were set in a tight line.

'And so you decided to ask an ex-gladiator trainer and a couple of slaves for help rather than come to me,' he said. 'Thank you, Marcus. Thank you very much.'

'Agron isn't a slave. And Scylax has some of the best contacts in Rome.' Both true, but that wasn't the point, and I knew it.

'Marcus did what he thought was best.' Perilla laid a hand on my arm. 'Besides, there wasn't time.'

My father sighed.

'No, I suppose not,' he said. 'You did very well, son, in any case. You deserve praise, not blame.'

I felt myself flush. 'I'm sorry, Dad. You're right. Maybe I should've gone to you first.'

He smiled gently. 'Two apologies in one morning, Marcus. You're improving.' I said nothing. 'So tell me more about Quinctilius Varus. You say he was intriguing with Arminius. I find that difficult to believe. Where did your information come from?'

I hesitated.

'Go on, Marcus. Tell him. Please.' Perilla's fingers tightened on my arm. 'He only wants to help.'

'Okay,' I said. 'I got it from Quinctilia.'

'Varus's sister?'

'Yeah. She had it from his deputy Vela, who passed it on to Nonius Asprenas.' My father had been rubbing his chin with his right hand. At the name his hand paused. 'You know the guy?'

'Oh, yes. I know Nonius Asprenas.' There was an odd catch to my father's voice that I didn't quite understand. 'And what precisely did Quinctilia say her brother had done?'

'I told you. She claimed he was taking bribes from the Germans.'

'In exchange for what?'

'Discouraging expansion north of the river. Turning a blind eye to what Arminius was up to. There was more to it than that, but that's general idea.'

My father leaned forward and placed his fingertips together as if I were one of his legal clients and we were discussing a case.

'That Varus was open to bribery is certainly credible, Marcus,' he said. 'Especially after the Syrian affair. You know about Syria, I suppose?'

'When he was nearly prosecuted for extortion?'

'Indeed. Nearly is the word. If it hadn't been for his connections—and of course the fact that Syria is an imperial province outside their jurisdiction—the Senate would have roasted him. As it was he was lucky to be given another chance; a fact that he himself would appreciate. I wouldn't dismiss the charge in principle, but I seriously doubt if Varus would have thought it worth the risk under the circumstances. If Augustus had ever found out that he was taking bribes, or even had reasonable grounds for suspicion, he wouldn't have lived to spend them.'

'Maybe that's so, Dad,' I said, 'but the way I think it worked it would've been pretty tempting. Varus might even have squared what he was doing with the emperor in the end. In any event the guy was guilty as hell. I've seen the proof myself.'

My father sat up. 'What kind of proof?'

'His own letter to Arminius giving him the details of his march from the Weser to the Rhine, including the detour through the Teutoburg. Route, dates, disposition of forces, the lot. And one more thing. He mentions the ambush.'

'What?'

'Sure. That's the point. Varus knew Arminius was going to hit him. Not as hard as he did, but still, that there would be an attack.'

'Where did Quinctilia get this letter?'

'I told you. From Vela. He sent it to Asprenas by courier just before the army set out.'

I felt him stiffen; and when he spoke again his voice was strangely quiet. 'You say Varus wrote this letter? You're sure of that?'

'Yeah, that's right, Dad. But I think Asprenas—'

'And Quinctilia herself is sure it's genuine?'

'Sure she's sure. She confirmed the handwriting herself.'

'She told you this as well? That she herself, personally, had recognised the writing as her brother's?'

I frowned. 'Look, what's all this about? Are you saying the old girl was lying?'

He shook his head. 'Oh, no. She wasn't lying. Or not intentionally so, anyway. You say you talked to her yourself? And you didn't notice?'

'Notice what?'

'Marcus,' my father said gently, 'the Lady Quinctilia is almost totally blind.'

I stared at him as the last piece of the mosaic in my head slid into place with an almost perceptible click. I remembered the pale eyes peering at me from close up when we had first met; remembered the way she'd stared past me, how she'd needed Asprenas's help to walk...

'How long?' I said.

My father understood the question, and its implications. 'I don't know. Her sight has been failing for years. Perhaps ten years ago it would have been good enough to read a letter and recognise the handwriting, although personally I doubt it.'

Not this handwriting. I remembered how cramped it had been and how close together the lines were. Still, that was something I could check for sure. Agron would be able to tell me; he'd been connected with the family for years. I yelled for Bathyllus, and he came out of the house at a run.

'You know where Agron hangs out, Bathyllus? The big Illyrian?'

'Not exactly, sir. But I can always ask at the Lady Quinctilia's. They'll...'

'No. No. Don't do that. He's got a blacksmith's shop in the Subura. Metalsmiths' Row, near the Shrine of Libera. You know it?'

Bathyllus sniffed. 'Not intimately, sir, no.'

Jupiter! The little guy was as big a snob as Callias! 'Find

it. Find Agron. I don't care if you have to comb the whole of the Subura for him, just find him, okay? And don't go near the Lady Quinctilia's place for any reason. You understand?'

'Yes, sir,' Bathyllus said stiffly. 'Of course, sir. Is there a message?'

'No message. Just a question. Get the answer and bring it back to me. Ask him when the Lady Quinctilia began to lose her sight.'

'Couldn't I send someone else, sir? After all, the Subura isn't exactly…'

'Beat it!'

He beat it. I turned to face my father.

'You're right, Dad,' I said. 'Quinctilia just said the handwriting was genuine. She never said she'd authenticated it personally. Which means that someone else did, someone she trusted absolutely.'

'Asprenas,' Perilla said.

I nodded. 'Asprenas. We've only his word for it that he got the letter from Vela. And if no one else but Quinctilia has seen it then it could easily be a forgery.'

My father cleared his throat.

'Quite possibly,' he said. 'It would not, at any rate, be the first that Nonius Asprenas was guilty of.'

Got the bastard!

'Tell us, Dad,' I said.

CHAPTER 41

My father didn't look at me. Instead, he picked up an olive from the plate in front of him and began carefully to cut the stone out with the point of a knife. I understood very clearly what was happening. Asprenas was one of the inner circle: good family, well connected. Guys like him were immune to criticism, to outsiders at least, and here I was an outsider. Marcus Valerius Messalla Messalinus was about to do the unthinkable: break the unwritten code that demanded that the circle protect its own.

'The rumours began just after he got back from Germany,' he said. 'Oh, they had no connection with his conduct during the campaign. In that sense he was a hero. He'd done all they say he did, brought his legions back in time to stop the Germans crossing the river and breaking the frontier. No one ever accused him of not being brave, or resourceful, or a good soldier.' The stone came free. My father set down the gutted olive, picked up another and repeated the same slow, careful process. 'That was when Asprenas began to produce certain documents. Bequests in the form of cash and property that he claimed had been made by colleagues who had died in the massacre. Nothing very big, taken individually. Taken together they represented quite a tidy sum.'

I remembered Agron's blacksmith's shop; the one that hadn't cost Asprenas anything because he'd inherited it from a dead friend. 'And these documents were forged?'

'It was...suggested.' My father was the perfect lawyer. 'Strongly suggested, in some cases. But in no case did the next-of-kin know anything about the bequests previous to Asprenas's lodging of his claim.'

That made sense. How the bastard had expected to get away with it altogether I couldn't imagine. Or maybe he'd just gambled—rightly, as it turned out—that his military reputation would protect him.

'I should say, of course, that no formal charges were made,' my father went on. 'If the documents were forgeries they were virtually perfect, and as a result, although there were several informal challenges, in the event they came to nothing.'

'But the rumours persisted?'

'The rumours persisted. Have persisted.'

'And the only guys who know the truth are lying unburied on the wrong side of the Rhine.'

'Indeed.'

'So what kind of money are we talking about?'

'Taken together, the bequests must have totalled two or three million.' I whistled. That sort of fraud was major league stuff. I knew a dozen young rakes who'd sell their grandmothers to a waterfront whoremaster for half the amount. 'Mind you, Marcus'—my father set the knife down on the table—'I'm not saying that proceedings should have been initiated. But the connections with your incriminating letter are, shall we say, significant.'

'In other words everyone knows Asprenas is a crook and a forger but no one can prove it. Or wants to prove it.'

Dad didn't answer; which was an answer in itself.

'He may be a crook,' Perilla said. 'But is he a traitor?'

'Yes. He has to be.'

'Oh, come on, Marcus! You'll have to do better than that!'

'Especially if you want to take this to the emperor,' my father added. 'Asprenas is Tiberius's man. More than that, he's useful: an established figure, a proven administrator, a military success. Tiberius wouldn't want to lose him and he certainly wouldn't condemn him without very firm proof. Yes, Tiberius will give you a fair hearing, Marcus, I guarantee that; but I tell you now that he'll ask for more than your opinion and a mishmash of unsupported theory. He'll need a properly presented legal case. Have you got one?' Then, when I hesitated: 'Well, son? Have you?'

Put up or shut up, his voice said. I temporised.

'Dad, we talked about keeping back information once. When I asked you about Julia. You remember?'

'Yes, of course. I told you that responsibility meant knowing when not to pass on information where it would cause more harm than good.'

'Yeah, right. Well, I'm really going to make your day. I'm going to apologise a third time. You were right. I can't take this to the Wart, not unless I have to. It'd cause more trouble than it's worth.'

'Marcus, if you know that Asprenas was responsible for the German disaster then it's your duty to tell the emperor.'

'That's the problem. It wasn't just Asprenas who was responsible. There was someone else involved. Someone more important.'

'If you're talking about Varus I don't suppose that after all this time Tiberius would—'

'I'm not talking about Varus. I mean the empress. I'm talking about Livia.'

That shut him up, as I knew it would; but if I'd expected him to look shocked I was forgetting that Valerius Messalinus was first and last a politician. He leaned back and regarded me steadily.

'That would certainly make a difference,' he said.

'Yeah. I thought it might.'

'Although the emperor and the empress tend to go their separate ways these days I doubt if Tiberius would take kindly to being told his mother is a traitor.' He allowed himself a wintry smile. 'Not as far as any unexpected imputations of treachery are concerned anyway. Besides, the information would cause grave complications. Political complications. If it is susceptible of proof.'

'I can make a good case, yeah,' I said. 'A circumstantial case, sure, although maybe the letter would help. There must be examples of Varus's handwriting on file we can compare it with. But I don't want to stir things just for the sake of it.'

'Good, Marcus. Very good. You'll make a politician yet, my boy.' I grinned. I couldn't help it. 'So what do you want? What would you settle for?'

'How do you mean?'

'Politicians make deals. It's our purpose in life. So what exactly would the price of your silence be?'

'I want Ovid's ashes brought back to Rome, Dad. That's all I've ever wanted. No more, but no less.'

My father was silent for a long time, his fingers drumming on the table in front of him.

'Very well,' he said finally. 'And you would like me, I suppose, to act as your broker. With the empress.'

I tried to speak as calmly as I could. 'No. I want you to arrange a private appointment. No slaves, no secretaries. Just the two of us, me and Livia.'

My father stiffened. 'No!'

'Marcus, if you're right she'll kill you!' Perilla's eyes were wide. 'Even if you're wrong she'll kill you. It's not worth it!'

'Sure it is. Look, I've thought this thing through, okay? And going straight to Livia's the only way I can see of settling it once and for all.'

'Why don't you just confront Asprenas? Force him to tell the truth?'

'That wouldn't do any good, Perilla. I've no concrete proof, remember? He'd just deny everything and go to Livia himself. And how long do you think I'd last after that?'

'But...'

'Hold on. I hadn't finished. Let's say I have insurance.'

'What kind of insurance?'

'Say I write the whole thing down. What I know. What I've guessed. Names, dates where I can give them. I leave it with someone I trust. If anything happens to me it goes straight to the Wart.'

'And if Tiberius already knows?' my father put in quietly.

Yeah. Nice one, Dad. I'd been hoping that no one except me would think of that.

'He doesn't,' I said.

'Would you wager your life on that?'

I swallowed. Put up or shut up. 'Yeah. Yes, I would. The Wart may not be a lot of things, but he's straight. He's straight, and he's army.'

'Very well, son.' My father's voice took on a strange cold formality. 'If you're absolutely certain that this is what you want I'll arrange an appointment for you with the empress as soon as possible.'

'Marcus!'

'It's okay, Perilla. I know what I'm doing.' Yeah. Like a flea playing footsie with an elephant. 'There's just one more thing, Dad.'

'Yes?'

'The document. If you can hang on for an hour or so you can take it with you.'

He frowned. 'I'm sorry, Marcus. I don't understand.'

'My insurance policy. I want it to go to someone I can trust. Someone who'll make sure the Wart gets it if he has to. I'm sorry, Dad, but you're elected. If you agree, that is.'

We looked at each other for a long time. Finally he cleared his throat.

'Of course, son,' he said. 'Go and write it out now while I talk to Perilla.'

I went through to the study and left them to it.

My father hadn't been gone long with the precious document tucked into the fold in his mantle when the last two bits of proof I needed arrived—the first from Agron via Bathyllus, the second from Callias. Quinctilia's eyesight had started to go a dozen years before, since when she'd relied on a secretary to read her letters to her. The litter slaves who'd kidnapped Perilla, Callias said, had belonged to a certain Curtius Macer. Macer had sold them cheaply after buying a matched set of Nubians at a bargain price from Asprenas. And Macer, Bathyllus informed me, was second cousin to Asprenas's wife.

Two straight bull's-eyes in a row, and two too many for coincidence. We'd found our fourth conspirator. My only problem now was to nail the bastard where it hurt and come out the other end myself with a whole skin.

My father sent round details of the appointment later that day. The empress would see me an hour before noon the following morning.

People had died of old age waiting for imperial appointments. Maybe I was just lucky, maybe I'd got a last-minute cancellation. Or maybe Livia wanted to see me as badly as I wanted to see her.

The short walk to the palace was one of the longest I'd ever taken. At least Perilla was out of it. I'd sent her to Baiae, to stay with a friend who owned a sizeable yacht and owed me a favour. If the worst came to the worst she could leave Italy fast. Marseilles isn't exactly the hub of the universe, but the seafood's good, and the climate would be a lot healthier than Rome's until Livia was safely dead.

The two Praetorians on the door gave me a suspicious look, and I wondered if they were the same guys who'd almost thrown me out on my ear the last time I'd visited this part of the

Palatine; but maybe it was my imagination. These gorillas all look the same anyway. Big and mean. I walked between them and gave my name to the secretary at the main reception desk. He checked his list, then looked up. His eyes were bureaucratically blank.

'That seems quite in order, sir. Her Excellency will see you immediately.' He snapped his fingers and something large and hairy materialised out of the woodwork. 'Hermes, take the gentleman to Her Excellency the Empress's suite.'

Without a word the messenger-ape shambled off through the labyrinth leaving me to follow as best as I could. The maze of corridors would've had Daedalus tearing his beard in envy. If the interview went badly and I had to run for it I'd have no chance. Finally, after walking for a good five minutes, we ducked down a short corridor and into a waiting-room grander than the ones we'd passed so far. A little guy in a very smart lemon tunic sat polishing his nails at a desk beside two imposing panelled doors.

The messenger-ape spoke. It was like having your pet dog suddenly quote Plato. 'Marcus Valerius Messalla Corvinus to see Her Excellency the Lady Livia.'

The guy in the tunic got up. He took me by the arm none too gently and propelled me towards the panelled doors. A discreet knock, a less-than-discreet push in the small of the back, and I was inside. The doors closed behind me and I was alone with the empress.

Livia sat beside a large desk. It was the first time I'd seen her close to, and she seemed—I'm not exaggerating here, nor was the feeling part of my nervousness—not quite real, not quite alive. Her face was an elaborate cosmetic mask like actors wear, or hired mourners in a funeral procession, and her eyes were…dead. That's the only word I can use. Not empty, or dull, or even lifeless.

Dead.

'You asked to see me, Marcus Valerius Corvinus.'

Her voice was dead, too.

I swallowed. 'Yes, Excellency.'

Maybe I'd made a mistake. If so it would be the last I ever made. My insurance policy suddenly seemed pretty thin. Thin and juvenile.

'And the purpose?'

Jupiter! I was close to panic. How do you accuse the mother of a reigning emperor and the wife of his deified predecessor of treachery to the state?

I think you betrayed Varus, Excellency. I think you caused the death of fifteen thousand men and the loss of three Eagles and almost lost us Germany just to give your son a better chance at the purple...

She was waiting. I cleared my throat. 'I've discovered some...irregularities, Excellency. In connection with the conduct of Lucius Nonius Asprenas.'

I'd expected the name to cause a flicker in the dead eyes. It didn't. I began to sweat.

'Irregularities?'

'Yes, Excellency.' I paused for effect. 'Treasonable irregularities.'

She just stared at me. Maybe I was wrong after all, I thought. There was nothing in her eyes, no guilt, no unease. Nothing. A fly buzzed across my face and settled on the desk in front of her. Jupiter, if I was wrong now wasn't the time to find out.

'Treason is the province of the emperor,' she said. 'Your appointment was with me.'

'I believe Asprenas was working for Your Excellency.' Did I say that? The mask set. Silence stretched between us like an overtuned lyre string. Finally, she spoke.

'You came to the palace some time ago enquiring about the poet Ovid. Is there a connection between that and your present impertinence?'

She was testing me, I knew. This was crucial. I had to convince her that I knew everything. Even if I didn't.

'Yes, Excellency. There is.'

'Then perhaps you would be good enough to explain it to me.' A flick of her finger indicated the visitor's chair. It was old Egyptian, and pretty frail—maybe even part of the stuff Augustus had brought back from Alexandria after Cleopatra had her run-in with the asp. I sat cautiously. The chair creaked.

'Now, young man. What are these "treasonable irregularities" that you say Nonius Asprenas was responsible for? And why should he be working for me?'

Her eyes were like iron spikes. 'Asprenas was a member of the Paullus plot, Excellency. He represented—claimed to represent—his Uncle Varus, whom your late husband—'

'The Divine Augustus.'

'I'm sorry, Excellency.' Shit, my hands were starting to sweat. I wiped them on my mantle. 'Whom the Divine Augustus had appointed to the German command.'

'You're saying that Varus was involved with Paullus and Julia?'

'No, Excellency. Not directly involved.' I paused. 'Not that there was much to be involved with.'

'How do you mean, young man?'

I could feel the sweat beading my forehead now, but I didn't wipe it off. She knew I was nervous. Sure she knew. Just as I knew that I had to keep my dignity because it was the only defence I had.

'The conspiracy was a fake, Excellency. It was intended to

destroy Julia as the rest of your husband's line had already been destroyed.'

The mask-face didn't move, but the eyes behind it glittered. 'Destroyed by whom?'

Jupiter! This was like juggling with razors! 'That's not for me to say, Excellency.'

'Very good.' Was there the trace of a smile on her thin lips? 'Go on, Corvinus.'

'May I speak frankly, Excellency?'

'I was under the impression that you already were.' I moved nervously and the chair creaked again. Suddenly I smelled camphor—an old smell, the smell of age. Livia or the chair? Old age, old bones, old crimes.

'The problem was that Augustus wouldn't believe another adultery charge,' I said. 'His daughter, the Lady Julia's mother, had been exiled for the same reason, and it was too pat. Even with Junius Silanus's confession to back it up the evidence would have been shaky. What was needed was something more...significant. Something Augustus would take seriously, even although he could never make it public.'

'And that was?'

'Proof that Julia was a traitor.'

Livia said nothing. The fly hesitated, rubbed its front legs together and began to crawl across the vast expanse of desk that lay between us.

'The problem was, Excellency,' I went on, 'that Paullus and Julia were on their guard. They knew they'd been targeted. Also, they weren't content to sit and wait. Sooner or later they'd have got through to Augustus, convinced him, if he didn't know it already, that his successors' deaths weren't just bad luck and that they could offer a viable alternative to your son.'

I could feel the sweat pouring off me now.

'That alternative being?'

'Postumus. Julia's brother. Your husband's grandson.' Her lips pursed.

'Postumus was a moral degenerate, Corvinus. Augustus knew that. My husband would never have agreed to him as a successor.'

'Yes, Excellency. But it's just possible that—latterly—the emperor had begun to suspect he had been... misinformed about his grandson's character.'

'Misinformed by whom?'

Again the challenge. Again I ignored it.

'Julia and Paullus weren't traitors. Not in the true sense of the word. Even if they had wanted to conspire against Augustus, they knew it would only be playing into their enemies' hands. Yet the plot was real enough. It happened. Why?'

'You tell me. This is fascinating.'

'There was a conspiracy, Excellency, only it was a conspiracy with the emperor's full approval. Or so Paullus and Julia thought. Its intention was to set the succession on its proper course.'

Livia sat forward. The fly, perhaps seeing the movement as a threat, stopped and flexed its wings.

'Its *proper* course?'

Fool! 'I'm sorry, Excellency. Perhaps I should have said, "to follow the Julian line".'

'I see.' She leaned back again. 'We'll let that pass. But your interpretation of the Paullus plot seems a little far-fetched, young man. If you don't mind my saying so...'

'I don't think so, Excellency. I have proof.'

'Then by all means let me hear it.'

'Paullus and Julia were approached by Asprenas, who was Quinctilius Varus's nephew; and Varus was Augustus's man.

Asprenas tells them he represents the emperor. Augustus will appoint Varus as commander in Germany. He'll then allow Postumus to "escape" from his island and take refuge with the Rhine legions. Paullus and Julia will do the same. The military situation being what it is, Augustus will permit himself to be pressured by the Julian party's supporters into a reconciliation with his grandson which will develop in time to his appointment as successor.'

The fly twitched nervously in the sudden silence.

'This is theory, Corvinus. You said you have proof.'

'I can prove it,' I lied.

'You're mad.'

I shook my head. 'No, Excellency. I don't think so.'

'Paullus and Julia would never have believed Asprenas. Not without a clear sign that he was my husband's representative.'

'But he did have a sign.'

'Namely?'

'The emperor's own signet ring.'

'The Sphinx seal never left Augustus's hand.'

'Not the original, Excellency. The ring you yourself gave him. Your own copy, which you used to seal documents in your husband's absence.'

The silence was total. Finally, Livia broke it.

'I could have you killed, Corvinus,' she said softly. 'I could call my guards and you would not leave this room alive. You know that, don't you?'

'Of course.' I tried to speak with more confidence than I felt. 'But you won't, Excellency.'

'Why not?'

'Because I didn't come here unprepared. If I die your son will learn the truth behind the Varian massacre. And if that happens, Excellency, I wouldn't give a gnat's fart for your own chances of living the month out.'

Her hand flashed down. The fly, startled, rose an instant too late and was a smear of blood on the desk top. Livia leaned towards me. For an instant, before she brought herself under control, I thought that she meant to attack me physically; but then she sat back again in her chair.

'Very well, Corvinus,' she said. Calmly, as if nothing had happened. 'Go on.'

'Thank you.' Again I wiped the sweat from my palms. 'Asprenas didn't wear the ring openly on his finger when he arrived at Paullus's house. I know that from the door slave. But once he was alone with the conspirators he slipped it on as a reminder to Paullus and Julia whose agent he was. Or rather whose agent they thought he was. In reality Augustus knew nothing about the conspiracy until he was told, and by that time the evidence was damning because it was genuine. Paullus was executed and Julia was exiled for adultery.'

'If what you say is correct then they could have exonerated themselves by explaining the true situation to the emperor.'

'Were they given the chance? And would Augustus have believed them if they had been?'

Livia's mouth set, and she didn't answer.

'It was all too probable, you see. And the facts were undeniable.'

'But why the adultery charge, if as you say my husband would not credit it?'

'The emperor's own granddaughter publicly charged with treason? You of all people, Excellency, should know how damaging that would be to the state.'

'Indeed.' Again the tight lips twisted into what was almost a smile. 'I take your point, Corvinus. In theory, at least.'

'Thank you, Excellency. Augustus, if nothing else, was fair. Knowing that the charge was false, he let the "adulterer" Silanus off as lightly as he could. Besides, Silanus was the one who revealed the conspiracy. He deserved some reward.'

'Junius Silanus was exiled, young man. And his political career was terminated. Hardly a negligible punishment for someone in his position.'

'Not true, Excellency. Silanus left Italy of his own accord and he was never interested in politics. The punishment was no punishment at all, and the emperor knew it.'

'So you say. Yet you claim he was rewarded.'

My left leg was beginning to twitch. Slowly, without taking my eyes from hers, I stretched it out and began massaging the thigh muscle.

'I've seen Silanus's estate, Excellency. Suburban villas that size don't come cheap.'

'Junius Silanus belongs to a very old and wealthy family.'

'True. Which is perhaps why a few months afterwards the emperor gave his own great-granddaughter in marriage to Silanus's cousin. Or was that simply coincidence?'

Livia said nothing. She stared at me, unblinking.

'Which brings us, Excellency, to what happened to the fourth conspirator. Nonius Asprenas.'

Call it imagination if you like; but when I spoke the name I swear the room itself held its breath. Livia's eyes were dark pools of hate, staring into mine.

'Nothing,' she said, 'happened to Asprenas.'

'That's right, Excellency. Would you like to tell me why?'

The silence lengthened. Finally she said: 'No, Corvinus. No, I would not.'

CHAPTER

43

eah. Just that. A straight refusal, the last-ditch reply of someone who was guilty as hell. If I'd had any doubts about being right, that put the lid on them. I'd got the bitch and both of us knew it. The spasmed muscle in my leg suddenly quietened.

'Very well, Excellency,' I said. 'Then I'll tell you. The solution's simple. Asprenas wasn't punished for his part in the plot because Augustus didn't know he was involved. Silanus never mentioned him. He'd been instructed not to by you, because Asprenas was needed for something else. Or am I wrong?' I paused for an answer that didn't come; then said softly: 'Only unfortunately Silanus wasn't the only person who knew about Asprenas, was he? There was someone else whom you couldn't instruct. Not one of your own people. A neutral outsider, a personal friend of Julia's who knew Asprenas by sight and guessed what was going on.' Silence. Total, absolute silence. I felt as if I was walking on glass. 'How did Ovid find out, Excellency?'

I didn't think she would answer, but finally she did: drily, clinically, in a voice devoid of emotion.

'He called round by chance with a book Julia wanted and saw Asprenas and Paullus coming out of the study together. I don't know the details, but they were incriminating.'

'So after wrestling with his conscience, like a good citizen he decided to report what he'd seen. Only the report was never made because he talked to the wrong person.'

'He came to the palace shortly afterwards.' Livia's voice was matter-of-fact 'The emperor was engaged and it was easy to have him brought to me. He didn't realise his mistake, of course. Not until much later.'

'So you had to get him out of Rome, fast. Permanently. You couldn't risk Asprenas's name being linked in the emperor's mind with the idea of conspiracy. And if Ovid had still been around when news of the German disaster broke he might've put two and two together and gone to the palace again. To Augustus himself this time.'

'Ovid was a fool.'

I shook my head. 'No, Excellency. He was only a poet mixed up in politics, doing his best as he saw it.'

'A well-intentioned bumbler can cause far greater harm than a conscious enemy. As, Corvinus'—she almost smiled—'I'm sure you yourself appreciate.'

I ignored the barb. 'So you had a quiet word with Augustus. Jupiter knows what you told him—that Ovid had been screwing Julia himself while they recited pornographic poetry together; that he was secretly fifty different kinds of pervert and was better off dead. And the emperor, who disliked Ovid and his poetry at the best of times, believed you. Or maybe he didn't think it mattered.'

Livia's mouth twisted. 'Oh, he thought it mattered, young

man! My oh-so-strait-laced husband was at heart a hypocritical frustrated libertine who castigated the vices of others precisely because they were his own. The Ovid I showed Augustus was his secret self, performing the acts that he would have performed if he had had the courage. What could the poor fool do but exile him?'

A cold finger touched my spine. I'd been given a glimpse of Livia's real face; and I knew that the most dangerous thing I could do was let her know she'd shown me it.

'Let's talk about Germany, Excellency,' I said.

She didn't answer, but I felt her stiffen.

'Frontier provinces were Augustus's responsibility. He made the policy decisions and took the glory or the raps personally. You would agree?'

'Yes.'

Was it my imagination or was she beginning to show signs of nerves herself?

'So if someone wanted to create a major embarrassment for the emperor the frontiers were the place to do it.'

No answer again; but her expression was set hard under the thick make-up.

'Okay, so which frontier would they choose? Forget the southern provinces. Parthia's keeping her head down at present, so the east's out as well. The Danube's possible, but that's Tiberius's stamping ground, and the person I have in mind wouldn't want him involved, especially after the Illyrian revolt.' Still no response, but I could see a trace of moisture on the caked powder of her forehead. 'That leaves Germany, Excellency. And Germany is perfect because Augustus is responsible for it all the way down the line. He makes the policy, he assigns the legions, he chooses the governor. And if anything does go wrong there your son Tiberius is close by to save the situation. Am I right?'

'Corvinus, I swear to you...'

I waited, but that was all she said. Her mouth had shut tight as a clam.

'You want to take over, Excellency?'

'No.' The moisture on her forehead had gathered into a bead of sweat that was dragging a runnel through the powder. 'Go on.'

'Very well.' I shifted my weight, and the chair creaked like old bones rubbing together. 'So let's talk about Varus. His appointment to the German command was your suggestion, wasn't it?'

'Varus was a natural choice. He was a proven administrator with wide military experience, loyal to my husband...'

'That doesn't answer the question, lady.'

Her eyes flashed. 'I told you, Corvinus. He was a natural choice. That should be enough.'

'Sure he was; but not for the reasons you've given. You chose Varus because first he was rotten as a bad fig where money was concerned and second because his nephew was Nonius Asprenas.' Her mouth was tight as an iron trap. 'When they got to Germany it was Asprenas's job to encourage the old man's greed, see to it that he made himself unpopular with the natives, maybe even lay himself open to a charge of maladministration. Only that wasn't enough for your purposes, was it? You needed something that would really smack the emperor in the jaw. You needed Arminius.'

Silence. Her eyes glared at me through the whiteness of the powder. I went on.

'Arminius was pure gold. Ambitious, two-faced as Janus, a natural actor and a natural liar. Roman-educated, Roman-trained. Plausible. Asprenas was to be your pimp, introduce the two, make sure they ended up in bed together.'

'An intriguing metaphor. You are speaking metaphorically, I trust?'

'Luckily for him, that part turned out to be easy. Varus saw a quality in Arminius that he'd always respected but never had himself: commitment. Varus took it for commitment to Rome, but that was his bad judgment and Arminius's good acting; and when the time came it swung the balance, because the old guy wanted to believe Arminius could be trusted.' I paused. 'So. By the time he gets to Germany Varus is pretty well softened up. Arminius comes to him and spins him a fairy story about creating a client-kingdom between the Rhine and the Elbe...'

'No fairy story. The concept was quite sound. And we needed a change of policy.'

'Sure. Okay, if you say so. Anyway, Arminius offers Varus a pretty big retainer for his co-operation, and Varus, who trusts his motives, agrees. The scam's very profitable, and it doesn't even rub his conscience up the wrong way. Then comes the crunch.'

She'd tensed herself again. We were on the most sensitive ground of all here, and I knew it.

'Arminius tells Varus that he needs one last favour: a military embarrassment to consolidate his hold over the tribes. On the march back to Vetera he's to allow himself to be decoyed into the Teutoburg. There Arminius will attack him but allow him to withdraw with his army intact.' I paused again, and then said softly: 'Only that wasn't the real agreement, was it, Excellency? The attack wasn't going to be the farce the old guy was expecting. When Arminius hit it would be for real.'

I'd got through to her at last. The mask cracked completely, and the frightened woman showed through.

'It was a mistake!' she whispered. 'We wanted a humiliation, not a massacre!'

'Sure.'

'Believe me! Arminius swore that the attack would be a limited engagement!'

A limited engagement. I felt like throwing up all over the bitch's marble flooring.

'Three legions,' I said quietly. 'Fifteen thousand men butchered, just so your boy could take a step nearer the purple. How the fuck do you sleep at night, lady?'

But the mask was back in place and the empress had herself under control again.

'I use poppy juice. I always have done,' she said. 'And in any case bad dreams are a small price to pay for the safety of Rome. Which brings us to yourself. What is your price, young man?'

The suddenness of the question took me by surprise.

'My price?'

'The price of your silence.'

'Nothing, Excellency.'

'Nothing?'

'A handful of ashes. You would call it nothing.'

She stared at me so long I felt the sweat breaking out on my forehead. Then she said, very quietly: 'Don't presume to dictate my own values to me, Corvinus. Political advancement would be nothing, property or money would be nothing. Ovid's ashes are not nothing.'

'Did you hate him so much, Excellency?'

'He nearly ruined all my plans for my son, all my plans for Rome. Had he been a politician we could have dealt with each other, but he was not. He was a well-meaning bumbler who wouldn't have understood bargaining if it had hit him in the face. Yes, I hated Ovid so much. I still do. I would have had him killed, only Tomi was worse.' She stood up, and for the first time

I realised how small she was; small and frail. I could have reached over and snapped her in half like a rotten branch. 'You will have your handful of ashes, young man. But never believe that you have let me off lightly.'

I stood too. As if at a signal (had she given one, somehow?) the doors behind me opened and the secretary was there waiting to escort me out.

'Goodbye, Valerius Corvinus,' Livia said with stiff formality. 'I will see that the necessary arrangements are made.'

I bowed and turned to go. I had almost reached the door before another thought struck me.

'One more thing, Excellency,' I said. 'I want a girl.' She stared at me and I heard the secretary's sharp, scandalised intake of breath. Then for the first time the empress smiled.

'Any girl, Corvinus?'

'A special girl. You know the one I mean.'

'Yes. I know the one you mean. It will be arranged.'

I bowed again, and left.

CHAPTER

44

But the day wasn't over yet. When I got home Bathyllus met me in the lobby.

'You have a visitor, sir,' he said quietly.

'Yeah?' I stripped off my cloak and my mantle and handed them to him. 'Who's that?'

'I took the liberty of showing him into your study. I thought perhaps you would prefer to talk in private.'

The study door was closed. As I opened it, the man inside turned...

Asprenas.

My hand had reached for the dagger at my left wrist before I remembered that I wasn't carrying it. You don't, usually, on visits to the palace. Asprenas had caught the movement. He smiled and shook his head.

'No, Corvinus,' he said. 'You're quite safe from me now, especially since you've chosen to handle this thing sensibly. It's over. And if I'd wanted to kill you I would hardly choose your own house to do it in.'

Without taking my eyes from him I half turned.

'Bathyllus! Some wine. I'll talk to you later.'

Then, to Asprenas, 'You're not welcome here. Get out. Now.'

He pulled up a chair and sat down. 'Don't blame the slave. I twisted his arm.'

'He should've known better.' I sat down myself, far enough away for safety. Also I didn't want to breathe the same air as he did any more than I could help.

'You've just come from your interview with the empress.'

'Yeah.'

'And she told you that our intention was to humiliate Varus and through him the emperor.'

I nodded.

'I thought she might. By the way, I'm glad you chose Livia and not Tiberius. It relieves me of my obligations.'

I gripped the arms of my chair, hard, to stop my hands shaking with disgust.

'So what do you want?' I said. 'Tell me, then get the hell out of my house.'

He smiled. 'I don't want anything. I have everything I need, thank you. But I thought perhaps you deserved congratulations. And, perhaps, some final clarification.'

'What sort of clarification? If it's about what you did to Varus you can save your breath.'

'That's precisely what it's about.' He leaned back in his chair, completely at his ease. 'Admissions first. Yes, I arranged things on Livia's behalf with Arminius. Yes, I forged the letter we showed you. That ought not to have been necessary, but my uncle persistently and categorically refused to incriminate himself in writing. And yes, of course I was wholly responsible for the attacks on yourself and for the Lady Rufia's kidnapping. These last the empress knew nothing about, although she would have approved if she had. However, I cannot leave you with the impression that Livia is totally innocent—I mean innocent of fifteen thousand deaths. I'm not that altruistic.'

There was a knock at the door: Bathyllus with the wine. I sent him away.

Asprenas leaned forward. 'Corvinus, do you honestly think that Livia didn't know what Arminius intended to do? Yes, trouble in Germany would have damaged Augustus. But Livia wasn't interested in simple damage. She wanted to destroy him.'

I couldn't believe this.

'You're saying that Livia intended a massacre from the start?'

Asprenas was smiling.

'Of course she did. I had my orders before I left Rome. Not the details, of course, simply the broad outline. Arminius, too, although he was acting for himself just as much as for Livia.'

'You're wrong, Asprenas. Not even Livia is that much of a bitch.'

He stared at me. 'Think, boy! Isn't it obvious? She had to do something because her position was becoming desperate. Augustus had woken up to the fact that he was being manipulated. Postumus was still alive and a growing threat. Augustus had to be destroyed while her influence over him still held good.'

'So why didn't she poison the guy, like the rest of his family? Don't tell me she had scruples.'

'She couldn't. Augustus still hadn't formally recognised

Tiberius as his successor. She had to smash the emperor's confidence in himself and make certain that it was Tiberius that he turned to. You can see that, can't you, Corvinus?'

I remembered the stories of how Augustus had reacted when the news of the massacre had reached Rome; how he had woken in the night, screaming.

'Quinctilius Varus, give me back my legions!'

'Yeah,' I said. 'I can see that.'

'So you believe me?'

'I don't know.' I shook my head dully. 'I don't know any more.'

He got up. 'You believe me. You have to, because it's the truth.'

'You want to swear that?'

His eyebrows rose in surprise. 'If you wish.'

'Would it mean much if you did?'

'Not a lot; but I will if you insist.'

I felt my gorge rise. 'Get out of my house, Asprenas. Get out now.'

He shrugged and turned, then paused, his hand on the doorknob.

'I'm glad I didn't succeed in killing you, Corvinus. I'm not a killer. Not in cold blood, anyway. Once was enough.'

'Once?' I said—and then remembered Davus, lying with his throat slit under a pile of grain. So that had been Asprenas himself. I was surprised he'd told me.

'Oh, by the way,' Asprenas was still smiling, and completely relaxed, 'there aren't many of us who know about the Varus affair, and we're a privileged group. The empress has to keep us sweet. She hasn't much influence with her son these days but she can still manage a favour or two. You're on your way up, young man.'

My fists clenched; but I couldn't've so much as touched the bastard.

'I'm not interested in politics, Asprenas,' I said. 'Not your sort, anyway.'

'It's your duty, son. You owe it to the state. Just remember I told you.'

The door closed quietly behind him. After he had gone I had the bath slaves scrub me until my flesh was raw. Then I got drunk.

CHAPTER

45

We buried him in December, the day before the start of the Winter Festival, in the garden of his villa outside Rome. He had no mausoleum, not even a stone, but that wasn't important: the earth was Roman earth, not the hateful frost-locked soil of Tomi. There were only four mourners, if mourners is the right word on what was after all a happy occasion: myself, my father, Perilla, and his widow. The Lady Fabia Camilla watched the ceremony with vacant eyes; but when I'd lowered the small casket into the narrow hole she threw in after it a single handful of dried rosebuds. I filled the hole in, laid the cut turf on top, and stamped it flat.

'Rest quietly, Father,' Perilla whispered beside me. 'You're home now.'

We walked back to the house through the bare-branched orchard.

'He wrote most of his poetry here in the garden.' Perilla was smiling, as if she saw not a bleak December day but the sharp yellow of narcissi against a pale blue cloudless sky. Perhaps she did. 'He would have approved. *Every place has its own fate.*'

From her tone I knew it was a quotation, but it wasn't one I knew. Maybe one of his own lines.

'Dine with me today?' My father laid one hand on my shoulder, the other on Perilla's. She smiled.

'Yes, Father.'

Did I answer him, or was it Perilla? I can't remember now. In any case it didn't particularly matter.

AUTHOR'S NOTE

The main characters in *Ovid* are historical. I have, however, taken some minor liberties with them for reasons of plot.

First, the real Valerius Corvinus was much older than I have made him: he and his Uncle Cotta were joint consuls for AD 20 (the year after the story closes), which would put him in his early thirties at least.

Junius Silanus was still abroad at the time of the story. Tiberius did not authorise his recall until the following year.

Perilla in Ovid's poetry is simply 'Perilla'. The rare family name Rufia becomes common only at a later date, and I gave her it for reasons of my own. It has no connection with the last name of her husband.

Suillius Rufus gets a very bad press in the historians. He was banished under Tiberius, recalled by Caligula, and became a notorious informer for Claudius's wife, Messalina. On the other hand, he and Perilla (so far as I know) were happily married with children. Rufus could not possibly have been, as I imply, the 'false friend' who attempted to deprive Ovid's wife of his estate and whom he calls Ibis in his poems.

Nonius Asprenas I have *not* libelled, in character at least. The charge against him of appropriating 'legacies' after the Varian disaster is made by the historian Paterculus, who served in Germany shortly afterwards and would have talked to men who knew him. Paterculus also mentions, when describing the massacre, the 'base behaviour of the camp commander Ceionius, who advised giving up and preferred a criminal's death by execution to that of a soldier in battle', and contrasts it with the conduct of the noble Eggius. As such, he was the natural choice for a villain.

Lastly, I feel guilty about the picture I have given of the palace bureaucracy, which is far more appropriate to the reign of Claudius (AD 41-54) than to that of Tiberius.